Also by Laurel Blount

The Johns Mill Amish Romance series

Shelter in the Storm
Strength in the Storm
Courage in the Storm

Home from the Storm

Laurel Blount

BERKLEY ROMANCE
New York

BERKLEY ROMANCE
Published by Berkley
An imprint of Penguin Random House LLC
penguinrandomhouse.com

ISBN: 9780593200261

First Edition: December 2023

Printed in the United States of America
1 3 5 7 9 10 8 6 4 2

Book design by George Towne

*Dedicated to my grandson, Russell Brock,
who has brought us such inexpressible joy.
May God guide and bless you always.*

Home from the Storm

Chapter One

CALEB HOCHSTEDLER HADN'T PRAYED FOR MORE than two years, but here on a secluded Florida beach, on this windy June morning, he figured he'd give God one last chance.

Gott, let Trevor Abbott be in this house. That's all I'm asking. I'll take it from there.

He sensed no particular answer, heard nothing but the steady crash of the waves behind him. Not surprising. He and God weren't exactly on speaking terms.

Caleb squinted up at the wooden house, set high on stilts, windows glowing in the last darkness before the dawn, and he set his jaw.

Truth was, he didn't much care what God had to say anyway. If the coward who'd murdered his parents was holed up inside this house, Caleb would drag him all the way back home to Johns Mill, Tennessee, and toss him on the courthouse lawn, trussed up like a hog ready for the butcher.

He moved up the steep steps soundlessly, the way Milt Masterson had taught him. Technically, he wasn't supposed to be moving at all. Milt had made himself very clear.

"I'll circle around and come up on the place from behind," the bounty hunter had said before they'd parted company. "Try to act like you've got some sense and keep out of sight until I give you the go-ahead. You hear me, Amish?"

Caleb had nodded. He'd heard just fine. But as *Daed* had often pointed out, hearing and listening were two different things.

Caleb respected Milt because the man was a legend in this business, but he was in his late fifties, a good thirty years older than Caleb, and the shrapnel he'd caught in his leg in Afghanistan slowed him down more than he liked to admit. The old wound troubled him more as the years went by, and that was the only reason he'd hired Caleb to tag along and help out with jobs. Milt was tough as nails, and Caleb had learned a lot from him, but the criminals they brought in were usually thieves or drug addicts who'd skipped bail.

Not killers.

In any case, hunting Trevor Abbott was Caleb's personal mission, not a paid job. He didn't want Milt to get hurt, and besides, he wanted—he needed—to deal with Trevor himself.

Trevor had destroyed everything that had mattered in Caleb's life. There was nothing he could do about that. Not now. All he could do was see to it that Trevor didn't go unpunished.

And he would see to it. Whatever it took. Because when all the light in Caleb's world had flickered into darkness, one lone spark had kept burning.

Justice. He wanted justice. It was the closest he could come to making things right. It wasn't near enough, but it was the only hope he had left.

He'd made it to the top of the steps, and he paused, scanning the windows. They were veiled with filmy curtains, and although lights were on, he saw no movement. Likely, Trevor was still in bed, and he'd just left the lights burning.

Wasteful and lazy. *Ja*, that sounded like Trevor.

Caleb crossed the deck, putting his heel down first, then rolling his foot forward as Milt had showed him. His heart was pounding, his fists clenched and ready. According to the information Milt had gleaned from his collection of under-the-table sources, Trevor had been hiding out here for weeks. The black car parked underneath the raised house was the make and model they'd been told to expect.

All signs were looking good.

Except one.

Caleb froze as his gaze zeroed in on the front door. It was ajar.

His blood chilled. Trevor might be lazy and wasteful, but he wasn't careless. If he was inside this house, that door would have been closed and locked tight.

Which meant Caleb's quarry had slipped through his fingers. Again.

Fury washed over him. Abandoning stealth, he strode the rest of the way to the door and kicked it wide open. It blammed against the wall, the noise echoing through the empty cottage.

A muffled protest came from somewhere below the house. Milt wasn't happy, but at the moment, Caleb couldn't have cared less. He stepped inside and scanned the room.

Somebody had left in a hurry. The house was what his *mamm* would have called "out at the elbows." Nothing was in its rightful place.

Doorways offered glimpses of a kitchen, bedroom, and bathroom. The rooms were decorated in calming shades of blue and green, but every surface was cluttered with debris. Somebody had been holed up here awhile, all right.

Just not quite long enough.

Caleb made a frustrated noise and punched the wall beside him. His fist went through the Sheetrock, leaving a jagged hole.

"Settle down!" Milt barked from behind him. The older man limped across the deck, breathing hard and scowling. "How many times I got to tell you? Temper fits don't solve nothing."

Caleb shot him a startled look. In a strange way—for just one fleeting minute—Milt had sounded a lot like *Daed*.

"He's not here," Caleb said.

"I figured that out about five seconds before you kicked this door in. Your boy's switched vehicles. Another car was parked down below, gone now. Can't tell much about it, because thanks to the wind and that rain we had, the tracks ain't clear. But the fact that there's anything left to see at all means he ain't been gone long. I'd say we missed him by a whisker."

Caleb clenched his jaw. Knowing that only made it worse. "He knew we were coming."

"Seems so. You run your mouth to somebody?"

"No," Caleb answered shortly. He knew better. Besides, other than Milt, he didn't have anybody to talk to these days.

"Well, I ain't, either, but somehow he found out we were closing in."

"What about the people you've been getting your information from? Could one of them have tipped him off?"

Milt shrugged. "Most of 'em ain't exactly model citizens, so that's a possibility. But I'd say it was unlikely. It's in their best interests to stay on my good side. If you're done punching walls, let's go through the house and see can we get any idea where this guy's headed. We spooked him, and he tore out in a hurry. Could be he left something behind he didn't mean to. You start here, I'll search the bedroom." Milt brushed past him into the house.

Left alone in the living room, Caleb took a minute to examine the damage he'd caused. The hole was the least of it. The drywall had split along its seam, leaving a crack the height of the wall. He tested the edge of the split with his finger, noting how easily it moved. Poor workmanship. Whoever had built this house had cut corners and skimped on screws. Not smart on a rental property. When he'd worked construction back home, he'd done plenty of repair work on rentals. *Englischers* didn't take such good care of what didn't belong to them. Sometimes they didn't even take care of what did.

Caleb didn't hold with that. *Daed* had always said that a wise man looked after what was his.

The memory jabbed at his conscience, as memories of his father often did. He was trying to live up to that teaching, in his own way, as best he could, but one thing was for sure. Nobody back home thought of him as wise. Far from it. When he'd left Johns Mill to track down Trevor, Caleb's Plain community had all shunned him, even his own family.

Even . . .

He cut that thought off short, but not before pain stung him like a wasp.

Every now and then, the lonely ache of his memories kept him up at night, wondering if maybe he'd been wrong to leave, like she . . . like they all . . . believed. Then he would think of his parents, imagining their last terrified moments, and his resolve would stiffen.

No, he'd see this through. Somebody had to stand up for the gentle people of the world. And since he'd never been the gentle sort himself, that job had fallen to him.

It had come at a high cost, though, and not just for him. He'd done what he could to make up for that, even after . . . everyone . . . had turned their backs on him. He had a stack of returned letters and uncashed checks to prove it.

It proved something else, too. He didn't have as much back home belonging to him as he'd once hoped.

Pushing that train of thought aside, he estimated the cost of the repair to the wall in his head. He pulled out his wallet and stacked a pile of twenties on a nearby table, anchoring them down with the base of a seahorse-shaped lamp.

There. Done.

All of life's fixes should be so simple.

"Pills in here," Milt called from the bedroom. "Looks like a prescription, but no name on the bottle. I'll take a picture and we'll see what it is. Whatever it is, he ain't taking it. Bottle's still near full, and he left it behind."

Milt resumed searching the dresser drawers. He'd likely be finished soon, so Caleb had better get busy himself.

He made short work of the living room and the kitchen, sifting through nondescript piles of trash. Fast-food wrappers and pizza boxes, a half dozen empty beer bottles, some discarded change, and a few wadded-up dollar bills.

He leaned one shoulder against the doorframe, scanning the rooms and trying to think the way Milt had trained him to.

Trevor had been here awhile. Some of the stuff in the pantry and fridge was expired.

He wasn't hurting for money. The discarded cash and car told him that, and the rental itself backed it up. A private place on a beach like this would be pricey, more proof that Trevor's wealthy parents were secretly sending money to their fugitive son.

Stephen Abbott was a lawyer, a smart one, so probably he'd left no trail. Even if he had, Caleb doubted it would've made much difference. Abbott had powerful friends and deep pockets.

He'd take a look in the bathroom. Maybe—

"Amish?" Milt stood in the bedroom doorway, an odd expression on his face. "This Trevor fellow. He killed your parents because he was obsessed with your sister. Ain't that what you told me?"

"That's right. My twin sister, Emma. She worked at my parents' general store, and she made the mistake of being nice to him."

Emma had always been too softhearted. She'd felt sorry for Trevor, and he'd latched on to her with the dangerous desperation of a drowning man. When *Daed* had gently discouraged him, Trevor had returned to the store and shot both *Daed* and *Mamm* in front of Caleb's terrified younger sister, Miriam.

"Yeah." Milt scratched his jaw and sighed. "You better come look at this."

Caleb followed Milt through the bedroom, glancing around. Not a large room, and mostly dominated by a queen-size bed, its covers rumpled. A big window overlooked the ocean, the waves glinting with the morning sunlight.

Milt halted in front of a closet with folding louvered doors. He shot a warning look in Caleb's direction.

"Keep a lid on that temper, now," he cautioned. Then he folded the doors open.

Caleb's heart lurched. The back of the closet was papered with photos of a young Amish woman. He leaned inside, his eyes moving from picture to picture, his mind unwilling to believe what he was seeing.

The woman wasn't looking at the camera and didn't seem aware her picture was being taken. The images weren't very good, but they were clear enough. His gaze lingered on the neat, dark hair smoothed under the *kapp*, the smooth curve of her cheek, and the sweet tilt of her head.

During the happiest time of his life, he'd seen this face every day. That had been a long while ago. Seeing her unexpectedly now, here, made so many feelings and memories rise up and wash over him that he couldn't think straight.

Hard on the heels of that came fear, sharp and ice-cold.

Because in each photo, a circle had been drawn around the woman's face with a red marker.

"I take it that's your sister," Milt said grimly.

It took Caleb a minute to answer.

"No," he said. "That's my wife."

Chapter Two

TWO HOURS LATER, MILT NODDED AT THE MIDDLE-aged waitress who'd refilled his coffee mug. He waited until she'd vanished into the diner's kitchen before speaking.

"I'm still trying to wrap my head around the idea that you're married, Amish. All this time we been working together, you never said nothing about a wife."

Caleb stirred a splash of cream into his coffee. He didn't want to talk about this, but there was no way around it, not now.

"If you'd known anything about Plain people, you'd have figured it out." He set down his spoon and tugged on his short beard. "Only married Amish men grow beards."

"That so?" Milt leaned back against the red vinyl booth, his eyebrows raised. "I reckon that explains why you never would shave that fool thing off."

When they'd first started working together, Milt had suggested he ditch his Amish clothes and get rid of his beard—or at least grow a mustache to go with it.

No offense, but in them clothes and with that scruff on

your face but nothing on your upper lip, you kinda stand out. In this business, that ain't a good idea.

A strange thing to hear from a man sporting a straggly gray ponytail, a jagged knife scar across one stubbled cheek, and two full sleeves of tattoos. But in time, Caleb understood that, in Milt's line of work, those things helped him blend in and gain the trust of the people he needed to talk to.

Caleb had traded his Amish clothes for jeans and T-shirts, and he'd even bought a truck and learned how to drive. But he'd refused to shave, even though his heart ached every time he caught sight of his reflection.

He figured he deserved that.

"So? Tell me about this woman of yours. What's her name?"

"Rhoda." The name felt strange on his lips now.

"That ain't a name you hear every day, is it? Well, you picked yourself out a real pretty one. Seeing as how I'm old enough to be her dad, I reckon I can say that without getting myself punched in the face."

"Don't count on it."

Milt chuckled, but then his expression got serious. "It ain't good, that boy having her pictures pinned up like that."

Caleb tightened his lips. "I know."

"You recognize the place where she was at?"

"Yes." Caleb pulled one of the photos out of his jeans pocket and unfolded it on the table.

"Whoa, now!" Milt frowned. "You shoulda left that right where you found it. I told you, I called in a tip. Cops'll go over that place with a fine-tooth comb, and you stole a piece of evidence."

Milt hadn't given his name, and he'd called from a phone that couldn't be traced. This was an off-the-books job, and he didn't want to answer a bunch of questions.

"I left the rest behind." He hadn't wanted to. He'd wanted

to rip every picture of Rhoda off that wall. "This was taken in her parents' bakery. Or what used to be her parents' bakery, back home in Johns Mill. They leased out the business and moved north not long after my parents were killed."

"So it's an old picture?"

"At first I thought so. But look here." He pointed to something just visible on the wall behind Rhoda's head. "See that? It's a calendar. Open to June of this year."

Milt squinted at the photo. "Seems like she's come back home." He shot a look over the picture at Caleb. "You're married to this good-looking girl, but you didn't have no idea where she was?"

"We haven't talked to each other in . . . a long while."

"You two getting a divorce?"

The waitress returned with their breakfasts. She made small talk as she set the plates of eggs and grits down, double-checked their coffee mugs and brought Milt a few packets of grape jelly for his toast.

When she was finally gone, Milt went on, "If you are splitting the blanket, you'll get no judgment from this corner. I got two ex-wives myself."

Caleb picked up his fork and prodded his scrambled eggs. He wasn't particularly hungry. "Amish people don't divorce."

Milt was peeling the top off his plastic packet of jelly. He paused, looking at Caleb. "Like not ever?"

"Not ever."

Milt whistled. "So two young folks goof up and get married that shouldn't. They got to live with that mistake for the rest of their lives? That don't seem too sensible, if you ask me."

"The church wouldn't ask you. Or anybody else." Caleb set his fork down. Ordering breakfast had been a waste. There was no way he could eat right now. "But sometimes there's not much sensible about it, no. And it's harder for us because I'm shunned." Milt still looked confused, so he explained. "The way we live . . . it's not like it is for you

Englischers, where women can support themselves easy. A married woman can work, at least until she has children and it gets too busy at home, but it's the husband's job to take care of his family's needs. But because I'm shunned, Rhoda isn't allowed to accept a glass of water from my hand, much less take money from me. None of my family can."

Milt stared, the triangle of toast in his hand forgotten. "You're kidding me."

"No."

The older man shook his head. "I had a great-uncle who belonged to one of them snake-handling churches, but I never heard of nothing like this before. So how'd you get yourself—what'd you call it again?"

"Shunned."

"Shunned." Milt repeated the word slowly, testing it on his tongue. "What'd you do?"

"It's more what I wouldn't do." He'd hoped that would be enough, but from the expectant look on Milt's face, it wasn't. "I wouldn't obey the church."

"You wouldn't do as you was told?" Milt snorted. "No surprise there."

Caleb ignored the jab. He couldn't argue with it anyway. He'd skirted the church's rules as long as he could remember, at least the ones he thought were silly or self-destructive.

Which was most of them.

That had caused some problems over the years. The Amish church took a stern view on rebellion—and Caleb's parents hadn't been big fans of it, either. But mostly he'd skated by.

It wasn't until after his parents' deaths that things had come to a head. He'd point-blank refused to follow the church's mandate to forgive Trevor Abbott for the murder of his parents, and he'd insisted on doing whatever it took to bring their killer to justice.

That hadn't gone over well. Justice, it turned out, wasn't something the church cared so much about.

Worse, it also turned out that Caleb wasn't someone Rhoda cared so much about. When she'd had to choose between him and her father, she'd made that plenty clear.

"That's it?" Milt prodded, breaking into his thoughts. "You just blew off some rules?"

"Where I come from, that's enough."

"And you're telling me that got you set crossways against your own family." Milt chewed a bite of toast and thought that over. "Including that pretty little wife. Seems like a shame. Can people ever get themselves un-shunned?"

"Some people can, *ja*. But probably not me."

He'd thought about that—a lot. Especially at first. But slowly he'd come to suspect that there was no road back, not for him.

He should never have joined the church in the first place. He'd realized he wasn't cut out to live Plain by the time he was eighteen. He'd only delayed telling his parents because he'd known how it would grieve them.

Then he'd fallen head over heels for Rhoda Lambright, their bishop's only daughter. And the minute she'd said she loved him back . . . well. He'd squashed down his doubts right quick. With the prospect of having Rhoda for his wife, he couldn't join the church fast enough. Rhoda was all that mattered. With her by his side, he'd figured he could put up with anything, even a bunch of fussy rules he didn't agree with.

He'd miscalculated, badly. He'd willingly chosen Rhoda over his own beliefs, but she hadn't returned the favor. When he and the church had parted ways over his parents' murders, he'd pleaded with Rhoda to leave with him. But like always, she'd chosen her father's side, not his.

The long and the short of it was, he'd made a *schtupid* mistake, and mistakes had consequences. He'd heard *Daed* say that a thousand times, and it was true. These consequences hadn't fallen to him alone, though. That was what bothered him the most.

"What are you going to do?" He looked up to find Milt studying him. "You got a plan worked out? Because—" The other man's phone buzzed, and he picked it up off the table, glancing at the screen. "I got to take this. "He slid out of the booth. "Sit tight. I'll be right back."

Caleb watched him walk outside the diner to take the call, well out of earshot. Likely it was one of the people who'd tipped them off about Trevor. Milt was always close-mouthed about his network of sources, probably why he had so many of them.

He studied the picture of Rhoda, straightening it gently with one finger. She was standing behind the counter at her parents' bakery, her forehead puckered as she slid a plump cinnamon roll into a cardboard box. Her face was circled by an angry red smear.

He'd never seen a photo of his wife before. Except for the red scrawl marring it, this one looked so normal and so real that he could almost smell the warm, spiced air of the bakery and the sweet, clean scent of the soap she liked. As he looked down at his wife's face now, his pulse quickened just as it had the day he'd walked in and seen her working, just like that, a shaft of morning sunlight falling across her face.

She'd been wearing a plum-colored dress, and she'd looked so . . . perfect. He'd stood stock still and stared at her like he'd never seen her before in his life. Which was silly, because of course he had. Plenty of times. Rhoda was Emma's best friend, and she'd been in and out of the Hochstedler home for years.

He'd done his best to give her a wide berth, though. She was the bishop's daughter, and Caleb was always in trouble with the deacons as it was. The last thing he needed was for

Rhoda to carry a tale home to her *daed* about something else he'd said or done wrong.

He'd privately wished Emma had chosen somebody else to be friends with. To make matters worse, it was soon plain to see that his older brother, Joseph, had his eye on Rhoda as a potential wife.

Joseph was steady and hardworking, but he wasn't much *gut* at talking to girls, so Caleb wasn't sure that Rhoda even knew that herself. But sooner or later, he'd figured his brother would speak up, and he and Rhoda would make a match. In Caleb's opinion, the two were well suited to each other, although he wasn't looking forward to having anybody related to the bishop as a permanent part of his family.

That was all the thought he'd given to Rhoda Lambright—right up until that morning.

But that day—he was never sure afterward what was so different about it. He only knew that he'd walked in the bakery with his heart firmly in his own possession, just as it should be. But when he'd walked out again, his heart—and all the rest of him—had belonged to Rhoda.

It was as simple and as complicated as that.

When Milt slid back into the booth a few minutes later, his face was troubled. "That was a friend of mine who has some law enforcement connections. He ain't heard nothing new about Trevor, but he says he'll let me know if he does. But he thinks, same as me, that this ain't a good sign, us finding those photos."

"No, but Trevor couldn't have been hanging around a bakery in Johns Mill taking pictures. It's a small town. People would have recognized him."

"Somebody else could have sent him the photos, though." Milt leaned over the table, his eyes holding Caleb's. "Because maybe—and here's the worrisome part—he wanted 'em. Could be Trevor's got wind you're hunting him, and maybe he's decided to make this personal. Teach you a lesson by going after your girl." Milt leaned against the back of the booth, frowning. "Maybe you and your missus ain't on speaking terms, but you'd better warn her. Like you did your sister when we thought Trevor was headed up that way last year."

Caleb winced. That was the last time he'd seen his twin sister, Emma. It hadn't gone well, and it had turned out to be a false alarm. Trevor hadn't even shown up.

His gaze drifted back to the photograph. "Likely Rhoda won't listen. Nobody paid much attention last time, and since it turned out I was wrong, they'll be even less likely to listen to me now. But you're right. I have to try. So I guess we're heading to Tennessee."

"Sorry, Amish." The older man shook his head. "I didn't mind helping you out with this—you know that. But there's a paying job I got to see to. Cash is running low, and I need to get some bills back in the old coffee can."

"I understand. I'd appreciate it if you'd keep your ear to the ground, though, and let me know if you hear anything new."

"That I can do. And listen here. You watch yourself. Having those pictures on the wall like that, not half hidden, and not ripping 'em down before he left . . ." Milt clucked his tongue. "He's getting sloppy. I took a picture of them pills. They're some kind of antipsychotic, according to the internet. And he ain't taking them. Could be this guy's getting close to having himself a breakdown. And that's when the really bad stuff starts to happen."

Really bad stuff. Caleb studied Rhoda's image, so sweet and unsuspecting. Part of him wanted to run straight to her to see for himself that she was all right—and keep her so.

The other part of him wanted to shy clear of what had caused him such excruciating pain. Every corner of Johns Mill held memories of his parents . . . and of the sweet, too-short time when Rhoda had loved him back.

But how he felt didn't matter. He had to warn Rhoda and keep her safe, if she'd let him. And if Trevor was headed to Johns Mill, Caleb needed to get there ahead of him, set a trap, and wait. It was the best chance of ending this cat-and-mouse game once and for all.

Long story short, he was going to Tennessee. He might as well get started.

"I'll be careful," he assured Milt. He slid out of the booth, eager to get to his truck and on the interstate. Trevor already had a couple hours head start.

Milt stood, too, sticking out his hand. When Caleb took it, the older man clamped down with a firm grip.

"I'm sorry to part company with you, Amish. You got a hard head and a short fuse, but you're one of the good guys. You get yourself in a fix up there, you call me, you hear? I'll come. You got my word on that. Now, go on. I got breakfast covered. You best get on the road."

Caleb nodded his thanks and headed for the door. And as he passed the front of the diner, he glanced through the window. Milt had settled back in the booth, pulled Caleb's untouched breakfast over, and was scooping the food onto his own plate.

In spite of his worries, Caleb found himself fighting a grin. *It's a sin to waste gut food. Mamm* had told him that a thousand times growing up.

In fact, she'd told him that at breakfast that very last morning, scolding him for leaving a scrap of sausage on his plate. Then she'd ridden off in the buggy with *Daed*, heading to work at the general store.

As Caleb strode toward his truck, his smile faded into a grim determination.

Chapter Three

RHODA HOCHSTEDLER BENT TO CHECK THE PAN OF apple turnovers baking in the oven.

"They're not quite brown enough yet, but close," she told her morning helper, Edna Raber.

"I can ice 'em when they're done," Edna volunteered. "Then I'll mix up more snickerdoodles to replace that batch I burned this morning."

Edna had felt so bad about that. The elderly widow had been a faithful worker when Rhoda's parents had run the bakery, and she'd gratefully accepted an offer of a part-time position when it had reopened. But she was in her late seventies now, and not in the best of health. Lately she'd been making a good many mistakes, and Rhoda couldn't afford to waste any more ingredients. The bakery was running on a shoestring these days.

"That's all right, Edna," she said gently. "It's nearly time for you to go home. I'll manage."

"I'll get these bowls and pans washed up anyhow before

I go. This quiet spell won't last long. It's near ten, and folks always come in around then, ready for a snack. You'll be too busy up front to fiddle around back here."

Rhoda glanced at the clock ticking on the wall, and her heart skipped. Was it already that late? She made sure the cooling rack was ready and set the plump sleeve of vanilla icing handy by, ready to drizzle over the hot treats.

She hoped they browned quickly. The twins would be waking up soon, hungry and a little cranky as they usually were after a nap. The days when she brought the children to work were always harder.

Rhoda often left Vonnie and Eli with her sister-in-law, Naomi, who cared for them along with her own little daughter, Elizabeth. But Naomi had a doctor's appointment today, and Joseph planned to take Elizabeth out to his woodworking shop while his wife was gone. Rhoda couldn't very well ask her busy brother-in-law to mind her two children as well.

Naomi and Joseph had been so kind already, inviting her and the twins to stay at the Hochstedler family farm while the apartment over the bakery was finished. She certain sure didn't want to cause them any more trouble than she had to.

She checked on the turnovers again, dabbing at her perspiring forehead with one dark green sleeve.

It was a blessing to be busy, she reminded herself. She'd known running the bakery all by herself would be hard. Hadn't she worked here ever since she was a *youngie*, after school and during the summers? She'd remembered how demanding this work could be.

And if she hadn't remembered, goodness knows, *Daed* had certainly warned her. Isaac Lambright had been discouraging this plan since the day Rhoda had proposed it, three weeks after he'd suffered a heart attack at their dinner table.

We should wait, Isaac had advised. *In a few months I will be well enough for us to move back and reopen the bakery together as we'd planned.*

Rhoda loved her father, and she prayed he was right. But life had taught her how suddenly sweet hopes could sour. When things didn't work out as you'd planned, it was no use wringing your hands. You prayed, you cried, you accepted the troubles *Gott* had seen fit to send you, and then you rolled up your sleeves and got to work.

They needed the bakery up and turning a profit soon, especially since Isaac wouldn't be able to work too hard for a while. And of course there were the hospital bills that wanted paying.

So she'd stood her ground with her father for only the second time in her life. She sure hoped this worked out better than the first time had.

To Rhoda's astonishment, *Mamm* had taken her side.

It's a schmaert *plan,* Ida had said. *The Hershbergers weren't good managers, and the bakery's trade has fallen off badly. Rhoda knows the business as well as we do. She can get things started up again while you recover, and she'll have Edna to help her. Caleb's family, too. They are kind people and feel badly about the fix their brother left Rhoda in. Besides, it is only for a short time. Soon enough, we will follow.*

It wasn't easy, trying to build the bakery's business back up and take good care of her children as well. But Rhoda—much to her guilty surprise—found she rather liked making her own decisions for a change. Even small things, like what display shelf to put the cookies on or what flavor of muffins to bake of a morning.

After her marriage had fallen apart, she'd been forced to rely on her parents for support. As grateful as she was, moving into their home had felt like stepping back into a well-padded cage. She knew her *daed* loved her dearly, but to him, she was always a *dochder,* someone to be sheltered and directed, not really a grown woman and a *mamm* capable of making her own choices.

Of course, since one of her choices had put her in this fix, she could hardly blame him. He'd advised her not to marry Caleb, but she'd not listened. She'd pay for that mistake for the rest of her life—they all would. But this time on her own had made her think that perhaps—just perhaps—she should carve out a little breathing room for herself and the *kinder.* A bit of space between herself and her well-meaning father might be a very healthy thing.

That was why she'd suggested that the empty rooms above the bakery be turned into an apartment. Fortunately, her brothers-in-law, Joseph and Sam, had readily agreed to do the work for nothing, which had appealed to her father's love of a good bargain. Of course, he'd not expect her to keep on living there once he and *Mamm* were back in town.

But the more Rhoda tasted independence, the more she prayed she could talk him into letting her keep this elbow room.

The bell on the bakery door jingled, startling her out of her thoughts. Someone was here, and the turnovers still weren't quite right. But in the time it took her to wait on the customer, they'd likely burn, and she couldn't trust Edna to watch them.

"Just a minute," she called, hurrying to slide the turnovers out of the oven. Another minute or two would've been better, but they'd just have to be a bit pale. "Don't ice them," she instructed Edna firmly. "They're too hot just now. I'll see to them later."

Wiping her hands on a towel, she moved toward the shop area, peeking into her father's old office as she passed the door. Vonnie and Eli were still asleep on their pallets, but as she watched, Eli flipped over and stuck his thumb in his mouth. He always got restless just before he woke up. She wouldn't have very long.

She winced when she saw who was waiting. Dora Byler

was a former schoolmate, and she'd never been one of Rhoda's favorite friends. The sharp-faced young woman was scanning the scanty array of pastries in the glass case. She frowned as Rhoda took her place behind the counter.

"I wanted some caramel sticky buns, but I see there's nothing but crumbs in that tray."

"*Gut mariye*, Dora." Rhoda offered the greeting Dora had skipped. "*Ja*, I'm sorry. Those went real fast this morning."

"You should make more of them," Dora returned tartly. "So others don't have to go without."

"Next time I will." Rhoda forced a smile. "Since I'm just getting the bakery going again, we're carrying a limited selection. I've some fried pies, though, peach and blueberry both. You bought a half dozen of those on Monday, I remember. Would you like some more? I'll throw in an extra one of each flavor."

"You can keep them. I gave the last ones to our pig. The pastry was tough, and the fruit filling wasn't near sweet enough."

Oh, dear. Edna had made those. Rhoda should have tasted them before selling any.

"I'm so sorry. I'll refund your money." When Rhoda moved toward the cash box, the other woman shook her head.

"*Nee*, that's all right. In your situation, you need every penny. But I have to say, I expected better. Those were worse than Arleta Hershberger's, and hers were terrible. I told my Irvin that I couldn't believe you'd made them. Poor Rhoda always had a real *gut* touch with pastries, I said."

Rhoda could feel her cheeks stinging. *Poor Rhoda.* That was a bit hard to take.

"How about some of these cinnamon rolls? I believe you'll like them better. And I'd like you to take them at half price to make up for the pies."

"I suppose I will. I want to support your business, but

these better be good. My Irvin doesn't mind how much I spend usually—he's such a generous husband—but he says we can't go buying pastries that are going to end up in the hog trough."

"Then maybe you should bake your own, Dora. See if your husband likes those any better."

For one horrified second, Rhoda thought she'd spoken her uncharitable thought aloud. Then she saw Mary Yoder, the owner of the quilt shop across the street, walking in the door, her pleasant face set in uncharacteristically stern lines.

"*Gut mariye*, girls," she said briskly. "Rhoda, I popped over for one of your chocolate cookies. I've been thinking about it all the morning." She shook her gray head ruefully. "I didn't have so much trouble resisting temptation when the Hershbergers were running this place. But now that you're back, I can't stay away."

Rhoda smiled. "I'm so glad. Just let me finish up with Dora here, and—"

"Never mind," Dora cut in sharply. "I don't think I'll take the cinnamon rolls after all. I'll try to come back in a day or two, if I have the time. And Rhoda? I'm praying for you and your poor children."

It took Rhoda a second, but she managed another smile. "*Denki,* Dora. That's real kind of you."

Mary offered Dora a tight-lipped smile, which faded the minute the other woman was safely out of the door.

"Ugh," Mary said. "That girl gets under my skin. I'm sorry. I'm afraid I cost you an order."

"Don't fret yourself." Rhoda slid open the back of the case to retrieve one of the cookies. She deliberately chose the biggest, with plenty of pecans. "I think she mainly came in here to complain."

"Even so, add her cinnamon rolls to my order. And six more of those cookies, too."

"You don't have to do that," Rhoda protested.

Mary chuckled. "Like it's such a hardship for me to take home extra treats! And don't you worry. You'll have this business booming in no time. Now let's talk of pleasanter things. Any word from Miriam? I've missed her help at the quilt shop while she's been away with that handsome new husband of hers. Do you know when they'll be back?"

"Not yet, but we expect to hear from them soon." Miriam was Caleb's younger sister, and three weeks ago, she'd married horse trainer Reuben Brenneman. In spite of her trying morning, Rhoda's lips curved up at the memory.

That had been such a happy day. Bittersweet for her, because it brought up memories of her own wedding. But Miriam's joy had been so hard won that it was impossible not to feel glad for her.

"I'm looking forward to having her back at work, that's for certain sure." Mary lifted her eyebrows behind her round spectacles and smiled. "At least until she gets too busy at home."

Womanly code for *until the babies start arriving.* Rhoda felt a painful pang of envy. She'd always longed for a big family. It had been real lonely, growing up as an only child in a community where large families were common, and she'd prayed that one day she'd have a houseful of little ones to love.

She pushed the feeling away. She was very thankful for her two children. Given her circumstances, she easily could have ended up with none at all, and how empty her life would have been.

She hoped *Gott* would bless Miriam with lots of healthy, happy babies. She'd rejoice with her over every one and with Emma and Naomi, too, as their families grew. These three women were like her own sisters, and she'd not begrudge them any joy.

The minute Mary was out the door, Rhoda was back in the kitchen, pastry bag in hand, drizzling icing in a steady stream over the turnovers. The turnovers were still a bit too hot, and the icing lines weren't as crisp as she'd have liked, but they would have to do. Edna had finished the dishes up and left, and Rhoda was secretly relieved.

She wasn't sure how she was going to manage Edna, but she'd need to figure something out. Everything this bakery offered needed to be tip-top quality. Dora wasn't the only one who'd complained about the Hershbergers. They'd damaged the bakery's reputation so badly that Rhoda's first job in Johns Mill had been to order a new sign, renaming the place Lambright's Bakery.

She and her parents hoped that would encourage their old customers to come back. Business had fallen off dramatically after *Daed* had leased this place to the Hershbergers and moved to Pennsylvania.

They'd moved because of her, and it hadn't been an easy decision. Nothing had been easy during that terrible winter. The grief over Caleb's parents had been fresh and raw, and the *Englisch* media had camped out around the Hochstedler home, causing all sorts of problems. It had been a very dark time, made darker by her husband's stubborn refusal to let go of his anger and submit his will to the church—and her growing certainty that he never would.

She'd tried to talk to him. Her father had, too. All their pleas had fallen on deaf ears. Caleb was too hurt and too angry with Trevor, and with the church and with *Gott* Himself, to listen. The worry of it all had made her physically sick—although now, looking back, that could have been the beginnings of her pregnancy making itself felt.

But she hadn't known that then. All she'd known was that her husband was pulling away from everything she believed in. She'd sensed his leaving, the way she could sense a snowstorm brewing long before the first flakes fell.

And she'd known he'd ask her to go with him.

Her *daed* must have known that, too, because he'd sat her down and talked to her plainly about what would happen if she followed Caleb away from the church. She'd never forget how her father's deep voice had trembled as he hammered home the penalties for breaking the vows she'd made when she was baptized.

You must not leave with him, Rhoda. If you stand firm, he may come back when he suffers the full consequences of his foolishness. But if you go with him, if you cushion the edges of that pain, he will likely not come back, and you will be shunned, just as he is. And that will break our hearts, your mamm's and mine.

She was their only child. What could she do? So when Caleb had asked, she had said no, although she'd wept watching the man she loved beyond measure striding away from her. She'd hurt him badly, she knew. Her unwavering trust in her father's guidance had long been a sore spot between them. Caleb had never understood that her father was also her bishop, that her loyalty to him was loyalty to her church and to *Gott*.

Loyalties, she learned, that her new husband didn't share.

After he was gone, her parents had made hasty arrangements to visit relatives in Pennsylvania. A change of scenery, they'd said, would do them all good. But she knew they were worried over how hard she was grieving. They feared if Caleb came back and asked again, she might change her mind and go with him.

But Caleb had never come back.

The turnovers went blurry, and Rhoda blinked hard until they came into focus. She readjusted her grip on the icing bag and went back to work, her lips pressed into a determined line.

She tried not to let herself think about Caleb too often. She couldn't change the sorrows in her past, and it was a sinful waste of time to dwell on them. Better to focus on what she could do something about, like caring for her children and making this bakery profitable again.

The bell jingled again just as she finished the last turnover.

"Coming!" Setting the icing bag aside, she stepped quickly to the sink to wash her sticky hands.

As she hurried back toward the front, she cast another quick glance at the twins as she passed the door. Still sleeping, but now Eli was halfway off his pallet, and Vonnie's small rump was sticking up in the air. She pulled the door closed, hoping they'd doze a little longer.

"I'm sorry to keep you waiting." She slipped around the corner into the store, wiping her damp hands briskly on a towel. "I'm shorthanded today, and—Oh!"

She stopped short, staring in disbelief at the man who stood in front of her, unsmiling, his once-familiar face set in new hard lines, his green eyes wary.

It was as if he'd stepped right out of her troubled memories. Her heart went suddenly, painfully still.

Caleb.

Chapter Four

THE PICTURES HADN'T TOLD HIM THE WHOLE TRUTH. Rhoda didn't look exactly the same. Like the painted sign over the front door of the bakery, she'd changed. The rosy-cheeked girl he'd married had turned into a woman. Her features were sharper, and the innocent softness he remembered was gone.

Guilt rolled in his chest. Their marriage hadn't been kind to her. It hadn't done him any favors, either. He'd hurt her by leaving. She'd hurt him by staying.

It had been a mistake, just walking in like this. The shock of being in the same room with Rhoda after all this time had hit him hard. He couldn't seem to move or speak. He couldn't do anything but stare at her.

She stared back, her face blank and stunned.

He should say something. The problem was, he had no idea what. He'd been driving all night, pushing past exhaustion with truck stop coffee and determination. All he'd wanted was to get here, see Rhoda face-to-face and reassure himself that she was all right, that Trevor hadn't gotten to her first.

He had no idea how he was going to explain this, no idea how to get her to listen to him.

All he could do right now was look at her. Because even with that new hardness in her face, when she'd gone white as a sheet, her brown eyes huge, Rhoda was still the prettiest woman he'd ever laid eyes on.

"Caleb?"

Hearing her whispering his name again cut at him.

"*Ja*, it's me, Rhoda." It was the first time he'd spoken an entire sentence in *Deutsch* in a very long time.

Except, of course, in his dreams.

"It's you," she repeated. Her face crumpled, and she stumbled toward him.

Without thinking, he held out his arms to her the way he'd done a hundred times. She ran into his embrace, as if the past couple of years hadn't happened at all. As the familiar warmth of her body nestled against his, such a fierce joy washed over him that his knees nearly gave way.

He rested his chin on her crisp *kapp*, pressing her close. He shut his eyes, drinking in the sweet, familiar scents of soap, vanilla, and sugar. Part of his mind was shouting warnings at him, but he didn't care. He didn't care about anything in the world, except for this.

Except for her.

She was crying. He could feel her gentle shudders against his chest, and it tore at him. Because in a minute, she'd start asking questions, and—

What was that?

A stealthy rustling was coming from Isaac's old office. Caleb's blood went cold. Leaning down, he whispered in Rhoda's ear.

"Who else is here?"

She stiffened and stepped out of his embrace, scrubbing the back of her hand across her eyes.

"Wh-what—" she stuttered. "Why—" Her eyes skimmed over his clothing. Jeans and a shirt. *Englisch* clothes. She darted a worried glance at the office door.

And she didn't answer his question.

"Why are you here, Caleb?" Rhoda's voice shook, and she pitched her words low, as if afraid of being overheard.

He frowned. Rhoda was hiding something. Somebody was in Isaac's office, of that he was certain sure. His wife had never tried to deceive him—or anybody else—before. Not ever. And her face was tense with fear.

Suspicion prickled across his shoulders.

"I need to talk to you." He kept his eyes on her, but his attention was on the closed door. Another soft sound.

Rhoda crossed her arms in front of her apron, her lips trembling. "That's why you've come back after all this time? To talk?"

Another quick flick of a glance to the left. The tears sparkling in her dark eyes did nothing to settle his nerves. He'd always hated to see her cry.

"We can start with that."

She straightened her shoulders and lifted her chin. "There's nothing for us to talk about, unless you're ready to make things right with the church." She swallowed. "Are you?" She shifted her position, angling herself in front of the office.

Milt had taught him to check for the little tells that let you know what was really going on, no matter what people were saying. The way Rhoda was behaving reminded him of how people acted when they were stonewalling you, assuring you the person you were looking for wasn't there, that they hadn't seen him in weeks. Distracting you by loud complaints about what you were doing at their house, when they knew perfectly well why you were there.

While they did that, the person you were looking for—a person they either loved or were deathly afraid of—was sneaking out a window somewhere.

And right now Rhoda seemed very much afraid, which would make sense if Trevor was skulking in Isaac's office. Could be Caleb hadn't gotten here quite quick enough.

But he was here now. He stepped around her.

"Caleb?"

Without answering, he headed for the door. She followed, pulling at his sleeve.

"Please," she choked out. "Don't—"

"Run," he muttered through clenched teeth. He broke free from her grasp and kicked the door open.

Two small children were bedded down on muddled nests of blankets on the office floor. At the loud noise, they sat up, looking at him with wide, startled eyes.

Then they started screaming.

He staggered to the side as Rhoda pushed past him. She went to the wailing children—a boy and a girl—murmuring reassurances in *Deutsch*.

"It's all right," she said over and over. "Don't cry. Everything's all right."

Both children held up their arms, sobbing frantically, flexing their fingers to be picked up. "*Mamm! Mamm!*" Rhoda knelt beside them, gathering them close, whispering into their ears.

Realization dawned, followed by a wave of shock so strong that Caleb's knees turned to jelly. He sagged against the doorframe.

Mamm? If she was . . .

That meant *he* was . . .

"Rhoda—" He sounded like a strangled frog.

"Go away." Her voice was clipped and hard. This time when she looked at him, something more than tears sparkled in her eyes—something he'd never seen there before.

Defiance.

"Can't you see how frightened they are? You've scared them half to death. You need to leave, right now!" It wasn't a question—or even a request. It was an order.

Caleb's brain was in survival mode, his whole world shifting and reforming in a way that made it impossible to think straight. He wasn't sure of much right now, but one thing he knew already.

He wasn't going anywhere.

"They're mine." Bewildered hurt rose in him, laced thickly with anger. "You were pregnant when I left. And you didn't . . ." He trailed off, unable to believe what he was about to say. "You didn't *tell* me."

Rhoda's cheeks had gone from pale to bright red. She held herself stiffly, facing him down like a small hen defending her chicks. "By the time I knew for certain, you weren't here to tell."

"*Rhoda*." He took a step toward them, and the little girl's cries turned back into shrieks.

Rhoda pressed her cheek against the top of the child's head. "Please." She pitched her voice to be heard over the screams. "Leave us alone. They're only little, Caleb! They don't understand."

She held his gaze as she spoke, her dark brows drawn over her eyes in a straight, no-nonsense line. But the wobble in her voice gave her away.

Orders and threats would never have gotten him out of that room, but that little tremble was a different story. Rhoda had been scared earlier. He hadn't been wrong about that. But it wasn't Trevor who'd frightened her, who had her gathering her children close.

It was him.

The sweet familiarity of before, of holding her in his arms again as if nothing had changed, vanished like dew on a hot summer morning.

Nothing was the same between them.

The woman he remembered, the woman he'd loved, would never have feared him. She'd been the one who'd always seen the good in him, who'd innocently expected blessings from his hand, when others only expected trouble.

He'd tried his best to live up to that trust, but in the end, trouble had come to Rhoda through him, although he hadn't meant it to be so. And now everything had changed.

He had to swallow three times before he could speak.

"All right, I'm leaving for now. But Rhoda? I'm coming back. Soon. We need to talk."

She looked as if she might cry, but when she answered, the telling wobble was gone.

"Bring the bishop with you. I won't be talking to you without him here. Now, go, and shut the door behind you. Ssshhh," she whispered to the snuffling *kinder*. "Everything is all right now."

Caleb backed into the bakery and closed the door. He stared at it in disbelief, trying to gather his scattered wits.

He—Caleb Hochstedler—was a father. Those two babies in that room—those tiny children calling Rhoda *mamm*—they were his. He knew that was true, that it had to be true. But the fact bumped against his stunned brain and heart, like a bird against a windowpane unable to get inside.

How could Rhoda have kept such a thing from him? And for so long, too, for at least . . .

Caleb did some clumsy calculations in his head. The children had to be just shy of two years old.

Almost two years, then, plus the months of her pregnancy.

His stomach rolled. He had some thinking to do—a lot of thinking, as soon as his brain cleared. Once he had his feet back under him, he'd piece together a new plan from the shattered bits of the old one.

Because this . . .

This changed everything.

He left the bakery, heading for his truck. When he cranked it, he realized he had no idea who now served as bishop in Johns Mill. Not that it mattered.

He wasn't talking to any bishop, not right now. Not until he'd had a few words with his brother Joseph.

As he drove to his late parents' farm, bitterness and disbelief built in his chest. Rhoda should have told him about his children. She could have. His post office box address had been on all of his letters. She should have sent word to him the minute she'd been sure herself. That went without saying.

She hadn't, and her father would be behind that. Caleb was sure of it. Rhoda had gone along with her *daed* in this—even in this—as she always did.

That was bad enough.

But his family must have known about the children, too. All of them, including the brother he'd asked special to look out for Rhoda. And none of them—not one—had told him.

He arrived at his old home. As Caleb pulled into the drive and jammed the truck into Park, his gaze zeroed in on the chicken house. Right there, in that little coop. That's where he'd asked Joseph to look after Rhoda while he was gone.

He'd had to force himself to ask. He'd trusted that Joseph would see to his sister-in-law's well-being. But he'd also known that Joseph had once had feelings for Rhoda himself.

Since then, his brother had married Katie Lapp's *kossin* Naomi Schrock. He'd found that out the last time he'd been in Johns Mill hunting for Trevor. He remembered Naomi dimly. A frail little thing, best he recalled, but with a sweet way about her.

But still, she was not Rhoda.

He jumped out of the truck, slamming the door behind him loud enough to make the hens squawk. The place looked different, he noticed with a pang. Naomi's flower beds, for instance, were smaller than *Mamm*'s had been, although they were just as carefully weeded. A vivid memory of his mother kneeling in the dirt, industriously yanking weeds, rose up in his mind, and he quickly turned away, toward the old dairy barn.

When he'd left, the stone building behind the house had been unused and full of cobwebs. The Hochstedlers had been dairy farmers for generations, until *Daed* had given it up to open a general store downtown catering to tourists. He'd had little use for the barn then.

Now, though, it boasted a freshly painted door and a sign out front advertising Joseph's woodworking business. Joseph would be working on this weekday morning, so Caleb headed in that direction. He pushed the door open without knocking.

It looked nothing like he remembered.

He'd spent nearly every morning of his teenage years in this barn, helping with milking, cleaning up muck, dealing with cows. Now tables and woodworking equipment were everywhere, and projects in different stages were stacked against the wall. Instead of smelling like cows and milk, the air smelled of newly cut wood and varnish. The place was neat and organized, with enough space for two or three men to work.

But Joseph was working alone, bent over a spinning lathe. When Caleb banged the door shut, his brother looked up. He stopped pumping the foot pedal, and the spindle slowed.

Trust Joseph, Caleb thought irritably, to use a foot-pedaled lathe, even though the church allowed electric tools in a business like this. Joseph had always been a stickler for rules.

For a few seconds, the brothers regarded each other silently. Then Joseph pulled off his safety glasses and set them on his worktable. He moved carefully and methodically, his face unreadable.

"Caleb," he said. "This is a surprise. What—"

"I wouldn't bring up surprises just now, if I were you. You knew." Caleb crossed the room in three long strides until he was a scant yard from his brother.

Joseph stood his ground without flinching.

"What is it that I knew?" He spoke quietly, but Caleb saw the muscle jumping in his brother's cheek. Joseph was not half so calm as he seemed.

"Don't play *dumm*. I've been to the bakery and seen for myself. You knew about the children. *My* children. And Rhoda's."

Joseph nodded. "*Ja*, I knew. Everybody knew. Twins are not so easy to hide."

"So everybody knew but me." The next words stuck in his throat, but he forced them out. "Their father."

He was a father. It didn't seem possible.

"You've reason enough to be upset." Joseph sounded tired. "But little cause to be angry. I thought of trying to reach you. But it was Rhoda's job to tell you such news, and if she didn't see fit to, I didn't think it my place to interfere."

"Not your place? You promised you'd look after her."

Irritation sparked in Joseph's eyes. "And so I did. So I am doing yet. She's staying here with us, her and the *kinder*, while we fix up another place for them to live. Naomi helps with the twins as much as she can so Rhoda can get the bakery going again. Your wife's gone without nothing I can provide for her, and she's welcome to it. This I have done, and gladly, because Rhoda is my sister-in-law. I have not failed your *fraw*, Caleb. That fault lies with you."

The truth of that didn't make it any easier to hear. But still . . . if he'd only known . . . "You should have gotten word to me."

"You should not have left," Joseph countered bluntly. He spoke with such certainty that Caleb's temper flared.

As usual, Caleb was the only one at fault in his brother's eyes. It had always been so, and it irritated him now as much as it ever had. Struggling for self-control, he tightened his hands into fists.

Joseph didn't miss the gesture. His eyes narrowed.

"You want to strike me for telling you the truth? Go ahead. You know already that I will not hit you back. But fighting with me will not change the facts, and I doubt it will make anyone think you should have been told about your children sooner."

Caleb made himself take a long, slow breath. As aggravating as his brother was being, he had a point. Caleb deliberately opened his hands, pressing his palms flat against his jeans.

"I don't want to hit you, *bruder.* But I do want to know about . . ." He forced himself to speak evenly. "About my children. I want you to tell me everything."

Joseph shook his head stubbornly. "That I will not do."

"Joseph—"

"I told you before. This was Rhoda's secret to keep, and now it is her explanation to give. Whatever you want to know, ask her. But"—Joseph's voice grew sterner—"mind yourself, *bruder.* Step carefully and watch your temper. You have hurt your *fraw* badly, and you've broken your vows not only to her but to the church. And from the look of those clothes and that truck I see through the window, your heart has not changed. Has it?"

Caleb was silent. After a second, Joseph sighed.

"Until it does, you are shunned and an outsider here. Rhoda and her children must come first with us."

Her children. Caleb's heart chilled as he studied his brother, who returned the gaze without blinking.

"So that's the way it is," he said slowly.

"That's the way you have chosen for it to be," Joseph retorted. "If you decide you want to make a different choice, you will have to talk to the bishop. Abram King serves us now. You'll remember where he lives. In the meantime, I will keep praying for you, as I've done all along. We all will. Now I need to get about my work."

He put on his safety glasses, picked up his chisel, and started the lathe spinning.

Caleb watched in disbelief for a minute, but his brother pointedly ignored him. Finally Caleb gave up. He left the old dairy barn and stalked across the yard to his truck, feeling even more frustrated and bitter than before.

That hadn't accomplished much. Except now he knew who the bishop was.

He climbed in the truck and started the engine. He let it idle while he tried to think.

At least there was no sign of Trevor so far. He'd check around some more, though, to make sure Rhoda was safe.

Rhoda and the children. His children.

A chill went down his spine. He didn't have only Rhoda to protect now. There were the little ones, too.

Judging by today, he wasn't particularly welcome here. But welcome or not, he needed to stay close by until he found out what Trevor was up to. And no doubt that meant jumping through whatever hoops Rhoda and the bishop set up.

Gritting his teeth, he shoved the truck into gear and pulled out onto the highway. Fine. He'd drive out to Abram King's first thing tomorrow morning. He honestly didn't care what the man had to say, but Rhoda did.

So, *ja*, tomorrow he'd see Abram. Afterward, he'd have a long talk with his wife, and then he was going to meet his son and his daughter. Finally.

And nobody—not Trevor Abbott, nor his brother, and certainly no Amish bishop—was going to stand in his way.

Chapter Five

CALEB KNEW EXACTLY WHERE ABRAM KING'S FARM was. He'd driven down this road a hundred times.

He still almost missed the turn.

He'd thought he was used to how much faster he got places in his truck, but it was different when on a road he'd never traveled except in a buggy. The drive that would have taken him half an hour was over in less than ten minutes.

That was part of it. But he was also still reeling from yesterday. He'd expected this trip to be . . . hard.

He'd had no idea.

Caleb tightened his grip on the steering wheel.

After leaving Joseph yesterday, he'd poked around Johns Mill, keeping his head down, trying to avoid being noticed. He'd walked by his *daed*'s old general store, but it was closed. A handwritten sign in the window said it would be opening back up in three days.

Then he'd driven to the neighboring towns and checked at motels, asking questions. He'd used all the skills Milt had taught him, but he'd found no sign of Trevor anywhere.

Afterward, he'd driven back to his father's farm. He'd parked on the side of the dark country road, just out of sight of the house where Joseph's family and Rhoda and the twins—his children—were sleeping. He'd dozed in the front seat, waking instantly whenever a car passed by.

That hadn't happened often. Just before dawn, he'd seen lamplight twinkle through the dark trees, shining from his *mamm*'s old kitchen window. Satisfied that everything was all right, he'd started the engine and driven to a convenience store at the edge of the county. He'd spruced up best he could in the restroom and bought himself a cup of strong coffee so he'd be wide awake for this meeting with Abram.

It wasn't a good idea to meet with any Plain church leader unless you had all your wits about you.

He had no intention of being kept away from his children, not by the church or anybody else. The idea of them—of two babies belonging to him—was still unsteady . . . fragile and new, like a chick fresh-hatched from an egg. He wasn't sure yet how to handle any of this, but he knew one thing already. It was his job to provide for those little ones, to look after them and protect them, best he could.

He planned to do that, once he'd figured out how. But he also knew his wife—or at least, he thought he still did. If her bishop told her to steer clear of her troublemaking husband, she would.

He couldn't let that happen.

Caleb turned into the trim, well-kept farmyard and killed the engine. He probably should've borrowed somebody's horse and buggy, he realized belatedly. Showing up here in a pickup wasn't likely to win him any points.

Although, maybe this particular bishop wouldn't mind as much as most would've. He recalled Abram as a chubby man with an easygoing nature and a knack for farming. Caleb had liked him, even after he'd been chosen to be a minister. Usually that would have been reason enough for Caleb to cut a wide berth around a fellow, but Abram hadn't become as serious and high-minded as most men did. At least, not best Caleb remembered, but then, he'd never paid much attention to Abram.

In any case, it was too late for second guesses now. Caleb got out of the truck. He didn't bother heading for the house. A farmer wasn't likely to be inside once the sun was up. He'd check the barn first.

Sure enough, Abram was inside, dressed in work clothes. He was leaning against the plank walls of a large stall studying its occupants, a skinny red cow with wicked-looking horns and a shaggy gray donkey.

He turned as Caleb approached, and his eyebrows disappeared under his bangs.

"Caleb." The sound of his name spoken aloud in Abram's familiar bass voice made goose pimples pop out on Caleb's arms—and gave his jumbled emotions another stir. "Welcome. I heard the car, but my wife hired a driver to take her to her sister's this afternoon. I thought maybe Birdie had gotten her times mixed up. I'm sorry I didn't come out to meet you."

The apology was something of a surprise. So was the fact that there was no disapproval on Abram's face—not yet. Only curiosity.

"I figured you'd be expecting me."

"*Nee*," Abram said. "Or rather, I'm surprised to see you today. But *ja*, I've been expecting a visit from you ever since Rhoda returned with the *kinder*." The cow lowed irritably, and the bishop turned toward the stall. "Steady there, Lula." He turned back to Caleb. "You'll have seen your *fraw* already, then?"

"I have, yesterday. She sent me here."

"I see." The bishop drew in a long, thoughtful breath. "I'd invite you inside, but I have to keep an eye on these two for the next little while. You all right with talking out here?"

"I don't care where we talk."

A smile played around Abram's lips. "Or what we talk about, I'm thinking. You've only come to get this part out of the way, ain't so? What I say matters very little because you've decided already what you will and won't do." When Caleb's eyes narrowed, the bishop chuckled. "Five sons," he explained. "And more than one stubborn boy in the bunch. I know it when I see it."

"You're right." Since Abram seemed to have a grasp on the situation, Caleb saw little point in starting off with an untruth. "I don't much care what the church thinks about this, and I have made up my mind that I won't be shut out of my children's lives. But it matters to Rhoda that she stay in your good graces, so I've come, hoping you and I can work out an arrangement that will suit us both."

"So you're a stubborn man but also an honest one." Abram gave a philosophical shrug. "*Gut.* That's not much, maybe, but it's enough to make a start."

"I want to spend time with my children." *And protect them and Rhoda from Trevor the way I couldn't protect my parents.*

He didn't say the last part aloud. He had no reason to think Abram would be sympathetic to his concern about Trevor. Rhoda's father certainly hadn't been. Caleb had heard so many lectures about trusting *Gott* that he could have preached a sermon on the topic himself.

Nodding, Abram picked up a wisp of clean hay and stuck it in his mouth. "Of course you want to spend time with your little ones. And so you should."

Caleb crossed his arms, waiting for the other shoe to drop. Surely this wasn't going to be that easy.

Suddenly the cow bawled again and charged at the donkey, horns lowered. The donkey sidestepped her, regarded her with his calm gaze for a second, then turned away and went on placidly chewing hay.

Caleb frowned at the animals, his attention distracted. "What are you doing with these two?"

Abram shot him a sideways look, chewing his own hay as calmly as the donkey. "Making a start." When Caleb only stared, the bishop chuckled. "Forgive my little joke. Lula there is a good cow. Fine pedigree and young enough to have years of calves ahead of her. But she was mistreated where she was before, and she has no patience with men nor with other animals. I tried putting her in with the rest of my herd and ended up having to get my bull stitched up by the vet. She gashed him with those horns of hers."

Caleb considered the cow. Thanks to the long years working at the dairy with his *daed*, he knew cows well enough to appreciate the good lines of this one. But he also noticed the white around her eyes and the stiffness of her stance.

Ja, that was a real *gut* cow there. That was also a real angry cow there.

There were ways to deal with that, but most of the time, cows that started off hard to manage stayed hard to manage. *Daed* had happened across a few mean ones over the years, mostly picked up at sales or auctions. He'd never kept them long. Ill-tempered cows were more trouble than they were worth.

He started to say so, then decided against it. Telling Abram what to do with his animals probably wasn't a good idea. Instead, he asked a question.

"Why's she in there with that donkey?"

"It's a little experiment I'm trying. She needs calming, Lula does, and Domingo's good at that. Of course, just at the moment, she's none too fond of him, but I think she's already starting to come around. Opposites." Abram slanted a look at his visitor. "It's funny, ain't so? How often *Gott* uses opposites to bring about balance?"

Caleb ignored the question. He certain sure didn't want to get into a discussion about God with a bishop. Best to change the subject. "I thought donkeys were known to be stubborn animals."

"You're thinking of mules. Besides, this donkey is a special one. I borrowed him from my friend Reuben Brenneman. He uses Domingo to help calm jittery horses. You'll know Reuben, of course." When Caleb didn't answer, Abram prodded, "Your new brother-in-law."

Caleb jerked around to stare at him. "Brother-in-law? I have no brother-in-law at all, new or old."

Abram lifted an eyebrow. "You have some catching up to do. You've got two of 'em by my count. Sam Christner, to start."

"Sam?" Caleb's heartbeat sped up as his overtaxed brain worked through that information. "So he finally married Emma, then. I knew he wanted to, but with his eye trouble, I wasn't sure he would." He thought it over and decided he approved. "He'll be *gut* to her," he murmured, speaking mostly to himself. "He always was silly over Emma, even back when we were in school together."

"He is silly over her yet," Abram remarked, smiling. "And she feels the same for him. They're running your parents' store together, although they've closed up shop for a few days. They've gone on a trip just now to attend the wedding of one of Sam's *kossins*. There've been a good many weddings happening just lately." Abram studied him. "You'll not have known, then, that your sister Miriam was married last month?"

"Our Mirry's *married*?"

Caleb thought he'd been shocked often enough by now that he'd be immune to it, but this news floored him yet again. The last he'd heard, his younger sister didn't even have the courage to set foot off the family farm. She'd witnessed their parents' murders, and she'd been so traumatized that she'd lived in terrible fear afterward.

Even now, the memory of Miriam's suffering made him feel sick to his stomach. It had been miserable to watch, and none of them could find any way to calm her. Now Abram was telling him his baby sister was married—to some fellow he'd never even met? How was that possible?

"Happily married, *ja*. She's doing much better these days, your *schwesdre*." Abram spoke gently. "You'll be glad of that, I'm sure."

Glad. Was he glad? He supposed so. He seemed to have gone numb.

It was so much, all at once. He was a father. Little Mirry was married, and so was Emma. Rhoda was so afraid of him that she'd shut him out of his children's lives.

The sick feeling in his gut grew stronger.

"Rest easy. Reuben's a *gut* man. I should know." Abram chuckled again, a rich sound. "He lived here for months while he was preparing to join the church."

Caleb looked up sharply. "He wasn't Amish?"

"He was and he wasn't. Born Plain, but hadn't been baptized because he thought he wanted to live *Englisch*. Came here, met your sister, and decided different." Abram smiled. "Of course, given that, I had to be sure he was joining for the right reasons. Falling in love's no reason to join the church. Love makes a savory sauce, but there must be strong spiritual meat to pour it over." He waited a beat. "You've found that out for yourself, ain't so?"

There was only mild curiosity in Abram's question, but Caleb flinched. The bishop had a point. Caleb and Rhoda had both paid a high price for that lesson. Falling in love was a very poor reason to join the church.

A horrifying idea occurred to him.

"You don't expect me to live here with you, do you?"

Abram guffawed and slapped his thigh, making Lula moo and stomp one hoof. Even the calm donkey raised his gray head to regard the bishop with a puzzled look.

"*Nee*," the older man said when he could speak. "I don't think that'll be necessary in this case. And good thing! Such an arrangement would likely be the end of both of us. Anyhow, your situation is different. Reuben was a man outside of the church wanting to marry one of our own, so naturally I had to be careful of that. You already are married."

Caleb was getting tired of dancing around the truth. "I'm also shunned," he pointed out. "Which I'm guessing is going to be a big problem."

Reuben wouldn't have been, not if he'd never been baptized. Whatever obstacles Miriam's new husband had faced here, shunning wouldn't have been among them.

Miriam's husband. Caleb shook his head. That would take some getting used to.

"*Ja,*" Abram agreed calmly. "It'll complicate matters some. Unless you've come home prepared to make full repentance for your actions?"

When Caleb didn't immediately answer, the bishop shrugged and sighed. "I figured that was too much to hope for just yet."

"Shunned or not, I want to see my children."

"And so you will, with a few guidelines in place."

Finally they were getting to the heart of this. Caleb braced himself. "What guidelines?"

"That we should talk about with your *fraw*, all of us together. She's at the bakery working now, *ja?* We'll go there," Abram announced.

"Now?" Good. He wanted to get this settled.

"No better time. I believe I can leave Lula and Domingo together all right. If she hasn't already gored him, I don't think she will. Besides," Abram added with a smile, "it's been a while since breakfast. A cinnamon roll and a cup of *kaffe* would just about hit the spot. I'll hitch up the buggy, and we'll drive over together."

Caleb shook his head. "Thanks, but I'll drive my truck."

"That would be quicker," Abram conceded. "But I cannot ride with you, as you know. That's forbidden. So you will have to wait for me. Is that all right?"

"I guess so."

"While you are waiting, maybe it would be best if you did not talk to Rhoda about this matter further. No sense stirring a stew without the cook on hand to supervise."

Again, that rich, rolling chuckle. “Although,” he added thoughtfully, “you might go on and order me that cinnamon roll. They are very nice, and they sell out fast.”

Then to Caleb’s astonishment, the bishop gave him a friendly clap on the back and whistled for his horse.

Chapter Six

SOMEBODY RATTLED THE BAKERY'S DOOR HANDLE. Hidden in the kitchen with her children, Rhoda bit her lip. It was past time to flip the sign to **OPEN**, and she couldn't afford to miss her morning sales.

But she was in no frame of mind to deal with customers, not yet. Her heart was racing, her knees were wobbly, and there was no way she could chitchat about the weather and make change.

So she stayed inside the kitchen, out of sight of the street, watching her children play with some wooden toys their *onkel* Joseph had made for them.

Vonnie was walking carved animals up the ramp into a hollow Noah's ark, babbling to herself. In spite of her churned-up feelings, Rhoda smiled. Her daughter was a sweet child, easily entertained and easily pleased.

Meanwhile her twin brother fought with an oversized painted top, trying to make it spin. This had been an ongoing struggle since Joseph had given them the toys a week ago.

The twins weren't quite old enough for the tops, but Eli was never one to give up without a fight. Rhoda watched her son wrap his fingers around the chunky stem of the toy, trying to make it whirl. It flopped over. He pushed his lips out and tried again.

And again.

Yesterday evening Eli had grown so frustrated that he'd yelled and thrown the top, narrowly missing his *kossin* Elizabeth's head. Rhoda had spoken to him sternly, her heart lodged in her throat. She'd brought the twins—and their tops—with her to the bakery today. It would make her work harder, but it wasn't fair to ask Naomi to cope with Eli's temper.

At least that was the reason she'd given. But she knew—and Joseph and Naomi had also known—that she wanted to keep the twins close by because of Caleb. She wasn't sure yet what her stubborn husband might do.

Eli had inherited that stubbornness. That was becoming clear, and it sometimes kept Rhoda up at night, fretting. She knew what heartache such obstinance could cause, not only for her son but for those who cared about him.

She squeezed her eyes shut. *Please Gott, help me to bring my son up so that his strength of will is a blessing instead of a fault.*

She'd prayed that prayer a thousand times, and she'd keep on praying it. If she'd learned one thing during these hard months, it was to lean on *Gott*, even when He seemed silent. Surely, in His *gut* time, He would answer her.

Although probably not in the way she expected.

She'd prayed for Caleb all through these months, too. Prayed for that moment when he'd see the error of his ways and come home.

She'd kept praying, even as the *when* in her thinking had shifted to *if*. *If* she saw her husband again. *If* he ever came home. Her prayers had begun to focus on acceptance, on building a life without Caleb, for herself and their children.

She believed what *Daed* had told her. Unless Caleb came home for the right reasons, it was probably best that he stay away. Otherwise, his return would only cause more trouble and heartache.

But yesterday, the minute she'd seen him, what had she done? She'd run straight into his arms before talking to him, before even asking why he'd come home.

It certain sure wasn't because he'd found out about the twins. There'd been no mistaking the shock on his face when he'd realized they were his. Rhoda touched that painful memory lightly, then dropped it as she would a hot biscuit.

Nee, he'd not come because of the children. And he clearly hadn't come back to make his repentance, either. So why *had* he come?

Could it be . . . had he come back, finally after all this time . . . for her?

She'd been turning that possibility over and over in her mind since yesterday. And she didn't trust the way her heartbeat skipped at the idea that Caleb still . . . cared. She'd been led astray by her heart before, and she had two innocent souls to protect now. She couldn't afford to be so foolish, not again.

For the first time since she'd returned to Johns Mill, she wished her father were here. She'd leaned heavily on her *daed*'s wisdom since Caleb had left. She'd considered calling and leaving a message at their *kossin*'s store. But this news would likely upset him, and she didn't want to do that, not when his health was still so uncertain.

Anyway, she knew already what he'd say. *Daed* would tell her to rely on the church for guidance, so that's what she'd do.

She didn't have quite the confidence in Abram King as

she did her own father—that was natural enough. But he was the leader *Gott* had chosen, and she would mind what he said. If Caleb wanted to make his repentance—which she very much doubted—Abram would know how to go about that. If Caleb wanted to remain outside their faith but have some contact with his children, those arrangements would be Abram's responsibility to oversee. Hers was only to obey.

That would likely be hard enough.

A series of raps on the door made her jump, so hard and firm that she knew before looking who it would be.

Sure enough, Caleb stood on the sidewalk, looking at her through the glass. He didn't smile and wave as he would have back when they were courting. He only held her gaze, waiting for her to open the door.

He was alone. Either Abram hadn't told him what he wanted to hear and he'd gone off mad, or he hadn't visited the bishop at all. With Caleb, either was possible.

She would have to stand her ground with him about involving the church in this. Her heartbeat faltered. All of her life, she'd been taught obedience, first to the church, then to her father. Once she'd married, she'd expected to obey her husband.

But of course, she'd trusted in her husband's commitment to obey their church as well, as he'd vowed to do. That trust had been misfounded. Now, obedience to one meant being at odds with the other. Nobody had taught her how to handle that.

She glanced back at the twins, still happily absorbed in their play. Then she said a quick prayer for strength, squared her shoulders, and walked to the door.

The minute she opened it, Caleb stepped inside. She locked the door behind him, then turned to face him, braced for battle.

Caleb had the strongest will of any man she'd ever met.

She'd have to make things clear from the get-go. Otherwise, he'd roll over her like a marble rolling pin, smashing all her objections flat.

She took a steadying breath—and wished her knees would stop shaking. "Caleb, I told you—"

"I know what you told me," he interrupted. "And I've done what you asked. Abram's on his way."

Her argument sputtered like a damp candle wick. "Abram's coming? Now?"

"He wants to talk to both of us together, he said. And he wants a cinnamon roll."

Rhoda blinked. This was unexpected. Well, not the cinnamon roll. Abram never came into the bakery without buying some sort of sweet treat. More than one if he was out from under his wife's watchful eye.

But she'd expected Abram to talk with Caleb privately first and then with her. She wasn't sure how she felt about all of them meeting together so quickly. She needed to speak freely, and with Caleb sitting beside her, that would be difficult.

"Rhoda?" Caleb looked at her, an uncharacteristic uncertainty in his green eyes. "I did what you asked. I'd like a favor in return."

"What?"

"Abram said you and I weren't to . . . talk about anything until he got here, but while we're waiting, I'd like to see the little ones." He shifted his weight from one boot to the other. "I hardly even got a good look at them before. If you don't mind, I'd rather meet them now, while we're alone."

Rhoda hesitated, sympathy warring with concern.

She needed Abram here. She wasn't sure how to deal with this. And she certain sure needed to know what had brought her husband home and what his plans were before this went much further. The idea of Caleb being part of the twins' lives while living among the *Englisch* and thumbing his nose at church rules . . . that worried her.

On the other hand, she could understand Caleb not wanting to meet his son and daughter under the eye of the bishop. He'd never felt comfortable around church leaders, and for good reason.

"All right," she conceded. "They're in the kitchen."

Caleb crossed the bakery in a few long strides, but he stopped short at the kitchen doorway.

Rhoda paused behind him, unsure what to do. Best, she decided after a second, to do nothing. She would step in if the children showed any signs of being upset. But Caleb would have to handle the introductions himself. She had no idea how to go about it.

He took a step in the children's direction—then paused. He turned to Rhoda, and the raw pain on his face made her catch her breath.

"What?" she whispered, alarmed.

"I don't . . . I don't know their names," he ground out roughly.

She swallowed. "They are called Vonnie and Eli."

"Vonnie and Eli." Her husband's eyes locked onto hers. "Short for Lavonia and Elijah? You named them after my parents?"

She cleared her throat. "There were two of them, a boy and a girl. It just seemed . . . right."

His gaze stayed fixed on hers, his chest rising and falling. "That was . . . that was kind of you. Especially since . . ." He trailed off. "It was kind of you," he repeated.

"I loved your parents very much," she reminded him softly.

He didn't answer. He tightened his lips and glanced away, but not before she'd seen a suspicious glitter in his eyes. The only time she'd ever seen Caleb weep had been on the day of his parents' funerals.

The memory made her heart ache. She'd wanted so desperately to help him during that terrible time, but she hadn't known how.

"Go ahead," she prompted him gently. "Speak to them."

He walked forward, slowly, and her heart constricted. Caleb was a sudden sort of a man, in all his ways, thoughts, words, and actions. He was holding himself back, doing his best not to startle the twins.

He knelt in front of them. His nearness finally captured the twins' attention, and they studied this strange fellow, their eyes wary.

"Hi there," he said. "I'm sorry I scared you earlier. I just . . . I'm your *daed*, and I've come a real long way to meet you."

The twins exchanged a glance.

"*Daed*?" Vonnie tried out the word.

Rhoda watched Caleb try twice before he could answer. "*Ja*," he managed. "That's right, sweetheart. You're Vonnie, ain't so?"

The tiny girl nodded.

"And you must be Eli."

Eli said nothing, examining the stranger with a suspicious expression. He was always slower to warm up to folks.

"Want me to show you how to do that?" Caleb reached for the top. Eli snatched the precious toy away, hiding it behind his back.

"Elijah," Rhoda scolded. The child shot her a guilty look. Sharing wasn't something that came easily to him. Reluctantly, he laid the top in front of his father.

"That's a nice one," Caleb said. "Your *onkel* Joseph will have made it, I'm guessing."

Eli didn't answer.

"*Ja*," Rhoda said. "Your brother's been very generous."

Caleb nodded shortly, and Rhoda couldn't tell if he was happy or annoyed to hear of his brother's kindness. Maybe both.

"Spin!" Eli urged impatiently. Intercepting another look from Rhoda, he added, "Please?"

In answer, Caleb set the top twirling. Eli and Vonnie smiled, watching the stripes on the top blend as it teetered merrily across the smooth tabletop. Caleb's eyes moved from his son to his daughter and back again, as if he couldn't look at them enough.

Rhoda crossed her arms over her chest, pressing back the feelings that threatened to spill out. Maybe she should have told him about the babies. She could have. He was still writing and sending those checks back when she'd discovered she was pregnant—with twins no less.

She'd planned to tell him. She'd believed Caleb might come back if he knew she was expecting—or at least she'd hoped so. But then her father had stepped in and taken charge.

When Gott changes Caleb's heart, he'll come back on his own, Isaac Lambright had told her. *Then he'll know of his children, and he can start being the father he should be. But as long as he stays in rebellion, best maybe not to stir this pot with such news. His letters are upsetting you, and the doctor says you must rest and be calm. From now on, we will send them back unopened.*

She'd been so heart-hurt then, and not feeling well. Her pregnancy hadn't been easy, and her doctor had made worried remarks about stress and her blood pressure. Besides, she'd never have ended up in this predicament if she hadn't ignored her father's warnings about Caleb in the first place.

So she'd never read another of Caleb's letters. She'd simply handed them to Isaac to be returned. She'd listened to her father's advice, and she'd obediently followed the course he had laid out for her. In a way, she'd had little choice. She couldn't accept money from Caleb, and she wasn't well enough to work, so her parents had been her only means of support.

But now, watching Caleb meet his children for the first time, she found herself wondering something. Something she'd wondered many times during her courtship and marriage, but not near so often since Caleb had been out of her life.

She wondered if maybe her father had been wrong.

Chapter Seven

Caleb played with the children until Abram arrived. Rhoda kept a watchful eye as she busied herself with various tasks in the kitchen. She tried not to think about all the sales she was missing, all the baked goods that would need to be discounted tomorrow if she couldn't sell them fresh. Today those were the least of her worries.

She was relieved when Abram knocked on the door.

"The bishop's here," she called as she went to let him in.

Caleb was sitting on the floor beside the children's table, patiently spinning the top. He nodded, not looking too pleased.

Abram came in the bakery, his round face beaming. "*Gut mariye*, Rhoda. It truly is a *gut* day for you and the *kinder*, *ja?* Caleb has come back."

Rhoda managed a weak smile. "I guess that depends on why he's come back."

Abram's own smile dimmed, and he nodded. "He did not tell me, either. Still, him coming at all is a good sign, and that's what we will focus on. Now, let's sit down and have ourselves a talk. Also one of your nice cinnamon rolls, I'm thinking. Or maybe two."

This time Rhoda's smile came easily. It was hard not to appreciate an enthusiastic customer like Abram. He was a bakery owner's dream.

"I'll put them on a plate for you."

A second knock sounded behind him. "That'll be my Ann. I asked her to cancel her plans with her sister so she could help with the twins. She can take them to the playground for a while and then drive them out to Joseph's. If that's all right with you, of course."

"*Ja*, that's fine with me." Rhoda had been wondering how they'd carry on such a serious conversation with the twins underfoot. She knew Ann King well and trusted her, so this was a good solution.

"But," Abram murmured hastily as Rhoda went to unlock the door again, "maybe I'd best have only one of those cinnamon rolls. My Ann is not so fond of sugary foods." The chubby bishop and his spare-framed wife had an ongoing battle over his sweet tooth.

Ann greeted Rhoda pleasantly, explaining that Mary Yoder had stopped her on the sidewalk, slowing her down. She sent her husband a stern *behave yourself* look as she passed him on her way into the kitchen. When he smiled innocently, she rolled her eyes. Ann King was nobody's fool. She knew her husband couldn't visit a bakery without indulging, but she seemed prepared to accept the situation philosophically.

She greeted Caleb with a cautious courtesy, gently interrupting the lesson on top spinning. She took charge of the twins, and soon the three of them were on their way to the park.

Caleb stood, watching the children through the big windows until they were out of sight. Then he followed Abram and Rhoda into the office, pulling up a chair with a resigned air.

Rhoda unfolded a second metal chair for herself, and Abram settled behind the big desk, a fat cinnamon roll and a steaming cup of coffee in front of him. He sighed happily and took a big bite before speaking.

"So," he said after he'd swallowed, "this will feel strange, I'm thinking. It's been a while since you two have seen each other, ain't so?"

Caleb and Rhoda shared quick glances, and her cheeks heated.

"*Ja*," she said. "That's so."

"And as we discussed earlier, much has changed since you went away, Caleb. Your brother's and sisters' marriages, and their *kinder* coming along."

"*Kinder*?" Caleb glanced up sharply.

Rhoda and Abram looked at each other.

"Your brother has a daughter, and Emma has a son," the bishop explained.

Caleb looked as if he were about to speak, but finally he nodded without saying anything. Rhoda felt for him. It was his own fault he'd missed so much, but it must feel bewildering, facing so many changes all at once.

"Of course," Abram went on, "your own *kinder*—they will be your biggest concern. The whole world changes for a man when he becomes a father, ain't so?"

Rhoda was watching Caleb out of the corner of her eye, and she saw him tense. "I wouldn't know. I only found out about the twins yesterday."

"And here you sit, together with your wife and a bishop, talking." Abram scraped icing off his plate with his fork. "Not something you would have easily agreed to before, I think. Already, being a father has changed you. However," he continued, his voice sounding more serious, "some things do not change. The church doesn't shift easily, and you've set yourself at odds with our rules for a long while. So." The bishop leaned back in his chair. The cinnamon roll had vanished, and the plate was scraped clean. "There are things we must talk about and some questions I will have to ask. Starting with this one. Have you come back intending to draw your wife and your children away from their faith?"

Rhoda held her breath, but Caleb didn't flinch. "No."

"Do you mean them or any other member of our community physical harm?"

Caleb's eyes narrowed. Rhoda could tell he didn't like the question, but he kept his voice civil. "No, I do not."

"Are you prepared to respect our faith while you are here? *Nee*"—he held up a silencing hand when Caleb started to speak—"I did not say follow it. I asked if you will respect it, if you will allow Rhoda to continue in her service and obedience to the church and to her community unhindered. Are you prepared to do that?"

This time Caleb's answer took longer, but after a second or two, he nodded. "*Ja*. That I will do."

"*Gut*." Abram nodded. "I have other questions, but I'll not be asking them yet. There's no point in asking a man who doesn't know the answers. As you said, you've only just found out about the twins—and many other things. You have much to think over, many things to decide. That will take some time."

"That's so." Caleb shot Rhoda a quick, sideways glance. "But this I know already. I want to be a part of my children's lives."

"Of course." Abram shifted his weight in the office chair, which squeaked an alarm. "You'd be a poor excuse for a man if you didn't want that. We will start by making those arrangements and deal with the rest later. For this, you must be close by, ain't so? Where are you thinking of living, Caleb? Not with me," he added with a chuckle. "As I said, I don't think that would work well for either of us. But I'm sure we can find you another place to stay nearby."

Rhoda sneaked a glance at her husband's face. He studied the bishop, his expression blank.

"You expect Caleb to live here?" she asked. "In Johns Mill?"

"That would seem the most sensible thing," Abram replied.

"I'm willing to stay close by," Caleb said. "The closer, the better."

Abram appeared satisfied with that answer, but Rhoda wasn't. If the bishop wouldn't ask, she'd do it herself. "For how long?"

Her husband set his jaw. "I'm not leaving anytime soon."

"And that is enough for today," Abram announced firmly. "In *Gott*'s good time, we will learn what the future holds. Now," he went on, "while you are here, you must have a place to sleep. Normally, of course, you would stay with your wife and family, but this is an unusual case. Rhoda, you're still living with Joseph, ain't so?" The bishop cocked his head thoughtfully. "Not such a good idea, maybe, for Caleb to stay there as well." He pounded on the table, making them both jump. "There is an apartment upstairs, isn't there? Above the bakery? I believe I heard you are having it fixed up."

"That's true," Rhoda admitted cautiously. "We're planning to live there, the twins and me, once it's ready."

Abram hoisted himself to his feet. "Let's go take a look," he said. "It may be just the thing."

Rhoda wanted to protest. The place wasn't yet finished. Besides, Caleb living right above the bakery where she worked every day, in the space she was fixing up to be a home for herself and the twins?

She wasn't sure she liked that idea. And she was positive her father wouldn't.

But she silently rose to her feet. She couldn't argue with a leader of the church. Besides, since the space wasn't ready to be lived in, there was no harm in showing it. She never thought she'd be thankful for how slowly the renovations had proceeded, but now that was a blessing. Abram would soon see for himself that his idea wouldn't work.

She led the way to the door at the back of the kitchen, opening it to reveal the wooden staircase leading upstairs. Faint odors of fresh wood and paint drifted down.

Those hopeful smells, mingled with the familiar scents of the bakery kitchen, steadied her. The upstairs apartment and its promise of future independence had lent her comfort for the past few months. Caleb's arrival hadn't changed that—and likely wouldn't.

Everyone knew Abram loved to go after lost sheep, but he'd never met one like her husband. Sooner or later, the bishop would have to face the truth. Caleb couldn't rejoin their community until he humbled himself before the church, and Rhoda knew better than most how unlikely that was.

Very.

She motioned for Abram and Caleb to go up the stairs first, taking a moment to collect her wits before following. The apartment wasn't large, but it was plenty big enough for Rhoda and the twins. A living area–kitchen combination was located over the bakery showroom itself, and the rest of the space, three small bedrooms and a bathroom, was arranged over the large industrial kitchen.

Originally, they'd only planned two bedrooms, one for her and one for the children. The twins had slept in the same room since birth, and with only one dividing wall, Joseph said, the apartment wouldn't seem so cramped.

Rhoda had agreed to all his other suggestions, but she'd insisted on adding another bedroom. The extra work made the renovations take longer, so she'd felt guilty over her stubbornness. Joseph and Naomi had been welcoming and kind, but it couldn't be easy having three additional people under their roof.

But since the twins were a boy and a girl, sooner or later

they'd do better in their own rooms. And if she managed to keep her newfound independence from her parents, she'd need this apartment for many years to come.

The night Joseph had agreed to her plans, she'd lain awake in the old farmhouse where her husband had spent his boyhood, crying softly into her pillow so as not to wake the twins slumbering nearby on their cots. She'd not understood why she'd cried—she hardly did that anymore, and she should have been pleased. But for some reason, she'd missed Caleb that night more than she had in a long, long time.

The memory unsettled her, and Rhoda took her time going up the stairs. When she reached the apartment, Caleb and Abram had already finished looking around.

"It needs some work yet," Abram was saying. "But you don't seem the sort who needs much comfort, and you can keep plenty busy up here while your *fraw* works in the bakery. You being a carpenter and having nothing else to do, the work should get finished real quick."

"Joseph and Sam are doing the work on the apartment," Rhoda protested quickly. Both men turned to look at her.

"Sam can see well enough to do construction work again?" Caleb asked.

Rhoda expected Abram to answer, but the bishop only looked at her expectantly.

She cleared her throat. "Not so *gut* as to work at a job, but well enough to help out here if Joseph guides him some. They've both been so kind, fixing this for me. I don't want to appear ungrateful by changing plans now, even if that would get the work done faster."

She also wasn't too sure how pleased Joseph and Sam would be to see Caleb, but that didn't worry her near so much as her father's likely reaction if he heard Caleb was involved in the apartment work. He might very well insist on shutting down the whole thing.

She couldn't very well explain that, though, so she stayed uncomfortably silent.

Abram cleared his throat. "Caleb, would you wait downstairs, please? I'd like to have a word with Rhoda."

Caleb didn't look too pleased, but he nodded. "All right."

The bishop waited while Caleb clumped down the stairs. Then Abram closed the door at the top of the steps.

"Rhoda, I'd like to ask you a question, and I want you to answer honestly." He waited for her nod. "I know your *mann* has a reputation for being hotheaded, so I must ask. Has he ever taken his temper out on you? Do you fear him? Is that why you don't want him helping with this work?"

"No." Rhoda shook her head. "Caleb has never raised a hand to me."

Abram smiled. "*Gut*. That relieves my mind."

"But this work has all been planned out. Besides, I'm not so sure Joseph and Sam will be happy to have Caleb's help, and they have been so kind. I wouldn't like them to be upset." She decided to go ahead and say it. "I don't believe my father would approve, either. And since this building belongs to him . . ." She trailed off, hoping Abram would understand the situation without further explanation.

"I see." Just as Rhoda relaxed, the bishop went on. "But many hands make light work, and your brothers-in-law are busy men with families and concerns of their own. I'm sure they'll accept whatever skilled help they can get." He sounded very certain. "As for your father, of course he is upset about how you've been treated. That's understandable. But the best remedy for that is for Caleb to make his peace with the church. That may take some time, so for now we must keep him near, keep him involved. I will write to your father, explaining that. He is a wise man, and I'm sure he will set his personal feelings aside and join us in our prayers that this plan will work." He paused, as if choosing his next words carefully. "You have been a very *gut* and obedient *dochder*, Rhoda, always. But now you are also a wife, and you must think first of your husband, *ja?*"

Abram's voice was as kind as always, but Rhoda felt a tiny sting, as if she'd been gently scolded.

Caleb had often accused her of putting her father before him, but she'd always insisted it was the church she was putting first. Now that the church and her father seemed likely to be on opposite sides of the fence, she wasn't sure what to do.

"*Ja*, of course," she whispered after a second. "My husband comes first."

"*Gut*. So?" He waited a second, eyebrows lifted. "Do you have any other objection?"

Rhoda shook her head miserably.

"Then I think my idea is best. Caring for you and your children is rightfully your husband's responsibility. You cannot accept money from him, but there is nothing I know of that prohibits him doing this work in return for being allowed to stay here. *Gott* has brought Caleb back here for some purpose. Perhaps he will not stay, but until he decides, we must not give up hope." He considered her soberly. "Will you do as I ask in this matter?"

Rhoda managed a nod. "Of course."

"We are agreed, then. He will stay up here and do the work that's needed. He can spend his evenings visiting you and the *kinder* at your brother's home."

"At Joseph's?" She wasn't sure how well that plan would go over, either.

Abram nodded. "Being with family will do him good. Of course, since he is shunned, there will be some inconveniences, but I trust Joseph to manage that. Also Caleb must meet with me once a week while he lives among us, and we will explore his objections to our faith. All of us will plant these seeds together and see what sprouts. *Ja?*"

"All right." She might as well agree. Whether she liked this idea or not, the church had spoken, and she had to obey.

An understanding sympathy shone in the bishop's eyes.

"You do not trust your husband, I know. Maybe you do not trust me so much, either. That is all right. For now, it will be enough to trust *Gott*," he said. "And to pray very, very hard."

He patted her shoulder gently, then started down the steps.

CHAPTER EIGHT

"I'LL SEE YOU DAY AFTER TOMORROW THEN, CALEB? Early afternoon, say around two." Abram was watching Rhoda put cookies into a bag for him to take along. "Some of those chocolate ones, too, *ja?*"

"Two?" Caleb didn't like the thought of meeting with the bishop every week, but Abram seemed to consider that settled. "Won't that keep you from your afternoon work?"

"Not if you help me with it." Abram smiled. "Plenty of work to do on a farm, as you well know. My boys are leaving home one by one, so I'm always grateful for an extra set of hands. Besides." He accepted the plump bag from Rhoda with a happy nod. "Working side by side makes hard talks easier, I've found."

Caleb hesitated, but it wasn't as if he really had a choice. "Fine."

"I'll be expecting you."

Abram was an affable fellow, but Caleb heard a hint of steel in those words. Rhoda must have heard that, too, because as soon as she'd let the bishop out of the door and locked it again, she turned to face Caleb.

"He'll expect you," she warned. "And if you don't show up, he'll come looking. He's an easygoing man, Abram is, but he means what he says."

"I could tell. Don't worry. I'm going."

Rhoda's expression didn't relax—her brows stayed pinched over her nose. She hadn't liked the idea of him staying upstairs in the apartment. He'd seen her face when Abram had suggested it.

"Rhoda—" he started gruffly. He wasn't sure exactly what he was going to say, but whatever it was, she didn't give him the chance.

"I'm sorry, but I have work to do," she said. "I've already lost the morning. Ann's driving the twins straight to your brother's, and there's things I'd like to get done while they're not underfoot."

She didn't want to talk to him right now. Rhoda had always been like that. When big things happened, she would need some time to herself to think. It had worried him slightly in the first days of their marriage, how she would retreat into herself, and he'd tried to push her a time or two. But he'd learned over time to wait it out.

"All right," he said. "You do what you need to do. I'll go back upstairs and look around. I'll have to rig myself up a place to sleep, and I want to make sure I see everything that needs doing yet before I talk to Joseph tonight."

"You're coming to Joseph's tonight?"

She sounded surprised. He frowned.

"Abram said I should." *And don't you want me jumping through his hoops?*

Maybe Rhoda heard the unspoken question, because she flushed. "I know. But maybe it would be better to give it a day or so and let things settle a bit."

Clearly she wasn't happy about the prospect of spending so much time with him. Hurt pricked at him, but he pushed it aside. Rhoda was the one who'd wanted to involve the bishop in their business.

"I'm none too happy about visiting with my own children under my brother's eye. But Abram wants it that way, and I want to be with the little ones. I'm sorry if that doesn't suit, but if I have to follow the rules I don't like, then so will everybody else."

The flush on her cheeks deepened. "Of course. But Abram didn't set a day for this to start. And"—she hesitated, looking very uncomfortable—"Joseph has been very kind to us, Caleb. You two don't see eye to eye, and it's important to keep peace in the family. Waiting would give us all a chance to settle our minds and pray. Then when we do get together, it will have a better chance of going well."

Caleb felt annoyed—and impatient. He didn't much like hearing his wife praising his brother so highly. And Rhoda's talk of praying felt like ants in his boot—painful and irritating, something to kick away.

Praying had always worked better for her than it did for him.

"All right," he said, exasperated. "I'll wait until tomorrow. But no later. The twins need to get to know me, and I'll need to ask Joseph how he planned to finish the work upstairs." He paused. "That apartment. You really want to live up there?"

"We can't stay with Joseph and Naomi forever. It's a nice enough place, and convenient to the bakery."

He couldn't argue with the convenience. But the nice enough? He wasn't so sure about that.

"It's small," he said. "And likely to be hot in the summertime, being up high and with lower ceilings."

"It's plenty big enough for the twins and me. And we'll just have to do our best in the summer."

"There's no yard for the children to play in." A thought occurred to him. "And where can you keep a horse, living in town? There's no barn out back."

"The children like to play in the park down the road," she said. "It's not the same as just letting them run out the back door, but it'll do. And Sam gave us Maude to use, his *aent*'s old mare. When I'm working, I leave her down the road at Edna Raber's farm. You remember Edna. She worked for my parents for years, and she helps me out some days, in the mornings. Edna's had a hard time since her husband passed, so I pay her a little extra for letting me put Maude in her pasture. It's a good arrangement for us both."

"Jerry Raber's farm is a fifteen-minute walk from here. You're walking that every morning in the dark? With the little ones?" He didn't like the idea of her alone on the road, especially not so early when the light wasn't good.

"Not every morning. When Edna's working, I leave Maude here until she's ready to go home. Her granddaughter Cora lives with her, and she drops Edna off in the morning, and then Edna drives Maude back for me when she leaves at lunchtime. And oftentimes Naomi keeps the twins while I work."

"You still have to walk over in the afternoons, though." When she was worn out from working all day. "That must be hard on you."

"You're thinking *Englisch*," Rhoda said impatiently. "A fifteen-minute walk's no walk at all, and I have a wagon I can pull the twins in if they're tired. Anyhow, it's a pleasant, easy road with almost no traffic. Remember? We used to—" She stopped short, and her cheeks went a darker pink.

It was true they used to walk together down the country lane leading to the Raber farm, slipping away from the bakery and her father's disapproving eye. They'd dawdled on that pretty road many an afternoon. There'd been a little meadow just off the road in Jerry Raber's pine woods that had been their special place. They'd often slipped there to be alone together. He'd stolen many a kiss in that meadow, and that was where he'd asked her to marry him.

"*Ja*," he said softly. "I remember." Their glances caught for a moment, and then she looked away.

"Anyway," she went on briskly. "This arrangement will do for the time being. Now, I'm sorry, but if there's nothing else you need to talk about, I'd better get to work."

Caleb hesitated. There was something he needed to talk about. He needed to tell her about Trevor. About the pictures pinned up in the closet and why he was so worried about her taking a walk she'd taken a thousand times before.

He needed to answer the first question she'd asked him. *Why are you here?*

She'd not asked again. Him finding out about the children had been a distraction for both of them.

He didn't want to tell her. She was keeping him at arm's length already, and bringing up Trevor certain sure wouldn't help. But she needed to know. He studied her face, trying to think of the gentlest way to bring up the subject.

"Speaking of work, have you had any trouble at the bakery since you came back? I mean, with reporters and such?"

She'd started setting out ingredients on her steel table. She shook her head. "They're mostly gone now. A few show up now and then, but if you don't answer their questions, they go away."

"I thought maybe with the movie coming out in a few weeks, they'd start hanging around again." A movie had been filmed in Johns Mill by *Englischers* hoping to capitalize on the country's fascination with his parents' murders. He'd caught glimpses of the advertisements for it here and there, and they made him sick to his stomach.

Rhoda sighed as she scooped flour into her mixing bowl. "Not yet, but Abram talked to us about that after church a couple of weeks ago. He says we'd best be prepared for another wave of visitors. Emma and Sam are thinking of closing the store for two weeks around that time, just to miss the worst of it." She glanced up. "They're running your *daed*'s store now. It was Joseph's idea. It's work Sam can do, and it's going well."

"Abram told me. Maybe you should close the bakery, too."

"Oh, nobody's ever paid much attention to me. It's Emma and Miriam they're interested in." She shook her head as she reached for the bag of sugar. "Why they'd want to make such a movie in the first place, I can't imagine."

"Money." That was the short answer. But he had his own ideas about why this movie had been made—and so quickly. From what he'd seen in the advertisements for it, it was strangely kind to Trevor and hinted of dark secrets hidden in the Amish community. It annoyed him, how they were twisting the truth. But it didn't surprise him.

"Making money from such a tragedy." Rhoda sighed. "It seems wrong. But then, I've heard plenty of Plain folks talking about how business has picked up since all this started. Even the Hershbergers did better with the bakery while the movie crew was in town. The *Englischers* aren't the only ones profiting. Abram says it's *Gott*'s way of bringing good out of the badness, but I still feel guilty when—" She glanced up, as if suddenly aware what she was saying. "I'm sorry. It must be hard for you, hearing about all this. I didn't mean to speak of it so lightly."

She looked genuinely upset, and his heart stirred. Rhoda never hurt anybody if she could help it.

"What they are doing is not your fault. If you can make a little money from their foolishness, I have no problem with you doing so. I just don't want you to be bothered." He hesitated, but he was too close to what he wanted to know to stop now. "You know how people do. *Englischers,* I mean. Making nuisances of themselves. Coming in and taking pictures and all of that."

He waited, but she seemed absorbed in mixing up some kind of dough, and she didn't answer. He tried again.

"You've probably had that happen, *ja?* Somebody coming in and taking pictures of you?"

"I suppose. I pay no attention."

That wasn't helpful. "Is there anybody who does that often?"

She stopped stirring and looked at him over her shoulder. "You mean like a reporter?"

"Maybe a reporter. But anybody. Have you noticed someone coming in more than once, taking your photograph?"

"I don't know." She studied him, her dark eyes suspicious. "Like I said, I pay no attention. *Englischers* know we don't like to be photographed and that we won't give permission if we're asked, so mostly they don't ask. They just take the pictures. They try to be sneaky, but we see. But what can you do? Best to just let it go. They don't understand, and fussing over it is bad for business."

"Will you tell me if you notice someone doing that? Taking your picture?"

She rested the spoon against the side of the bowl and turned to face him. "Why?"

"Because—" He stopped.

She waited, her expression expectant and slightly annoyed. The comforting scents of cinnamon and vanilla hung in the air, mixed with the clean smell of lemon dishwashing liquid. There was a dusting of flour on the front of her apron.

And he just . . . couldn't. He couldn't tell her about that awful closet, about those angry red circles around her face.

"Never mind."

She studied him. "Is it that you're worrying more now?" she asked. "Because of the children?"

He wasn't entirely sure what she meant, but that was a question he could answer honestly. "*Ja*, I am worrying more."

She nodded. "I felt the same way after the twins were born. As if suddenly the whole world was on my shoulders."

The whole world. Guilt and anger kicked him squarely in the stomach. He should have helped her carry that load. It was his place and his right.

"I wish I'd been there."

"I wished that, too," she said quietly. "But at least I had my parents with me. I'm thankful for that."

Caleb had been wondering about something. "Why didn't Isaac and Ida come back to Johns Mill with you?"

"They plan to come when they can. *Daed*'s not well right now. He had a heart attack a while back."

"I'm sorry." He honestly was. Caleb had often disagreed with his father-in-law, but Rhoda was devoted to him. He knew the pain of losing a beloved parent, and it wasn't something he'd wish on anyone.

"He's getting better, thankfully. It's just taking time, and they have all sorts of things to wrap up in Pennsylvania. They'll move here as soon as they can. They don't like being apart from the grandchildren."

That made sense. Ida and Isaac had always doted on Rhoda, and surely they were over the moon excited about the twins. But he was still puzzled.

"It's a hard life for you, looking after the bakery and the children on your own. Why didn't you wait until your parents could come with you?"

For a second, he didn't think she'd answer. "The bakery business had fallen off under the Hershbergers. We needed to build it back up as soon as possible, so I came ahead."

"And your father agreed to that?" Caleb couldn't keep the doubt out of his voice. "You coming here alone?"

"I'm here, aren't I?" Rhoda retorted with a stiff shrug.

That didn't really answer his question. "When he does move back, will he be all right with you living separate from them in those rooms upstairs?" He thought that unlikely, knowing Isaac.

She'd picked up her spoon again, avoiding his gaze. "We haven't talked it over yet. But I think the apartment would be a sensible choice for me and the twins, even after *Mamm* and *Daed* move back. It'll be handy for me to be so close to the bakery. I could do the early work, so they could come in a little later. And living apart means we all wouldn't be so . . ." She seemed to have some trouble choosing her words. "Up under one another's feet," she finished finally.

Caleb couldn't quite believe what he was hearing. Rhoda wanted some space between herself and her father. Finally.

He didn't know how he felt about that. On the one hand, her desire for a little independence was a *gut* thing and, in his opinion, long overdue. If she'd started down this road earlier, things might have turned out differently.

But she hadn't, and here they were.

Still. Good for her.

"I hope your father will listen to you. He should. You're taking the bit in your teeth," he said quietly. "And you're making all this work, hard as it is. Not one woman in a hundred could do half so well."

She looked up, a surprised gratitude shining in her eyes. For a second—just a second—it felt like the old days. The familiarity of it made Caleb's heart jump in his chest.

"If I have done anything well, it is because *Gott* has helped me. I near worried myself sick at first, when you . . . left. And again after the twins were born. And then later, when *Daed* was in the hospital. I'm learning to trust the Lord and submit to His will." She hesitated, her eyes pleading with him. "It's truly the only way to find peace, Caleb."

He'd stopped relying on God a good while back, but he wasn't about to share with Rhoda, nor with Abram, how badly his faith had been shaken. His disagreements with the church had him in enough trouble without digging that hole any deeper.

"I'd best go upstairs and let you get back to work," he said.

Rhoda's hopeful expression fell.

"Fine. I'll likely be busy out front, so just go out the back door in the kitchen when you're ready to leave." She kept her eyes on her mixing bowl.

"All right. I'll be making a list of materials I need, and I'll spend tomorrow collecting them. After that, I'll likely be here working every day."

She nodded without looking at him.

"*Mach's gut*, Rhoda. I'll see you tomorrow evening."

He listened as he walked away. He listened all the way up the stairs. But she never answered.

Chapter Nine

"DON'T WORRY YOURSELF, RHODA. WE WILL TRUST *Gott* and take this one step at a time. It will all work out."

Naomi's voice was calm, and she was setting the supper table with brisk efficiency, but her forehead was puckered. And Joseph hadn't come in from the barn, although the evening chores should have been finished long ago.

They were all *naerfich* about Caleb coming by this evening.

Yesterday afternoon, when Rhoda had driven her borrowed buggy into the drive, Ann's had been parked in the yard. The bishop's wife was in the kitchen having a hushed conversation with Naomi and Joseph while the twins played in the living room with their *kossin* Elizabeth.

When Rhoda walked in, the trio abruptly stopped talking. Joseph avoided her eyes, his expression grim. Naomi's face was pale, but she'd offered Rhoda her usual sweet smile.

"Ann was catching us up on the news," she'd murmured.

Looking a little embarrassed at having been caught gossiping, Ann had quickly taken her leave, and they'd all stood in the kitchen looking at each other.

"So," Naomi had said finally, "Caleb will be meeting with the bishop. That's good news."

"It is news," Joseph said dryly. "Whether it is good remains to be seen." He'd listened as Rhoda explained the bishop's plan. When she'd finished, he'd sighed.

"I suppose we'll see how it goes. With Caleb, you never know."

That was true. Even though he'd told her he'd not be by the bakery today, Rhoda had startled every time the door had opened, expecting him to come striding in. Naomi had confided that she and Joseph had felt much the same, here at home.

Now that it was near the hour they expected him, everyone was on edge.

Her sister-in-law had spent her nervous energy cooking. She'd roasted a chicken, and she'd asked Rhoda to carve it while she put the plates around the table.

Rhoda wasn't so good at cutting up a whole bird. Her mother preferred to do that task herself, so she'd had little practice with it. She suspected that was why Naomi had assigned her the job. She needed to concentrate, and in a strange way, that calmed her.

"I know everything will work out," she said now, setting another slice of meat on the platter. "One way or the other. But I can't help worrying."

"Worrying does no good," Naomi reminded her. Then she sighed. "But *ja*. Joseph is also worried. He and Caleb had words the other day, and it troubled him."

That explained the crease in Naomi's normally smooth brow. A youth spent coping with a heart defect had taught her patient acceptance. It took a great deal to ruffle her calm, but anything that upset her beloved husband would certainly do it.

"Joseph loves his brother, of course," Naomi went on. "We've both been praying for Caleb to return. But now that he's back, there are so many feelings to sort out. Things have been hard between the two of them since . . ." Naomi stopped short, then added, "For a while."

Rhoda glanced up, wondering how much Naomi knew about the beginnings of the tense feelings between her husband and his brother—and the part Rhoda herself had played.

Back in their school days, Emma Hochstedler had been her best friend, and the Hochstedlers one of her favorite families. As the years passed and everyone approached adulthood, she couldn't help noticing that this family included two handsome young men.

Joseph was the quieter one. He hardly spoke, and when he did, his words were often clumsy. But Rhoda had noticed how his eyes had followed her, how quick he was to offer his help at any opportunity. She knew the signs boys gave when they were thinking of a girl in a special way, and she was secretly flattered.

Ida and Isaac had noticed, too, and they'd conveyed a silent approval. Joseph was a kind young man and a steadfast member of the church. He wasn't the sort who hurried, but sooner or later, Rhoda had expected him to ask her to take a drive in his buggy. When he did, she'd planned to say yes.

But one day while she was still waiting for that invitation, Caleb, Joseph's quick-tempered, fun-loving brother, had walked into the bakery, just like he'd done dozens of times. But that particular morning, he'd looked at Rhoda as if he'd never laid eyes on her before in his life.

And she'd looked back.

Right then and there, for reasons she was never able

to fully explain, Rhoda's girlish daydreams had changed direction.

Joseph didn't change course near so easily. She'd seen the wounded surprise in his eyes the day he'd found out she was riding home from singings with Caleb, and she'd noticed the looks that passed between the brothers.

She'd felt bad about that, but she'd been so certain that *Gott* meant for her and Caleb to be together. She'd not been the only one. Caleb's parents had thought so, too, believing her influence would firm up their son's faith and keep his heart here in their community.

They'd all been wrong, of course. But back then, things had been different.

She pushed her memories aside. There was nothing she could do about past mistakes. Besides, maybe she and Caleb hadn't turned out so well, but Joseph clearly hadn't been meant for her. He and Naomi were one of the happiest couples she knew. Whatever spark he'd felt for Rhoda had sputtered out long ago.

But the rift between the two brothers had simmered on.

Rhoda sighed. "I think this is the best I can do with this chicken."

Naomi glanced at the pile of meat on the platter and nodded her approval. "You did a *gut* job."

"Should I throw the bones away, then?"

"*Nee*, I'll put them in the refrigerator, and tomorrow I'll boil them up with some carrots and celery to make chicken broth." Naomi was a frugal and sensible housewife. Nothing went to waste under her watchful eye. "I'll pop in a few cloves, too. That's my secret—" She broke off, her busy hands going still. Rhoda frowned and followed her gaze.

Caleb stood in the kitchen doorway.

He nodded politely at Naomi, looking uneasy. His gaze drifted to Rhoda, holding hers for a couple of seconds, then he scanned the kitchen.

"Everything looks different," he murmured, as if speaking to himself.

Rhoda's heart tightened with sympathy. Her husband had grown up in this house. The kitchen had been his *mamm*'s domain, and the place where she spent most of her time. He'd not seen it since shortly after his parents' funerals.

As Joseph's wife, Naomi had taken over this space, slowly replacing Lavonia Hochstedler's preferences with her own. The room was clean and bright and pleasant, but it would not be the kitchen Caleb remembered.

"*Ja*, we have made a few changes," Naomi said gently. "But one thing is the same. You are welcome here, Caleb."

He blinked and refocused his attention on her. "*Denki*. I came to . . . to see the children for a while. I guess Rhoda told you about that. Sorry, I didn't plan on interrupting your supper."

"You aren't interrupting," his sister-in-law replied. "Vonnie and Eli are in the living room with Elizabeth."

"Elizabeth?" Caleb looked toward the open living room door.

"Our daughter," Naomi explained. "Your niece. She's a little younger than the twins, but they play together real well. Go see for yourself."

Caleb didn't hesitate. He headed straight for the living room. As he passed Rhoda, he paused as if he were going to speak, but he seemed not to know what to say. In the end, he gave her a quick nod and continued toward the children.

He carefully approached the twins and knelt on the rug beside them. Vonnie looked up and grinned.

"*Daed*," she said happily.

The emotions Rhoda had been squashing for two long days splashed up like water in a bumped bucket, and she made a soft, choked sound. Naomi swiftly set the last spoon in its place. She drew Rhoda to the side, where Caleb wouldn't be able to see, and enfolded her in her arms.

"It's all right," she said fiercely into Rhoda's ear. "It must feel like a great deal right now, but I truly believe this is a *gut* thing, him coming home, a great chance. You and Joseph must believe it, too." She pulled back, her hands on Rhoda's arms and looked her in the face. "Especially you. You must show Caleb that you believe it."

"What if I'm not sure I do believe it?"

"Try not to let him see that. He needs us to believe so he can believe himself. It wouldn't be easy for anybody to come back home and ask for forgiveness, but for a stubborn fellow like your *mann*, it's even harder."

"That's what I think, too," Rhoda whispered. "That it will be too hard for him. And maybe too hard for me, too. I don't know what to do, Naomi."

"Well, when we don't know what to do, we pray. What is too hard for us is not too hard for *Gott*, and He knows already what the future holds." Naomi tugged her back so that they could see through the living room doorway.

Caleb was sitting cross-legged on the floor, Vonnie in his lap. They were rolling a plastic ball across the rug to Elizabeth and Eli in turns.

As Rhoda watched, Vonnie tried to push the ball forward. Caleb gave it a secret nudge with his fingers, and it rolled to Elizabeth. Delighted with her success, Vonnie clapped her hands and grinned.

Caleb grinned, too, pressing a kiss on the crown of his daughter's head.

The lump in Rhoda's throat swelled so that she could barely breathe. Naomi had tears in her eyes as well.

"That," she whispered, "that is the best reason you have to hope, Rhoda. Love. His love for the twins, the love they'll have for him. In time, your love for each other will come back, too. It's still there, waiting, buried under hard feelings and hurt. And love always hopes, you know. The Bible tells us that."

Rhoda nodded, dashing away her tears.

"Now"—Naomi released her with an affectionate pat—"supper's ready. Joseph should have already come in, but since he hasn't, I'd better go get him." She sighed. "Caleb's not the only one in this family who can be stubborn." Her lips twisted into a half smile. "I'll be right back."

"All right."

After Naomi had gone, Rhoda stowed the chicken bones in the refrigerator and washed and dried her hands. Still holding the towel, she walked back to the living room doorway.

Caleb was so absorbed in the twins that he didn't notice her at first, and she was glad of the chance to watch him unobserved. It made her heart do funny things seeing him sitting on the floor like that, her children—their children—clambering over him. Laughing.

It hurt her and made her happy all at once, and she didn't know what to do with the jumble of feelings. It reminded her of when she'd been in labor with the twins—the pain and the joy and the fear all mixed up together.

And a hollow, awful loneliness. That had been there, too, and it was here with her now.

He looked up, his green eyes connecting with hers. Then he looked down at the twins and then back at her. He didn't speak, but somehow, she understood his feelings, the way she had before his angry grief had built a wall between them.

Aren't they wonderful? She heard the words as plainly as if he'd spoken them—so plainly that she opened her mouth to answer.

Before she could, the kitchen door swung open, and Joseph came in, followed by Naomi. He glanced at his brother, his face expressionless as he hung his hat on the peg by the door.

"Joseph," Naomi murmured.

Her husband shot her a look. Normally he could never resist Naomi, but all he said was, "We should eat."

Caleb rose to his feet. He picked Vonnie up in his arms, and Eli stood beside him, clutching his pant leg. Her husband studied his older brother, who'd gone to the sink to wash his hands.

"Hello, Joseph."

Joseph's shoulders tensed, but he didn't turn. He was looking for the towel, which Rhoda belatedly realized she still held. She hurried over, holding it out like a peace offering.

"I'm sorry," she said.

"You," Joseph said, in a voice loud enough for Caleb to hear, "have nothing to be sorry for."

"But I do." Caleb spoke from the other end of the kitchen, his voice measured and tight. "Is that what you're saying?"

"I've said nothing to you at all," his brother pointed out.

Naomi squeezed her husband's arm so hard that Rhoda saw her knuckles whiten. But all she said was "It's time to eat. I'll get Elizabeth." She went to pick up her daughter, who was playing with the ball on the living room floor.

"*Daed* eat?" Vonnie piped up from Caleb's arms.

Joseph looked at the little girl, his expression softening. He was fond of Vonnie and Eli.

"I don't think—" Caleb started.

But Joseph interrupted him. "You are welcome to eat here, *bruder*. With us and with your wife and your *kinder*."

Caleb had been in the process of leaning down to set Vonnie on her feet, preparing to leave. He straightened, considering his brother.

"Do you mean that?"

"I don't say things I don't mean."

"Hungry," Vonnie murmured plaintively. She patted Caleb's cheek. "Eat?"

Caleb's gaze shifted from his brother to his daughter.

"*Ja*, *liebschdi*. It's time to eat." He looked at his brother again, this time with a warmer expression. "*Denki*," he offered awkwardly.

Some of the stiffness ebbed from Joseph's face. "You are still my brother," he said. "And Rhoda's husband. This is where you belong. Where you have always belonged, whether you have the sense to know it or not."

"I'll set another plate," Naomi said quickly, settling Elizabeth into her seat.

"On a tray." Everybody froze, looking at Joseph, who returned their stares steadily. "He can eat here, and welcome, but he's shunned, and it's not allowed for us to sit at table together. Not until he makes his confession in front of the church. He can have his supper in the living room."

Rhoda held her breath as Caleb studied his brother, his expression unreadable.

It was wrong, of course, to break the rules of shunning, at least in the eyes of the church leaders. But people often bent them when nobody was around to see. Even her father as bishop had tended to overlook such transgressions—unless people made a show of them.

And, oh, she felt for Caleb just now. To be shamed and set apart so, in his father's house, in front of his children, the children he was trying so hard to win over.

It was a hurtful thing.

But as *Daed* had often reminded her, shunning was meant to be hard, meant to show the person the consequences of their wrongdoing. And this was Joseph's home and his decision, not hers. She clenched her fingers in front of her apron as she waited to see what Caleb would say.

"Don't trouble yourself, Naomi." Caleb set Vonnie down gently, but there was nothing gentle in his expression. "I'm not hungry. I'll go and leave you to your suppers."

Rhoda had no idea what to say. She pressed her lips together and stayed silent as Caleb strode through the house and out the door.

Vonnie and Eli watched wide-eyed. When the door shut behind Caleb, they stuck their fingers in their mouths, and Vonnie began to whimper.

If Caleb had heard her, maybe he'd have turned around, but he was well out of earshot. Rhoda felt a twinge of exasperated sorrow. The twins, especially Eli, usually took a while to warm up to somebody new. It had taken them two weeks to get comfortable with Joseph, even though he'd been unfailingly kind to them. Yet Vonnie had glommed on to Caleb almost immediately, and even Eli seemed to be softening some.

Well, she couldn't fault them. It hadn't taken Caleb long to win her over, either, back at the start of things.

"Joseph." Naomi's voice was pained. Her husband threw her an uncomfortable look, but he raised his chin.

"I am sorry, too, Naomi, but this situation is of Caleb's own making. We'd best be clear from the start. My brother never met a rule he wouldn't bend. If we let him start out skirting the church's guidelines, it'll only make things harder for all of us later."

"I know Caleb's never much liked rules, but that doesn't mean he can't learn how to submit himself to them, given some time and some grace. But one thing's certain sure. You're not going to win your *bruder* back by squabbling over the *Ordnung*, Joseph." Naomi's soft voice was uncharacteristically firm.

She was right. Rhoda knew that with absolute certainty. There was something in Caleb, some deep-running stubbornness that caused him to set himself against rules. It was as if he had to try his strength against them, like the way her *daed*'s old billy goat had tested every fence they put him in.

That goat had never stayed penned up for long. Finally, her father, exasperated at finding the animal munching on his wife's flowers again, had put him in a stall where he couldn't possibly escape. He'd gone out that evening to find that the goat had butted his head bloody against the wooden walls.

Ja, Rhoda thought sadly, Caleb was much the same.

The noise of a buggy rattling into the yard at a high speed made all of them look in that direction. Joseph made it to the door first, Naomi and Rhoda right behind him.

Emma and Sam's buggy was just coming to a stop outside the back door. Emma sat in it alone, looking disheveled, and the horse was panting as if he'd been driven hard.

Caleb, almost to his truck, halted and turned.

Joseph glanced at his wife, a question in his eyes.

"I called her neighbor Birdie," Naomi admitted, "and left a message, when I heard Caleb was here. I knew she would want to see him as soon as she got back from her trip."

Joseph drew in a breath and nodded wearily. His wife patted his arm.

Emma set the brake and jumped down. She rushed around the front of the buggy and stumbled to a stop, facing her twin brother, who'd halted in front of his pickup, watching her. He didn't change expression, but he squared his shoulders as if bracing for a blow. In spite of everything, Rhoda's heart ached with sympathy—for both of them.

Emma and Caleb were twins, and they'd always been close. Emma had been hurt almost as badly as Rhoda by her brother's choices. And Caleb . . . well. Being shunned by Joseph would be difficult enough, but facing Emma would be a different thing altogether.

For a few seconds nobody breathed. Then Emma made a short, strangled noise and rushed at her twin. In two seconds, she was in his arms, her narrow back heaving with sobs.

Caleb held his sister close, murmuring in her ear, soothing her. The stubborn tightness in his face had relaxed into a gentleness that cut at Rhoda's heart.

"Love," Naomi said quietly. "Love is the strongest pull in this world. If anything can change Caleb's heart, it will be that. We'd all do well to remember it."

Without looking at Rhoda or Joseph, she turned and went inside.

Chapter Ten

Caleb held his twin against his chest until her sobbing slowed. Unlike their younger sister, Miriam, Emma had never been much of a crier. She was likelier to snap at you than to fall apart.

Having her crying in his arms made his heart hurt. He'd caused the whole family grief, he knew, but the sorrows he'd dealt to Rhoda and to Emma bothered him most.

Finally, Emma drew back, wiping at her eyes. "This will teach you to stay away for so long," she scolded with a self-conscious sniffle. "Your shirt's going to need a good washing. You should've worn a raincoat maybe. You must have known how happy I'd be to see you."

Caleb glanced down at the tear splotches on his shirt, and his heart lurched.

"You're happy. So far you're the only one."

His sister's eyes filled with sympathy. "Give them time,"

she murmured. "It's been hard, Caleb. We've all been so worried. There's been no word from you for such a long time. We feared something had happened to you."

The gentle reproach in her voice irritated him. After all, like Rhoda, Emma had been exasperated with him the last time they'd spoken, and she'd suggested that he not contact her until he was ready to come home for good.

But he'd left a way for her to contact him. He'd wondered why she hadn't, and he wondered more now.

"I gave you a phone," he reminded her, "so you could call me if you needed to. You never used it." *And you should have.* He didn't add that out loud, but he thought it.

"Oh!" Emma looked taken aback. "That was . . . broken."

Caleb knew Emma nearly as well as he knew himself. There was something she wasn't telling him. "How?"

Again, the quick flick away of his sister's eyes. "What difference does that make now? Anyhow, we can talk about it later. Come on." She tugged at his arm. "Help me unhitch the buggy, and we'll go inside."

He glanced at the house. Joseph stood in the doorway. Rhoda was behind him peering over his shoulder. Caleb's heart sagged.

"I was just leaving."

"Leaving? But why? Aren't you staying for supper?"

"Not if I have to sit separate, being shamed in front of my children, no."

"Be fair, Caleb." Emma glanced at the house. "You know Joseph. He's always followed church rules, right down to the letter."

"*Ja*," Caleb agreed grimly. "Believe me, that I know."

"Then you shouldn't be mad. I know Joseph sticks to the straight and narrow more than most, but you need to have a little patience with him—with all of us. I'm over the moon to see you, Caleb, but you gave us no warning. Likely

Joseph would have handled this better if he'd known ahead of time, if he could have thought it all through."

"If you and Naomi could have softened him up, you mean."

A smile tickled around his sister's lips. "That too." She drew in a breath. "All right. We'll not push this any further today. Why don't you come eat with Sam and me? At the table," she whispered with a wink. "We're living over at Sam's *aent* Ruth's old house." She lifted an eyebrow at him. "You'll remember where that is."

He'd shown up there unexpectedly a couple years back, startling Emma and Sam in the barn. He'd been on Trevor's trail then as well, but he'd come up empty-handed. That was when he'd given her the phone she was acting so skittish about.

He made a mental note to follow up on that as soon as he had the opportunity.

"*Ja*, I remember." Caleb looked toward the silent house. Joseph had disappeared, leaving Rhoda standing there alone. When she caught his eye, she swiftly turned and vanished, too.

His sore heart throbbed, but he made himself shrug.

"All right," he decided. "I'll come." Maybe Emma's enthusiastic welcome hadn't healed the aching spot in his heart, but it had soothed it some. It would be nice to spend more time with her.

"Is that yours?" Emma gestured toward the pickup.

"It is. You and Sam all right with me parking it in your yard?"

His sister kept her face carefully bland. "Of course. Would you rather I ride with you or follow along in the buggy?"

Caleb was startled by the offer. It was strictly forbidden for Emma, a member of the church in good standing, to ride in a vehicle driven by someone who was shunned. And while he might think following nitpicky rules in the privacy of a home was silly, riding openly in a truck through town was an entirely different matter. Emma would be asking for trouble doing such a thing, and he couldn't allow that.

"No," he said firmly. "Drive the buggy. You'll likely be needing it, and I'd rather not leave Joseph with the care of your horse. I don't want to give him any more reasons to complain about me than I have already."

"All right." Relief flickered across Emma's face. "You go ahead, and I'll follow fast as I can."

"Not too fast. That horse looks winded. You take your time. I can catch up with Sam while we wait for you." He wanted a quick word with his brother-in-law anyway without having Emma within earshot.

"Sam will be glad to see you. He has lots of news to share." Something in Emma's smile, something secret and happy, put Caleb's senses on high alert.

Sam, he suspected, wouldn't be the only person he'd find waiting for him at that little house. Unless he was mistaken—and he didn't think he was—he'd find another little niece or nephew waiting there as well.

He felt suddenly exhausted. So many changes. Little Miriam was married, and Emma was a *mamm*.

And he was a father himself. He still wasn't used to that idea, and every time he remembered, his heart jolted. It was like the time he'd stupidly touched an electrified fence when he and Milt were chasing a fellow wanted on drug charges. Masterson had laughed about that for weeks.

Caleb hadn't laughed. He'd been furious. It had hurt, and he hadn't liked the way the pain had come out of nowhere. Pain and surprise made an unpleasant combination.

"All right," Emma was saying. "I'll run inside and speak to everybody, but I'll be following soon enough."

"Soon enough," he agreed. He cast one more look toward

the house. No sign of Rhoda or anyone else. He firmed his lips. "I'll get going, then."

As much as he'd enjoyed seeing Emma, he was thankful to be alone with his thoughts on the short trip to his sister's new home. He sorted through his feelings as he drove swiftly down more roads he was used to traveling in a buggy.

Usually, he liked the speed and the convenience of driving. He liked the sense of power in the pedal under his boot, so different from sitting in a plodding buggy while *Englischers*' cars roared past. But right now he wouldn't have minded a slower drive and some extra thinking time. He needed to settle down.

Being at Joseph's had reminded him sharply of why he'd left here in the first place. He just wasn't cut out to be Amish. They believed in things he didn't—like pointless rules. And they didn't believe something he believed with all his heart.

That evil shouldn't be forgiven and overlooked but fought.

He'd believed that before he'd left, but living out among the *Englisch* had brought the lesson more firmly home. The nastiness that lurked in some men's souls couldn't be tolerated. It needed to be brought to account.

He'd written that to Rhoda shortly after he'd left, explaining what he believed—or trying to. School had never been his favorite thing, and he wasn't too good with a pen. But he'd taken pains over those words because he'd wanted her to know how he felt. He'd wanted her, if she could, to understand.

She'd never answered him except for the one short note telling him there was no point writing until he was willing to repent and come home. The words had been in Rhoda's handwriting, but it was her father Isaac's voice Caleb had heard when he'd read them. It was the only reply he'd ever received. After that, he'd only got his own letters back, unopened.

A person could never understand if they weren't willing to listen, if they couldn't imagine that there could be any truth other than what they believed themselves. Rhoda had always been a good Amish girl. He'd known it before he'd married her. She'd never leave the church. Not for him. Not for anybody.

He'd always known that—or he'd thought he had. But during those first dark days after his parents' deaths, he'd come to understand Rhoda's blind loyalty to the church—and her father—on a different level. More than anything then, he'd needed the comfort of the woman he loved. The one who'd seen good in him when no one else had, who'd drawn closer to his side even when others warned her away. He'd needed the unquestioning love of this woman, the bishop's pretty daughter who'd chosen him—troublemaker Caleb Hochstedler—over his perfect church-abiding brother.

Instead, she'd parroted her father's sermons back to him, withdrawn from him, refused to listen to anything he said that didn't line up with what Isaac said. He'd slowly come to understand then that she'd never really chosen him at all—not the real him. That was as much his fault as Rhoda's. More, because he'd hidden parts of his heart in order to be sure of winning hers.

He'd not liked leaving her without support, and he'd tried to soften the financial blow he'd caused. She—or more likely Isaac—hadn't allowed that. He'd accepted their decision because he'd felt he had little choice in the matter.

Now, with the children, everything was different. He couldn't leave Rhoda and the twins alone and unprovided for simply because he'd lost his faith. The church, though, would insist that he do exactly that. As the wife of a shunned man, Rhoda would suffer as long as he lived, and so would their children.

That wasn't acceptable, but repenting before the church

would mean professing beliefs he just didn't have—and then living by them for the rest of his life. He couldn't do that, either.

He took his hand off the steering wheel and ran it roughly through his hair.

He honestly didn't know what he was going to do.

Chapter Eleven

THE HOME EMMA NOW SHARED WITH HER HUSBAND was a small white-painted house, farther from the rest of the Plain community than was usual. When Caleb had met Sam's *aent* Ruth, he'd understood why her brother had provided her with a home none too close to his own. She'd always been a sharp-tongued woman, and he'd been surprised to find out that Emma was living there and caring for her.

He'd discovered that the summer before last, after he and Milt had heard that Trevor might be back in the area, stalking Emma. Caleb had hidden in Ruth's barn for a time, keeping an eye out, but he'd seen nothing out of the ordinary—except for a romance blooming between his twin sister and Sam Christner.

He'd not expected that, but after he'd left, he'd felt relieved. Even after the buggy accident that had damaged his eyesight, burly Sam was a fellow to be reckoned with, and it was plain to see that he loved Emma beyond all reason.

If life had taught Caleb anything over the past few years, it had taught him that the world was full of danger. With Sam close by, Emma would be as safe as anybody could be.

When Caleb pulled into the drive, Sam opened the front door and stepped onto the porch, squinting at his visitor. A small tow-headed boy was perched on his forearm.

Caleb smiled. That would be Emma's son, the nephew he'd not known anything about.

"Sam," he called, suspecting that Sam's eyesight wasn't good enough to recognize him. "It's Caleb."

"*Hallo.*" Sam started down the steps, as if he could see the same as always. But Caleb had grown used to noting details—it was something Milt stressed over and over again. So he noticed how Sam trailed one hand along the railing next to the steps and how he jutted an elbow out to snag on the shrubs planted in front of the house, keeping him centered on the straight path leading to the drive.

He noticed something else, too, a resigned expression on Sam's face, as if he were about to visit the dentist. Looked like Emma's husband didn't share his wife's excitement about her prodigal brother's return.

"Emma told me to come," Caleb explained.

"I figured. Although I wasn't expecting you—nor Emma, either, at least not anytime soon." The big man hesitated. "Where is she anyhow?"

"Coming," Caleb assured him. "Driving the buggy back."

"Is she now?" Sam said slowly. "That wonders me. I figured all your family would be visiting together."

Caleb chose his words carefully. "It didn't work out so."

"*Ach*, well. Your coming so unexpected-like has stirred up everybody's feelings. Emma was beside herself when she heard the news. She couldn't hardly think straight, and I'm sure the rest are the same. They've been real worried over you."

There was no mistaking the disapproval in Sam's voice. Probably wiser to turn this conversation to a safer topic. Caleb nodded at the child in Sam's arms. "Who's this little stranger?"

The distraction worked. Sam's broad face creased in a

smile as he looked down at the baby. "This here is Jonas, our boy. Jonas, this is *Mamm*'s brother, Caleb. Your *onkel*."

The boy looked curiously at Caleb out of round eyes the same shade of blue as Emma's own. His hair was Emma's, too—a warm shade of yellow. The rest of him was all Sam.

Young as the boy was, and he couldn't be a year old yet, he already had his *daed*'s sturdy build and broad face. Even the way he sat up on his father's arm, strong and straight, spoke of Sam.

It was strange, Caleb thought, seeing his sister's features mixed with those of his friend in this child. Strange but sweet. His mind flicked back to his own son and daughter. The twins were a mix of him and Rhoda, too, just like this little one. Eli had Rhoda's brown eyes but sandy hair like Caleb's. And Vonnie's hair was her *mamm*'s dark brown, but her eyes were a very familiar shade of green.

The memory of their little faces made his chest ache. "Hello there, Jonas," he managed around the knot in his throat.

Maybe Sam guessed what he was thinking because the other man's expression softened.

"Come inside the house." He led the way back up the carefully leveled walkway. "I'm surprised Emma let you out of her sight long enough to drive the buggy back."

"She wanted to ride back in the truck with me, but since we'd have to go straight through town to get here, I didn't think that was such a good idea."

Sam pulled the door open, standing back to make room for Caleb to pass. "You were right. And I thank you for telling her so."

"Well"—Caleb shrugged, feeling uncomfortable—"sometimes my sister's soft heart gets the better of her common sense."

"It wasn't just that." Sam followed him into the living room and shut the door behind them. "She's been feeling bad about how you two left things, how she snapped at you that day in the barn. Blaming herself for your staying gone and sending no word." Sam's tone made it clear what he thought of that. "She's been praying hard that you'd come home, and here you are. So she didn't care if she was seen breaking church rules by riding with you. Other folks would have cared, though, and there'd have been a ruckus about it, likely. I appreciate you stepping between my wife and that kind of trouble."

My wife. The claim—and the warning—in those words was clear. Caleb nodded shortly. He didn't much like being reminded of how much trouble he could cause here just by doing something simple like driving somebody around. But when word got around that he was back, folks would be watching for things like that. There had always been people all too willing to tattle whenever he stepped out of line.

Sam settled Jonas on the braided rug and set out a toy barn and some carved wooden animals for the little boy to play with. Caleb picked up a chubby pig and looked it over. Like the toys he'd seen back at the bakery, these showed signs of his brother's careful workmanship.

"These are well made," he said.

"*Ja*," Sam said. "Joseph turns out such wooden playthings for the store whenever he has a spare minute. We can barely keep 'em in stock, they're so popular. He makes plenty for our own little ones, too. Jonas here has a cupboard full already. And Naomi has to make sure Joseph doesn't spoil their Lizzie with too many play pretties." Sam paused. "Eli and Vonnie get their share, too. Your *bruder* would never let those two babies go without."

Not like you. The words weren't spoken aloud, but again, Caleb could guess what Sam was thinking. His brother-in-law had little patience for men who made trouble for women and children or who shirked their God-given responsibilities. No doubt, in Sam's opinion, Caleb had done both.

Caleb took his time answering, watching his nephew

gnaw on a wooden horse. "*Ja*," he said after a minute. "I saw such toys at the bakery, and I figured where they'd come from. That was kind of him."

"He's a kind man. I know it may not seem so just now, to you. But he is. And it's not only the twins he's looked after. He's taken great care of Rhoda, too, since she's come back home. I helped as I could, but most of it fell to him because I can't do such things as well as I used to." The big man made the confession with a simple honesty that brought Caleb up short.

For all the many years he'd known Sam, the man's strength had been his purpose. He'd used it, best he could, to protect those he cared about. His family, his friends, his neighbors. Now, through no fault of his own, he wasn't so able to do that, and Caleb knew that must grieve him. Caleb lifted his chin and met his brother-in-law's dimmed eyes. If Sam could admit his weakness so openly, Caleb should be strong enough to do the same.

"I'm thankful for his help. And yours. I left Rhoda in a bad fix."

"*Ja,* you did," Sam agreed bluntly.

Caleb flinched, but Sam was right, and there was no point dodging the truth. "An even bigger fix than I realized. I didn't know about the babies, Sam. I wrote to her and got a post office box so she could write me back. She only wrote to me once, then my letters starting coming back unopened. She never told me she was expecting."

Sam used his boot to nudge a wooden cow closer to his son. "*Ja,* we figured it was so. Emma said all along that if you'd known about the twins, you'd have come quick. Miriam too. They'd have told you themselves, if they could have found a way to get word to you. They didn't know about that post office box. Emma tried asking Rhoda how to contact you once, and . . ." Sam shook his head. "I don't know what was said, but both of 'em ended up crying.

Emma said she'd never bring you up again with Rhoda, not until you were back home. And now you are. If you don't mind my asking, how'd you find out?"

"I didn't. I mean," Caleb amended when Sam's eyebrows went up, "not until I got here."

The other man's wide brow furrowed as he thought this over. "Maybe that's *gut*," he decided. "That you came back only because of Rhoda herself. After what you said in the barn that day when you were last here—about how it was a mistake to marry her because you weren't cut out to live Plain, I'd wondered if you ever would."

Sam's tone was warmer now. That made it hard to be completely honest, but Caleb needed somebody to know the whole truth. Sam, who'd always been the protective sort, was the likeliest to understand the situation.

"I did come back because of Rhoda, but there was something more to it. I was worried. I found photographs of her in a house where Trevor Abbott had been staying."

Alarm flashed across Sam's face like lightning. "You found what?"

"Photos of Rhoda, lots of them. He'd pinned them up in the closet of a house he'd been renting in Florida. We nearly had him there, Milt Masterson and I. He's a bounty hunter I've been working with."

Sam listened without interrupting as Caleb told the story. When Caleb mentioned the red circles around Rhoda's face, his brother-in-law flinched. He stayed silent, though, until Caleb had finished.

"So you came because you think Trevor's heading back to Johns Mill?"

"He might be. Milt believes this movie business is pushing him toward the edge again, and we can trust Milt's instincts. I wouldn't blame you for not trusting mine. I was wrong before, thinking that Trevor was planning to come here. But—"

He broke off. Sam had been looking at Jonas, his brow wrinkled in thought. But at that, he glanced up sharply.

"What?" Caleb prodded.

"He was here," Sam admitted. "Trevor. Just after you left last time. He . . . surprised Emma in the barn."

"*Vass?*" He spoke so sharply that Jonas looked up, his eyes wide. Sam shot Caleb a stern look, then gently cupped his son's head with one large hand, settling him. When the child had gone back to his playing, Caleb spoke again, more softly.

"Trevor was here?"

"He was. Things got sticky for a few minutes, but it turned out all right. He made some threats and broke that phone you gave her, but that was the sum of it. I talked him down, and between the two of us, Emma and I got him off the property before anybody got hurt." Sam tightened his lips. "That was the best I could do. But that's in the past, and there's little good to be had raking it back up again now. You didn't answer my question. Is that the only reason you came home? Because of Trevor?"

"Like I said, I came because I was worried about Rhoda. I wanted to make sure she was all right and to warn her and the rest of you to keep an eye out, to be careful. Then I saw the twins, and as you can guess, the conversation got sidetracked. For the last few days, Trevor Abbott's been the last thing on my mind."

"I suppose I can understand that well enough." Sam's chair creaked as he leaned back, his face troubled. "But Naomi told Emma you were talking with the bishop about settling things with the church. Emma was over the moon about it. Now you're telling me that's not so? That you haven't agreed to such a thing?"

"I agreed to meet with Abram," Caleb admitted. "That's all so far."

"So far." Sam fell into a thoughtful silence. For a few

seconds, the only sounds in the small room were the clock ticking on the wall and the pulse pounding in Caleb's ears.

Caleb was thankful for a moment to gather his wits. He was stuck on the fact that Trevor had been here and gotten close enough to Emma that he could've hurt her. He hadn't, but that was to Sam's credit, not to Caleb's.

Something else was worrying him, too. If he and Milt had been right back then, that increased the likelihood that they were also right now. The back of Caleb's neck prickled, and he rubbed it, thinking hard.

"There's Emma," Sam said suddenly, a split second before Caleb caught the sound of buggy wheels crunching over gravel. "Best we be talking about something else when she comes inside. But before that, I need to know something. What are you planning to do now that you know about the twins?"

"That's the question. I don't know."

"Don't you?" His brother-in-law made an impatient noise. "Then I'll tell you. You need to stay here and be a husband to your wife and a father to your children."

Sam's exasperation stung like salty water in a cut. Once, he and Sam had respected each other, even when they didn't see eye to eye. Those days, it seemed, were gone. "It's not that simple."

"It's simple enough. There's nothing holding you back from it but pride."

"This has nothing to do with pride."

Sam made a scoffing noise. "Doesn't it? To stay, you'll have to admit you were wrong to chase Trevor. You'll have to humble yourself before the church and ask for forgiveness. You're telling me your pride's not kicking up a fuss at the thought of that?"

Maybe it was, a little. But he'd have done it anyway, except for one thing. He lifted his chin. "What if I'm not sure I am wrong?"

Sam frowned. "If you don't think you're in the wrong, you're not thinking at all. Just look at the damage you've done, at the kind of hurt you've caused—"

"I know the hurt I've caused." Caleb interrupted. "You think I don't want to erase the pain I caused Rhoda? To fix it somehow? Of course I do, Sam." To his shame, his voice cracked on the words. "Of course I do," he repeated more steadily. "But I don't see how I can without heaping more mistakes on top of the ones I've already made. I hid my doubts about the church because I knew Isaac wouldn't let me within ten feet of his daughter if I wasn't a church member. And I just couldn't face life without her, Sam. I'd have done anything. Maybe you don't understand that."

"You've been living life without her for more than two years, seems to me," Sam muttered. "Better for the both of you if you'd done that to start with." He tilted his head toward the window, and they heard more noises as Emma brought the buggy to a stop. Her husband's expression softened, and he went on thoughtfully, "But, *ja*, I understand well enough how a man behaves when he's neck deep in love with a woman. But to lie about your beliefs to marry her . . . and that's what you did . . . it's—"

"Wrong." The word didn't begin to cover it. "*Ja*, I know. I learned that the hard way. But now, if I want to be a part of my own family, I'll have to lie again, Sam. Because my feelings about the church haven't changed. Well," he amended grimly, "they have. But not in the way you all had hoped."

Sam's jaw firmed. "You should tell Rhoda so up front. If you don't, I'll have the job of it, and I'd rather not. I'm already going to talk to Emma and try to let her down easy. I'll wait a day or two, give her some time to enjoy your homecoming. But I'll be telling her. Emma's in my care now, and I'll not have her deceived. Rhoda and those babies are your concern."

Caleb exhaled slowly. "You're right. I'll talk to Rhoda. I'll tell her why I came back . . . and how things stand with me." That wasn't going to be an easy conversation. "But I'd rather not do it right now. I'd appreciate a little time, Sam. Time with her and my children before—" Before he upended everything again.

"A little time," Sam agreed cautiously. "Not too long, though. Then you'll be honest with Rhoda about why you came back and how things stand between you and the church." He waited for Caleb's nod before adding, "She's not the only one you should be honest with, either."

"Rest easy. I've no intention of misleading that round little bishop of yours."

"*Nee*, I meant that you should be honest with yourself." A smile played around Sam's lips. "Our round little bishop can take care of himself."

"He's a far cry from Isaac Lambright, that's for certain sure," Caleb observed dryly. "The *youngies* here now have it easy, I'm thinking."

"You're thinking wrong. Abram seems a softheaded fellow sometimes, but if you try to pull the wool over his eyes, you'll find yourself set on your heels right quick. If you doubt me, ask your new brother-in-law when he and Miriam get back from their trip next week. He can tell you."

"Tell you what?" Emma bustled through the door. Her face was flushed and her bonnet was askew, but she was smiling. "Sam, would you finish unhitching for me? I started, but I couldn't wait another second to get inside. I see you've met our Jonas! Were you surprised?"

"Best surprise in the world," Caleb assured her.

His twin beamed. She swept her baby up in her arms and snuggled him close. "Were you a good boy while I was gone?"

"He was that. Good as gold." Sam rose to his feet. "I'll see to the unhitching."

"I'll help." Caleb got up, too, but Sam shook his head.

"I can manage all right by myself, and I expect Emma would rather you stay inside with her. She'll want to spend as much time with you as she can." *Seeing as how you're likely to leave again before too long.*

Sam didn't speak that last part aloud, but Caleb read it in the other man's face as plainly as if he had.

"You can help me get the supper together," Emma suggested happily. "Because you're eating with us. At the table," she added firmly. When Caleb cocked an eyebrow at her, she smiled. "It's fine. Isn't it, Sam?"

Sam shrugged. "I don't see why not. There's nobody here but us, and I reckon it's one blessing about my eyesight not being so good as it used to be. Folks tend to make us allowances."

Ja, Caleb thought, likely they did. The church tended to be sympathetic toward those with physical disabilities, and in such special cases, neighbors were quick to lend a hand—and to generously ignore an occasional sidestepping of the rules.

"You're spending the night, too," Emma went on. "I can roll the baby's crib into our room just as easy, and you can sleep in the spare bed."

"I don't know. I'm supposed to be bunking up in the apartment above the bakery." Although, since Rhoda wasn't staying there, it probably wouldn't matter so much for him to spend the night someplace else. He'd seen no sign of Trevor anywhere, and it would be nice to sleep in a bed rather than on the floor—or in the cab of his truck.

"Well, you can stay here for one night anyway. Right, Sam?"

Sam paused with his hand on the doorknob. "I have no objection. You can stay and are welcome. Of course, I figure you'll be wanting to spend most of your time with Rhoda and your children, ain't so? I expect you'll have a lot of things to talk with her about."

"That's so, *ja*," Caleb answered.

Sam didn't answer in words. He just gave a short nod as

he closed the door behind himself, but he communicated his meaning well enough.

He'd meant what he'd said. He expected Caleb to have that honest talk with Rhoda. Soon. And he would.

But he wasn't looking forward to it.

Chapter Twelve

RHODA WIPED HER BROW WITH HER SLEEVE, THEN resumed ladling the blueberry muffin batter into the tins she'd placed on the steel bakery work area. She'd better hurry. The sun was already up, and she could hear Eli making his fussy noise behind her. In a minute, he'd be crying, and then Vonnie would likely follow suit.

She'd had to bring the twins with her again today. This time it was Elizabeth who had a checkup, and Rhoda didn't want to ask Naomi to wrangle three children in the doctor's office.

"It's all right, Eli," Rhoda said firmly. "Settle down and play with your toys. *Mamm*'s got to get her work done."

Her words made no difference. The twins didn't like the safety corral she'd set up in the far corner of the kitchen, even though she'd padded the tile floor well with old quilts and given them plenty of toys to play with. They'd not been here twenty minutes, and already they were restless. Not good, considering the problems Rhoda was dealing with this morning.

Edna had sent word by her granddaughter, Cora, that she was down with a stomach flu. Rhoda had been counting on Edna to make today's muffins—she had no trouble following that familiar recipe—but now she'd have to find the time to make them herself.

Eli's fussing grew louder behind her. She set the filled tin to the side, flipped the big oven on to preheat, and began filling the second tin. She had time to make only one kind of muffin today. Blueberry muffins were always a big seller, and she wanted these fresh and ready to go when she opened the store in two hours.

"These will be done soon," she called cheerfully over her shoulder. "Then you can sit at the table and have your breakfast, *ja?*"

Hopefully they'd sit. Sometimes when she had to bring them along, they'd lose interest in their food too quickly and toddle around the bakery, getting under her feet and in her way. She suspected this morning wasn't going to be one of the better ones.

That was too bad. She dabbed at her forehead again. She hadn't slept well at all. She'd tossed and turned in her bed at Joseph's home, thinking about how badly Caleb's visit had gone yesterday evening.

She didn't blame him for feeling hurt, but he'd certainly not shown any sign of the humility he'd be needing if he intended to stay. He hadn't spent the night here last night, either. She'd tiptoed upstairs and checked. Probably he'd stayed with Emma and Sam, sidestepping the bishop's instructions.

She wondered if he'd even show up for his meeting with Abram today. It wouldn't surprise her if he didn't.

The back door opened, and she glanced over her shoulder to see Sam ushering in Emma, who had Jonas cradled in her arms. Caleb followed them. His green eyes sought hers for a second. Then he looked away, toward the twins in their makeshift playpen.

"*Gut mariye*, Rhoda," Sam said. "Caleb asked me to talk him through what needs doing upstairs. Said he didn't get much chance to talk it over with Joseph. Figured we'd come early and get that done before Emma and I open the store."

Rhoda bit her lip as she bent to slide the muffin tins in the oven. "That's fine," she said evenly. She set the timer, squared her shoulders, and turned around.

Caleb had walked to the playpen. Eli lifted up his arms pleadingly, and his father made a move to pick him up.

"Don't," Rhoda said sharply, adding belatedly, "Please. If you're going upstairs with Sam, you won't want them underfoot distracting you. I need them to settle down and be content where they are. I have a lot on hand today and no help."

"I'll set Jonas in there with them." Emma plopped her sleepy son onto the folded quilt inside the barricade. "The *kossins* like playing together. That'll keep them happy for a few minutes anyway."

Caleb looked down at Eli, who, just as Emma had predicted, was distracted by his cousin's arrival. Caleb smiled and tousled his son's hair, and Rhoda's foolish heart melted.

That was another thing that had kept her awake last night, remembering Caleb and the twins together. She'd always felt so wistful watching Sam and Joseph with their *kinder*, and she'd wished that Vonnie and Eli had their father's love, too. Seeing them with Caleb had given her a glimpse of what that would have been like.

What it should have been like.

Sam cleared his throat. "Come on then," he said to Caleb. "Rhoda's right. I have work waiting for me, and as you'll soon see, you have plenty as well."

The two men clumped upstairs. Emma walked over to Rhoda's side, scanning the bowls of dough and the greased pans sitting ready.

"How can I help?" Emma had plenty of her own work to

do, but she never hesitated to offer an extra pair of hands wherever she could.

"You could punch down that wheat bread there and set it to rise in the pans for baking," Rhoda suggested. Emma nodded and moved to the sink to wash her hands.

They worked in silence for a few seconds, the only sounds the babbling of the children's voices behind them and the heavy thumps of the men's boots overhead.

"Caleb ate supper with us last night," Emma volunteered. "And then he spent the night."

"I guessed as much." Rhoda measured flour and sugar into another big stainless steel bowl. Now that she had some help, she could squeeze in a batch of banana nut muffins, too. "I'm sure he was comfortable at your house."

She kept her voice carefully neutral, but Emma tensed. "You mean because we had a bed for him to sleep on or because we're willing to wink at the rules?"

"That's your business."

"No." Emma quickly measured out another lump of dough, shaped it, and plopped it into the waiting pan. "It's all our business, Rhoda. We're a family."

"*Ja*," Rhoda agreed. "We are, and I'm very thankful. I'm not so sure about Caleb, though."

"Rhoda," Emma started, but Rhoda shook her head stubbornly.

"I know you mean well, Emma. And I know you love your brother, and of course you hope for the best where he's concerned. But you didn't see what happened yesterday. He hardly stayed any time at Joseph's."

"Well, this has all been difficult for him. I mean, finding out about the twins . . ." Emma went silent for a second, her hands skillfully folding another lump of dough into a smooth loaf. "It was a shock."

And Emma blamed her for that, although she'd likely never admit it. They'd argued over it once, the fact that Rhoda wouldn't get in touch with Caleb about the babies.

Rhoda stripped several overripe bananas of their skins, dropping the soft fruit into another bowl. "I'm sure it was," she conceded. "But it shouldn't have been any shock to him to find out that there are consequences to being shunned. I know it's hard, and I don't blame him for not liking it. Still, he can't expect everyone to ignore the rules and act as if nothing has changed."

Emma shaped two more loaves before she answered. "It's a hard thing," she said carefully, "coming home after you've been away. It was hard for me. And it's been hard for you, too, I think. It's even harder for Caleb." She tucked the last loaf in its place and turned toward Rhoda, her face earnest. "But underneath all that stubbornness and temper, there's something else. Something strong and good. You know that. You saw that in him, back before. You said as much to me."

She had. Rhoda flushed at the memory. She'd been so starry-eyed back then, so in love with the handsome man with the fiery temper who looked at her as if she were the only person in the world worth looking at.

So, yes, she'd praised him back then, to her parents and to anybody else who dared to suggest that Caleb Hochstedler wasn't the fellow she should be spending her time with. *There's a sweetness to him*, she'd said. *Deep down. A trueness and a goodness. You just have to know where to look.*

She felt uncomfortable now recalling those words. How people must have laughed at her—and worse, pitied her—when Caleb had left so soon after their marriage.

She mashed the bananas with extra force. "I didn't know what I was talking about."

To her surprise, Emma took gentle hold of her elbow, stilling her arm. "It must seem so now," her sister-in-law whispered. "I have nothing but sorrow and sympathy for what my brother has put you through, *schwesdre*. But you were right about him back then. People say love is blind, but it isn't, not really. Love sees us the way we're meant to be and overlooks the broken places. That's all."

Rhoda blinked back tears and mashed even harder. Goodness, she was crying or getting mad all the time lately.

"Anyway," Emma went on, "he's come back now, and I know he cares about you still. And those babies. How could he not? God's given him—and us—another chance, I think. Please, Rhoda, try to see him the way you used to. Be kind. Maybe he doesn't deserve it of you, but isn't that when the church teaches us that it's the most important to offer kindness? When the other person can't raise himself up enough to deserve it?"

"Grace"—Rhoda murmured the word—"is what it's called." She'd heard plenty about grace at home growing up. Although now that she thought about it, none of those talks had been directed at Caleb. And he'd certainly needed more grace than most in her circle.

"*Ja*, that's what's needed. Give my brother some grace," Emma pleaded.

"I don't have much of that left in me, Emma."

"Then give what you do have, and let us see what *Gott* can do with that. Maybe He will multiply it like the loaves and the fishes, and make it enough."

Rhoda shrugged miserably, unsure how to answer.

They heard heavy footsteps on the staircase, and a second later Sam poked his head out of the doorway.

Emma immediately moved to the sink to wash away the stickiness of the dough. Whenever Sam was around, Emma wasn't far from his side. He rarely needed her help, but Emma stayed close anyway, just in case.

It was sweet, although this morning, something about that quiet, unquestioning devotion made Rhoda's heart ache.

"All right," Sam said. "I've explained things to him, and he knows what to do." He looked in Rhoda's direction, zeroing in on her location easily as always. "Caleb's a fine carpenter, so there's no doubt the work will be done right.

And he has nothing else to do, so it'll be finished a lot quicker, that much is for sure. Plus, I'll rest easier knowing that somebody's here with you." He almost seemed to be speaking that last sentence to himself.

"Why?" Rhoda asked, frowning.

"Oh, the tourists and the reporters," Sam explained hastily. "They'll be starting up again, making nuisances of themselves. Best to have somebody around."

Rhoda raised an eyebrow. In her experience, Caleb was the one likeliest to cause problems. But she remembered Emma's plea for grace, so all she said was, "It'll be a blessing to have the apartment ready sooner."

"All right, then. Emma, we'd best get on to the store, *ja?* We're just down the street, Rhoda, if you should need us. Remember that."

"*Denki*, Sam. And thank you, too, Emma, for helping me get this bread set to rise."

"*Du bisht welcome*." Emma collected Jonas from the playpen, sent Rhoda another imploring look, and the three of them left.

As she mixed the batter for the banana muffins, a floorboard overhead creaked, and Rhoda cast an uncertain look toward the ceiling. She didn't much like the idea of Caleb being upstairs working all day, but she didn't suppose there was much she could do about it.

Behind her, Eli made another unhappy noise.

"Out," he demanded.

She glanced over her shoulder to see him shaking the wooden barrier while his sister looked on, wide-eyed.

"*Nee*, Eli. *Schtopp!*" she told her son sternly.

He scowled at her, his little brows lowered stubbornly. For a second, he looked so much like Caleb that her heart caught in her throat.

How was she going to raise such a son alone? Caleb had been blessed with two wise parents, yet he'd skirted trouble all his teenage years. How would a boy with such a personality fare with only a *mamm* to guide him?

She'd have to be extra strong, she told herself. When Eli shook the wooden safety gate again, she spoke over her shoulder. "*Mamm* is busy now. You must play nicely with your sister, Elijah."

Eli had no intention of playing nicely. He didn't like being confined. Another trait he had in common with his father, Rhoda thought ruefully. And when he was unhappy, he had no problem making other people unhappy, too. Already Vonnie's face was puckered, and she was tuning up to cry.

Another creak overhead, followed by the sharp thumps of a hammer. The noise did Vonnie in, and she began to sob.

A headache throbbed over Rhoda's right eye. *It will be all right*, she told herself. But her hands shook as she slid the tray of muffins into the oven.

This was shaping up to be a very long day.

Chapter Thirteen

CALEB PAUSED, TWO NAILS IN HIS MOUTH AND HIS hammer poised over the window trim he was nailing into place.

The children—*his* children—were screaming their heads off.

He listened for several seconds, but the noise didn't stop. He spat the nails into his hand and walked to the door that led downstairs.

He lingered there, trying to hear. Rhoda was talking to the twins. He couldn't make out what she was saying, but he could hear the desperation in her voice.

She was overwhelmed.

When he'd walked in with Sam and Emma this morning, Rhoda had already been hard at work, her cheeks rosy, and she was wearing a dress in a pretty dark green. Seeing her standing there with a mixing bowl in front of her, stirring batter, strands of hair escaping from the bun under her *kapp* . . . it had jolted him painfully back in time.

He'd walked in on her just so more than once after their marriage. They'd spent the first month staying in relatives' homes, ending up at the last in his own parents' house. Rhoda, ever the good girl, had always risen early and helped get breakfast started.

He remembered watching his new wife working in other folks' kitchens, wishing he could walk up behind her, gather her into a hug, and give her a kiss. He hadn't done it, of course. Rhoda was shy and always worried about what other people thought.

So he'd bided his time, longing for the day when they'd be in their own home as man and wife and could do as they pleased. They'd nearly made it. Then his parents had been killed, and the world had fallen apart, taking his marriage with it.

The children were still fussing. Caleb weighed the hammer in his hand—and his options.

He could stay up here and do the work he was supposed to be doing. Or he could walk downstairs and offer his help. Likely Rhoda wouldn't accept. She'd sure snapped at him when he'd started to take Eli out of the playpen earlier.

But letting them cry on and on like that . . . Caleb hadn't paid much attention to how people looked after their babies, but he didn't think any parent he knew would have allowed the crying to go on for so long.

He'd go downstairs. Maybe Rhoda would bite his head off again, but she needed help, whether she wanted to accept it from him or not.

He set the hammer and nails aside and went down the steps, pushing open the door that led into the roomy kitchen. Rhoda stood at the long stainless steel counter, taking muffins out of a baking tin. At least he thought they were muffins. They were burned black, and the bitter smell of smoke hung in the air.

The children stood behind the wooden fence, wailing.

Eli's face was turkey-red, and his mouth was wide open as he yelled for all he was worth.

Mad as a cat in a water bucket, Caleb thought with a grin.

Vonnie stood behind her brother sobbing miserably, her eyes wide. She wasn't mad, Caleb realized. She was frightened. His grin vanished, and he started in her direction.

"It's all right," he murmured. When he reached the playpen, he gave his hands a quick wipe down his pants and reached for her. "Come here, sweetheart."

Maybe he moved too fast. Or maybe it was because Vonnie was already upset, but she shook her head and moved away from him. When she stepped backward, she tripped on a toy and plopped onto her bottom. For one split second, both she and Eli stopped howling. Then Vonnie began wailing again, louder this time.

"It's all right," Caleb repeated. He leaned into the playpen, intending to scoop her up when Eli slapped at his father's outstretched hands.

"*Nee!*" the toddler objected loudly.

"Elijah!" Rhoda dropped the tin onto the counter with a clatter. In a flash, she was beside the playpen. "We don't hit people!"

"It's not his fault," Caleb said quickly. "He was trying to look after his sister. I was reaching for her, and—"

"That doesn't matter." Rhoda knelt on the other side of the playpen, holding her son's gaze. "It's *never* good to hit people, Eli. It's not the way we behave."

She wasn't looking at him, but Caleb could feel waves of exasperation and disapproval coming off her. And she'd contradicted him, flat out and openly. It set him back, that, because it was such an un-Rhoda-like thing to do. She'd never have done that in the past, no matter how strongly she disagreed with whatever he'd said or done. She'd only have pleaded with him softly, her dark eyes hurt and hopeful.

He'd never been able to resist Rhoda when she looked at him like that, no matter how convinced he was that he was right. He'd given in every time, to the point that his relatives had ribbed him about it.

Only once had he turned a deaf ear to Rhoda's pleas. Once he'd walked away. The last time.

Rhoda released Eli's hands, giving her son a final stern look. Eli frowned back, his brows low over his dark eyes. He didn't look convinced about the whole no-hitting-no-matter-what rule, and Caleb didn't blame him. He'd never been convinced about that one, either.

"Pick her up," Rhoda said.

She was talking to him, Caleb realized. "What?"

"You were going to pick Vonnie up. Go on and do it. Eli has to learn that he's not the boss. If he gets his way by hitting people, he'll only do it again."

"I don't want to scare her—" Caleb started.

"You already have," Rhoda pointed out wearily. "Pick her up."

He scooped Vonnie up into his arms. Eli made a move in his direction, but Rhoda quickly intercepted it.

Vonnie went stiff in his arms. She used her two small hands to push against his chest, levering herself as far away from him as she could.

That bothered him, but right now, something else was bothering him even more. The twins weren't the only ones who'd been crying. Rhoda's eyes were red-rimmed, and silvery tracks of spent tears trailed down her cheeks.

"What's wrong?" he demanded, forgetting for the moment that he had no right to ask her such questions.

"Nothing."

He waited a beat, bouncing Vonnie up and down gently, trying to soothe her. "Doesn't the church frown on lying?"

Rhoda flushed. "I'm not lying. There's nothing wrong, not really." She dabbed at her forehead with one sleeve.

"I've just got a lot of work to do, and I burned the blueberry muffins."

Maybe he was missing something, but that didn't seem worth crying over. "Can't you make another batch?"

"I'll need to open up soon. I should have paid closer attention, but it's hard keeping an eye on the children and the baking, too."

Well, yes, of course it would be. In the old days, there'd been at least two people working here all the time, often three or more.

Vonnie's crying ebbed into a miserable snuffling, and Eli glared up at him, his lips in an angry pooch. Caleb's children didn't like him too much this morning. Not so surprising. They'd hardly spent any time with him

Rhoda didn't seem to like him much, either. Looking at the situation she was in now, overworked and struggling to do the jobs of three people while minding her children, he couldn't blame her, either.

"I could watch them."

She looked at him then, her expression confused. "What?"

"Upstairs. I could watch them so you could get your work done." He thought fast. "The smaller bedroom is finished. We could block off the doorway with this here." He jiggled the wooden play yard. "They'd have plenty of room to play. I'd be within sight. I'm working in the kitchen, and it opens right up to there."

For a minute, he thought she'd refuse, but then she glanced over her shoulder at the ruined muffins and up at the clock, ticking its way toward eight.

"All right," she decided. "They may not like it, but they don't like being down here, either, so I don't see that it'll make any difference."

It didn't sound as if she had too much confidence in him, but she'd agreed, and he wasn't going to push his luck.

"You watch them for a minute," he said, "while I take this apart and get the room fixed up."

Rhoda nodded. "I'll change their diapers real quick while you're doing that."

Diapers? He hadn't even thought about that. Good thing she had.

Upstairs he quickly cleared out the smaller of the three bedrooms, moving a few boards and some scattered tools. Then, for good measure, he grabbed a broom that was leaning against a corner in the tiny kitchen and swept the floor.

He removed the door from its hinges, setting it carefully to the side. Then he grabbed a screwdriver and went back downstairs.

Rhoda and the children had vanished, but the soothing murmur of her voice came from the office. He felt a guilty twinge of relief that she was handling the diaper side of things. He could deal with it if he had to, but it seemed a little up close and personal for a pair of kids he'd only just met.

He worked fast, removing a panel from the wooden play yard and carrying it up to the apartment. He made a couple more trips for the quilts and toys, and ten minutes later, when Rhoda called from the base of the stairs, he was nearly ready.

"Come on up," he called, frowning as he rigged a makeshift gate in the doorway. It wasn't perfect, but it would serve for now, low enough for an adult to step over, but high enough that the children would be safely contained.

Rhoda took longer to get upstairs than he expected. When she finally made it to the top, she was carrying Vonnie and leading Eli patiently by one hand as he negotiated the steps.

Caleb mentally gave himself a kick. He should have offered to help bring the kids up. He finished setting the last screw with a battery-operated drill. Then he set the tool safely to the side and walked over. The children seemed happier now, probably because each of them held half a cookie in one hand.

Rhoda craned her neck, looking past him at the room as

he took Vonnie out of her arms. To his relief, his daughter allowed this without a protest, although she looked at him uncertainly.

Rhoda looked uncertain, too.

"Come see," he invited. "They'll have a nice play space up here while I'm working. They won't be able to come to any trouble, and you can concentrate on your baking and your customers downstairs."

Rhoda peered into the bedroom and gave the wooden gate a good shake. It barely budged.

"I screwed it to the doorframe. I'll putty up the holes," he told her. "Once we don't need the gate anymore. You'll never be able to tell it was there."

She nodded, her eyes scanning the quilt he'd thrown over the floor and the scattering of toys. She nibbled on her lip.

"It'll be all right," he assured her.

Rhoda sighed and seemed to come to a decision. She bent her head toward the children.

"You're going to play up here," she told them in a firm, encouraging tone. "It'll be wonderful fun, but you must be real *gut*, and not bother Cal—" She stopped and swallowed. "Not bother *Daed* while he's working. *Mamm* will be right downstairs, and I'll bring up another snack for you in a while."

Daed and *Mamm*. Hearing himself coupled up with Rhoda like that made his stomach do funny things. In a strange way, it reminded him of that moment when he'd walked out of this very bakery after seeing Rhoda—really seeing her—for the first time. He'd stood frozen on the sidewalk for a minute, such a tangle of longings in his stomach that he hadn't known what to do. But he'd known that he wanted to do *something*—wanted it more than he'd ever wanted anything in his whole life.

Caleb watched the twins. Neither looked happy, and Vonnie's forehead was starting to pucker. That wasn't good.

If the babies started crying before Rhoda even got downstairs, she'd never stick to this plan.

An idea occurred to him.

"Wait just a minute," he said. He set Vonnie down beside Rhoda, and the child quickly gathered a fistful of her *mamm*'s skirt. He grabbed up a couple of sawhorses and stepped over the wooden fence to put them in the room. He picked up one of the faded quilts, gave it a snap, and draped it over the top of the sawhorses, creating a little tent, open at the front.

"There." He turned to the children. "Now you have a playhouse."

The twins considered the offering with cautious interest. To sweeten the deal, Caleb picked up a painted wooden stove and tucked it inside.

"See, Vonnie? You can cook like *Mamm.* And, Eli—" Quickly Caleb brought a little workbench over, made so that a child could hammer pegs into holes. "You can work like"—it took him a second—"like *Daed.*"

Rhoda glanced at him, and their eyes met. Her cheeks flushed a pretty pink, and she looked away quickly.

Vonnie held up her hands to Caleb, flexing her fingers. She wanted to be picked up and put in the room.

He swung her up and over the fence beside him. Before Eli could protest, Caleb picked him up, too. Then he stepped over the fence to stand beside Rhoda.

The twins toddled around and explored the space, dipping in and out of the makeshift tent as they babbled to each other.

"That was a *gut* idea," Rhoda admitted softly. "But," she added, "they don't stay interested in anything for long at this age, so they may fuss in a bit."

"If they do, I'll handle it," he assured her. "You'd best go downstairs and get to baking, *ja?* Don't you have muffins to make?"

The reminder worked. Rhoda cast one last concerned look at her children and then slipped downstairs. Caleb noticed that she left the doors at the top and bottom of the steps wide open, no doubt so she could hear if there was any trouble.

After an hour or so, Caleb wondered how Rhoda ever got any work done with the twins around. Not because they were fussing. The tent idea had been a good one, and they played happily for a long while. But because they were so much fun to watch.

Every few minutes he found himself pausing in his work trimming out the windows just to check on them. They threw him a few cautious glances, but they seemed to feel safe in their little enclosure, and they soon went about their play without paying him much attention. He worried that the drill's noise would bother them, but even though they startled the first few times, they ignored the sound afterward.

Rhoda must've been busy below, because soon the scent of banana muffins drifted up, making his stomach rumble. Not long after, he heard the soft murmur of voices as she opened the store and began dealing with her customers.

Around ten, she came up with warm muffins and milk for the children.

"I always give them a snack about now," she explained. "We don't eat lunch until late because I have to close up for that, and I don't want to miss customers wanting to pop in during their own lunch breaks. This will tide them over." She stood at the gate, the laden tray in her hands.

"Let me help you." He moved to take the tray from her so she could manage her skirts as she climbed over the barrier, but before he reached her, she quickly set it down on the floor.

He felt a flash of irritation. Passing things back and forth by hand with a shunned person was against church rules, but it wasn't as if anybody was watching them. He waited until she'd climbed over, then picked the tray up and set it over the barrier for her.

On the floor. He'd play by the rules, silly as they seemed to him.

"*Denki*," she murmured, sounding relieved. Then she turned her attention to settling the children with their snacks.

The muffins smelled wonderful *gut*. Banana walnut had always been his second favorite, right under the lemon poppy seed with drizzled icing. His stomach growled, and he covered the noise with a cough.

"Hello?" An unfamiliar female voice called from downstairs. Caleb stepped to the top of the stairs and peered down. An *Englisch* woman stood in the kitchen looking irritated. When she saw Caleb, she complained, "There's nobody working, and I need some rolls."

"She'll be with you in a minute," he said. "But you're not supposed to be back in the kitchen. Go wait in the front."

"Caleb." Rhoda hissed under her breath. He turned to see her clambering back over the barrier, nearly tripping in her hurry. "You have to be polite."

"I was polite. She has no business coming around back." He didn't bother to lower his voice.

"I'll be right there, Mrs. Anderson," Rhoda called breathlessly. Brushing past Caleb, she pattered down the steps.

Caleb clenched his teeth as he picked up the drill and turned back to the window in the kitchen. Rhoda shouldn't be at the beck and call of pushy *Englischers*, women who thought nothing of stepping behind a counter where they clearly weren't supposed to be instead of waiting a few minutes.

He glanced over his shoulder. The twins had plopped down on the quilt and were eating their muffins and swigging milk from brightly colored cups with little spouts. They looked content, and a little of the weight in Caleb's stomach lifted.

Rhoda was just doing good business. He'd seen his *daed* do the same at the dairy, more than once. Being polite when somebody crossed a line because that's what it took to earn the money to put food on the family table.

He hadn't understood it so well back then. In fact, sometimes he'd secretly despised his father for being so gracious when the milk company representative never bothered to be anything but rude in return. But now, finally, he understood things a little better.

He'd be nice, too, if that's what it took to feed the two little ones behind him. He suddenly wished he hadn't been quite so stern with the *Englisch* lady.

"Caleb?"

He'd been so lost in his own thoughts that he'd not heard Rhoda climbing the steps. He braced himself for a chewing-out, but instead she'd brought him a mug of steaming coffee and a fat muffin on a plate.

"Here." She set the offerings on the counter beside him. He could see at a glance that the coffee was exactly as he liked it—lightened up with the smallest splash of cream.

She'd remembered how he took his coffee. A lump rose into his throat, and he felt good and awful both at the same time.

He meant to say thank you, that's all.

"I'm sorry, Rhoda," he blurted out instead.

"Oh, well." She gave a tired shrug. "You're forgiven. I don't suppose it matters much, anyway. Mrs. Anderson is too busy to make her own rolls. She'll get over her hard feelings and come back quick enough." She turned and started toward the steps.

He almost let that stand, but he'd come this far. He might as well see this through.

"No. I mean I'm sorry for this. For all of it. For you needing to work so hard and having to manage our little ones all by yourself."

She'd stopped two steps away from him. She didn't say anything, and the silence stretched out tensely between them.

"I did what I felt I had to do, but I never meant—" Caleb stumbled to a clumsy stop. But this was something he needed to say, so he made himself finish. "I never meant to hurt you, Rhoda. Truly."

He saw her take a broken breath, saw her shoulders hitch. But she still didn't turn around.

"Well, you did hurt me," she told him. "Truly." She went down the steps without looking back.

He knew, because he watched her until she was out of sight.

Chapter Fourteen

RHODA DARTED A GLANCE OVER LYDIA ZOOK'S SHOULDER, up at the big clock ticking on the bakery wall. Only fifteen minutes until five, when she could shoo out the last customers and lock the door.

Finally.

When her parents had been running the bakery, this had been one of their busiest times. People often popped in to get something to go with their suppers—a dozen fresh rolls or a loaf of bread, and maybe some cookies or a cake for dessert. Normally she'd be sorry to see only one customer waiting in line at this time of day.

Not today. She'd never been so thankful to see a workday end in her life, and she'd had some challenging ones with the twins underfoot. For once, they weren't the ones running her ragged. They'd been happy as could be upstairs with Caleb all day. They'd come down for some lunch and to take their naps in the office, but other than that, they'd played in the apartment the whole day.

No, today it wasn't the twins giving her trouble. It was

all the nosy women coming in wanting the scoop about her husband's return. Like Lydia, who'd been dragging out her purchase for several extra minutes.

She and her husband ran Zook's, a grocery store down the street. Lydia always liked to know the latest news, and Rhoda's situation had drawn her like an ant to spilled sugar.

"It must be a shock for you, Caleb coming home so unexpected-like." Lydia's eyes were bright with curiosity. "But a real happy shock, if he's planning to stay."

"Mmm." That wasn't exactly a question, Rhoda told herself, so she wasn't being impolite by not answering it. She put another sugar cookie in the white box. "That makes an even dozen. Is that all you need, Lydia?"

"Maybe a few gingersnaps," the other woman said without so much as looking in the display case.

"I've already put three gingersnaps in there, remember? And the box is near full." Rhoda closed the white lid, tucking its tabs into place. Without giving Lydia a chance to protest, she quickly figured up the cost.

Fortunately, the last customer was an *Englisch* fellow, so at least he wouldn't be likely to ask her any personal questions. Once she had him taken care of, she'd be done for the day.

"*Mach's gut*, Lydia."

"*Mach's gut*." The other woman left, an air of disappointment hanging over her like a cloud. Rhoda couldn't help feeling a bit smug. The women who visited Zook's tomorrow eager for the latest gossip would just have to do without.

"May I help you?" she asked the *Englischer*. He looked vaguely familiar, which meant he'd likely been here before. *Gut*, she thought. Maybe he'd know exactly what he wanted to buy, and this would go quick.

He smiled, showing a lot of very white teeth. "Everything looks so good, I'm having a hard time deciding."

Well, so much for that hope.

"Take your time," she said politely, although she wished devoutly he'd hurry up. If he didn't, somebody else would wander in, and she'd be stuck that much longer. "The cookies are all popular," she suggested. "And the breads. I'll sell you any of them at half price since I'm about to close for the day."

Hint, hint.

"That's nice of you. I'll take a loaf of that wheat bread there, I guess. And a dozen cookies."

Good. Rhoda reached for the bread, then unfolded a box for the cookies. "What kind?"

"Surprise me," the man said.

She'd give him some oatmeal raisin, Rhoda decided. There were a good many of those left. And some chocolate chip pecan cookies, too. Everybody liked those.

"Sounds like you've had a surprise yourself," the man remarked.

She'd do half of each, Rhoda decided. "What?"

"Your husband coming home." He offered another toothy smile. "I couldn't help overhearing."

As Rhoda bent her head back over her work without answering, her heart began to stutter. Best she could recall, neither she nor Lydia had said anything about Caleb being her husband.

She darted a quick look at the man, who seemed unperturbed by her silence. He'd probably just put two and two together, she decided. He had his phone out now. That wasn't unusual. Her *Englisch* customers often fiddled with their phones while they waited. But as she watched, his thumb tapped the phone once. Then he moved it slightly and tapped it again.

Rhoda frowned. Was he taking her picture?

She turned her head as far away as she dared and fumbled with the cookies, scooping them into the box with none of her usual care.

She knew the sort who often took pictures—tourists, usually women, intrigued by her clothes and her lifestyle. They meant no harm.

This man, though, was different. She figured up the purchase as fast as she could, annoyed by how her hand trembled on the pencil.

"It's fifteen dollars and thirty-two cents," she said.

"You're nervous." The man smiled again. "You shouldn't be. I'm not going to hurt you. But maybe it's not me you're scared of. I hear your husband's got quite the temper."

Her skin prickled.

"Fifteen dollars and thirty-two cents," she repeated. She lifted her chin. "Do you want the cookies and bread or not?"

"You're charging me full price. You said I could have the stuff for half. Remember?"

He was right. She'd made a mistake. "I'm sorry."

"Not a problem." Opening his wallet, he plucked out a bill. He placed it on the counter, scooting it in her direction with one finger. "I don't mind paying full price. I'll even go a little extra, if you'll sit down and have a talk with me." He leaned in close. "There are people who'd give a lot of money to hear about how that hotheaded husband of yours has mistreated you."

Rhoda firmed her lips. "I'm not talking with you," she said. "But you can still have your discount."

"No." A voice spoke from behind her, low and definite. "He can't."

She glanced over her shoulder to see Caleb approaching, his face like a thundercloud and his eyes glittering like green ice. He picked up the bill resting on the counter. Fifty dollars.

"You blew your chance at a bargain," Caleb said. "But you don't have to pay this much, either. Not if you tell me who's paying you to take pictures of my wife."

"I can't do that." When Caleb took a step in his direction, the man held up his hands. "Nothing personal, man. Just doing my job."

Caleb scanned him, his eyes narrowed. "You don't look like a reporter."

The man shrugged. "Didn't say I was."

"We're keeping this." Caleb stuck the money in the cash box. "Add it to your client's bill. Now, get out."

"Caleb," Rhoda whispered.

"If he's not a reporter, then he's a private investigator, Rhoda. Sent here to snoop around, likely by the Abbotts." He turned his attention to the man. "That's right, isn't it?"

"No comment." The man chuckled. "Fine. Keep the money. Plenty more where that came from." As the *Englischer* lifted the phone for another photo, Caleb's hand moved swiftly. The phone skittered across the floor, leaving the man staring at his empty fingers. He studied Caleb with raised eyebrows.

"Looks like they were right about you," he said.

"Pick up your phone," Caleb ordered. "And get out."

"Here." Rhoda held out the bag with the cookies and bread.

Both Caleb and the stranger looked at her with some surprise.

"He paid for them," she explained simply.

The man chuckled again and accepted the bag. Then he scooped up his phone and left, whistling as he went.

The minute he was out on the sidewalk, Caleb crossed to the door and snicked the lock shut. He also flipped the sign and snapped off the lights. Then he turned to look at her. "Has he been here before?"

"I think, maybe so." She swallowed as Caleb's expression darkened. "He looked familiar. But he hasn't been here much, or I'd have remembered him better."

"Have any other folks been coming around, asking questions?"

Rhoda thought of Lydia and sputtered a laugh. "A few, *ja*."

"This isn't funny, Rhoda."

"No, you're right. It isn't." It wasn't funny. It was unsettling. Caleb shouldn't have smacked the man's hand, of course, but she couldn't help being thankful that he'd come in when he had.

A worrisome thought occurred to her. "Where are the twins? They shouldn't be left alone."

"They're all right. They're safe upstairs in their play area. I'm about ready to knock off for the day. I came to get you so I could show you what I've done on the apartment before you leave."

"I've a ways to go yet. I still have to get everything cleared up for the night. It'll take me a good hour or so. If you need to go someplace, bring the twins down here."

Caleb shook his head. "*Nee*, that's all right. Just come upstairs when you're done."

After he'd climbed back up the steps, she went through the motions of shutting down the bakery for the evening, one well-practiced step at a time. The routine soothed her frazzled nerves.

Today's troubles had started with Mrs. Anderson's irritated question. *Who on earth was that rude man?*

Rhoda had opened her mouth and realized she had no idea how best to answer. *He's fixing the upstairs apartment. I'm sorry—what can I get for you today?*

That explanation and a discount on her favorite rolls had settled Mrs. Anderson, but the Plain women who'd come in afterward weren't so easily satisfied. They knew perfectly well who Caleb was. What they wanted to know was how Rhoda felt about her husband's return—and what was going to happen next.

Rhoda didn't know the answer to either question. The only thing she knew was that since Caleb had come back, her whole life felt topsy-turvy.

Topsy-turvy had always been Caleb's specialty. He'd started turning her life upside down the day they'd taken notice of each other. She hadn't minded so much at first. In fact, she'd rather liked it.

There'd been something different about Caleb Hochstedler. Something that made her catch her breath and press her hand to her stomach whenever he looked at her. Lots of boys had looked at her before, but none of them had ever made her feel like Caleb had.

The memory made her sad. She'd been so very happy for a while. Then her life had turned upside down and, like a badly whipped meringue, had plopped into a sad, wasteful mess.

It took her an hour to get the kitchen to rights. Then she squared her shoulders and went upstairs.

She hadn't heard any hammering for some time, so she was curious to see how much work Caleb had gotten done. When she reached the top of the stairs, she heard him talking quietly.

"*Ja,* there you go. Give it a good pound."

Give what a good pound? Rhoda peeked around the door.

Caleb knelt on the floor in the play space, watching Eli smack a wooden peg with the little hammer Joseph had made.

That wasn't her favorite toy. Eli had smashed a finger more than once, resulting in yells and tears. She watched as her son, his tongue sticking out of one side of his mouth, lifted the hammer and hit the peg again.

"*Gut!*" Caleb gently moved Eli's left hand out of the danger zone. "You'll hurt yourself, though, if you don't keep this hand out of the way. Try it now."

Eli's hammer hit the peg with a satisfying whack. The little boy grinned up at Caleb.

Caleb smiled back and tousled his son's hair. "You've the makings of a good carpenter."

Rhoda's eyes lingered on her husband's face. Oh, she remembered that smile, and it still made her stomach catch.

She glanced quickly away, looking around the apartment—and her mouth drooped open.

Caleb had been busy.

The whole place looked . . . finished. All the trim was up. Not only up but painted, too. He'd cracked the windows open to let out the fumes so that only the faintest scent lingered in the air. Even the wood scraps and sawdust had been swept into a neat pile.

Forgetting herself, Rhoda pushed the door wide and walked in, inspecting the details one by one. Caleb had done more in a day than the other men could have managed in a week. She couldn't believe it, but the apartment was near ready to move into.

"*Mamm!*" Vonnie called. Rhoda turned to find Caleb and the twins watching her. She felt her cheeks flush.

"You've got everything done!" She reached to touch the window trim.

"Careful!" Caleb pushed himself up and stepped over the little fence. "It's likely not dry. I only finished about an hour ago. But by tomorrow it'll be *gut*."

"How did you get this done so fast? And with the twins to watch, too?"

"They were little trouble. And this is what I do, Rhoda. I'd be a pretty poor worker if I couldn't knock this out in a day."

"I can't believe it." Rhoda couldn't stop the smile spreading over her face. She hadn't realized until this minute how much she was looking forward to moving into her very own home.

Naomi and Joseph had been so kind, and she'd focused on how grateful she was to them—and she was grateful. She hadn't allowed herself to dwell on all the little inconveniences that came with living in someone else's house.

But now that the end was in sight, the feeling of relief was sweet.

She'd better enjoy it, because Abram had already sent his letter to her father, explaining his arrangement with Caleb. Her parents' plans to move here had likely sped up. She wanted to prove to them that her living above the bakery could be a good situation for them all. That would be easier to do if everything was already settled and running smoothly when they arrived.

She smiled at Caleb. "*Denki*. It's kind of you to see to all this."

A warmth kindled deep in his eyes, but he didn't smile back. "It's not kindness. It's my job, looking after you and the twins, and I intend to do it."

He sounded so grim that her smile faded.

"Anyhow," he went on. "Don't get too excited. It's not finished yet."

She frowned, looking around. "What's left to do?"

"Odds and ends. Better locks, and I want to replace that hollow core door at the top of the staircase with a solid wooden one. I'll install some alarms, too, on all the windows and doors. I learned how, working among the *Englisch*. Nothing fancy, just something that'll make a big noise if somebody tries to come in."

She blinked, confused. "Alarms?"

"*Ja*. This is a business. People may think you have money here and try to break in. And it's clear folks can't be trusted to stay where they belong. Like that *Englisch* woman today. Best if you have some sort of bell that tells you when somebody's where they oughtn't to be."

A bell? Rhoda wasn't sure what to say. "There's one on the front door to let me know when customers come in. That's the only bell we've ever needed."

"Because nobody was living upstairs," Caleb explained. "And your father was usually here when you and your *mamm* were working. Don't worry about the cost. I'll pay for the alarms myself."

She was shaking her head before he finished speaking. "Wouldn't such bells be electric? I don't think the church will allow that."

Caleb sighed. He didn't say, *Who cares?* but she read it in his expression. "You've got electricity down in the bakery."

"*Ja*, of course," she said defensively. "It's a business. That's allowed. There's no electricity upstairs, though."

"So I'll power the upstairs alarms off batteries. I can figure that part out. You need the alarms, Rhoda. It's not just about money. I may not always be here to run off people like that man earlier."

Rhoda tossed him an exasperated look. "And you think a bell's going to do that job? I doubt it."

"Rhoda—"

There was no point arguing about this. "Talk to Abram."

"What?"

"Talk to Abram about your bells and alarms. If he says it's all right, then I guess it is. You're meeting with him tomorrow anyhow, ain't so? You can bring it up then."

"All right, I will," Caleb said, looking determined. "There's something else I want to talk to him about, too."

"What's that?"

"I've been thinking," Caleb said. "Today went all right, didn't it? With me watching the *kinder*? We could keep doing this for the next few days while I finish the work upstairs. That'll give me plenty of time with the twins. Naomi won't have to do you the favor of watching them, and I won't have to hang around at Joseph's in the evenings."

"That's not what Abram said to do."

"Everybody says he's a sensible man. Hopefully he'll see the sense in this."

Rhoda studied the stubborn set of her husband's jaw. She wasn't so sure. In her experience, bishops didn't like having their instructions ignored, even good-natured ones like Abram.

"I guess you can ask him."

"I will. And I'll still come to Joseph's tonight after supper, like I'm supposed to," Caleb added.

He didn't sound too happy at the prospect, but Rhoda wasn't the only one who had experience with bishops. Caleb had lived Plain long enough to know he'd have a better chance of swaying Abram's mind if the other man saw that he'd made an attempt to follow instructions first. "Tomorrow I'll explain my idea to Abram. If he agrees, then it'll be all right with you?"

"I'll abide by whatever the bishop says."

It was the only correct answer to that question. But as she gave it, a tickle went up her spine. Of course she'd obey whatever decision her bishop handed down. That went without saying. It was just . . .

She wasn't so sure how she felt about this idea. And Abram was unlike any bishop she'd ever known. There was just no telling what he might say.

Chapter Fifteen

THAT EVENING, CALEB SAT ON THE LIVING ROOM floor playing with the twins, his back to the kitchen, where Rhoda and Naomi were clearing away the dishes.

He'd arrived at Joseph's house just after supper, as promised. He'd expected his brother to disappear to the barn or his workshop for the duration of the visit. Joseph didn't shy away from trouble, but he made a policy of not looking for it.

However, to Caleb's surprise, his brother was lingering in the kitchen, He'd walked to the living room doorway more than once, peering inside.

He was there again now. Caleb sensed that without turning around. He'd learned to be aware of what happened behind his back. *Watching your six*, Milt called it.

The children were trying to put together a chunky puzzle of a monkey. Vonnie was good at it, considering each piece carefully before fitting it in place. Usually she was right, although her fingers weren't always deft enough to line up the edges. More than once, Caleb had helped nudge the piece into its spot. Vonnie didn't appear to mind his help.

Eli, though, wasn't so *gut* with the puzzle. He was better with his fingers, but not near so patient. He chose pieces at random, trying to jam them in where they didn't go.

Caleb tried to help him, too, but Eli was in an irritable mood, snatching the pieces away. Finally Caleb had left him to work on his own, and the child had grown more and more frustrated.

Right now, he was trying to fit the monkey's tail on top of its head. When it wouldn't cooperate, his lips pooched out.

"Bad!" The toddler threw the piece across the room.

"*Ach*, now," Caleb said reprovingly and then stopped short.

How many times had his father said that, in just the same tone? Ach*, now, Caleb. The cows won't let their milk down any faster with you banging the buckets around.*

Ach*, now, Caleb. Let your sister have the last piece of the candy. We men must take special care of the women, always.*

Ach*, now, Caleb. You mustn't blame your brother for giving you the cold shoulder. You knew well enough that he'd set his heart on Rhoda Lambright far before you took any notice of her.*

"Eli!" Rhoda hurried in from the kitchen. "We don't throw things. Besides, that's Elizabeth's puzzle, not yours. Let's find the piece before it's lost for good." She took her protesting son by the elbow, leading him toward the corner of the room where the piece had landed.

"Takes after his *vadder*, that one," Joseph murmured from the doorway.

Caleb glanced up. There was no condemnation in his brother's eyes, only weary amusement as he watched Rhoda helping Eli retrieve the piece.

"Maybe so," Caleb agreed. "I never much liked puzzles."

"You never had the patience for them," Joseph pointed out shortly.

Ah. There it was.

"No." Caleb set Vonnie on the floor and rose to his feet. "I'm not a patient man. For instance, I'm getting tired of waiting for you to stop hanging around that doorway and come out with whatever it is you need to say to me."

"The children are overtired." Rhoda walked up, the puzzle piece in one hand. Her eyes darted from him to Joseph and back again. "They had a busy day. I think they'll need an early bedtime tonight. I'm sorry, Caleb, but—"

"That's all right." Temporarily distracted from his standoff with Joseph, he knelt and tweaked Vonnie's tiny nose. "I had a real *gut* time today, and I'll see them both again tomorrow. I've some cleaning up to do, and a few odds and ends. They can stay upstairs with me again."

"After you meet with Abram," Rhoda reminded him.

He'd sent word to the bishop that he'd be coming first thing in the morning. He wanted to get this talk out of the way. Abram had sent a message back for him to wear work clothes. No telling what he was going to be roped into helping with.

"After that, *ja*."

Rhoda nodded. "Say good night," she instructed the twins.

"Good night," they parroted and then allowed themselves to be led to the stairs.

"Good night," Caleb responded. He watched the trio mounting the steps slowly. They were too big for Rhoda to carry them both, so she was carrying Vonnie and leading Eli by the hand.

Eli was rubbing his eyes, his small mouth still shaped into a pout. He tried to jerk his hand away from his mother's grip, and she wobbled, nearly losing her balance.

"Here now!" Caleb was across the room in a heartbeat, and before anybody could protest, he swept Eli up into his arms. The cranky child immediately began to howl, but Caleb ignored that, focusing on Rhoda's startled face.

"I'll carry him up for you."

"Oh, but—"

"Best hurry up. He's not likely to get any quieter standing here. I'll follow you."

Although she looked uncertain, Rhoda started up the steps. Judging by the rigid set of her shoulders, she wasn't happy. She wasn't the only one. Eli struggled in Caleb's arms, working himself into a full-fledged fit.

Caleb pressed Eli snugly against his chest so that the little boy couldn't kick. "Settle yourself," he told his son firmly.

The minute Rhoda was safely at the top of the steps, she turned. "I can take him now."

"I've got him," Caleb countered firmly. "You're sleeping in Miriam's old room?"

When Rhoda nodded, Caleb led the way down the hall, turning into the room that had been, for a time, more than a bedroom for his younger sister. It had been a sanctuary—and a kind of prison.

For weeks after witnessing her parents' deaths, Miriam had been too terrified to step outside this room. She'd still been in that state when he'd left home, and he'd been worried about her.

Now she was married and away on a trip with her new husband. Caleb still couldn't wrap his mind around that. He was anxious to meet this Reuben, curious about the man who'd coaxed his sister back out into the world.

Miriam's room didn't look much different. The furniture was the same—a bed, a chest of drawers, a nightstand, and a chair. Even the quilt on the bed, a big star pattern consisting of little diamonds in shades of blue and green pieced together, was one he recognized. Miriam had made it, back before his parents' deaths.

He did notice a few changes. The chest of drawers had been scooted to the side, making room for two cribs. They were lined up end to end across from the window, where they could catch the breeze on a hot summer night. New items were neatly arranged on the nightstand. A glass for water, a comb, a book marked with a ribbon. All placed just as Rhoda liked them. He remembered that from their marriage, and the sight of the familiar odds and ends made an aching knot form in his belly.

"Caleb?" Rhoda paused in the doorway, her dark eyes watchful and worried. "*Denki.* I can manage from here."

He didn't want to leave. "I don't mind helping."

"Oh, I'm used to handling bedtime alone. And Eli's already calmed down."

Caleb glanced at his son. Eli had stopped struggling, that was true. Temper had ebbed into tears, and he snuffled against Caleb's shirt.

"*Ja,*" he agreed quietly. "He's all right now."

Rhoda hesitated another telling second before walking into the room. The flush of color on her cheeks made it clear that she was uncomfortable being alone here with him. The knot in Caleb's stomach twisted tighter.

There'd been a time, when they'd been traveling around paying obligatory visits to relatives after their wedding, when they'd been relieved and secretly delighted to escape to whatever spare room they'd been allotted. It was the only space and time they had to be alone.

He'd been so impatient back then for them to have a house of their own. But right now he'd give a great deal to have a few moments of those old visiting days back again.

To have his wife look at him the way she used to. With trust and love instead of uncertainty and fear.

"Caleb?" Rhoda prompted.

"I'll be going, then." He set Eli down in one of the cribs. "I'll see you all tomorrow."

"After you talk to Abram."

Irritation prickled. Why did she keep reminding him of that? "*Ja,*" he agreed shortly. "After that."

As he passed her on his way to the door, he paused to touch his fingertip to Vonnie's nose. The little girl promptly sneezed, and he and Rhoda both chuckled at the same time.

Their eyes met, and for one sweet second, his splintered world pulled itself back together. Then Rhoda's expression shifted from amusement back to worry, and she edged past him, moving toward the cribs.

"Good night, Caleb," she said without looking at him.

"Good night."

He pulled the door closed and went downstairs. He'd hoped Joseph would have given up and gone out, but his brother was standing by the kitchen sink with Naomi.

"I guess I'll be leaving." Caleb started toward the door, hoping to make it outside before anybody objected.

He wasn't quick enough.

Naomi turned toward him, her sweet face concerned. "No need to rush off. Stay on and visit. Rhoda usually puts the little ones to bed and comes back down for a little while. It'd be nice for us all to spend some time together. We could sit in the living room."

Caleb smothered a sigh. That sounded . . . uncomfortable. During their courting days, he'd spent a few evenings sitting next to Rhoda in a living room under her father's stern gaze, trying his best to look respectable. It had always set his nerves on edge.

Back then he'd been willing to do whatever it took to spend another minute or two with Rhoda. He liked better having her all to himself, off in their meadow maybe, where they could linger together unwatched. But even their time together under her parents' eyes had been sweet. He remembered how Rhoda would dart glances his way, looking at him from underneath her lashes, her lips curving up just the tiniest bit.

Every time she'd done that, his insides had gone gooey. He'd have sat on that sofa until the cows came home, hoping for another of those little looks. If Isaac Lambright wanted to glare at him over whatever book he was reading that evening, that was a small enough price to pay.

Now, though, the glances Rhoda sent his way were different. They still did things to his insides—but nothing that made him happy. When Rhoda looked at him now, his heart ached with an unbearable heaviness. That one shared look over Vonnie's sneeze was the exception.

"*Denki*, Naomi," he said now, "but I'm tired."

"Well"—his sister-in-law sounded disappointed—"I can understand why. Rhoda said you did amazing work today. The work of five men, she said. We could hardly believe it, could we, Joseph?" When her husband didn't answer, she murmured, "Such a blessing to have your help. If you're ready to go, we won't stop you. But, Joseph, isn't there something you wanted to talk to Caleb about before he left?"

Her husband looked uncomfortable, but he nodded. "There is, *ja*. I'll walk outside with you."

"All right." The last thing Caleb wanted to hear right now was some lecture from his brother, but there didn't seem much he could do about it.

"So?" he asked as soon as they'd reached the yard. "What did you want to talk about?" As he spoke, he reached into his jeans pocket, pulling out his keys.

Joseph glanced at them. His mouth tightened, but when he spoke, his voice was carefully even. "Miriam got word to us that she and Reuben expect to be home on Friday. We're meeting them over at their farm and having a supper."

"Ah." Caleb braced for the explanation of why he shouldn't be there, or what rules would be in place if he was. "And?"

"We're hoping you'll come. It would be *gut* to have the whole family, and it would mean a lot to our sister to see you."

Caleb lifted an eyebrow. Not what he was expecting. "I'd like to see Miriam," he conceded cautiously. "And meet this Reuben she's taken such a shine to. He's a good man?"

"He is." Joseph's answer was quick and certain. "He's a

hard worker and an honest fellow. At first I wasn't sure of him. He'd never joined the church, and he carried some grudges that . . ." Joseph paused, glancing at his brother. "But it turned out all right. Abram thinks highly of him."

"I care more what Miriam thinks."

Joseph looked as if he were going to argue, but instead he lifted a shoulder in a shrug. "I suppose you'll find that out on Friday, if you'll come. Will you?"

Caleb hesitated. No doubt there would be the usual fuss over rules related to his shunning, especially if there were other people there. And there almost certainly would be. But he already knew his answer, so there wasn't much point in holding it back. "*Ja*, I'll be there."

"I'm glad."

Caleb doubted that. "Anything else?" He jingled the keys in his hand.

Joseph didn't miss the gesture. A muscle jumped in his jaw, but he nodded. "There is one other thing."

"And that is?"

"I need to ask for your forgiveness."

Caleb blinked. He'd been prepared for his brother to say just about anything—except that. "Why?"

Joseph took his time answering. He'd always had trouble with finding the right words, and he and Caleb had tangled many times when Joseph had said something too bluntly. He was being careful now, and that meant this mattered.

"It's hard," Joseph said finally. "Waiting on things. Especially things you want really bad."

Caleb's mind flicked back to the beach house, to finding Trevor gone when he'd hoped his long search would finally be over. "That's true enough."

"We've been waiting for you to come home for a long time. Praying for it. Hoping for it. But when you finally did . . ." Joseph looked back at him, meeting his eyes. "When you did, I didn't know what to do." He scrubbed a hand across his face. "I was afraid to believe it, I guess.

And so maybe I wasn't as . . . welcoming as I should have been. I'm sorry."

Caleb felt suddenly awkward—and guilty. "That's all right."

"*Nee*. It's not. As your brother, I should have been the first to celebrate. The first to believe that this marked the start of good things," his brother continued doggedly. "You hurt us, Caleb. Leaving like you did. No." He held up a hand when Caleb started to speak. "I know your reasons, and I don't want to argue over them again now. But pain—it makes you too suspicious sometimes. Too slow to trust when a person tries to make amends. I'm not offering that as an excuse," Joseph went on, "just a reason."

Caleb thought of the wariness in Rhoda's eyes. "I understand." Then, because he knew what his brother was waiting for, he added, "You're forgiven."

"*Denki*." Joseph looked relieved. "I am thankful, Caleb. Thankful that you've come home and that you've been willing to meet with Abram and follow his instructions. And pleased to see you're working so hard to get to know your children and mend fences with your wife. You have made a *gut* start."

"Does this mean you're going to lighten up on the rules a little?"

"Probably not," Joseph answered honestly, but Caleb noted a glint of humor in his eye. "You and I are different in how we look at rules. They are a protection for people like me and Naomi. And Rhoda, too. Keeping danger out and good in. To you, they are a restriction, keeping you from something you want." He lifted his chin. "Before you left, you asked me, remember, to look after Rhoda. Ain't so?"

"That's so."

"And so I've done. So I'm doing yet, best I can. Asking you to follow our rules about shunning is part of that."

"You're protecting my own wife and children from me. Is that what you're saying?"

Joseph never lied, and he didn't lie now. "That's what I'm saying, *ja*. And I'll keep on doing it. Until I see there's no more need." Joseph glanced at the truck parked near his barn and winced. "Drive safe, *bruder*."

He climbed the steps and went into the house. Caleb stood alone in the yard for a second, his eyes straying to the second floor, to Miriam's old bedroom. From this angle, he couldn't see inside, but likely Rhoda was near finished getting their children ready for bed.

He clenched his hands around his keys so tightly that sharp edges dug into his palm as he stalked to his truck. Once inside, he picked up his phone off the seat. After it had rung inside his pocket and made Vonnie cry, he'd taken to leaving it in the truck when he was around the children.

He had a voice mail. He tapped through the procedure to listen to it and frowned as Milt's gravelly voice spoke into his ear.

"Got some news, Amish," the bounty hunter said without preamble. "I've put out some feelers. Your boy's in your area, they say, and something big's brewing. I'm on a job, and that's all I know, so no sense calling me back. I'll get in touch when I hear more, but in the meantime, watch yourself and that pretty wife of yours."

A click and the call disconnected. Milt didn't believe in wasting words.

Caleb glanced back at the house, a shiver tickling up his spine. He dropped the phone on the seat and started the engine, unable to shake off his uneasiness.

So, Trevor was in the area, and he'd been careful enough that Caleb hadn't seen any sign of him. That wasn't good. He sure hoped the "something big" Milt had caught wind of didn't involve Rhoda.

Or his children.

At the thought of the twins, Caleb stiffened. Did Trevor know about them? Probably. Almost certainly. Someone, maybe Trevor's father, was feeding him information, likely with the help of that man Caleb had run out of the bakery earlier.

Caleb pulled the truck out onto the road, but he drove only a little way before turning into the dirt side road leading into the pastures where *Daed* had run his milk cows. Aaron Lapp now leased them from Joseph, and his beef cattle were bedded down in the short summer grass. They looked at him curiously as he locked the truck and started back up the road toward the Hochstedler farmhouse.

He wouldn't spend tonight on the side of the road. He needed to be closer.

He didn't walk fast. He didn't want to get to the farm until Joseph had finished the evening chores and gone inside for the night. Then Caleb intended to settle himself in the barn and keep an eye on the house. He'd left his bedroll back at the bakery, but that didn't matter. He wouldn't be sleeping much.

Joseph had kept his word to look after Rhoda—and would continue to keep it. But he put too much stock in church rules. They could only go so far to keep a woman and her children safe.

Caleb was prepared to go the rest of the way.

Chapter Sixteen

WHEN CALEB DUTIFULLY SHOWED UP FOR HIS MEETing with Abram the following morning and found the bishop preparing to paint his barn, he almost groaned out loud.

This was even worse than he'd expected.

"Hot time of year for painting." Shading his eyes, he peered up at the stout man perched on the fourth rung of a wooden ladder.

"*Ja*, it is." Abram chuckled. "That's why I'm starting early, and on a day I have help. Open that bucket of paint, and pick up a brush for yourself. You can do the low work while I paint up top. We can get a good bit of this job done while we talk. Mind you don't get any paint on your clothes. They look too fancy for painting."

Fancy. Smothering a yawn, Caleb pried open the lid, dipped a brush in, and scraped it against the side of the pail. Only here would faded jeans and a T-shirt be considered fancy.

"So." Abram brushed the red paint onto the barn wall. "You don't look as if you slept well last night."

"I didn't."

"Is the apartment uncomfortable?"

"The apartment isn't the problem." That was true enough. He'd have been plenty comfortable in the bakery apartment, if he'd slept there.

Abram slanted him another glance. "Conscience troubling you?"

"No."

"Something must be, or you'd not have asked to meet with me this morning." Abram swiped another board. "But you can take your time with the telling. The more of this barn we get painted, the more pleased I'll be."

"I don't want to tell you anything. I want to ask you something. Two things, actually."

Abram grunted as he dipped his brush in the paint. "*Gut.* Questions are *gut.* That is what we are here for, you and I."

"Is there any reason I can't install alarms in the bakery? On the windows and doors, I mean, in case someone tries to break in?"

If he'd expected some reaction from the bishop, he didn't get one. Abram calmly continued painting. "Is there any reason to install them? Has the bakery been robbed before?"

"Not that I know of, but there are more *Englischers* in town than usual. When that movie opens in two weeks, there's likely to be another rush of tourists pestering my family."

"And you think Lambright's Bakery may have trouble?" Abram clambered down his ladder, scooted it to the left, then climbed back up again, pail and brush clamped in one hand. "I have to say, I wasn't too worried about that. I suspected there might be problems at your parents' old store, though. I've spoken with Sam already. They're planning to close for the week the movie comes out, which I think is wise. Maybe longer, depending. There are sure to be folks wanting to get in and see where it all took place." He clucked his tongue sadly as he swiped another swath of fresh dark red over the faded paint. "It is a shame for them to lose their profits, but it can't be helped. We will all be thankful when this movie nonsense is finished and this is over."

"Nothing will be over until Trevor Abbott is in jail." Caleb slapped more paint on the barn with extra-hard strokes, thinking fast.

Maybe he should tell Abram everything now. All of it, what he'd found in the cottage, why he'd come back to Johns Mill, what Milt had heard about Trevor being close by. That would come out soon enough anyway, once Sam told Emma. Better, maybe, if he got ahead of it.

"Careful," Abram warned. "You'll get splats on your clothes. As for the rest of it, there are two ways to put sorrows behind us. One is to wait for them to pass, and another is to move ourselves forward, putting them behind us." He dipped his brush again. "You've been stuck on Trevor and the past for more than two years, and that hasn't helped you or your family. If you want to make a future with Rhoda and the children, you have to move on." He spoke with the certainty common to Amish bishops—as if there couldn't be any other way of looking at something except the way they saw it.

Caleb set his jaw and promptly scrapped his idea of explaining everything to Abram. He kept forgetting this odd little man was a bishop. He had plenty of experience tangling with bishops, and he'd never come out on the good side of it.

Besides, he'd had almost no sleep, and while he was in no particular mood to help this man paint his barn, he'd far rather do that than endure another lecture on forgiveness and trusting God. And he could smell one coming.

So he held his tongue. For a few seconds there was no sound except the slippery slick of the paint sliding across the rough boards.

"You know," Abram went on finally, "it can be an admirable thing to stick with something you believe in, not minding when others don't agree with you." He dabbed his perspiring forehead with a rag he'd slung over one shoulder. "This you have certainly done, when many men would have backed down."

Caleb paused, his brush in mid-swipe. That sounded almost like a compliment, and he felt a sudden, silly rush of warmth at the approval. Then he tamped it down.

Bishops didn't pay compliments. Especially not to him.

"So?" he asked brusquely. "Can I install the alarms or not?"

Abram sighed. "You want these because you are worried about your *fraw* and the *kinder* being there alone?"

"Yes, especially at night."

"I see." Again, Abram climbed down and repositioned his ladder. "And although the bakery has never had such things, you feel it's necessary now because of the fuss about the movie?"

"That's right." Mostly.

Abram continued to paint. "When will the apartment be ready for them to move into?"

"It's near ready now. I'll finish it up in a day or so."

Abram paused his painting, looking down at Caleb with raised eyebrows. "You have done quick work. That's *gut*." The older man considered, his lips pursed thoughtfully. "I will think on this and let you know."

Caleb tightened his grip on the brush handle—and his patience. "It would be easier to install the things now rather than later," he pointed out.

"*Ja*, maybe. But easier is not always best. And quick is not always wise."

"But—"

"I have answered your question," Abram interrupted. "As best I can for now. I will give you the rest of my answer soon. Now I have a question for you."

Caleb fought the urge to argue. Only the fact that it would do absolutely no good kept him from it. Abram was considering the alarms, and that was more than a lot of church leaders would have agreed to. Best to be quiet for now. There'd be time to argue later if he said no.

Besides, he still had to bring up the question of spending his time with the children at Lambright's Bakery rather than at Joseph's.

"What do you want to know?"

"As I said, you have a strong mind. That's a fine thing to have, when it's pointed in the right direction. But you've set that mind against the church. Why?"

Caleb stopped painting to stare up at Abram. "You know why."

"I do not. Oh," he went on calmly, "I know why you are angry with Trevor Abbott and why you want him to be punished for the crime he committed. And I understand how your unwillingness to forgive and to leave justice in the hands of *Gott* has caused you to be at odds with the church. This I know."

"Then I don't understand what you're asking me."

"Your trouble with the church started long before that. You've been butting heads with the rules as long as I can remember. What started it?"

Caleb paused, considering. It was a strange question, one nobody had ever asked him before. His mind went back, thumbing through years of memories. Then he stopped and shook his head.

"I don't know," he said impatiently. "What difference does it make anyhow?"

"I think it might make a good bit of difference." Abram finished painting the last boards on his side, put the brush in the bucket, and climbed carefully back down the ladder. "All folks struggle with forgiveness. It can be a very hard thing. But still, most men would not have left a young wife and a grieving family behind as you did. Think on it, and see what you remember." Abram sighed and rolled his head from side to side, stretching his neck. "But thinking, like painting, is hard work, and you're too tired for such today. Finish up this wall, then take yourself back to the bakery. Spend time with your *fraw* and your *kinder*, and make an effort to get along with your brother, however much he's annoying you."

When Caleb shot him a startled glance, Abram chuckled.

"Five sons," he reminded him. "And no two of them alike."

"I wanted to speak to you about that. Rhoda needs help with the twins while she works. I'd hoped I could spend time with them there instead of driving out to my brother's every evening."

"You can certainly spend time with them during the day," Abram agreed. But just as Caleb relaxed, he added, "But you should still visit your brother's house as well. It is not so pleasant for you there as staying at Emma and Sam's home maybe, but it is important to mend all your fences, not just the easy ones."

"How did you—" Caleb started. The bishop only winked.

"I have—"

"Five sons." Caleb finished the sentence with him. "I know."

The bishop chuckled. "I'll come to town Saturday and talk to you and Rhoda both. I'll give you my decision on these bells you want then, and we'll work out a visiting schedule. Of course, there's church to talk about as well."

Church? Caleb shook his head, alarmed. "I don't—"

"Not today," Abram interrupted. "That we will talk about some other time. But if you plan on trying to get out of going, you'd best come up with a real good reason." Abram winked. "Now get on with you before I decide I need help painting the back of this barn."

Caleb didn't need to be told twice. He washed up quick at the outside spigot, and in short order, he was back in his pickup heading for the bakery.

As he drove, his mind sifted through the conversation he'd just had. Abram King wasn't like any bishop Caleb had dealt with before. His talks with other church leaders had involved long, dry lectures with sharp eyes on his face to make sure he was registering the proper feelings about the trouble he was in.

Nobody had ever asked for help painting a barn—nor had a bishop ever asked him any questions, much less such a strange one. He was glad Abram hadn't pushed for answers, because he was wrong. Maybe Caleb had been at odds with the church for years, but that wasn't why he wanted Trevor caught so badly.

That had to do with what had happened the day he'd told *Daed* what Emma had talked to him about in private. About her worries about Trevor's increasing attention. About the gifts he insisted on slipping into her belongings whenever she turned her back and the way he always seemed to appear wherever she happened to be. And about how he paid little attention to her polite protests.

Emma had felt sorry for the scrawny *Englischer*, but then, Emma felt sorry for everybody. Caleb didn't, and he could read between the lines.

If Emma was telling him this much, there was more she wasn't telling. His sister always softened things. Caleb had suspected that this Trevor was a bigger threat than he appeared to be, and he'd made that clear to his father.

When dealing with other people, particularly with *youngies*, *Daed* had been a gentle fellow. Caleb, flushed with the status of a newly married man, had taken it upon himself to give his father advice. He'd told him to make it very clear to Trevor that Emma was off-limits.

More than likely, that advice had gotten his father—and his mother—killed.

He pulled his mind away from that aching regret as he parked at the back of the bakery. When he walked inside, he glanced toward Rhoda's makeshift corral, but it was still missing the piece he'd taken upstairs, and the children were nowhere in sight.

He should have fixed that back before leaving to talk to Abram, he realized. Without it, she'd have had no way to keep the children nearby but out of trouble while she worked.

The low musical sound of Rhoda's voice came from the front of the bakery where she was waiting on a customer. Caleb hesitated at the bottom of the steps, chewing the inside of his cheek.

Likely that's where the children were, underfoot while Rhoda was trying to work. Maybe he should go get them. By now, everybody in Johns Mill would have heard of his homecoming, so nobody would be surprised to see him. He'd keep his head down, scoop up the twins, and scuttle upstairs.

Decision made, he started toward the front of the store.

Rhoda was busy behind the counter. A line of customers wound around the store, *Englischers* and Plain alike. The children stood beside her, looking overwhelmed by the noise and the people. Vonnie had her fingers stuck in her ears.

Rhoda was smiling and talking pleasantly to the customers, but a worry line creased her brow, and there was a tightness around her mouth that Caleb didn't like.

She was working too hard, but since she'd not accept money from him, there wasn't much he could do about it. He knew she needed the cash these customers were putting into her money box. The least he could do was to get their babies out from under her feet.

He slipped quietly behind her and over to the twins. They looked up with wide eyes.

"*Kumm*," he whispered. "Let's go upstairs and leave *Mamm* to her work."

Vonnie immediately lifted her arms to be picked up, but Caleb had expected her to cooperate. He was more worried about Eli. His son must have been tired of being cooped up behind the counter because he took the hand Caleb offered without complaint.

"Good boy," he said approvingly.

Rhoda finished making change for an *Englisch* lady before catching his eye. He tensed, expecting a sharp look, but to his surprise, her expression softened.

"Thank you," she said. "They will be much happier upstairs, and it's so busy down here, I can hardly keep up."

"You're welcome."

For a second, they smiled at each other, and then Rhoda blinked. "I . . . um . . ."

"Need to get busy." Caleb glanced over the crowd. "We'll see you in a while, and—" He broke off short and frowned. "Hey! You there! What are you doing?"

"Caleb!"

He barely heard Rhoda's protest. His attention was fixed on the young *Englisch* man sliding a phone back into his pocket.

Caleb dropped Eli's hand and thrust Vonnie into his wife's arms. He brushed past her and around the corner, elbowing his way through the crowd, who watched him, slack-jawed.

The young *Englischer* flushed red and started for the door. He made it four steps before Caleb had him by the arm.

"Why were you taking pictures?"

"I—I—" the man stammered. "Look, you can't just come out here and start grabbing people."

"Give me your phone."

"I'm not going to—"

Enough of this. Caleb dug in the man's pocket while he yelped a protest. He brought up the phone, which, he saw, was still in its camera mode. Quickly Caleb flicked through the photos. The last five were of Rhoda, from different angles, zoomed in close.

He tightened his mouth. He must not have made himself clear with that last fellow. He'd make sure this one understood him and that he carried a message to whoever was paying for these pictures.

"Who are you taking these for?" Caleb still had the fellow by one arm, and he gave him a shake.

"Nobody! I mean, you know, just me."

"I heard they don't like to have their pictures taken," an *Englisch* woman murmured in a shocked tone. "But this seems a bit extreme."

"Why," Caleb repeated through gritted teeth, "are you taking pictures of my wife?"

"Your wife? Oh, man, I'm sorry, okay? I'll delete them. I was only . . . you know." The *Englischer* was yammering desperately. "She's just . . . she's really pretty. I didn't know she was married, honest."

He sounded miserable—and embarrassed. He was telling the truth. Caleb dropped his arm.

"No more photographs."

"No problem. I'm leaving." The man retreated a few steps, holding up his hands. "And trust me, I won't be back."

Caleb turned to find the crowd staring, their faces a mixture of disapproval, astonishment, fear, and—in a few cases—amusement.

Rhoda was staring, too, and he recognized her expression. Shocked disapproval. It was a look he'd seen on her face more than once.

As he made his way back to the counter, people scurried to step out of his way. As soon as he rounded the corner, he gave the twins a quick once-over. Hidden behind the counter, they'd missed most of what happened, and they didn't look upset. *Gut.* He scooped up Vonnie and took Eli's hand again.

"We'll be upstairs," he told Rhoda.

She gave him a narrow-eyed look. Then she turned back to her customers, many of whom were quietly abandoning the line and heading for the door.

"I'm so sorry," she called. "How about a free cookie for everybody? Your choice."

Caleb frowned as he took the twins through the kitchen toward the stairs. Free cookies. She was bribing the silly people to stay in line. Better, in Caleb's opinion, if they all left, at least until this movie was a thing of the past.

He left the door at the bottom of the steps ajar. Once he had the children safely in their playroom, he'd make sure the door at the top of steps was open as well so he could hear what went on downstairs. He planned to keep a close check on Rhoda throughout the day, whether she liked it or not.

Milt had always said he had good instincts. A natural, that's what he'd called Caleb. Right now, those instincts were prickling hard. Maybe the man today hadn't meant trouble, but that changed nothing.

Trouble was coming.

Chapter Seventeen

RHODA MARCHED UP THE STEPS AN HOUR AND A half later, a snack tray in her clenched hands. She found Eli and Vonnie playing happily in their little room. Caleb was sprawled on the kitchen floor, his head under the sink.

Rhoda ignored him as she served the children their snack of cheese, crackers, and milk. Once she had them settled, she stalked back to the kitchen area.

"I brought some food and coffee." She plunked the items down on the counter.

"Sorry." Caleb pushed out from under the sink and levered himself up to a sitting position. "I know you're busy. I was about to get the children something to eat myself, but I noticed a leak under here, and—"

"I was busy, *ja*. Until you decided to pick another argument with one of my customers. Since then, I've barely sold anything. This is a small town, Caleb, and news travels fast. You have to be careful what you say and do."

Caleb sighed and got to his feet. "You don't have to tell me that."

"It's clear you need reminding." To her horror, she felt tears threatening. "I'm counting on this business, Caleb. I need the money."

"I know, and I'm sorry that I scared off your customers. I won't apologize for calling that fellow out, though. He shouldn't have been taking your picture."

Rhoda made an exasperated noise. "People do that sometimes, Caleb. They mean nothing by it mostly. We're curiosities to them, that's all. If you're running a business, you just have to put up with some things."

"Like strange men taking photos of your wife? I don't think I'll be putting up with much of that." He glanced at her. "Although he was right. You are pretty."

Rhoda had other things she'd been planning to say. She'd made a mental list downstairs as she'd watched the promising line of customers thin into a dribble.

Suddenly she couldn't think of even one of them.

You are pretty. She shouldn't care what she looked like. Beauty wasn't important, and to care about your appearance was vanity and pride and . . . all sorts of other bad things. But somehow hearing Caleb say those words again ebbed her boiling anger down to a simmer.

During that brief period of their marriage when they'd been together, he'd said that often. He'd lean over at some awkward time, usually when she was working under the eye of an older aunt or cousin, and he'd whisper in her ear, *You're so pretty.*

Her eyes stung. That was the hard thing about happy memories. They could hurt you worse than anything else.

"Rhoda?" Caleb's expression shifted into concern.

She opened her mouth to fuss at him, to tell him that this

was no time to be talking silliness. But for the life of her, she couldn't get any words past the heavy lump in her throat. All she could manage was a miserable noise that sounded like a hurt kitten.

In two seconds, Caleb had her in his arms.

"Shh." The warmth of his breath against her ear sent her heart into a spin. "You've had a hard day, but it's all right now."

Rhoda closed her eyes, and for a moment—just a moment—she almost believed that it was. Here in Caleb's embrace, breathing in the smell of his shirt and his sweat and the fine wood dust that had always clung to him and tickled her nose whenever he'd been working . . . everything did feel right again. It was as if the world had twirled backward, all the sorrows of the past wiped clean, the way she'd wiped yesterday's specials off her chalkboard with a damp rag, preparing for the new morning.

"I know you're worried about money." She had her head against his chest, and his voice rumbled in her ear. "But please. Close the bakery until all this movie nonsense is over."

The warm sweetness dissolved, and she pulled away from him. "I can't!" She scrubbed at her eyes, wishing for a tissue. "I need the customers."

"Not if they cause trouble. And they will, Rhoda. The kind of people the movie will draw here aren't the sort you'll want much to do with."

"I'm not making friends with them. I'm selling them pastries and cookies, and their money spends as good as anybody else's."

"So does mine."

"Caleb—"

"I know what the church says, Rhoda. But I'm here, ain't so? I'm meeting with the bishop and doing everything you've asked of me. Seems like it wouldn't be such a stretch to let me pay some bills for you, quiet-like, so you wouldn't be in the middle of all this mess." Caleb sounded both impatient and hurt.

"I appreciate you wanting to help, Caleb. Truly, I do, but—"

"It's more than wanting, Rhoda. I'm your husband, and I'm the twins' father. It's my job, seeing to the bills and making sure you're not bothered. That you're safe."

Then make things right with the church. The simple answer, the answer she'd given him time and time again, hung unspoken in the air between them. She knew Caleb heard it just as plain as if she'd said it aloud, because his jaw tensed.

She waited for a span of three breaths before she spoke. "What did Abram say about the alarms?"

"That he'd decide and talk it over with us when he comes by. We're to meet him on Saturday." He lifted an eyebrow. "To tell you the truth, I was a little surprised he didn't shut down the idea right away. Your fa—" He broke off. "Most other bishops I've known would have. But Abram seemed willing to think it over." A thoughtful gleam came into Caleb's eye. "I suppose I could ask him about the money, too. Maybe he could find some way around this whole shunning thing."

Rhoda's heart felt like a sore tooth hit with a blast of cold air. The way Caleb was talking, the way he was thinking still . . . he was never planning to repent. "I doubt it. Abram can be soft on some things, but he never gives way when it's important. Just like my father," she couldn't resist adding.

"Your father was never soft about anything." Caleb considered her for a moment. "Maybe," he went on, "you should ask Isaac whether or not you should close up the bakery."

Rhoda looked at him with some surprise. "That's a first. You certain sure never saw the use of asking *Daed*'s opinion before."

"I don't particularly want his opinion now. But he cares

about you. That much I know. And you'll listen to him a lot quicker than you'll listen to me. You always have," he muttered bitterly.

She lifted her chin and looked him in the eye. "Not always."

That was all she said, but it was clear from Caleb's expression that he knew exactly what she meant.

She felt suddenly uncomfortable. "I should get back downstairs. There won't be many customers maybe, but that just means I'd best not miss the ones who do come by."

When she turned away, he spoke behind her. "Rhoda?"

She glanced over her shoulder, and the sadness in Caleb's eyes made her catch her breath. He'd looked just like that when he'd heard his parents had died. The anger and the terrible, burning bitterness, those had come soon after. But at the very first, there had only been sorrow, so much of it that she'd yearned to comfort him.

"*Vass?*" she asked softly.

"Do you wish now that you'd listened to your father? About me?"

She was startled by the question. The truth was, she'd had some thoughts like that, back at the first. At her lowest point, she'd nearly said as much to Joseph—that she wished she'd waited for him to speak instead of marrying Caleb.

Thankfully, she'd caught herself in time, and she'd slammed the lid quick on those regrets. No good could come of going down such a path.

Besides, *Gott* had brought good out of it, just as He promised to do. If she'd not married Caleb, there would be no twins, and she loved her two babies with all her heart. And there had been those happy days—at the first. Days when her heart had held so much joy that the whole world had shimmered with it.

If she'd listened to her father, she'd have missed a great deal of pain, but she'd also have missed that.

She opened her mouth to tell him so. But then her mind

skipped ahead to the bleak and lonely years ahead of her if Caleb stayed his course—as he seemed very likely to do. A wave of weary grief washed over her.

"I don't know," she whispered.

Turning away from the pain in his eyes, she hurried downstairs to the safety of her work.

Chapter Eighteen

SINCE THE CUSTOMERS HAD THINNED, RHODA'S work didn't prove very distracting. At least the ones who came in didn't have phones in their hands. Word about Caleb's outburst had spread fast.

Until recently she'd never been sensitive about *Englischers* and their picture taking. Her father had told her years ago to pay no attention to it. If it got too bad, she was simply to turn away or find work to do in the kitchen.

But now, as upset as she was about the loss of today's promising profit, she had to admit . . . men with phones in their hands made her a bit more uneasy than they used to. She hadn't noticed this fellow—she'd been too busy. But she'd been watching for such things ever since Caleb had thrown the last man out—the one she'd recognized from before.

Was he connected to the movie somehow? Or Trevor? She didn't much like the idea of that.

The bell over the door jingled, and an Amish woman came in, shepherding four children. Rhoda smiled a relieved welcome and pushed her troubles out of her head for the time being.

"What can I get for you?" she asked cheerfully.

Those customers relieved her of a good many cookies, and they were the first of a steady trickle of visitors who kept her busy over the course of the afternoon. Not many, but enough that she didn't have much time to fret.

Caleb came downstairs with the children just as she was locking the door for the evening.

"Did you have a good workday?" he asked cautiously.

"Not as good as I'd hoped, but not as bad as it could have been," she admitted. She knelt down and gave the twins a cuddle. "I've missed you. Not," she added politely, "that I don't appreciate your *daed* taking such good care of you today."

"I've enjoyed it." Caleb's face softened as he looked down at his son and daughter. "But I'm through with the apartment. It's ready for you to move in to." He cracked a rueful smile. "It was done yesterday, really, but I found some things to tinker with just to drag it out a bit. I like spending my days with these two." He hesitated before adding, "You're going to this supper they're having tomorrow night, then, for Miriam and her husband?"

"Of course. It'll be nice to see them both and welcome them home. I only just got here in time for the wedding, so I barely met Reuben. He seems like a real kind fellow, though, and he's done worlds of good for Miriam."

"That's what everybody says." Caleb sounded as if he were reserving judgment, and there was a flinty look in his eye. He'd always been protective of his sisters.

"You'll like him," she promised.

"We'll see."

Rhoda smiled. "*Ja*, I suppose we will, tomorrow night. The supper, though. You know . . ." She trailed off, hoping he'd guess what she meant.

"*Ja*, I'll not be allowed to eat with the rest of you." He

didn't look happy about it, but he didn't look too angry, either, which was a relief. "I'll manage. But there's something else . . . I have a favor to ask you."

Oh, no. She hoped he didn't want her to help him bypass some rule or other. Not at a big gathering like this was likely to be. "What?"

"Probably easier to show you. Just a minute."

To his surprise, he went through the kitchen and out the back door. The children looked up at her questioningly, and she shrugged.

"I don't know," she told them.

A minute later, he was back, carrying a wad of cloth in his hands. As he got closer, a shock of recognition thrummed through her body.

"Those are your old clothes."

"That's right." Caleb looked down at the bundle in his hands. "They still fit, except the pants are too loose around the waist. I wondered if you'd mind taking them in."

"You're planning to wear these?" Rhoda tightened her fingers around the damp rag in her hands, dribbling soapy water onto the counter. "Why?"

"Well"—he shot her an uncertain glance—"I know Miriam's doing better now. But *Englischers* used to frighten her, and I don't want her to see me and think . . . I just figured it might be best for me to wear these tomorrow night. If you don't mind fixing them, that is."

"I don't mind." She swallowed a bitter lump of disappointment. It was kind of him, she told herself, to be so careful of his sister's feelings. She'd just hoped for a minute that maybe he'd been considering . . . "You'll need to try on the trousers so I can see what wants doing. You can go upstairs and change while I start cleaning up and getting the dough ready for tomorrow."

"All right."

As he started toward the stairs, she called after him, "Best try on the shirt, too, just to be safe."

He nodded and disappeared, and she heard him clumping up the steps. He made short work of it. She'd barely finished wiping down the counter before he was back downstairs in his sock feet, wearing Plain clothes.

Her breath caught so hard in her throat that she choked. He looked . . . he looked like her Caleb again, and a torrent of memories flooded over her. That green shirt . . . it matched his eyes exactly. She'd picked the material out on purpose just for that reason, and she remembered now the thrill she'd felt when she'd found it. And how she'd laughed when she'd held the material against his cheek later, gloating at how well she'd remembered the color.

And how he'd laughed back and leaned forward and—

All the might-have-beens she'd tried not to think about swirled around her in a whirlpool of grief. She stood, paralyzed, unable to do anything but stare.

"See?" He stuck his finger in the waistband of the pants, pulling them sideways.

Rhoda blinked and cleared her throat. "You're right. They'll need to be altered." She hesitated a second before walking closer.

Darting an uneasy glance up at him, she tested the fabric herself, pinching it together to get the feel for how much would need to be taken in. It wouldn't be too hard. An inch on each side.

"You're a good bit leaner." Her eyes skimmed the shirt. "But only around your middle. That shirt's barely big enough for you across the shoulders now."

Before she thought better of it, she reached up with both hands to smooth the taut fabric covering his broad chest. His muscles tensed under her fingers, and startled, she looked up into his face.

That was a mistake.

He gazed down, his eyes searching and holding hers. For one second they stood there, frozen together.

Then he folded her into his arms, pulled her close, and kissed her.

And just like that, all the sorrows and the worries and the hurts that lay between them dissolved. Nothing existed but the warm strength of Caleb's arms and the sweetness of his mouth moving over hers.

A loud clattering jerked Rhoda back into the world. She pulled away, flustered.

"Wh-what?" she managed.

Caleb was already halfway to the steel counter where she'd been mixing up tomorrow's bread dough. While they'd been . . . distracted . . . Eli had pulled over the tin of flour she'd had open. A giant cloud of pale dust filled the air, and both children were powdered white.

"Oh, dear!" Rhoda hurried to Caleb's side. "Eli! What have you done?"

Her son blinked at her, a little pyramid of flour on the top of his head. His sister stood beside him, equally floured, her little arms outstretched and a look of horror on her face. Eli sneezed, and Vonnie began to whimper.

"Eli!" Rhoda said again, tsking her tongue gently. "Just look at this mess! What a waste!"

Caleb gave a strangled snort. She shot him a questioning look, and he stared back, working his mouth oddly.

Then he gave up and started to laugh, his eyes twinkling into hers. And in spite of all the strangeness surrounding that kiss, Rhoda found herself laughing, too.

Eli, delighted that he wasn't going to be in trouble, chuckled as well. The pile of flour on the top of his head cascaded over his nose, making Caleb laugh harder.

Vonnie was the only one who didn't find any of this funny. Her whimpers escalated into sobs.

Caleb leaned over, apparently intending to scoop up Vonnie and comfort her.

"Don't!" Rhoda choked out. "You'll be covered in flour,

and I can't wash those clothes, take up the pants, and have them ready before tomorrow. I'll handle the children. You go upstairs and change into your *Englisch* clothes."

Caleb looked disappointed, but he nodded. "She's just scared. It made a loud noise, didn't it, sweetheart? Bang! And now you're all floured like one of *Mamm*'s rolls." He tweaked her nose gently. "You're one of the sweet rolls, though."

His daughter gazed at him with teary eyes, her sobs subsiding into shuddering breaths. "Mess," she murmured sadly.

"*Ja*, it is, but *Mamm* and I will fix it all up, don't worry." He looked at Rhoda. "I'll hurry and change, and then I'll be back down to help."

"*Denki*," she said. He held her gaze again, and one side of his mouth tipped up.

"No problem." His eyes dipped to her lips, and she felt her cheeks going pink again.

"Mess!" Vonnie said more insistently, and Eli sneezed a second time.

"Come on outside," Rhoda said. "Let's see how much of this flour we can brush off, and then we'll get about cleaning up the kitchen."

She felt Caleb watching her as she led the twins to the back door. Not until she was closing the door behind them did he move toward the stairs.

She dusted the twins, best she could, telling herself she was grateful for this interruption, messy as it was. She felt dazed. What on earth had just happened? They'd been talking very sensibly about clothes, and all of a sudden . . .

That, Rhoda thought wryly, was the problem with Caleb. Things seemed to happen all of a sudden with him—and he'd always had a knack for sidestepping her *gut* sense.

There'd sure been nothing sensible about that kiss. She didn't know what Abram would think about this, and she certainly didn't plan to bring it up. She suspected that kissing her husband would appear on the church's list of things not to do when a person is shunned.

By the time Caleb came back down, she had the twins as clean as she could get them and settled at their table while she swept up the spilled flour.

She also had herself back under control. More or less.

"You can leave those clothes there," she told him, careful not to look in his direction. "I'll take them with me and get them fixed up tonight." She paused, then added hopefully, "If you have any others you'd like me to alter—"

He shook his head. "These are the only ones I kept."

Her heart sank, and she swept a bit more briskly. "Oh."

"They were the only ones you made for me. Just after we were married. Remember?"

A sunburst of sweetness went through her, and she pressed her lips together hard to keep from smiling. "I do remember," she said softly.

"I remember, too," Caleb said, a funny tone in his voice. She dared a glance at him. He was studying the twins, still a little powdery. He murmured, as if speaking to himself. "I remember everything about those days."

The sadness in his voice tugged at her conscience. She needed to tell him something.

"Caleb?"

He looked over at her. "*Ja?*"

"I'm not sorry."

His eyes dipped back to her lips, and he smiled. "I'm glad to hear it."

She flushed. "That's not what I meant. I'm not sorry I didn't listen to my father about you. Even though you—" She gripped the broom handle tightly and looked him straight in the eye. "Even after everything. I'm not sorry," she repeated.

Slowly, a smile broke over Caleb's face—a real smile that went all the way up into his eyes.

"I'm not sorry, either," he said.

Chapter Nineteen

THE NEXT AFTERNOON, CALEB LEANED AGAINST THE living room wall in Miriam and Reuben's new home, waiting for the couple's arrival with what appeared to be half the Johns Mill Amish community. Delicious smells wafted in the air, and joyful conversations buzzed all around him.

Family and friends were eagerly anticipating the return of the couple, who'd spent the last few weeks since their wedding visiting relatives. From what he'd overheard, folks were particularly excited to see Miriam, and her amazing recovery had been gratefully described more than once.

Maybe it wasn't so polite to be listening in on other people's conversations, but since nobody was talking to him, he didn't have a lot of choice.

Rhoda had done her best, but she hadn't had the clothes ready last night. So he'd driven over to Joseph's first thing this morning to put them on. Then Rhoda had pointed out that it might not do so much good to show up in Plain clothes driving a pickup truck. She'd suggested they all ride over together.

He'd glanced at Joseph, who'd shrugged.

"There's room," was all his brother had said.

He'd almost refused. "Room" in a buggy didn't mean it would be comfortable. With all the adults and three *kinder* crowded in, it would be tight. And tense, too, likely.

He'd opened his mouth to say that he'd drive himself and make sure to park his truck someplace out of sight of the house. Then Rhoda had done something that changed his mind.

She'd picked a tiny fluff of lint off his shirtsleeve.

It was such a wifely thing to do. Such a simple, ordinary thing. She hadn't even looked up into his face when she'd done it. She'd been distracted by the twins and making sure the lid on her bowl of chicken salad was snapped down good and tight. But when he'd felt that featherlight touch on his arm, his insides had turned to mush.

"Fine," he'd said. "I'll ride along with you all."

Rhoda had looked at him and smiled, and just like that, he started thinking about kissing her again.

Which was nothing new. He'd been thinking about little else ever since it happened. When he'd come over last night, Rhoda had sat in the corner of the living room, bent over her sewing, her lips pursed as she let out the seams in his shirt. She'd been too busy to talk to him, so he'd occupied himself playing with the children.

But he couldn't stop looking at her. He'd sneaked quick glances, noticing how the lamplight gave her a warm, rosy glow. How she moved the rocker just a bit with the toe of her shoe when she paused her sewing. How she glanced up and smiled, her face bright with gratitude when Naomi offered her a glass of iced tea.

Naomi had caught him looking that time. She'd said nothing, and her facial expression hadn't changed, but there'd been something in her eyes, a little flash of knowing that had made him shift so that Rhoda was no longer directly in his line of sight.

He'd kept thinking about her, though.

Right now, she was working with several other women setting the long tables that had been put throughout the house, dipping frequently back into the kitchen to keep an eye on the various dishes being kept warm. Rhoda had always had a bright, quick way about her, and she never slacked when there was work to be done.

Right now, though, he wished that she'd pause in all her scurrying and come talk to him. Stand beside him maybe, as if they were a real married couple still. As if she cared about him.

"They're here!"

The cry came from the yard. Caleb started toward the front porch with the surge of people ready to welcome the newlyweds home but then thought better of it. Best not to push himself forward. He didn't know Reuben yet, and he had no idea how his sister's new husband would react to meeting his shunned brother-in-law. He certain sure didn't want to put Miriam on the spot, not with everybody watching her.

But he was as eager to see the couple as everybody else, and he positioned himself so that he had a good view through the front window. *Ja*, there they were.

His eye lit on Miriam first. His younger sister was perched on the edge of the buggy seat, laughing and waving with her right hand. Her left was hooked through the elbow of a broad-shouldered man who handled the reins with a lazy ease that spoke of skill and long practice.

Her new husband was smiling, too, but his smile was only for the woman beside him. When he pulled the buggy to a stop, he leaned sideways and said something to her. Miriam looked at him with so much love shining in her face that Caleb's heart rose into his throat.

Ja, this was all right.

Maybe he didn't know this Reuben well yet—although

he would make it his business to know him. But he already knew the most important thing.

His sister was happy.

Emma made her way to the buggy. After Miriam was handed down by her new husband, Emma whispered something in her younger sister's ear. Miriam's head went up, and she looked sharply toward the house.

One quick question to her sister, who nodded. Then Miriam let go of Reuben's arm and sprinted toward the porch.

Suddenly Caleb didn't care what people thought, or who might tattle or fuss. He shouldered his way through the crowd and was waiting when Miriam threw open the front door.

She halted for just one split second before launching herself into his arms so hard that he staggered backward.

Caleb heard himself laughing. His sisters sure knew how to welcome a fellow home.

Miriam was murmuring something in his ear over and over again. "You're here, you're here."

"*Ja*, I'm here, Mirry," he whispered back.

She pulled back, searching his face, her own wet with happy tears. "Just for now? Or for good?"

"I—" he started, but she shook her head.

"Let's not talk about it. Not today. I don't want to know. For this minute I just want to be happy. And I am, Caleb. I'm so very happy!" She paused and sniffed the air. "I'm also very hungry! I hope supper's ready!"

"It nearly is." Rhoda came up and held out her arms to Miriam, who gave her a hearty hug. "It's wonderful *gut* to see you!"

Caleb watched the two women smiling and chatting with each other. He couldn't get over how well Miriam looked.

It was such a change from the last time he'd seen her, not long after the funerals. Then, she'd been pale and shaky, her eyes wild with fear, startling at the least noise. He still remembered how he'd felt walking out of Miriam's bedroom, how the anger blooming in his chest had closed into a tight, throbbing knot.

It had never quite loosened up again. Until just lately, a little.

Seeing his sister smiling and laughing here in her very own home, so happy with her new life . . . well. It didn't make up for the past, but it made it more bearable.

His gaze strayed to Rhoda, as it always did whenever she was in the room. She was smiling, too, although her face didn't light up with her smiles like it used to. But, he thought, as Rhoda laughed at something Miriam said, his wife did look better than she had that first day when he'd walked into the bakery. He studied her for a minute, trying to put his finger on it.

There was still a wariness in her eyes, particularly when they lit on him. But she didn't look as weary and resigned as she had at first. Today she looked almost . . . hopeful.

"Come on." Miriam looped her arm through his. "Let's go and find our seats. I'm starving."

"Oh, but what about Reuben?" Rhoda put in hurriedly. "Shouldn't we wait for him?"

Miriam waved off her husband with an affectionate smile. "He'll be fussing over Breeze. He was so happy to see that horse when we got back. We'd boarded him at Abram's, you know, and our driver let us off there so we could drive ourselves home. Reuben was so glad to get his hands on a pair of reins again, he won't be thinking about supper for a while yet. Caleb, you can sit next to me. We've lots of catching up to do."

"Oh!" Rhoda cast Caleb an agonized look.

Miriam had forgotten that Caleb couldn't eat at the table with her—or with any of them. Maybe if it was just the two of them or only the family, rules might have been fudged a bit. But that was out of the question here with all these folks about.

"We'll catch up, Mirry, but first I want to meet this husband you've picked out. I think I'll walk outside and look him over. You and I can have our talk after supper just as well."

Miriam looked disappointed, but before she could protest, Rhoda put an arm around her waist, tugging her toward the biggest table. "I want to hear all about your trip. Did you go to the quilt museum?"

It was a *gut* distraction. His sister was an avid quilter.

"We did! And Reuben was so kind, Rhoda. He didn't mind how long I stayed there. There was so much to look at . . ." Chattering happily, Miriam allowed herself to be led away.

Caleb sensed many pairs of eyes watching him. He glanced around, and people suddenly found their shoes very interesting. They were waiting to see what he'd do now, given that he couldn't eat with them.

No doubt somebody—probably Emma—would fix him a plate and find him someplace to eat by himself. The idea of that took away most of his appetite.

He'd do what he said. He'd go outside and get a look at this new brother-in-law of his.

As Miriam had predicted, Reuben had slipped off to the barn. When Caleb walked in, the other man was putting the horse in his stall. He closed the gate and leaned on it, studying the animal.

He didn't seem aware he wasn't alone, so Caleb was startled when he spoke.

"You'll be Mirry's brother." The man shifted so that he was half facing Caleb. "The other one."

"I am." Normally Caleb would have offered a handshake, but he wasn't sure how strict this new fellow might be about such things. From what he understood, Reuben was a freshly minted church member, and sometimes those were the nitpickiest people of all.

Next to deacons and bishops.

Reuben grunted and nodded. His blue eyes skimmed Caleb quickly, and Caleb had the sense of being measured.

"If your horse needs attention, I'll be happy to see to him," he volunteered. "They're serving supper in there now, so you might want to go on in."

"There's not so much to do, and I like to manage my horses myself. No offense," Reuben added casually. "You can go in and have your own supper. Tell Mirry I'll be along shortly."

Caleb shrugged. "If you don't mind, I think I'll stay here for a bit."

"That's right." Reuben considered Caleb thoughtfully. "You're shunned. You can't eat at table with the rest of them. I'm surprised Mirry didn't get upset about that. She was real excited when she heard you were back in town, but she wasn't sure you'd be here tonight. When Emma told her you were inside, she lit out across the yard like a filly let out to spring pasture. I don't think she thought much about the shunning part of it beforehand. It wonders me that she didn't make some sort of fuss." He chuckled. "Folks think she's not the fussing type, but Mirry's got more spirit than most people realize."

"She might would have, once she realized. She asked me to sit next to her, but Rhoda distracted her. I slipped away out here before it turned into a problem."

"Believe in keeping the rules, do you?" The other man shot him a skeptical glance. "That's not what I'd heard of you."

Caleb spluttered a laugh. "Joseph's the rule-keeping Hochstedler. Not me. But there are a lot of folks in there. Most are nice enough, but there are a few fussbudgets. I didn't want anybody making trouble for Mirry, so I left."

"That so?" Reuben's expression didn't change, but Caleb sensed he'd passed some sort of test. "I owe you my thanks, then, for not getting my new *fraw* into trouble her first night home."

"No thanks owed to me. But I do owe my thanks to you. I've been told you're the reason my sister's in there laughing and surrounded by her friends instead of hiding in her bedroom back home."

Reuben didn't exactly smile, but the line of his jaw relaxed, and the corners of his eyes crinkled. "I'm only one reason. Like I said, Mirry's got plenty of spirit. She did most of the work on her own, with *Gott*'s help."

"Still. I'm in your debt."

"There's no debt between family." A shadow crossed his face, and he added, "Not between strong families anyhow. Folks warned me about you. Said you had a stubborn streak a mile wide, but that didn't scare me. I've come up against stubborn before. Now that I've met you, I believe you and I are likely to get along real well." Reuben moved toward him, one hand outstretched. "I'm glad to meet you, *bruder.*"

Caleb smiled. It was true what everyone had told him. This Reuben was a *gut* man. Mirry had chosen well. "Good to meet you, too."

"I have to say, I don't much like this. The shunning rules, I mean. Especially not here, in my house. Brings up bad memories."

"Why's that? You weren't shunned, they say."

"Only because I'd never joined the church in the first place. And I know it's not meant to be a punishment exactly. Abram explained it all to me while I was living with his family and getting ready to join the church. It's more a way to help somebody understand what they're losing, he says."

The knot in Caleb's chest clenched tighter. He'd thought he understood what he was losing when he left.

He'd had no idea.

It wasn't just the time he'd missed with the twins—memories of them as babies that he'd never have, although that sorrow cut at him. There were a thousand other things, things he'd taken for granted without realizing it. Seeing love and trust in his wife's eyes instead of worry and suspicion. The feeling of belonging, of knowing the people around him, how they thought and how they would act in any situation, even though he might disagree with them. It was the sense of rightness, of being in the world he understood. A world he'd been born to.

Reuben seemed to be waiting for his answer, so Caleb cleared his throat. "Maybe so."

"But I think it would feel like a punishment, especially if you had a certain type of man in charge. Abram's all right, but all of them aren't. Besides, no matter how you slice it, it's also a handy way to scare folks into behaving themselves," Reuben went on. "Me, I don't much like the idea of scaring people into anything. So, you back to stay?"

Caleb lifted an eyebrow at the abrupt question. Everybody back in the house over the age of ten had been wondering the exact same thing, but nobody except Mirry had had nerve enough to ask.

His new brother-in-law returned his gaze without so much as a blink. Apparently this fellow had plenty of nerve to spare.

"I don't know." That was the truth.

"You don't know," Reuben repeated. He shifted to face Caleb fully and leaned back against the wooden stall partition.

He didn't look particularly concerned by Caleb's answer. He seemed relaxed and curious, and somehow that made Caleb relax, too.

"Why'd you come back, then?" Reuben asked. "Before you'd made up your own mind what you wanted to do, I mean. Somebody tell you about the babies?"

"No. I didn't find out about them until I got here."

Reuben whistled. "That must have been a kick in the belly, finding out you were a father, unexpected-like."

A kick in the belly. Ja, that described it, all right. "It was."

"Seems strange to me, then, that you'd be coming back

here at all. I've heard you're the sort of fellow when he sets his mind to something, he don't turn loose of it so easy. They say Trevor Abbott is still hiding out somewhere, dodging the police. What made you give up on tracking him?"

His new brother-in-law obviously didn't believe in dodging tough questions. Caleb thought fast. The two days of grace Sam had given him were up already. Sam hadn't told Emma why Caleb had come back, but likely he would very soon.

"I've not given it up. Not yet. I heard rumors that Trevor was heading to Johns Mill, so I followed, but—"

A sharp intake of breath behind him had Caleb turning around. Rhoda stood in the doorway, a laden tray of food in her hands.

Her eyes were wide. She'd heard—and likely now she was scared to death. Caleb mentally kicked himself for talking so plainly.

"Rhoda—" he started, but she turned away and hurried out of the barn, the tray rattling loudly.

"Best you go after her," Reuben suggested. "I've not been married too long, but I've already learned that it's smarter to talk things over early when there's been some sort of a stumble."

"You could have told me she was standing there," Caleb muttered.

"She only came in at the last, but *ja*, I could have done. But of course, I had no way to know that you were keeping secrets from your *fraw*." He tilted his head. "You don't strike me as a *schtupid* man, but that seems a foolish thing to do. From what I've heard, there've been too many secrets between the two of you already."

Caleb felt a muscle twitching in his jaw as he battled with his temper. Maybe he wasn't going to like this Reuben as much as he'd thought. "I didn't want to scare her."

Reuben shrugged. "Like I said before, you'd have to go a long way to find a man who hates seeing folks scared more than I do, *bruder*. But like all things *Gott*'s made, fear's got its rightful place in the world. Some things we would do better to be a bit scared of. I have a feeling the man who has brought you back here might be one of those things. I've got Mirry, so don't worry yourself over her. And if you need help looking after your own, you let me know." He winked. "Now, get on with you. Like I said, when it comes to women, a smart man mends his fences quick."

Chapter Twenty

RHODA HURRIED ACROSS THE YARD, THE PLATES chittering on the tray in her hands. She needed a quiet place to sort out her nerves and think.

She settled on the washhouse. Nobody would be inside there today. Anchoring the tray against her stomach with one hand, she opened the door and slipped inside.

She set the tray on a little table and covered her eyes with her hands, pressing back the threatening tears. She hadn't meant to eavesdrop. She'd wanted to bring Caleb something to eat. He deserved it. He'd sidestepped the problem of not being able to sit next to his sister at table so neatly that Miriam hadn't even noticed.

Rhoda knew it bothered him to be excluded by his family and friends, so it had warmed her heart, seeing how he took care that his sister's homecoming not be upset by some kerfuffle over shunning rules.

She'd fixed his plate while the others settled down to their supper. A few women were up and serving the food, and although they'd said nothing, she'd felt their eyes on her as she'd worked. Ann King was in charge of pouring the tea and came back into the kitchen to refill her pitcher just as Rhoda was putting the finishing touches on the tray.

The bishop's wife had patted her shoulder and spoken clearly enough for every woman in the kitchen to hear. "You're a real *schmaert* girl to fix your *mann* some supper. Kindness will bring him back quicker than any rule ever could. Go on and take that to him, and don't worry. I'll keep an eye on the *kinder*."

Ann's words had given Rhoda the strength to straighten up and stop dodging the other women's glances. Right under their noses, she'd snagged Caleb an extra dinner roll and put a nice big pat of butter on the side of his plate, just as he liked.

She'd smiled. Many dinners like this, she'd thought, and she'd likely be letting those pants right back out again.

She'd held her head high as she'd walked across the yard, thinking that she wasn't too sorry that the children were happily eating inside under Ann's watchful eye. It wouldn't be so bad, she thought, to have a few quiet moments together, just her and Caleb.

Then she'd walked into the barn and heard—

"Rhoda?" Caleb eased open the wash shed door, his expression guarded. "Can I come in?"

"There's—there's not much room," Rhoda stuttered. There wasn't. It was a small shed, and the wringer washer and a table took up most of the space.

"We need to talk." Caleb slipped inside, closing the door behind him.

Rhoda wished he hadn't found her so quick. She wasn't ready to have this talk, not yet. But there was nothing for it. She could tell by the expression on her husband's face that he wasn't going away.

She tinkered with the cutlery on the plate. "Is it true?"

"*Ja*," he said gently. "It's true—or at least I think it is."

She looked up at him. "You think? Don't you know?"

"Well, no. Not for certain sure." He seemed puzzled by the question. "I mean, nobody's seen Trevor around here yet, and I've found no sign of him. But my old boss Milt's heard some rumors that he's here—or close by, and I trust his judgment."

"But that's why you came?" She looked back down at the tray and moved the butter knife a little to one side.

"I don't want you to worry." He reached for her arm. She stiffened at his touch, and his voice gentled. "Don't be frightened. He won't get anywhere close to you or the little ones. I'll see to that. If Abram won't agree to the alarms, I'll find another way. I'll sleep in my truck outside, if that's what it takes. If Trevor tries anything, I'll be waiting."

Rhoda drew in a deep, hard breath and raised her eyes to his. "You didn't answer my question. Is that the reason you came home? Because you were chasing Trevor Abbott and you thought this was where he was?"

He didn't seem to know how to answer—and that was answer enough.

"Don't be—" he started.

"Scared? I'm not." Rhoda spoke sharply. "I'm not scared of Trevor Abbott. He's a sad, sick boy who did a terrible thing. I pity him."

"You *pity* him." Caleb's voice was incredulous.

"Of course I do! And so should you. He's only young, but he's already ruined his life, and he has two murders on his conscience. I've prayed for him many times, that he'll repent and seek the Lord's forgiveness. If anybody should be afraid, it's him, not me. Someday he'll have to answer to *Gott* for what he did."

Caleb's face was tight and set. "*Gott* doesn't seem to be in any hurry to call him to account."

"Maybe that's because you were too ready and willing to take on that job yourself. Vengeance is His business, not ours. Our business is to—"

"Forgive. *Ja*, I know. Don't preach at me, Rhoda." He

dropped her arm and took a step back. "Trust me, I've heard it all before."

"Maybe you heard," she muttered. "But you never listened. I thought—" She stumbled at the admission but forced herself to keep going. She'd been foolish, and she'd best own up to it. "I thought you came back because maybe you still . . . cared for me a little."

"I did. I do. And more than a little."

Pained sincerity thrummed in his voice. She wanted to believe him. She really did. But she knew what she'd heard. "That's not what you told Reuben just now, when he asked."

"I didn't tell him the whole of it. I've not told anybody the whole of it."

"Tell it now."

Something guarded came into his eyes. "I don't want to scare you."

"I've told you, I'm not scared! I'm hurt. I've been hurt ever since you walked away and left me here. All alone! As if"—she sucked in a broken breath—"as if I didn't matter to you at all!"

"You've always mattered." Now his voice was edged with desperation. He leaned down so he was looking directly into her face. "You want to know why I hightailed it up here? Because in the last little nest Trevor had made for himself, I found photographs of you. Of you, Rhoda, working in the bakery. My wife. Pinned up all over a closet wall. And maybe that doesn't scare you, but I can tell you it sure scared me."

She stared at him, wide-eyed, trying to absorb what he was saying. "The pictures were from the bakery. That's why you came there first. You were looking for Trevor." She whispered the words. "That's why you kicked in the office door that day, and it's why you got so upset about people taking pictures." She was fitting the pieces together one by one, and she wasn't liking the story that was taking shape.

"Someone took those pictures of you I found. If I could

find out for sure who put them up to it, who was sending them to Trevor . . ."

"Why didn't you just tell me that? Or Abram?" Suddenly, understanding dawned. "You figured you might not be allowed to hang around if folks knew you were still all caught up with chasing after Trevor Abbot. It was . . . easier . . . if we all believed there was a chance you wanted to make your repentance. A chance that you still cared . . . I see," she whispered.

And she did. Oh, she'd been such a fool. Again.

"Excuse me." She attempted to edge past him toward the door, but he didn't budge.

"We need to finish talking about this."

"I am finished talking." She stepped outside.

Caleb, however, was right behind her.

"Rhoda—"

"Ah! There you two are!"

Rhoda froze. Abram was carefully descending the back steps of the farmhouse. Once safely on the ground, he walked toward them, his face wreathed in smiles.

She glanced back at Caleb. His expression was as uneasy as her own. Neither of them wanted to have a conversation with the bishop just now, but it didn't look as if there was any way out of it.

"Such a happy day!" Abram was perspiring in the heat, his rosy face looking as if it had been buttered. "Reuben and I have spent so much time together that he feels like one of my own sons. That makes this celebration even sweeter. What a blessing that this young couple will be settling down here among their family and friends."

He looked at them cheerfully, obviously expecting hearty agreement. Caleb apparently wasn't going to say anything, so Rhoda cleared her throat.

"*Ja*, we are very thankful to have Miriam and Reuben close by."

"Such a blessing," Abram repeated. His eyes went from her face to Caleb's and back, and his expression became more thoughtful. "But as it happens, that is not why I was looking for you. I need to attend an auction tomorrow, so I won't be able to meet as we'd planned, Caleb. But I have thought over your request for the bells and such. I do not think such things are necessary."

"You're wrong," Caleb told him flatly.

Rhoda sucked in a horrified gasp. "Caleb!" Contradicting a bishop . . . that wasn't something a person did.

But Abram only shrugged. "Maybe," he admitted.

"There's no maybe." Caleb brushed past Rhoda and faced off with the chubby man. "I have reason to think Trevor is hanging around here, that he's planning something. Something big, likely connected with the movie coming out soon."

Abram's brow wrinkled as he considered this revelation. "And you think this is going to be something bad? Something that could pose a danger to Rhoda and your children?"

"Of course I do."

The bishop pursed his lips and brushed some crumbs from his beard. "But you are only guessing. It might be bad. But something big can also mean something good, *ja?* It depends on how you look at it."

Rhoda cast an apprehensive glance at Caleb. He was staring the bishop down, and a muscle was jumping in his cheek. He wasn't happy, and her stomach clenched as she waited for the explosion.

Two seconds ticked by before he spoke. When he did, his voice was fierce but controlled. "Going by Trevor's past history where my family's concerned, I'm sure you can understand why I don't want to take any chances."

"*Ja*. That I understand. You want Rhoda and the *kinder* to be safe, and you fear that if they are alone, this Trevor may take advantage of that situation and try to harm them. In this, my friend, we must trust *Gott*. But—" he said, holding up one hand as Caleb started to interrupt. "I agree that taking some sensible precautions is a *gut* idea. The apartment is ready to live in now, ain't so?"

Rhoda and Caleb exchanged glances. Caleb nodded.

"It is."

"I have recently had a letter from Rhoda's father. He also is concerned." Abram cleared his throat. "About various things. He thinks it would be best for Rhoda to continue living with Joseph until he and her mother move here. He has asked me to tell you this and help you find someone to rent the apartment."

What? Her father had made such plans with the bishop without talking with her first, just as if she were some young *maidel* and not a married woman with children of her own? Rhoda's heart sank, and frustrated tears welled up in her eyes.

Well, now she was in a pickle. She didn't want to keep living at Joseph's, but if Abram fell in line with her father's plan, there'd be no way around it. It was just like *Daed* to do something like this, she thought irritably. He must have figured this was the quickest route to getting his way—simply have the bishop lay down the law and make the arrangements.

Caleb seemed to be undergoing some sort of inner battle, but finally, he nodded.

"That might be the best idea."

"Maybe. But me?" Abram was saying now. "I don't think so."

Rhoda glanced up at him, hope budding in her heart. "You don't?"

He smiled at her benevolently. "No, I don't. It is a good thing to have family close by, and it was kind and right for Joseph and Naomi to invite you to stay in their home while the apartment was being prepared. And I'm sure," he went on carefully, "that you all have enjoyed your time together. But families get stretched thin when guests stay too long, even much beloved guests. So I think it best that you and the children move into the apartment as you'd planned."

"Oh, I do, too! And I'm not the least bit worried about Trevor, honestly!" The words poured out of her in a rush of relief.

"You should be," Caleb argued. "Look," he said, turning back to Abram. "I know in your eyes I don't have any say-so here, but Rhoda's my wife, and the twins are my children, and I want them safe. Either tell her to stay with Joseph or let me install those alarms."

Rhoda held her breath, but Abram didn't seem perturbed by the heat in Caleb's voice.

"As it happens, given these unusual circumstances, there is a third way to solve this problem, and that's the idea I think best."

Caleb made an impatient noise. "Let's hear it, then."

"The best way for a man to protect his *fraw* and *kinder* is with his own presence and attention."

There was a confused silence, broken only by the singing of a frog hidden someplace in the damp wash shed. Evening was coming on, Rhoda realized vaguely. It would be time to go home soon.

"What do you mean?" Caleb was asking.

Abram smiled. "You will move into the apartment with them."

Chapter Twenty-One

RHODA AND CALEB STARED AT THE BISHOP, WHO looked back at them benignly. The frog had gone silent, as if he couldn't believe his ears, either.

"What?" Caleb managed finally.

"It's allowed," Abram said calmly, "for married couples to live together even when one is shunned. There would have to be certain amendments, of course." He coughed delicately. "Separate rooms," he explained. He looked at Caleb. "Since you are so worried about your family's well-being, it stands to reason that you'd rather be on hand yourself to see to them. So I'm guessing you'll have no objection to this plan?"

Rhoda was pretending to keep her gaze fixed on Abram, but she was watching Caleb out of the corner of her eye. He looked about like she felt . . . *ferhoodled.*

She did her best to school her features. Unlike Caleb, she couldn't argue with a bishop, no matter what crazy idea he might suggest. For the first time ever, though, she wished her husband would.

But for once, he didn't.

"I've no objection if Rhoda hasn't." She noticed he carefully didn't look in her direction.

"I—" Rhoda started, but Abram held up a hand.

"I will talk to Rhoda herself," he said. "Now, alone. Afterwards you two can work out the details."

Caleb nodded, still looking dazed. "All right."

"Wait," the bishop protested as Caleb started to walk away. Abram pointed at the table. "Don't forget your supper."

Caleb looked down at the tray Rhoda had fixed for him. His expression shifted as he took in the generous portions, the extra roll and the melting pat of butter, but he said nothing. He leaned close to Rhoda and picked up the tray. As he did, their eyes met, and a shiver ran down her spine.

Once Caleb was safely outside, she clasped her hands in front of her apron, dropped her eyes, and waited to hear what Abram would say. Her nerves were standing on end. Was he serious? She was expected to live with Caleb?

They'd been married only a couple of months before he'd left. He'd been gone far longer than that. She'd been slowly warming up to him, getting used to having him nearby again. She'd even started to hope that . . .

"Rhoda?"

Abram was looking at her. She blinked. "I'm sorry. What?"

"I can see my idea has taken you by surprise. That's why I asked Caleb to give us a moment to ourselves. I wanted you to have a chance to think this over and tell me if you have any concerns."

"Concerns?" She wasn't sure how she was supposed to answer that. Of course she had concerns. Plenty of them. But surely Abram already knew that.

"*Ja*. Before, when Caleb had first arrived, we spoke, you remember, in your wonderful bakery. I asked you then if you were afraid of your *mann*. If you feared his temper or felt that he would hurt you or your children. You told me you did not fear him." Abram paused. "Was this the truth?"

"It is the truth." She swallowed. "At least, it's true in a way."

Abram's gentle expression changed like lightning, and he frowned. "In a way?"

She clenched her fingers more tightly. "I don't believe Caleb would hurt us, not how I think you mean. It's true he has a temper, and he's been known to . . ." She hesitated, torn between telling the truth and the disloyalty of detailing her husband's shortcomings to a bishop. "He's been known to be less than forgiving sometimes when people provoke him."

There. That was about the nicest way she could put it.

Abram's face relaxed. "*Ja*. This I have heard."

"But he's never raised a hand in anger to me, nor to his sisters, nor to any child. I don't believe he ever would. But," she went on, her voice shaking, "there are other ways to hurt people."

The older man nodded. "You mean like leaving them behind. Which he's done already, putting you in a very difficult place."

She nodded miserably. "He only came back to Johns Mill looking for Trevor. He says he's worried about me and the children, and I believe he is. But it wasn't us that brought him home. It was Trevor."

"And this—the fact that he did not come back because of your marriage and your feelings for each other—this is a painful thing."

The sympathy in Abram's voice made shamed tears well up in Rhoda's eyes.

"It is," she whispered, annoyed at herself for crying. Goodness, she should be used to this by now. Hadn't she dealt with this embarrassment over and over again?

Mostly people blamed Caleb's own hotheadedness for

his leaving, and they'd shown her great kindness and compassion. But she'd sensed in others some suspicion that maybe she also was to blame somehow. Clearly, they wondered why a freshly married young man would be so quick to leave his wife behind.

"No matter what his reasons were," Abram went on, "he came back. And he found out about the twins, and I am glad he did. A man, even one who has left our church, has a right to know about his children. It wonders me why you didn't find some way to contact him. If you had, likely it would have brought him back to us that much sooner."

Caleb had said much the same thing. Rhoda felt her cheeks flushing, and she lowered her eyes and stayed silent.

Abram wouldn't let her off the hook so easily. "Didn't you want to tell him?" he asked.

She swallowed, but she had to tell the truth. "My father didn't think it a good idea."

There was a short, shocked silence.

"Isaac wanted Caleb kept in the dark? About his own children?" Now Abram was the one who didn't seem to know what to say. He furrowed his brow, thinking. When he raised his head again, he still looked troubled. "I've already disagreed with him about you and the apartment. It worries me that I must disagree with him again, about this. I have always respected your father and his judgment very much."

From the tone in Abram's voice, that respect had been sorely shaken. Rhoda opened her mouth to defend her *daed*, but the words died on her lips.

Because, she realized with some guilt, her respect had been shaken, too.

She'd felt the same back then—that *Daed* was wrong not to send word about the twins. She'd wanted Caleb with her so much, more than anything.

She should have insisted. But with Caleb gone, her parents were her only supports, and she'd needed them—badly.

Besides, she'd been taught all her life to trust her father's wisdom over her own. She'd only ever asserted her own will once—to marry Caleb. And afterward, her father had used every one of Caleb's stumbles to hint that she'd have done better to listen to him in that, too.

When Caleb had left her, he'd settled that question once and for all in Isaac's mind. After that, Rhoda had felt foolish for loving her husband yet, foolish for the desperate hopes still hidden in her heart.

Hearing Abram—a bishop himself, chosen by *Gott*—question her father's decision felt at once both dangerous and hopeful. As if a wall she'd been sheltering behind had crumbled, giving her not a glimpse of something scary but of something temptingly beautiful.

But even so, she owed her father some loyalty. He'd looked after her during a very dark and frightening time, when her husband was nowhere to be found.

"My father feared that Caleb would never come back to stay. While *Daed* was bishop here, he'd bumped against my husband's stubbornness many times and had come to believe that his heart wasn't fully committed to the church. And I was . . . very upset. Before the children came, it was . . . an emotional time." That didn't begin to explain what it had been like to go through her pregnancy alone, but it was the best she could do when talking to a man. "I think *Daed* feared if Caleb came back then, I might be persuaded to leave with him, and both I and the children would be lost."

"I see." Abram still didn't look convinced, but he nodded. "Well, in any case," he went on with some relief, "that decision was taken out of our hands. Caleb does know. And perhaps we should look for the hand of *Gott* in that." The bishop's tone grew at once gentler and firmer. "Our Lord doesn't much care for such secrets, I think. When we won't give them up, He has a way of uncovering them."

Rhoda thought about what she'd just overheard, happening into the barn at just the right—or perhaps just the wrong—moment. The bishop had a good point.

Abram drew in a deep breath. "I share your concerns, though, and those of your father. It is true that Caleb may not stay among us. It seems he has not been completely honest with either of us about his reason for coming, and that isn't a good sign."

"And if he leaves again, this time he won't just hurt me," Rhoda whispered. "The children are getting attached to him."

"The little ones may suffer," Abram agreed quietly, "but we can't shut all the pain out of our children's lives, no matter how much we want to. Likely it would not be wise to do so even if we could. *Gott* certainly doesn't shut all pain out of His children's lives, now does he?"

"No, He doesn't." She could personally vouch for that.

"With that in mind, I am going to ask you to try this living arrangement. For two reasons. Would you like to hear them?"

She nodded, although she couldn't imagine any reason that would make her feel this was a good idea.

"First of all, because Caleb tells me he wants to be near you and the children to protect you. This is a *gut* thing, to want to protect those we care about." When she opened her lips, he held up a hand, "I know. I know. He doesn't always show this in the wisest way. But . . ." He leaned forward earnestly. "The good intention is there, buried underneath his stubbornness and his quick temper. And it's something that can be built on."

Rhoda thought that over. Abram was right, she decided. It was what she herself had always felt about Caleb, what she'd tried unsuccessfully to explain to her father. Deep down within Caleb, there was a goodness that they didn't see. The things he did sometimes seemed bad, but they were never meant that way.

Of course, as she'd learned, that didn't make them hurt any less.

"You said there were two reasons. What is the other one?"

"The church is asking Caleb to forgive a man who has hurt his family beyond all reckoning. This is a tall order for anyone, but for a fellow like your *mann,* who's butted heads against the church's rules all his life and who feels such hatred for evil and injustice. Well, it is much harder for such a man to leave punishments in the hands of *Gott.* For him to do so will take a surrendering of the will that most of us cannot even imagine. And we aren't helping him. *Nee,*" the bishop sighed sadly. "Instead we are hindering him, I think."

Rhoda frowned. "What do you mean?"

"What is the best way to teach a child to behave as he should? Not by rules nor hard words. The best thing is to show him a good example, *ja?* And to love him as he learns to follow it. When Caleb comes home after making some decisions we feel are wrong, do we forgive him? Do we leave justice solely in the hands of *Gott*?" The bishop shook his head. "I think maybe we do not."

Rhoda blinked, confused. "But he's shunned. We're supposed to follow the rules about that, surely?"

"We are, *ja.* That's why shunning is such a dangerous thing. A very dangerous thing that should be used only as a last resort."

He spoke gently, but Rhoda could read between the lines. Abram didn't just question her father's choice not to tell Caleb about the twins. Abram didn't agree with the church's decision to shun Caleb in the first place.

Proof, maybe, that what her father had worried about was true: Abram's soft heart would cause him problems as a bishop. Of course, since Abram had a stepson who was also shunned, she supposed it was natural that he would feel so.

Abram went on, "But you are right, of course. What's done is done, and the church's guidelines on this are clear.

Caleb must repent of his actions and must demonstrate a changed heart to rejoin us. And do you know what changes hearts?" He smiled at her. "Love. In this case, it could be a man's love for a wife and children."

Rhoda swallowed hard. Arguing with a church leader went against everything she'd been taught. If you happened to disagree with something they said or did, you kept your thoughts strictly to yourself.

But in this case, given what was at stake, she had to speak. "Love didn't change his heart before," she said. "Not where the church was concerned, anyway. My father said that Caleb only joined the church so that I would marry him. He said that was why it didn't last, because a marriage wasn't enough to hold a man with such a rebellious temperament."

"Maybe not, but it started him on the path, and now his concern for you has drawn him back. Perhaps instead of being upset, we should look on the bright side. There are many roads to the places *Gott* means for us to go," Abram observed softly. "Some roads have more twists and turns than others, but if we don't lose faith, we will get where we are meant to be in the end."

Rhoda considered. Possibly Abram was right. Maybe she was looking at this in the wrong way.

With her heart in her throat, she asked the question she'd been wanting to ask for more than two years. "Where do you think Caleb is supposed to be, really? I . . . care for him very much, but he is so stubborn, and he disagrees with so many things the church teaches. Can such a man ever truly belong here with us?"

Abram gave her a fatherly pat on the shoulder. "That is what we are going to find out."

Chapter Twenty-Two

THE FOLLOWING SATURDAY AFTERNOON, CALEB WALKED out of the bakery and headed toward his truck. It was the first time he'd been alone for hours.

Today was the day the family had decided to get Rhoda's belongings moved into the apartment. Everyone had converged at the farmhouse well before dawn, sleeves rolled up and ready to work. The women had packed up the lighter boxes, those with clothing, bedding, and kitchen items, stowing them in the smaller buggies. Then they'd clopped off toward town. They'd spent their morning scrubbing out the apartment and getting it ready for the bigger items the men were bringing along.

He, Joseph, Reuben, and Sam had worked together to load up two wagons with the heavier things. It hadn't taken long. Rhoda hadn't brought much with her, so most of this furniture was either given to her or loaned.

The other men had talked as they worked, catching up on various odds and ends as they heaved bedroom and kitchen furniture into the wagon. Caleb had listened as he stacked empty drawers and chairs, fitting them carefully in place so they wouldn't rattle around on the drive.

It brought back memories, working alongside other men like this, everyone knowing what to do and doing it without complaint. He'd worked plenty out in the *Englisch* world, of course, but it was different there. The men on the construction crews where he'd temped had been a lot less efficient. They'd no shared understanding of how to go about such work, and Caleb had often grown frustrated when they made the simplest jobs take twice as long as they should.

But the work today went just as it was supposed to, and he'd labored with a sense of quiet satisfaction. Until Joseph had pulled him to the side.

"I need to speak to you," his brother had said. Caleb had tensed, expecting a reminder of some shunning rule. He'd tried to be careful, not handing things to the other men and only picking up what he could carry alone. But no doubt he'd missed something.

Then Joseph had surprised him.

"Stick close to Sam. He's determined to do his share, and mostly he manages real well. He misses things sometimes, though, like sharp edges and such, and a day like today will be hard for him, what with everything jumbled out of place."

"All right."

"But don't let him know you're watching out for him."

"Don't worry." That was the whole of the conversation, but as he'd walked back inside to pick up a nightstand, Caleb's heart had felt lighter.

It wasn't the first time Joseph had asked him to keep an eye out for someone else. *Mind Daed, Caleb, and be quick to lift those gates out of the way before he gets to them. He's not so young as he thinks he is.*

It was silly, really, how good it felt to have his brother asking for his help again. As he'd jumped into the wagon to rumble into town with his brother, with his brothers-in-law following behind in a second wagon, heading back to Rhoda and Vonnie and Eli, the whole world somehow felt . . . right.

For the first time in a long, long time, *he* felt right.

Sitting there on the rough wooden seat, smelling horse and hot canvas and sweat, he'd pushed everything out of his head and pretended that this was an ordinary summer day. That he was just a run-of-the-mill Amish man, working with his family, moving into a new home with his wife and his children.

The rest of the morning had gone by fast. They'd driven the furniture into town on two wagons, unloaded it, and wrestled it up the stairs while the women got lunch ready and kept the little ones out of the way. Then they'd eaten sandwiches and macaroni salad, with cookies from the bakery for dessert.

There hadn't been near enough places at the table, of course, and Caleb had been secretly grateful for that. It had seemed natural for him to sit on the floor with the twins to eat. Rhoda sat with Joseph and Emma at the kitchen table, little Elizabeth perched in the fourth chair.

He was glad to help Eli and Vonnie manage their food. He liked spending the time with them, and besides, Rhoda had been minding them all morning while trying to get the apartment cleaned up. They were overexcited by all the commotion, so he was sure her job hadn't been an easy one.

Fortunately, they were good and hungry, so they settled down to eat without much trouble. Reuben and Miriam had sat on the floor, too, leaning their backs up against the opposite wall and balancing their plates on their knees.

Caleb couldn't help watching them, marveling over the difference in his sister. He'd been thankful just to hear she'd overcome her fears enough to leave the farm. The fact that she'd also married had stunned him, but now he saw how closely the two changes were intertwined.

It was Miriam's love for Reuben—and his for her—that had brought her out of the darkness. She was happier than he'd ever seen her. She smiled and laughed easily with her husband, and Caleb didn't miss the sweet glances she sent toward the *kinder*. No doubt Miriam hoped he'd be an *onkel* again soon.

That idea brought a smile to his own face—and a little twist of envy. It must be nice to have the future stretched out in front of you, so joyful and uncomplicated.

Once lunch was over, everyone began packing up to leave. They had their own Saturday chores to see to, and the day was getting by. He'd walked out to retrieve his duffel bag of clothing from his truck, planning to stow it in the bedroom he'd been allotted.

"Caleb?"

Miriam hurried toward him. She beckoned him over to Reuben's buggy.

"I brought you something." His younger sister shot him a playful look. "Don't be mad."

"Why would I be mad?"

"You'll see." She pulled a package from the box strapped to the back of the buggy. "Here."

The bundle held several shirts and pants. All Plain. He riffled through them and glanced over at his sister with a raised eyebrow. "You got me new clothes?"

"Not new. Some are your old ones, the ones you left behind. Others I begged from Joseph and Reuben. I let them out and fixed them up so they'll fit you. Or close enough." She laughed. "I didn't ask Sam for any, although he'd have been just as happy to share. But his shirts and pants would have swallowed you whole, for all the muscles you've added in the past years. I hadn't time to do that much sewing."

He wasn't sure what to say exactly, but thanks seemed to be in order. "*Denki*."

"Rhoda mentioned that you had only the one outfit and that she'd made it over so it would fit better. She said you wore it for me." Miriam patted his arm. "And that was kind. But *Englisch* clothes don't scare me anymore."

"It doesn't look like much else does, either."

She smiled. "Not as much as it used to. When I offered to help Rhoda sew more clothes for you, she said she wasn't sure you'd be needing them."

Miriam left that statement hanging in the air. Caleb knew she wanted an answer about his plans, but he didn't have one to give her. Whenever he thought about the future, he felt like he was balancing on a beam, tilting first one way, then the other.

He'd felt that way for a while, but the feeling was stronger since the ride into town, sweaty and hot, sitting beside Joseph just like the old days. Since the time he'd spent working easily with his brother and his new brothers-in-law, understanding how they thought and what needed doing without being told.

Since seeing Rhoda and the twins smiling at him, happy and excited to see their new home taking shape. And then sitting down, not so separate this one time, eating a hearty, hard-earned lunch.

He'd remembered what it felt like to belong. And that feeling had kindled a longing in his belly that was hard to ignore. He wanted this. He wanted to stay here and wear these clothes and be a husband to his wife and a father to his children, like Sam had said. He wanted it so bad, he was sick with it.

But that feeling didn't change facts. He might feel at home working with his family, but he still didn't really belong here. He didn't agree with the church any more than he ever had.

When he didn't answer, Mirry frowned. "You can talk to me, Caleb. If you're worried about scaring me, you needn't be. Reuben told me already. About you coming back because you think Trevor may be here."

Apparently, Reuben really didn't believe in keeping secrets from his wife. Caleb scanned his sister's face, but she didn't seem upset. He hurried to reassure her anyway. "You don't have to worry about Trevor, Mirry."

"I'm not worried." She lifted her chin. "Well, not really. I still have some bad moments, but I'm not near so scared as I used to be. I'm more afraid that you'll leave again." She straightened her shoulders. "But I won't let myself think on that, either. I was real worried that Reuben would leave, but *Gott* worked everything out just fine. I've wasted too much of my life being fearful. So I won't worry, but I'll be praying for you, Caleb. Praying *hard*."

She made it sound like a threat. Caleb smiled.

"But," she went on, "whatever you end up doing, you'll need more than one outfit to wear. It'll be easier for Rhoda if you're dressed Plain and act as if you're at least considering staying. Especially now that you two are living together again. Otherwise people will talk."

He hadn't thought of that, but likely Miriam was right. Their new arrangement would cause talk enough. If he persisted in wearing *Englisch* clothes, it would stir up more gossip, certain sure.

"I'll wear them." He didn't mind the idea so much.

In fact, he didn't mind it at all.

He caught a flash of satisfaction in his sister's eyes, but she only nodded briskly. "Good. Now, you'd best get back inside if you want to say goodbye to everybody."

He did want to say goodbye, but probably not for the reason Miriam thought. He couldn't wait to be alone with Rhoda and their *kinder*, just the four of them.

He'd been looking forward to that moment ever since Abram had astonished him with the idea. He'd never imagined such a thing would be allowed, and he'd been fairly sure that Rhoda wouldn't like the idea.

He'd known when the bishop had shooed him off to talk to Rhoda alone that he was giving her a chance to object. He'd expected to be told that the whole notion had been set aside, but instead, Abram had gone on to speak to Joseph, and a moving day had been arranged.

The fact that Rhoda hadn't protested mattered more to

him than he wanted to admit, even to himself. And the chance to spend time with her and the twins out from under his brother's eye—that was something he'd been doing a good bit of daydreaming about.

Fortunately, for once, the family goodbyes didn't take very long. It seemed no time before the door had shut behind the last of their helpers, and he and Rhoda were alone in the freshly scrubbed apartment.

Except for the little ones, of course, but they were in their room napping. As excited as Eli and Vonnie had been all day, he'd figured they'd not be able to go to sleep at all. That showed how much he knew about children. They both fell asleep about the time their heads hit their pillows.

Rhoda was busy cleaning up after their lunch, and he helped by gathering the empty dishes and setting them beside her at the sink.

Once that task was done, he took a minute to look over the apartment. Their helpers had done their jobs well. Everything was bright, clean, and inviting. All the furniture was in place, the surfaces shone, and the rooms smelled pleasantly of lemon cleanser. A few homey touches added warmth and color, like the pretty quilts spread over all the beds. Miriam's handiwork, he was sure.

It wasn't large, especially not for four people, and he saw some potential problems, since originally this space hadn't been designed with an Amish lifestyle in mind. A farm with some green and space for a garden would have suited him better, and he still didn't like the flimsy locks or the hollow core door at the top of the steps. But those could be replaced—and would be as soon as he could manage it. All in all, it was a clean, safe place, easy for him to keep an eye on.

And it was theirs.

He wandered back into the kitchen. Rhoda was still working at the sink. After an awkward moment, he picked up a dishtowel and moved to stand beside her.

She looked at him. "What are you doing?"

"Helping." He offered a smile. "I have nothing else to do."

"I've been thinking about that." She wiped a glass with her dishcloth and then rinsed it well before upending it in the drainer. "Maybe you should get a job."

"A job?"

"*Ja*. Miriam offered to watch the twins for me on Monday. She might do it more often, if it seems to suit everyone. Since you're living here, you'll see them plenty in the evenings, and this way they'll be looked after during the workday. There's lots of construction work around, and I'm sure that fellow Sam you used to work for would be happy to hire you on."

Caleb dried the glass slowly. Since he had no idea where it went, he set it on the counter and reached for another one.

He didn't like this plan. Not the part about Eli and Vonnie being with his sister during the day. He'd miss them, but he supposed that was all right. Nobody would be pestering Miriam or the twins, not with Reuben around, and it would be better for the little ones not to be cooped up in the bakery all day long. That little accident with the flour had been funny, but what if Eli had grabbed at something hot? Or sharp?

Besides, as the release of the movie crept closer, his nerves were getting jumpier. He needed to keep a sharp eye out, and that was harder to do with the children underfoot.

But the idea of Rhoda being here alone, or with one elderly part-time helper, while he was off working some construction job? That he didn't like, not one bit, especially now that curious *Englischers* and reporters were trickling back into town. The bakery would be busier, meaning anybody could slip in unnoticed.

An idea occurred to him.

"I could work here maybe. Helping you."

Splash! The bowl Rhoda had been about to rinse slipped through her soapy fingers and plopped into the dishwater.

"Here?" She grabbed a towel and mopped up the splashed water on the counter. "But you don't bake. Besides, I wouldn't be allowed to hire a person who's shunned." Was he mistaken, or was there a hint of relief in her voice?

Hire him? The idea of him working for his wife—and baking—nearly made him laugh out loud, but when he answered, he kept his tone carefully serious. "I wouldn't work for pay. I'd just help out, like. Not with the baking," he added hastily. "You know I'd be little good at that. But with other jobs." He tried to think. "Cleaning up and fixing things." He'd seen a few things downstairs that could use a bit of repair, and those locks were top on the list. "Washing dishes maybe."

Rhoda looked uncertain. "Do you think Abram would allow it?"

Caleb chuckled. "He's allowing us to live in the same apartment. I'm pretty sure he'll not mind if I take the trash out and sweep your floors."

She shot him another worried glance. "Wouldn't you be bored doing that all day? And you'd have no money coming in. Won't that be a problem?"

"I have money saved. Enough that I can buy food and such for a good while yet." The money he'd made helping Milt had piled up some. He'd had little to spend it on. And Abram had agreed he could buy groceries. It was another reason he liked this arrangement—at least he could start providing for his family in that small way. "It wouldn't be forever. You're run off your feet here already, and it's probably going to be extra busy over the next few weeks. That is, unless you've changed your mind about closing the bakery while this movie nonsense is going on."

"I've not changed my mind." Rhoda finished rinsing some silverware and irritably chunked it into the cup on the dish drainer. "It may be a little unpleasant, but it'd be bad business to close up during the weeks I'm likely to have the most customers."

Bad business but good sense. Still, he wasn't going to argue about it. "Well, then I'd rather be on hand, in case there's trouble. You might as well put me to work."

"Of course." Rhoda tightened her lips as she fished around in the sink and pulled the plug. "You'll want to be here in case Trevor comes."

Caleb threw the dishtowel on the counter. Taking Rhoda's arms, he gently pivoted her around to face him.

"*Ja*," he said firmly. "I do want to be here. I plan to make sure nobody ever gets close enough to hurt you or our children. I can either stand around outside, or I can be inside helping out. That part's up to you."

Rhoda stared up at him. She was so close, and the warm softness of her arms under his hands made him long to gather her close and kiss her until they both forgot about this argument.

Until they both forgot about everything.

Instead he let her go, and she took a quick step backward.

"You know"—she looked at him, her dark eyes troubled—"you could have told me, Caleb, right off. You could have said about those pictures and all when you first came."

"Would it have made any difference if I had?"

"I wouldn't have been too worried, if that's what you mean. He came before, and he could have killed Sam and Emma both, but he didn't. But *ja*, it would have changed some things. I'd rather have understood that's why you came right from the start, that you were chasing after Trevor. I'd like to have known that before I—" She left her sentence unfinished. "I wish you'd told me," she repeated.

"I should've. I'm sorry."

She picked up the dishrag and began wiping the already clean counters. "I almost wish Trevor would show up." Her voice shook. "It's hard how this is dragging on and on, and I don't like how you're misleading Abram . . . pretending that you might rejoin the church."

"I'm not pretending." The words came out before he thought.

Rhoda froze in mid-wipe. When she turned to look at him, the disbelief in her eyes felt like a slap.

He waited for a minute, searching desperately for some way to explain his feelings to her. *Help me, Gott, to find the right words.*

He blinked, startled. The desperate prayer had formed in his mind naturally, like the old days, when he'd prayed like he breathed. When he'd believed that *Gott* actually listened.

He forced himself to refocus his attention on the woman in front of him. "I won't deny I came back here because of Trevor. Partly. And partly I came because of you."

She watched him, uncertainty plain on her face. Another slap—or it felt like one. Rhoda never used to look at him like that.

"Is that so? Would you have come to Johns Mill if I'd still been living in Pennsylvania? If you hadn't found pictures of me, but you'd heard Trevor was here? Would you still have come back then?"

They both knew the answer to that already, so there was no point in dodging it. "*Ja*, I'd have come."

He saw the hurt in her eyes as she nodded. "That's what I thought." She'd started to turn away when he spoke again.

"I'd have come, sure. But you'd not have found me meeting with any bishop, nor putting on these clothes." He plucked at the shirt he was wearing, one of Joseph's old ones. "Trevor's the reason I came. But you and our babies are the reasons I'm wanting to stay."

Rhoda's eyes flew wide, and she whirled back around so fast that the damp dishrag spattered drops of water on his shirt.

"Caleb? Is that true? You really want to—"

First he'd started back praying, and now this? He'd better

shut his mouth and do some hard thinking before he made this woman promises he wouldn't be able to keep.

Again.

"It's been a real long day," he interrupted desperately. "We're both tired. We should talk about this later, when we have our wits about us."

He left her standing in the kitchen, beat a hasty retreat to his lonely bedroom, and closed the door.

Chapter Twenty-Three

WHAT WAS THAT NOISE?

Just after midnight, Rhoda lifted her head from her pillow, her body taut, listening. But now the only sound she heard was the steady ticking of the battery-operated clock on her nightstand.

She was imagining things. She lay her head down on the smooth cotton pillowcase and closed her eyes. She was just a little skittish, she told herself. She'd always found it hard to sleep the first few nights in a new place.

Well, almost always. When she'd been married to Caleb, it hadn't seemed to matter so much. When they'd gone on their wedding trip, they'd stayed in three different homes, but she'd fallen asleep just fine, every night. Even at Caleb's sour *onkel* Melvin's home, where the mattress had been so lumpy, it might have been full of wadded-up socks. Even there, she'd fallen asleep like a baby, her head resting on Caleb's chest, his arms around her, and the steady beat of his heart under her cheek.

Rhoda shut off that memory quickly. Ever since Caleb

had surprised her by mentioning he wanted to stay, she'd struggled not to set her heart on that possibility.

He'd said they would talk about it. Until then, she'd pray for guidance and wait to see what *Gott* was up to. Unfortunately, although she tried hard to discipline her thoughts, hope kept sneaking in, bringing all her old dreams with it.

She turned over in the bed so she was facing the window. It was cracked, letting in a cool night breeze that fluttered the white curtains gently. That was nice, but the air coming in smelled like pavement. She missed the scents of the country, the green smell of trees and grass. She even missed the smells of horses and cows.

She couldn't complain, though. This apartment was a blessing from *Gott*. Besides, being in town had its good points. There'd be no more buggy rides into town in the dark hours before dawn. She'd simply get dressed and walk right downstairs. And since Caleb planned to drive the children over to Miriam's house, he'd have the job of collecting her borrowed horse, Maude. Rhoda wouldn't have to leave the bakery kitchen all morning, so she'd get plenty done.

This apartment wasn't the sweet little farmhouse she'd once dreamed of, but it was comfortable, affordable, and convenient. And if Caleb *did* stay, maybe they could find themselves a small farm not too far from town and—

There she went again.

She rolled back over, tugging at the light sheet and flipping the pillow to its cooler side. She needed to stop thinking and get to sleep. She planned to get up extra early so she could bake a few batches of sugar cookies first thing. Mrs. Anderson wanted some pretty ones for her daughter's baby shower. The dough was all made up, so that wouldn't be a problem. And Edna could help with the decorating. That would make her feel happy and useful. First thing tomorrow, Rhoda would roll them out, and—

She frowned, searching her memory. Had she put that sugar cookie dough in the refrigerator after she'd mixed it up last night? It needed a good chill. She didn't remember doing it, but probably she had. When you were busy, you often did routine tasks without thinking.

Yes, most likely she'd done it.

Five restless minutes later, she sat up and put on her slippers. She'd best go check.

She padded down the stairs, wincing at every creak. She didn't want to wake up the twins—or Caleb, of course. It was . . . strange . . . thinking of him sleeping just down the hall from her. So close again after all this time.

And yet so far away, too. Although maybe not for much longer, if—

She snipped off that train of thought and made a face in the dark, frustrated with herself.

A security light in the lot outside shone through the window of the kitchen, making it easy to see. There was no big bowl on the counter. A good sign. To make doubly sure, Rhoda opened the large refrigerator. The light popped on inside, making her blink. *Ja*, there was the dough, just where it needed to be. She could go back to bed and sleep peacefully now.

She hoped.

Another blessing about living here. If she'd woken up at Joseph's wondering about the dough, she'd have fretted over it all night. Now, she could easily pop down and check on things, and if she had forgotten something, it would be simple to fix.

She'd remind her parents of that when they tried to get her to move in with them once they resettled in Johns Mill. She knew that discussion was coming, probably sooner rather than later. She'd finally mailed them a letter yesterday, telling them about Abram's suggestion that she and Caleb share the apartment. She could well imagine her father's face when he read that. All his fears about her husband leading her and the children away from the faith would be rekindled.

Of course, they wouldn't blame her. When a bishop told you what to do, you did it. But this news would light a fire underneath their moving plans, certain sure. Ida and Isaac Lambright would get here as soon as they could, and that was likely to make things difficult. Her father and Caleb had always been like oil and water.

She wondered if it was wrong for her to pray that her parents would be delayed. Not forever, but just . . . for a while. At least until Caleb had made up his mind what he wanted to do.

She'd just pray that *Gott* would work it out for the best. That was always the wisest thing, and—

Rhoda froze halfway across the kitchen, her eyes fixed on the back door.

The little handle on the lock wasn't turned. And that wasn't right.

That door had been locked tight after Caleb's family had left yesterday. She'd seen to that herself, feeling a little like a hypocrite when she'd checked it twice.

She truly wasn't worried about Trevor, not much anyhow. She did believe he was just a boy, troubled in his mind, who had done a terrible, awful, tragic thing. But ever since Caleb had told her about those pictures he'd found, she'd paid a bit more attention to locks and such.

So, *ja*, she'd locked that door. She was certain of it.

She hurried over and twisted the lock, her heart in her throat. Then she walked quickly across the kitchen toward the stairs. She needed to check on the children. She went up the steps as swiftly as she could, afraid that at any moment, she was going to feel somebody grabbing her from behind.

When she made it to the top, she closed the door. By then her fingers were trembling so much, it took her three tries to turn its lock.

She finally managed it, but it didn't give her much comfort.

Caleb didn't like this flimsy door. One good kick, he'd said, and it would give way. He'd ordered a solid wooden door to replace it, but it hadn't come in yet.

She tiptoed to the twins' bedroom and peeked in. It was darker here, and it took a moment for her eyes to adjust. Eli and Vonnie were safe in their beds and sound asleep. She sent up a silent, devout prayer of thanks.

She glanced down the hall. Caleb's room was on the far end. He hadn't much liked that arrangement. He'd have preferred the front bedroom, putting himself between the door leading downstairs and herself and the children. But she'd not known that, and she'd asked Joseph and the other men to put her things in the room closest to the stairs. She'd figured that sensible, since she'd need to slip downstairs early to work. Caleb hadn't realized her plan until all the furniture was in place.

She'd apologized, and he hadn't insisted on changing, although he'd not been happy. Now she wished they'd gone to the trouble to switch.

She hesitated in the hallway. Everything seemed very quiet, but still . . . that unlocked door. She'd never be able to go back to sleep, not when she knew she'd fastened it.

She padded down the hallway to Caleb's room. His door was shut, and she stood there for a second, her fist poised to knock. Then she thought better of it—right now probably best to keep silent—and turned the knob, gently easing the door open.

This room was on the side with the security light, so she could see it clearly. The bedroom was empty, the covers thrown back, and the bedding rumpled.

Where was Caleb?

Her heart hammered as she fought a wave of panic. She hadn't realized until this moment how much she'd been counting on Caleb's comforting presence. She'd expected to walk down here, tell him about the door, and have him jump up and take over.

Instead he was nowhere to be seen. Had he slipped outside, leaving the door unlocked? That seemed unlikely, considering how worried he'd been about such things.

Unless.

She tiptoed to the window. Pushing the curtains aside, she peered down into the parking area behind the store buildings.

It took her a minute to find him. If she hadn't been looking down from the second story, no doubt she'd not have seen him at all. But there he was.

Caleb had dragged a chair out and positioned himself near the bakery's back door, behind a fence set up to screen off the dumpster. Rhoda wrinkled her nose. It couldn't smell very good right there, she thought. A poor place to choose to sit.

Or maybe not.

From where Caleb was sitting, he had a view of the entire area, and he was close enough to the door that nobody could get inside before he could stop them. But because of the fence, nobody entering the back alley could easily see him.

It was the perfect spot to keep watch.

She stood at the window a few more moments. He didn't stir the whole time, although the chair must have been uncomfortable. She thought about the twins sleeping peacefully not so far away, as her heartbeat slowly steadied.

Caleb was not a perfect man. He was certainly not an obedient Amish man. But still, there was real goodness in him. Other people couldn't see it so easily, but she knew it was there. He would stand discomfort and weariness for her sake. He would work in a bakery, doing menial jobs, just to keep her and their children safe.

While other men sidestepped trouble, Caleb went striding out to meet it. When he disagreed, he didn't stay silent, but spoke up, not minding who he was arguing with.

It did not make him a comfortable man to love. Carrying

and birthing the twins hadn't been so comfortable, either. But in the end, when she'd cuddled them in her arms, it had been well worth it.

She turned away from the window and walked softly to the door at the top of the stairs. Her fingers were steady now, and she was able to unlock it easily. She went downstairs and followed suit with the door in the kitchen.

Then she went back up to her bed, lay down, a peaceful drowsiness falling over her like a soft blanket. As she slipped into her dreams, the rhythmic ticking of the clock beside her sounded like a comforting heartbeat.

The next morning, Rhoda was well along in her baking before Caleb came back from dropping the twins off at Miriam's house. He walked in the back door looking frustrated.

"I wish all the businesses around here started as early as this one," he grumbled as he made his way to the coffeepot. "I stopped by the hardware store, but they won't open until ten. Ten o'clock on a weekday." He shook his head in disgust.

"Well, they're *Englischers*." She leaned over to open the oven. Warm sweet-scented air puffed against her face as she swapped one sheet of sugar cookies for another one. Edna would be here soon, and she wanted to have these ready for icing. "They get a later start than we do, most of them."

"Mmm." Caleb was too deep in his coffee mug to answer.

Rhoda hoped it helped. She'd made the coffee extra strong today. As far as she knew, Caleb had spent the whole night outside. When she'd awakened just before dawn, she'd heard his whistling softly in his bedroom.

The whistling had done funny things to her stomach. He'd always whistled like that in the mornings—something she'd discovered that first oh-so-sweet day of their marriage. She'd almost forgotten about that habit—until she'd heard the familiar tune again.

"What did you need at the hardware store?" She quietly plopped a bacon kolache on a plate and, on impulse, added a hot sugar cookie. Caleb had always liked sweets first thing in the morning. She set the offering on the counter at his elbow.

His mouth tipped into a weary smile. "*Denki.* Since Abram's being stubborn about the alarms, I'm going to get bolt locks for the front and back doors, and that solid door for upstairs is supposed to come in today, too. Before you go to fussing, remember: A sturdy door is no different from a good fence. It prevents problems as well as solving them."

"I'm not fussing," she pointed out. "Speaking of solving problems, after you eat your breakfast, could you look at that shelving unit against the wall? It's nice that it rolls, but I worry the twins will grab hold and tip it over on themselves. What do you think?"

She could tell that he liked being asked. "Best to have it fixed in place maybe. I can see to it, and by the time I get finished, the hardware store should be open."

"*Denki.*" She smiled at him, and he smiled back.

"*Du bisht welcome,*" he said. And as soon as he'd devoured the food and poured himself another cup of coffee, he set about anchoring down the steel shelving.

That kept him busy until midmorning. When she dashed back into the kitchen to grab a tray of sourdough loaves to replenish the display case—and to check on Edna's progress with the cookies—he told her he was headed to the hardware store.

"I won't be long," he said. Then he added, "And maybe, if you can find a spare minute or so, we can talk before Miriam brings the twins back home. Just the two of us."

Her heart leapt up in her chest. "*Ja*, sure," she told him, hurrying back out front.

A few minutes later, when she had a break between customers, she went back into the kitchen and inspected the shelves. The unit had been bolted to the wall, and all her supplies had been carefully put back in their allotted spaces. She tugged as hard as she could, but it wouldn't budge.

She smiled with satisfaction—and a little dab of secret pride. Caleb had always done real *gut* work. Even *Daed* hadn't been able to fault him in that.

And he certain sure wasn't lazy. He'd not said a word this morning about being tired, even though she could see the dark smudges under his eyes, and she'd caught him yawning more than once. He'd even helped her get the children their breakfast upstairs, and when Eli had sloshed half the milk out of his cereal bowl, Caleb had only chuckled wearily and mopped it up with a napkin.

Edna had finished icing the cookies and gone. Rhoda poured herself a mug of coffee and sipped it as she busied herself in the kitchen, keeping an ear out for the bell over the shop door. For the moment, business had slowed.

If Caleb hurried back, maybe they could have their talk now. In the meantime, she'd get everything she could do finished so they'd have plenty of time.

She went out front and straightened up swiftly. The small trash can she provided near the door was already overflowing with discarded napkins, so she took out the bag, twisted it shut, and headed for the back door.

When she tugged at the door, it refused to open. Caleb must have locked it when he left, she thought with an amused exasperation. She never locked this door during the workday. Deliverymen and her helpers often needed access to the kitchen. Besides, although she'd been nervous at night, surely in the daylight she was perfectly safe.

She'd have a word with him about that when he got back. She unlocked the door, pulled it open, and stopped short.

A man stood down the alleyway with his back to her, an *Englischer.* Her eyes skimmed his disheveled clothing, and she frowned. There weren't many homeless folks around Johns Mill, but this fellow sure looked as if he hadn't bathed or changed clothes in a while. Maybe he was hanging around hoping for a meal? She'd gladly offer him something to eat and even bag up some day-old items for him to take with him.

She started to call out to him, but before she could, he pulled a phone out of his pocket and snapped some pictures of something on the ground. As he leaned over to get a better shot, his shirt rode up. Rhoda's eyes widened, and her heart thudded hard.

Quietly she closed the door and twisted the lock into place. She hurried through the store, flipped the sign to **CLOSED**, and locked the front door, too.

Shaking, she leaned against the doorframe between the two rooms and prayed hard that the man would go away before Caleb returned from the hardware store. Because if he didn't . . . if Caleb found a rough-looking *Englischer* outside of her bakery taking pictures . . .

There was no way that man would walk away without Caleb confronting him. And this stranger had a gun tucked into the waistband of his pants.

Chapter Twenty-Four

CALEB LEFT THE HARDWARE STORE, BAGS IN HAND, heading down the street toward the bakery. His errand hadn't gone well.

The delivery of the door was delayed, and picking out the locks had taken longer than he would have liked. He still wasn't sure he'd found the best lock for the front entrance. He didn't want to mess up the looks of the antique door, so he'd combed through all the locks searching for a stronger one that would fit the same as the existing one.

He'd picked the one in stock that seemed the most similar, but if it didn't work, he'd need to return it and order another. It would mean another delay, and he wanted to get the place secure as soon as he could.

He had to get some sleep.

He'd spent another uncomfortable night, this time outside in a straight chair. Of course, he'd had little chance of sleeping anyhow. Not only had he kept replaying his conversation with Rhoda in his head, but Trevor Abbott hovered at the corner of his mind like a storm cloud, dark and heavy and ready to break.

Caleb couldn't shake the sense that fresh trouble was brewing. He smelled it coming, like a farmer smelled rain before it fell, so he'd decided to keep watch for a little while.

That little while had lasted until near about dawn. It had been a waste of time because nothing had happened. Except that he'd had a lot of time to think.

Mostly about Rhoda.

This setup of Abram's had his heart zigzagging like a squirrel on a highway. It felt very right and very wrong all at the same time. One moment he was loving this—being so close to Rhoda and the children, knowing they were safe and sharing all the little ordinaries of life.

The next minute she'd set something down instead of handing it directly to him or quietly shut a door, leaving him alone on the outside, and he'd feel a rush of frustrated sadness at how *wrong* this all was. It was like holding a level up to a board you'd nailed in place and seeing the bubble slip sideways. Your work might look straight, but that proved it was off-kilter, and it needed fixing.

He'd never in his life let a crooked beam stand, not on a job with his name on it. But the marriage that had his name on it? Right now, that was about as crooked and flimsy as it could be.

Maybe he didn't agree with the Amish church about everything, but he did agree that marriages were important. Marriages were the foundations of families, so they needed to be true-built. They had to stand the test of time, to bear the weight of generations of both joys and troubles.

They were worth fixing.

He wanted to fix his. He just wasn't sure he could. Staying

with Rhoda meant getting on his knees before the church and following their rules. All of them, whether he happened to agree with them or not.

He'd already planned to talk to Rhoda. There were some things they needed to settle between the two of them. But maybe . . .

Maybe he'd go see Abram this afternoon and ask his advice.

He shook his head at the absurdity of the idea. Him, Caleb Hochstedler, asking advice from a bishop?

Nobody in Johns Mill would ever believe he'd do such a thing, but oddly enough, he genuinely wanted to hear what Abram had to say. He suspected he wouldn't like a lot of it. He also suspected he'd better put on clothes he didn't mind getting dirty. Abram would likely set him to mucking out the pigpen or something.

Somehow, though, that didn't bother him so much. Time spent with Isaac had always set his teeth on edge, but he didn't mind spending time with Abram, even if it did involve a pigpen or two.

Caleb reached the front door of the bakery and bent to examine the lock. He'd check this quick and get on with his plans.

"It's closed."

A plump middle-aged Amish woman looked down at him through thick spectacles. He straightened as his mind worked to place her. Erma Miller, he thought. Her husband, Wayne, ran a little repair shop the next town over. He worked on everything from buggies to farm equipment to kitchen gadgets. They'd had a houseful of children, likely all grown now.

"Lambright's Bakery," Erma explained helpfully. If she recognized him, she didn't let on. "It's closed. I don't know why, but the door's locked. Try going to Miller's Café if you want something to eat. They're my husband's *kossins*, and the food's real *gut*." She offered him a smile and bustled off down the sidewalk.

Caleb turned his attention back to the bakery. The sign did say **CLOSED**, and—he jiggled the doorknob—it was locked up tight. He frowned.

Rhoda wouldn't close the bakery in the middle of a busy workday. Not without a really good reason. He leaned close to the window, shading his eyes so he could see inside.

Rhoda was huddled in the doorway between the shop and the kitchen. She was peering into the kitchen, and it was plain to see that she was terrified.

He tightened his jaw. *Steady*, he told himself. *Be smart. Be quiet. Be quick.*

He rapped softly on the glass, and Rhoda turned her head. When she recognized him, she cast one worried look back toward the kitchen then ran toward the front.

As she fumbled with the lock, he gritted his teeth, fighting the urge to pick up the big terra cotta pot of geraniums beside him and pitch it through the glass window.

When she finally got the door unlocked, he moved inside. She threw her arms around him and held on for dear life.

"It's all right." He didn't ask what was going on. He figured he already knew. "Where is he?"

"Out back," she whispered against his chest. "I was so scared you'd go there first before I could warn you. I didn't know what to do."

He could feel her shaking, and the adrenaline and concern whirling inside his chest solidified into a rock of resolve.

"I'm here," he said. "It's all right. Nobody's going to hurt you."

"I don't know if it's Trevor. I don't think so, but I couldn't see his face." She drew back to look up into his face. "But, Caleb, whoever he is, he has a gun. I saw it."

He disentangled her arms gently and pushed her toward the phone. "Go across the street to Mary Yoder's. Once you get there, call nine-one-one," he told her.

She looked at him blankly. It wouldn't have occurred to her to call the police. The Amish didn't rely much on law enforcement. It was one of the reasons they made such convenient victims.

"Nine-one-one," he repeated. "Tell them there's a man with a gun behind the bakery and give them the address. Tell Mary to lock up tight and then stay away from the windows and wait there for me to come get you."

"I'm not leaving you. And, Caleb, Sam and Emma are over at the store."

His heart constricted. *Emma.* But his first job was to make sure his wife was safe.

"Do what I tell you, Rhoda. Please. Go to Mary's and call the police." He didn't want her anywhere near Hochstedler's General Store, not if Trevor was in Johns Mill. "You can also call the store from Mary's and warn Sam to lock up."

She shook her head. "I can call them from here. I'm not leaving you, Caleb. If anything happened to you, I'd—" She broke off, her eyes going wide. "There he is!" she whispered shakily. "He's out front now, right on the sidewalk!"

Caleb stepped forward, tucking Rhoda behind him, and saw the man his wife was pointing at.

Relief hit him so hard his knees sagged. He started to grin as he walked across the bakery, and by the time he pulled open the door, he was laughing.

"You old rascal, you just scared my poor wife half to death. Rhoda"—Caleb drew the older man inside—"meet Milt Masterson. I worked for him while I was away."

"Ma'am," Milt said politely. "Sorry if I spooked you out back. I heard you open the door, and when you shut it so quick, I figured what must have happened. I was just taking a look around before I came in to speak to our boy here."

Rhoda blinked, obviously trying to recover her wits. She'd been badly scared, Caleb realized with a guilty pang. And small wonder. At the moment, Milt looked even scruffier than usual.

Caleb stepped outside to retrieve the bags he'd dropped on the sidewalk. Then he locked the door.

"Stay closed for a little while," he suggested gently. "Just till your nerves settle. How about you get Milt some coffee and a few of those cookies you made this morning?"

Rhoda tried twice to speak before her voice worked. "All right," she managed finally. "It'll—just take a minute. I'll need to make some fresh coffee. The pot's nearly empty."

"Oh, I don't need nothing, and—" Milt stopped when he caught sight of Caleb's face. Understanding glimmered in his eyes, and he cleared his throat. "Although a cup of coffee sure would hit the spot if it ain't no trouble, ma'am."

"It's no trouble at all. And it's—very nice to meet you," Rhoda said.

Caleb smiled. He'd been right to distract her with the refreshments. Already she seemed steadier. "Take your time. Milt and I need to do some catching up."

As Rhoda turned to fiddle with the coffee maker behind the counter, Caleb beckoned Milt toward Isaac's office. Once inside, Milt sank into a metal folding chair and scratched at his chin.

"I knew you came from these people, Amish, but I have to say, I never give it much thought." He shook his head. "I blew into town early this morning, and I been poking around some. Driving the roads and going in and out of stores and such. Never seen the like of it. Folks driving around in horses and buggies. Farms with wash hanging out on the lines, just like my old grandma used to do years ago. You musta felt like you stepped into a whole other world when you started running with me."

"I'd stepped into a different world a long time before I met you, Milt."

Milt nodded and leaned back in his chair, looking around the room like a man who had nothing in particular on his mind. Caleb knew that wasn't true. Something was up, or Milt wouldn't be here.

You couldn't rush Milt. He'd get to the point when he was ready.

"That's your wife?"

"Yes, that's Rhoda."

Milt grunted. "I don't usually hold with commenting on other men's women, but she's even prettier than her pictures. I believe did that girl belong to me, I'd have kept myself at home."

Caleb managed a smile. "Proves you're a smarter man than I am."

"That," Milt said calmly, "ain't ever been a question." He chuckled. "And let me tell you, it takes a smart man to get information around here. You Amish don't talk much, do you?"

"No. Well, to each other, yes. But not to *Englishers*."

Milt nodded. "Private folks. I can understand that. I tried to strike up a conversation with three or four Amish folks and got nowhere. Nice as pie, but not telling me nothing." He shifted in his chair. "But there's more'n one road to most places, ain't there? Driving them buggies, wearing them clothes, that all attracts people's attention. Maybe you don't talk to outsiders so much, but that don't mean they don't know your business. I talked to the owner of the feed store. He ain't no more Amish than I am, but he answered my questions right quick."

Caleb frowned. "What were you asking about?"

"You for starters. Found out you had some big news when you got here. Kids. Or so I heard."

"That's right. It turns out I'm a father. Twins. A boy and a girl."

"Yeah, that's what he told me, all right." Milt paused. "And you're sure they're yours?"

Caleb rose slowly to his feet. "Yes, I am. And if I were you, I wouldn't go any farther down that road."

The older man didn't budge. He looked up at Caleb and raised an eyebrow. "Well, that got your attention pretty quick, didn't it? Set back down. I ain't throwing no rocks, not at you nor your wife, neither. It was an honest question, but maybe not the politest one."

"And I answered it." Still irritated, Caleb sat back in his chair. "Honestly. Now answer a question for me. What were you taking pictures of out back?"

"Found some footprints in a little dried mud back there."

"I didn't see them." Caleb frowned, alarmed. How had he missed that?

"Not so easy to see." Milt chuckled again. "That's why I'm the boss and you ain't."

"You think it was Trevor?"

The amusement faded from Milt's face. "I do. There was a little bit of sand mixed in with 'em, too, likely from that beach. I'd guess our boy's been here at least once in the past few days. I'll send them pictures I took to you so you can see for yourself, although all things considered, it don't look like it's going to matter much."

Caleb's mind was racing. Trevor had been here—here, at the bakery, close to Rhoda and his children. And he hadn't even known. The idea made him feel sick.

And furious. At Trevor. And at himself. He should have—

Wait a minute. Caleb frowned as Milt's words registered.

"What'd you just say?" He glanced up to find the older man studying him calmly, waiting him out. "Why doesn't it matter that Trevor's been here?"

Milt grinned. "Been wondering when you'd catch that. Took you a while. Being around that pretty girl's got your brain addled. It don't matter 'cause I had a phone call from one of the folks I tap for info. He had some big news, the kind I figured you'd rather hear in person."

"What news?"

"Trevor Abbott's decided to turn himself in."

Chapter Twenty-Five

"He's going to do what? When? Where?" Caleb shot questions at Milt, one after another.

"Day after that movie releases, apparently. Going to be a big old spectacle, from what we hear. Lots of press, some kinda statement. On the courthouse steps here in town. The parents are setting it up."

Caleb sank back into the chair behind Isaac's desk. "He's turning himself in. Why?"

"Who knows? Sure is convenient timing for them movie folks since it's bound to get them extra publicity. But could be the boy's just tired of running. Even," he added wryly, "when you get to stay in nice digs and got money to burn, that still gets old. Lonesome too."

Something about Milt's tone didn't sound quite right. He cut his old boss a sharp look.

"You have some ideas about this."

Milt shrugged. "Me, I got ideas about everything. But this setup has some stink to it, you ask me."

"You don't think he'll really turn himself in?"

"Naw, I think he probably will. This whole thing's been laid out too careful—tying it to the movie release and all that. "You seen the trailer for it?"

"No."

"Maybe you ought to. Sure doesn't give the feel that Trevor's the bad guy, I'll tell you that. I figure his father's looking to capitalize on it all they can. I hear he's got his hands in a judge's pockets, too. If he can get a sympathetic jury . . ." Milt shrugged again. "It's the best bet, I'd say, to get Trevor off easy, considering he's up for two murders. That part of it makes sense."

Caleb's eyes narrowed. "What doesn't make sense?"

Before Milt answered, Rhoda pushed the door open, bracing a laden tray against her stomach.

"The coffee and the cookies," she explained.

Caleb jumped up. He started to take the tray from her, then thought better of it. "*Denki*," he whispered, moving aside so she could set it on her father's old desk.

"Thank you kindly, ma'am." Milt's face brightened at the sight of the steaming coffee and the iced sugar cookies. "This looks like a real treat."

"I hope you'll enjoy it." Rhoda shot an uncertain look at Caleb and then turned back toward Milt, clasping her hands in front of her apron. "I'm sorry I wasn't more welcoming. I didn't know you were a friend of Caleb's."

"Don't you apologize." Milt accepted the mug from Rhoda with a smile. "A woman's got to be careful in this world, and right now I sure don't look like a guy you'd want to turn your back on. Sorry about that. I had news I figured Caleb would want to know, so I came straight on. Didn't have time to change clothes or nothing."

"It wasn't your clothing. It was the gun mostly." Rhoda set his plate within easy reach. "I saw it, and it made me *naerfich*. Nervous," she translated.

"Guns make me plenty nervous, too, depending on who's holding one." He reached into the waistband of his jeans and produced the pistol. He laid it on the desk next to the tray.

Rhoda tensed, but Caleb knew Milt was trying to be kind. In his world, putting a weapon out in the open like that, out of easy reach—that was a gesture of trust. Since Milt didn't trust many people, Caleb had seen him do something like that only a scant handful of times. He must really feel bad about scaring Rhoda.

"If it makes you feel any better," Milt went on, "that there is my personal firearm. You can ask Caleb, I don't generally carry on the job. I'm licensed in a bunch of states, and they all got different regulations about that. Besides, most of the folks I go after ain't violent. Worst they're gonna do when they see me coming is run."

Rhoda listened, her forehead creased. "Why do you need a gun at all?"

Milt shot an uneasy look at Caleb. "Well, ma'am, in my business, a man tends to make enemies. Matter of fact, that's how your boy here and I met." He chuckled. "A meth addict's brother jumped me at a truck stop down in Georgia. "'Member that, Caleb?"

Caleb shot Rhoda an uncomfortable look. "I remember. Try that cookie, Milt. Rhoda grew up baking, and she's a born cook."

"They look real good, for sure." Milt took a bite, but unfortunately it didn't stop him from talking. "Yeah, I'll never forget that day. This fellow was wanted on drug charges, and he'd skipped bail in Mobile, see. Happens he had a wife he hadn't treated too good, and I managed to finagle a meeting with her at this truck stop. Poor little thing, she wasn't no bigger than a minute. Didn't look like she'd had a square meal in a while and couldn't have been much over eighteen. Already had two babies she was trying to look after. Fellow was holed up at her house, slapping her around some. She was willing to let me know exactly where to find him in exchange for grocery money. Guy's brother found out about it somehow." Milt whistled before taking another bite of cookie. "Now he was a piece of work. Mean as they come and half crazy, too. Him and a friend of his followed us to the truck stop and got the drop on me. His friend had a knife to my throat before I knew what was happening, while the other guy starting beating up on that poor girl while he dragged her to their truck. Then your husband here, he comes running up out of nowhere—"

"Milt—" Caleb shot a concerned glance at Rhoda. Her eyes were wide, and she was hanging on Milt's every word.

The older man paid him no attention. "And he tackles the guy dragging the girl. I mean a full-on body tackle. Got that girl loose and told her to run inside. That guy pulled his own knife and got in one slice across your man's chest—oh, no." Milt stopped as Rhoda sucked in a horrified breath. "Now, don't you get upset. It wasn't no big deal. Only a few stitches. And that fellow paid for it, I'll tell you. Guy was built like a brick wall, but our Caleb here beat the ever-loving tar out of him." Milt finished his cookie and grinned. "I hired him on the spot."

Clenching his jaw tight, Caleb picked up Milt's empty plate. He put it on the tray and nudged it toward Rhoda. "You can take this back to the kitchen now."

Milt meant well. He was telling this particular story because he thought it showed Caleb in a flattering light. He didn't understand that Rhoda wouldn't see it that way at all.

Rhoda picked up the tray, but she didn't budge. "Was the girl all right?"

Milt blinked. "She had a few bruises, but she was alive, which was a better outcome than I was expecting. If it hadn't been for Caleb, it all coulda turned out different.

Course our boy here always was quick to step between a woman and trouble. There was this other time, down in Atlanta—"

"That's a long story," Caleb interjected desperately. "And not one we have time for right now. You'll need to reopen soon if you're not going to miss out on all your day's customers, Rhoda. Why don't you go ahead? Milt and I will stay in here and finish talking, and I'll let him out the back when we're done. All right?"

Rhoda nodded, and when she glanced at him, there was something in her eyes that confused him. He'd expected shocked disapproval, but instead he saw a softness that hadn't been there in a long while. Before he could make sense of it, she turned back to Milt.

"It was very nice to meet you."

Milt stood. "Pleasure's all mine, ma'am."

Caleb opened the door for Rhoda and closed it behind her.

"I'd appreciate it if you didn't tell her any more of your stories, Milt," he said. "They'll only worry her."

The older man sank back into his chair and reached for his coffee. "Sorry. I didn't think about how such stuff might upset a lady like her. I'm a fish out of water here, Amish. I never seen nothing like this place. Do you know, I was poking around the back alleys up both sides of Main Street here, just scoping things out. At the end of the alley across the street behind some grocery-type store—"

"Zook's" Caleb supplied.

"Yeah. Behind there, I was looking for signs of somebody hanging around."

Caleb had already done that himself. "You find anything?"

"No. But while I was looking, this man came out the back door of his store, little short fellow. He had a wrapped up sandwich and a bottle of water." Milt shook his head. "Thought I was scrounging in the dumpster for food and wanted to give me a square meal."

Caleb winced. *Ja*, Eben Zook would have taken one look at Milt and figured he must be down on his luck. "Sorry. Johns Mill gets plenty of *Englisch* passing through, but they're mostly tourists. He wouldn't have known what to make of you."

Milt waved his hand. "Not what I meant. Dressing like this, I been offered food and money plenty of times, and I been given enough flyers about homeless shelters to wallpaper this room. Been nudged down the road by the police, too, more than once. Don't bother me. Like I told your lady there, I know I look rough. That's okay. It's part of my business. It was the way this little fellow did it—all respectful-like. He made it clear he wasn't gonna answer any nosy questions, but he gave me his name and asked me mine. Invited me to sit in his storeroom to eat."

Caleb nodded—and waited, not entirely sure what Milt was getting at.

Milt snorted. "You don't even see nothing special about that. Son, ain't you been paying attention the last couple of years? The rest of the world ain't like that. It's been a long time since I met a fellow like that little storekeeper. And it's been a longer time since I met a woman like that wife of yours." He shot a look up at Caleb and shook his head. "No wonder you hightailed it home so fast when you found out Trevor was eyeing her. I'd have done the same. There's something so . . ." He trailed off. "I ain't got the words," he decided finally. "But a man would do just about anything to protect a girl like that. Or a place like this. I don't blame you," he said. "Whatever you end up doing to keep 'em safe, I won't blame you a bit."

The opinion of a man like Milt wouldn't mean much to the bishop or to the church members here, but it meant something to Caleb. He set his own mug of cooling coffee to one side and leaned across the desk.

"Then help me," he said. "Tell me everything you've heard about this latest Trevor thing. Turning himself in all of a sudden, just when the movie's about to come out? His father's got to be behind that, and I don't trust it one bit."

"I don't, either." Milt leaned forward, propping his elbows on the desk. "I'll tell you what I think. But you ain't going to like it."

A few minutes later, Milt slipped out the back while Rhoda was busy waiting on customers. Caleb busied himself installing the new lock on the back door and replacing the sagging hinges on a cabinet, his mind replaying what Milt had said.

He watched Rhoda as she worked, listening to her gentle voice, and noticing how she treated the people who came into the bakery. Kindly, never rushing them. She murmured sympathetically as one elderly *Englisch* lady told her a rambling story about her recently deceased dog, and she tucked a free cupcake in the lady's order.

She also listened calmly to complaints from a few people who seemed to hold her personally responsible for how the bakery had gone downhill under the Hershbergers' management. And she cheerfully promised two different Plain women to help with fundraisers to benefit people in need, even though he knew she had little time to spare these days.

No. There were not many women in the world like Rhoda. Nor like his sister Miriam, who drove her buggy into town to drop off the twins, saving them the trouble of driving out to get them.

She waved off their surprised thanks. "I spent so long cooped up at home, I love being able to get out and drive to town. I'll never take that for granted again. I'll come pick them up next time, too," she offered, her tone carefully innocent. "I'm sure you two would rather spend all the time you can at home together."

Caleb shot her a sharp glance, and she winked at him saucily before turning away to accept Rhoda's offer of half a hummingbird cake to take home to Reuben.

After Miriam left, Caleb helped Rhoda tidy up the bakery.

Then he took the twins upstairs while she made up the dough she would need for the next day.

The twins had enjoyed a happy day with their *aent,* and they were already looking forward to spending the next day with her. Caleb felt secretly pleased when they squabbled over who was to sit on his lap while he told them a story. He managed to make room for both of them and concocted an involved tale about an ornery mule named *Schtubbich.* He managed to wrap it up just as Rhoda climbed the steps, a tray of wheat rolls in her hands.

She smiled at the three of them seated in the rocking chair. "I'm going to warm up these rolls and fry some ham slices for supper. It won't take a minute."

Caleb set the twins on the floor and got to his feet. "I'll help." He tugged over a little basket of toys and dumped them out in front of Eli and Vonnie. "Play nice together while *Daed* and *Mamm* get supper ready."

The twins settled down happily enough, reaching for their favorite toys.

Rhoda was watching him, her expression uncertain. "I can manage by myself," she said. "Like I said, it's going to be a quick meal."

"It'll be quicker with me helping," Caleb pointed out. "I'm not much of a cook, but I can fry ham. You've been baking since early this morning, and you've been run off your feet. You must be tired." He rummaged around until he found a skillet.

Rhoda hesitated, but finally she joined him in the kitchen. She heated the oven and slid in the rolls to warm before opening a couple of cans of green beans and corn. She flashed him an apologetic look.

"Sorry it's so simple," she said. "I got spoiled living with Naomi and Joseph. Naomi always prepared supper while I worked. Usually all I had to do was bring home the bread and dessert. I've got to get back into the habit of cooking again."

"This is fine," Caleb said gruffly. "Trust me, anything home-cooked is better than what I've been eating."

A peaceful silence fell between them, punctuated by the rattle of cans and spoons. "Your friend Milt was very nice," Rhoda offered cautiously.

"He's a *gut* man, *ja*, but I know he looks scary. I'm sorry he frightened you."

"That was my own silliness." She stirred the green beans and adjusted the heat. "I shouldn't have judged him by his appearance. The story about how you met him, that was true?"

"True enough." The ham was starting to sputter and spit. He moved it around with a fork.

He felt like sputtering himself. He wished Milt hadn't told that story. He could imagine what Rhoda was thinking. Milt's description was accurate enough—Caleb had punched the man. It had been the only way to get him to let go of the woman.

He didn't regret it. He'd done what needed doing. Isaac sure wouldn't see it that way, though, and whatever her father thought, Rhoda thought.

"I'm glad."

Her words took him so much by surprise that they didn't register at first. "What?"

Rhoda's cheeks had turned pink, and she kept her eyes down as she set the table. "I know it's sinful to use violence, but I can't help but be thankful you helped that girl. It would have been more wrong to stand by and do nothing."

"I thought so, *ja*." He studied her, the ham forgotten.

Those were the words he'd been waiting for. The ones he'd prayed to hear—back when he'd still prayed—secretly feeling guilty. It had seemed wrong to pray for his wife to disagree with the church she loved and trusted.

"I'm surprised you feel the same way, though," he added honestly.

She looked up, a troubled defiance in her dark eyes. "I

don't really know how to feel about it," she murmured. "I don't know how to feel about you. I don't know what to . . . do."

Her honesty settled in his stomach like a brick. "I don't know what to do, either," he told her. "I'm not sure what the right answer is for us. Or even if there is one. But I know how I feel about you, Rhoda. That's the one thing that hasn't changed. Not for me."

She took a minute before she answered him. "I can't say that's true for me," she admitted. "You . . . hurt me, Caleb. Worse than anybody has ever hurt me in my whole life. It's hard for me to trust you now, because if I do . . ." She trailed off and cleared her throat. "If I do, there's a good chance you'll hurt me again, by leaving. And the children, too."

"I don't want to hurt you. Any of you." He wasn't sure of much, but he was sure of that.

"Then don't go," she said softly. "Talk to Abram until you can make your repentance in front of the church and mean it. Do whatever it takes to find your way back to us. I don't know how that can happen, but I'm praying you'll find some way to do it. Because—"

He swallowed. "Because what?"

"Because although neither of us knows what to do right now, we both know what the right answer is. We're married, Caleb, and whether our reasons for marrying each other were smart or foolish doesn't matter. What's done is done. The right answer is to honor *Gott* by being true to what we promised."

She made it sound so simple. "Are you telling me you could love me again? That things between us could be like they were before?"

"No." She spoke gently. "I'm not telling you that. I'm not sure things can ever be like they were before, but that doesn't mean they can't be good. And when I said I didn't feel the same about you, I told you it was because I didn't trust you. Not because I didn't love you."

His heart leapt up like a startled deer. "Rhoda—" He moved toward her, but she stepped quickly out of reach.

"You'd best flip that ham there. It's about to burn, and—" A loud banging came from downstairs. They both paused, listening.

It happened again—loud, insistent bangs. The noise, Caleb realized, of a closed fist being knocked impatiently against a locked door.

"Somebody's at the back door," Rhoda said.

"Are you expecting someone?"

She shook her head. "Could it be your friend Milt again maybe?"

"He had business to attend to in Georgia, so I wouldn't think so. Here, mind the ham. I'll go see who it is."

She nodded, her eyes worried. "Be careful."

He smiled. "Trevor's not likely to knock on the door. Likely it's some *Englischer* who just remembered they need a birthday cake tomorrow."

Looking relieved, she picked up the fork he'd set on the counter, flipping the ham over expertly. "If it is Milt, you should invite him to supper. There's plenty to feed one more."

When Caleb reached the door, he paused. The apartment was cramped but bright and clean, and everything was in good repair. Eli and Vonnie played happily on the rug, toys strewn around them. His rosy-cheeked wife worked at the stove, her dark hair smoothed neatly under her kapp, the air smelling richly of food and comfort.

Of home. And love.

Because Rhoda still loved him. She'd said so, straight out. And one thing he knew for certain sure about his wife: She never lied.

Hope and longing crowded into his chest, squeezing it tight. This. This was what he wanted, more than anything, and it was within his reach. The only question was whether or not he was willing to do what it took to have it. To have them.

Just before Milt had left, he'd clapped Caleb on the back. *This here is a real special place, Amish, and it seems to have real special people in it. I'd want to protect them, too, if I was you. But if I had to leave all this behind to do it . . .* Milt had shaken his head. *I can't decide if you're a saint or a doggone fool.*

Caleb turned that same question over in his mind as he went down the steps. Whoever was at the back door was getting impatient. The banging was louder now and more insistent.

Nothing related to a bakery should be this big of an emergency, he thought irritably. But maybe this wasn't related to the bakery. Maybe it was Milt, come back again. The only reason he'd have done that was if he had important news.

The door was solid with no peephole to see out of. He'd change that, Caleb thought. First thing tomorrow. He didn't like opening a door blind, and he should have thought of it before.

"Who is it?" he asked, his hand on the lock.

The banging stopped, and there was a brief silence.

Then an all-too-familiar voice commanded, "Open the door."

Ice washed through Caleb's veins, and his hopeful mood evaporated.

This was not good.

He hesitated, but he had no choice. Bracing himself, he twisted the lock and pulled open the door.

Isaac and Ida Lambright stood outside, suitcases and bags at their feet. Isaac had a key in his hand, and his brows were drawn together in a disapproving frown Caleb recognized all too well.

"Hello, Isaac, Ida," he said evenly.

Rhoda's father flicked a glance over Caleb and tightened his lips.

"We have come to see our *dochder*." Isaac waved away a van that was idling in the alley, dismissing his *Englisch* driver. Then he brushed past Caleb, striding into the bakery kitchen as if he owned the place.

Which, Caleb realized with an unpleasant jolt, he did.

Chapter Twenty-Six

"IT IS VERY SMALL." IDA LAMBRIGHT WALKED BACK into the kitchen, her round face set in worried grooves. "And living right over the bakery? I don't know as I'll like that too well."

"But that makes it easier, ain't so?" Rhoda added plates to the table, trying to guess how well the dinner would stretch to two more people instead of one. "Not far to go in the morning, so I don't have to get up half so early."

"Early rising is a healthy habit." Isaac puffed up the stairs, lugging the last small suitcase. Caleb had brought up the others. He'd set them down in the living room without glancing in Rhoda's direction and then disappeared back downstairs. "This place will do for now, but I will start looking for a house soon."

Ida looked happier. "Maybe we can find one a little ways from town. After spending so much time crowded in with our *kossins*, it'd be nice to have some elbow room. Which bedroom is ours?"

Rhoda bit her lip. This was going to be a problem. "There are only three. The twins are in one, and I have the bedroom across the hall. Caleb's is at the end—"

"We will take that one." Isaac clomped down the hall.

Ida sent Rhoda a sympathetic look but said nothing. She almost never argued with her husband, even when it was clear she disagreed with him.

But somebody needed to speak up, surely.

"*Mamm*, please, would you dish up the dinner? I need to talk to *Daed*." Rhoda hurried down the short hallway, praying that she'd find the right words.

"You have fresh sheets?" Isaac put the case on the floor and gave the room a look-over. "Just set them out. Your *mamm* can fix up the bed after supper."

"I have sheets, but *Daed*, I wish you'd let me know you were coming. I'm real glad to see you and *Mamm*, but we've not made any arrangements."

"About Caleb, you mean?" Isaac shrugged. "He can stay with his brother or one of his sisters. Surely they will make room for him." Her father's tone suggested that he had some doubts about how glad Caleb's family might be to see him, but he obviously considered that his son-in-law's problem.

"I am sure they would, but Abram said he was to stay here. I don't know that we should make changes without checking with him."

"Abram." Isaac's expression made it abundantly clear what he thought about the new bishop's ideas. "I plan to talk to Abram about this matter soon. But for tonight, we will all have to make do."

From the tone in her father's voice, Rhoda understood that the "making do" would be arranged on Isaac's terms, not hers or Caleb's.

"If he won't go to his family," Isaac went on, "he can sleep in my office. It will be easy enough to make a bed for him on the floor there. Tomorrow we can make different plans." Her father nodded at the bedding. "Take the quilt and the pillows down. He might as well eat his supper down there, too."

"But—"

"He is shunned yet, *dochder*, your husband or not, and we will obey the rules in this house. Surely even Abram expects that much." He sighed. "I know it feels difficult, but when you soften the shunning, you only prolong the problem."

As he spoke, her father pulled the quilt and bedding off the bed, wadded it up, and pushed it into Rhoda's arms. Before she could protest, he stacked a pillow on top of it.

"Take it down," he instructed. "Your *mamm* will fix a plate for Caleb while you get everything set up in the office."

Rhoda stood there trying to think, her heart pounding. She didn't like this, but there wasn't anything she could say or do that would make a difference, not tonight.

Isaac and Ida had plenty of friends in Johns Mill, but they couldn't just show up on somebody's doorstep. Besides, there was no getting around the fact that this building, bakery and apartment both, belonged to her father. He had every right to stay here if he wanted.

But Caleb wouldn't like the idea of showing up at his siblings' homes so late in the day, either, although she was sure any of them would welcome him in. And she secretly worried they would think less of her for making their brother go begging for a bed at the last minute.

Finally, she turned without speaking and walked down the hall. The twins, excited to see their grandparents again, were crowded close to Ida in the kitchen, clutching her skirt. All three of them looked up as she passed.

"I'm taking these things downstairs," she said shortly. "I'll be right back."

Ida shook her head and sighed. Then she went back to dishing up the supper. The twins stared after Rhoda, sensing something wasn't right.

"*Daed?*" Vonnie piped up, her lilting voice making it a question.

Rhoda didn't pause to explain because she wasn't sure how to. She'd better figure it out fast, though. As soon as she got downstairs, she'd have to explain it to Caleb.

She found him in the bakery looking out the front window. He turned when he heard her behind him, his gaze dipping to the bedding in her arms.

His expression hardened. "That's for me, I'm thinking."

He sounded neither surprised nor pleased.

"We thought you could sleep in the office," she said. "Just for tonight. It's too late to make other arrangements for my parents. I'm sorry, Caleb. I didn't know they were coming—"

"Wouldn't have mattered too much if you had."

Rhoda's heartbeat sped up. He was already irritated, and things would only get worse when he heard Isaac's suggestion that he eat down here alone, too. It had always bothered him that her father disapproved of their match, and anytime she took *Daed*'s side, Caleb was unhappy—even when she had no choice, like now.

Oh, she wished her parents hadn't come. Or at least that they had waited just one more day. She'd felt so hopeful, just a bit ago, up in the apartment kitchen. When she and Caleb had been talking, she'd felt as if they were finally understanding each other.

Something had shifted in him since Milt's visit. She couldn't put a finger on exactly what. But she knew Caleb, and she was certain she'd seen a difference. She hoped it was because he was seriously considering staying.

Then her parents had shown up, and now, from the mulish look on Caleb's face, he was back where he'd started. Her father had always had that effect on him. She'd often felt like a wishbone, pulled between her *daed* and Caleb, trying to keep them both happy.

She'd never been very successful.

She went into the office. "I'll make you up a bed on the

floor. It won't be very soft, I'm afraid, but I'll do the best I can."

Caleb followed as far as the doorway. "I can do that. I've been managing for myself for a long time."

"Please." Rhoda's voice was thick. That lump of tears was swelling like a summer thundercloud. "Let me do it for you. I want to."

When she looked up into his face, their eyes caught—and held—for one painful minute.

"I'm sorry about this, Caleb," she whispered. "I really am. It's just for tonight."

"Don't fret yourself." He reached to take the bedding from her arms just as she leaned down to set it on the floor. Their hands brushed, making her breath catch in her throat and her heart skitter.

Maybe Caleb felt that, too. His face shifted.

"Rhoda," he started gruffly.

"*Dochder!*" Isaac's voice called from upstairs. "The supper is ready, and your *mamm* has fixed Caleb's plate. Come fetch it and take it down to him before it gets cold."

The warmth in Caleb's eyes cooled. "Don't trouble yourself. I'm not hungry."

"I'm so sorry," she repeated miserably. She was still holding a corner of the quilt, and she worried the fabric between her fingers. "You know how *Daed* is—"

"*Ja*, I know," he muttered. "Just like I know when it comes down to it, you'll choose him over me, every time."

"That's not true! I chose you, Caleb. I married you!"

"You married me, but you never gave me first place in your heart, Rhoda. You kept that for your father. As your husband, that place should have been mine. Even your church teaches that much."

Your church. So, as she'd suspected, they were back to that.

"*Gott* has first place in my heart, Caleb. But you came right after Him. I wish you could believe that."

He studied her. "You know one of the first things Milt ever taught me? Ignore what people say. Watch what they do. That shows you what the truth is and what really matters to them."

"Oh?" That hardly seemed fair. "And if I looked at what you've done—what lesson would I learn?"

His eyes flashed. "That I'll do whatever it takes to protect my family, to keep them safe. And," he added, holding her eyes, "that I don't much care who I make mad, not when I'm doing what I think is right."

"If family matters so much to you, why did you leave?" Tears were getting close, but she wouldn't cry. If she did, Caleb would go silent and awkward. He'd always hated to see her cry. "You couldn't change what happened to your parents, no matter what you did, and the rest of us needed you here, with us. It seems to me what really mattered to you was chasing after Trevor Abbott. And what good has that done? You've never found him, Caleb, not for all your looking. He may never be found, for all we know."

Caleb started to answer, then stopped short, a funny look on his face. Maybe because the tears she was trying so hard to keep back had a mind of their own. One rolled down her cheek, and she knew others were about to follow.

She had to get out of here.

"You never found Trevor," she repeated. "And you've lost so much, Caleb. We've both lost so much." She dropped the corner of the quilt, leaving it in a rumpled puddle on the floor. "You're right. You might as well finish making your own bed," she whispered. "You're the one who's going to have to lie in it."

She left him in the office, shutting the door behind herself with a firm click.

Back upstairs, her parents accepted Caleb's refusal of his dinner—and her reddened eyes—without comment. They sat down together at the table, the little ones pulled up on each side of Ida in their booster seats, just as they'd always done back in Pennsylvania. In fact, as Isaac bowed his head, signaling silently that it was time to pray, Rhoda felt as if nothing had changed at all.

She kept her head down, but she was too upset to focus on her gratitude for the food in front of her. She picked at her supper, trying to eat enough to keep Ida from commenting on her lack of appetite. Although for once, Ida might not have noticed. She was too overjoyed to be with her grandchildren again, laughing and talking with Vonnie and Eli while she helped them with their suppers.

The twins were happy, too. Even Eli beamed at his grandmother, and he ate his green beans without any fuss at all.

Rhoda cut her ham into tiny pieces, hoping she'd be able to swallow them. The meat was a little burnt, likely because she and Caleb had been so busy talking while it was cooking.

As she thought about their conversation, irritation flickered in her heart. Why had her parents shown up just now, today? Why hadn't they let her know they were coming? It would have been easy enough to do. One phone call to the bakery. Of course, she had her own suspicions about why things had worked out this way.

After supper, she and *Mamm* quickly finished up the dishes.

"I'll put the *kinder* to bed," Ida offered eagerly as she rinsed the dishcloth and hung it to dry. "You must be real tired after working all day. But don't worry. I'm here now, and I'll try to help all I can."

"You will be a great help." Rhoda gave her mother a hug. "You always are."

Ida smiled. "Come along, children." She held her hands out, and Eli and Vonnie each took one. "We must get washed up and brush our teeth, and then once you are settled in bed, I will tell you a story."

"Mule?" Eli asked hopefully.

Ida looked at Rhoda, eyebrows raised.

"Caleb's been making up stories for them about a mule named *Schtubbich,*" Rhoda explained.

"A stubborn mule," her father muttered from his chair in the living room. "This he would know plenty about."

"Isaac," his wife reproved softly.

Her husband *hmmphed.*

"Well," Ida said. "I don't know that story, but I can tell you a different one maybe. You must help me think up ideas."

She led the children away toward the bathroom. Rhoda hung the dishtowel in its place. Then she walked into the living room and sat in the chair across from her father.

He glanced over the top of the book he was reading. Then he sighed and closed it, marking his place with one finger.

He didn't seem impatient or irritated, only tired. That was the thing about her father that Caleb had never understood. *Daed* was not a bad man. He had his faults as all folks did, but he was a *gut*, kind father, and when he'd served as a bishop, he'd done his very best.

He and Caleb had never gotten along, but others—many others—had been thankful for Isaac's leadership. Like Sam and Emma, who'd spoken to Rhoda of Isaac's wise advice after Sam's accident.

It had grieved Isaac terribly to give that service up when he'd moved to Pennsylvania. Bishops served for life, as a rule, and he felt he'd failed the community of Johns Mill by leaving. It was a black mark on his conscience and would always trouble him.

But she'd been so ill and in such pain after Caleb had left. Her father had been deeply concerned about her, and so he'd made a very hard decision.

All her life, he'd done everything he could to help her. Now and then, people had hinted that Isaac had a bit of a blind spot where Rhoda was concerned, that maybe he loved her too much because she was his only child. She thought perhaps that was true. That sometimes made things very difficult, but it also made it much easier for her to forgive him and to follow his advice, even when she didn't much like it.

"So," he said now, "what is it you wish to say to me, *dochder*?"

"Why did you come here, *Daed*? Like this, I mean, without letting me know ahead of time. Is it because of Caleb?"

Her father seemed surprised by the question. "*Ja*, of course that is why. It worried me."

Rhoda made herself wait for a second or two before speaking again. "I am not a little girl, *Daed*. And you know my heart. I did exactly what you would have told me to do. I sent Caleb straight to the bishop."

"That you did." Now it was her father's turn to weigh his words carefully. "And while I was thankful you involved him from the start, I'd rather have been here myself. Caleb is a hot-tempered man, and I was concerned about what he might do when he found out about the children."

"He did nothing wrong, but *ja*. He was real upset to start with." Rhoda winced at the memory. "Maybe we should have told him about the twins, *Daed*. Abram wasn't pleased about that being kept a secret. He said Caleb had a right to know, and"—she swallowed, then pressed resolutely ahead—"I think he is right."

Her father raised his eyebrows and digested that bit of information for a moment.

"It is a serious thing to disagree with the man *Gott* has chosen to lead us," he said carefully. "But a man is only a man, and sometimes we make mistakes. Abram's stepson left the church, and I think maybe this makes him soft on those who stray in that way. Shunning is not meant as a punishment but as a lesson, and it is a lesson that loses its teeth when it isn't strictly upheld. Caleb could have known about his son and daughter easily enough if he had come home and humbled himself before *Gott* and his church as he rightly should have done. It is not our business to cushion the hard corners of sin for those who choose that path."

Having spoken his piece, he leaned back in the chair.

"You don't like Caleb."

He father looked surprised by her directness, but he didn't deny it.

"I fear him," he admitted quietly. "I see the damage he can do—to you and to the children. All of us have our weaknesses, those things that can lure us beyond *Gott*'s wise guidelines and into danger. For some, it is money. For others, lust. For Caleb, it is anger and pride. And for you, Rhoda, I think it is love."

She frowned at him, surprised. "But surely love is a *gut* thing, Daed."

"*Nee*." He shook his head. "Love is a *powerful* thing. The goodness of it depends upon its object. A person must be very careful who and what she loves. The love of money, that is evil. The love of *Gott*. That is *gut*."

"And me loving Caleb? You see that as an evil thing?"

"Not evil, no. Dangerous. It is very dangerous for a woman like you to love such a man."

Rhoda frowned. "A woman like me?"

Her father smiled sadly. "You have a strong will of your own, *dochder*. Just look at how you've started the bakery up again, all on your own while caring for two little ones. Not many women could do such a thing. I have seen this strength in you since you were little, and I have done my best as your father to shape and guide it wisely. For you to love such a man as Caleb Hochstedler, a man unwilling to submit his own stubborn will to Gott, this is like lighting a fire in a dry field—things can get out of control very fast. I have seen it from the start, and I have told you this. Even before you married, I warned you as clearly as I could." He sighed. "I wish I had been wrong. I hoped that I was. But I was not wrong, as we see."

"But he's come back." Remembering why exactly Caleb had returned, she hurried on to her next point, before her father could ask any questions. "And more important, he's stayed and met with Abram, just as I asked him to do. And I think—I truly think—he's considering staying."

Her father listened, but his sad expression didn't change. "Caleb I have known since he was a boy, Rhoda, long before you two took notice of each other. He's always been of his own mind, prideful and stubborn. Maybe he wishes to stay more now because of the children. But if he had truly surrendered to *Gott*, there would be no considering. Only doing. The indecision only shows that he is still unwilling to submit his will to *Gott*'s."

Rhoda's heart sank as she listened. There was something in what her father was saying. She didn't want to believe it, but she couldn't deny it.

"So, you think there's no hope?"

"There is always hope," her father said gently. "But the hope *Gott* sends sometimes takes forms we don't expect." He leaned forward, taking her hands in his own. "You have been given great hope, *dochder*. Eli and Vonnie are your hope now, two blessings brought out of sorrow. With Caleb gone, I, too, have been given hope—that my grandchildren will grow up loving and trusting their faith without his poor example to hinder them. I know it is hard for you, and if I could, I would take this cup of bitterness away. But we must all submit to the trials *Gott* sends. Even you."

"Caleb hasn't been a poor example to the children, *Daed*. Not once, the whole time he has been here. He's only been kind to them and loving." Her voice trembled as she remembered. "He could be a good father."

"*Could be* and *will be* are different things." Her father released her hands and sighed again. "A father's first and most important job is to shepherd the souls of his children, but Caleb seems unable to manage his own faith, much less that of his family. You have not listened often to my advice about Caleb. So you likely will not listen to this advice, either, but as a father who cares for his daughter's soul, I will give it anyway. Accept your lot, Rhoda. Be content with the blessings you have been given, and give up hoping for something different. If you don't, I fear you will end up harming not only yourself but your children as well."

Chapter Twenty-Seven

THE NEXT MORNING, CALEB WORKED ON REHANGing a cabinet door in the bakery kitchen, trying his best to tune out Rhoda and Isaac's conversation behind him.

If he didn't, he'd say something, and that wouldn't be a good idea.

Sleeping on the floor downstairs—and mulling over his argument with Rhoda—hadn't made for a restful night. Given his mood, anything he said would likely only make things worse.

"What are you doing, *Daed*?" Rhoda was asking now. Caleb ground his teeth and turned the screwdriver hard.

"Moving these cookies to the bottom shelf of the display case."

"I see that, but why?" Rhoda's tone was respectful, but Caleb heard exasperation hiding underneath the question.

He didn't blame her. She'd been experimenting with the placement of the different baked goods, rearranging them until she hit a winning combination. She'd been so pleased when sales had picked up, and he'd thought it a real smart thing to do.

"That is where we have always kept them," Isaac replied. He'd been rearranging things all morning, and although Caleb could tell Rhoda didn't appreciate it, she wasn't protesting.

He wished she'd stand up for herself. Her father had been making a nuisance of himself ever since Ida had left with Mirry and the twins.

Ida had been disappointed when Miriam appeared to pick up the children to spend the day at her home as planned. She'd been looking forward to spending the day with her grandchildren, but Eli and Vonnie were excited about going with their *aent*. They made it clear they didn't want to stay at the bakery, so his sister had invited the older woman to come along.

"We'll have a real pleasant day together," Miriam had promised cheerfully. "And it'll be nice to have your help with the twins. Many hands make light work."

Ida had happily accepted. And as soon as his wife had ridden away in the buggy, Isaac had begun making his presence felt. He seemed determined to undo every change Rhoda had made since she'd reopened the place.

It was irritating Caleb, but he was biting his tongue and attending to his own work. Rhoda had made it clear last night where her loyalties lay, so there was no point arguing with her about her father. There never had been.

Besides, as soon as he'd heard Rhoda coming down the steps early this morning, he'd come in, hoping to have a word with her alone. A word was about all he managed before her father had followed, but that was enough for him to see the difference in her.

Whatever Isaac had said to her last night had done the job. Rhoda was back under her father's thumb. Fresh wariness filled his wife's eyes whenever she looked his way.

He wanted to pull her aside and talk to her alone until that look ebbed out of her eyes again. He wanted to find some way to set things back to where they'd been before her father had elbowed his way back into their marriage.

No chance of that. Not right now anyway. They were all too busy.

The bakery was buzzing—lots of *Englischers* coming in. The upcoming movie release was already drawing curious people to Johns Mill. Caleb's carpentry work was in the kitchen, but he made frequent passes by the doorway, keeping an eye on the crowd.

It was about time to take another look. He finished screwing the hinge in place and tested it. It worked to his satisfaction, so he walked to the doorway behind the counter.

Rhoda stood there alone waiting on a line of customers. To his left, Caleb could see Isaac in the office rummaging through his old desk.

He felt a flash of annoyance. The only *gut* thing about having Isaac on hand was that Rhoda didn't have to work out front by herself. A man's presence deterred some of the worst nonsense, although not all of it. Isaac looked less sturdy than he had in the past, but he could have pulled a chair behind the counter and sat there. Instead, Rhoda's father had left her to fend for herself.

Nobody was taking this seriously enough. Milt suspected that Trevor's plan to surrender to authorities was a smoke screen for something else. What, he'd admitted, he didn't know. But it smelled fishy, he'd said.

Caleb had learned to pay attention to Milt's instincts. For the time being, he planned to stick as close to Rhoda and the children as he could.

Even if it meant bunking on a floor and putting up with his in-laws.

Maybe he could find something out front that needed a bit of carpentry work. The frame around the big window looked damaged along the bottom. If he took his time, he could spin out fixing that for most of the working day. Then he'd be on hand if anyone stepped out of line.

"Why have you moved everything?" The middle-aged *Englisch* lady at the front of the line sounded annoyed. "The cookies are hard to see way down there. Some of us can't bend over too well, you know."

"I'm sorry," Rhoda said. "We're trying some new things. I know it is hard when you're used to seeing everything in a certain place."

His wife, Caleb reflected, was a much nicer person than he was. And her patience paid off. The older woman looked mollified.

"I guess I don't need to see them. I already know what I like. I'll have a dozen snickerdoodles and a dozen oatmeal raisin cookies."

Caleb watched as Rhoda filled the order. The *Englisch* lady wasn't the only one who had to bend over so far. Rhoda did, too, and cookies were her biggest sellers. Her back would be aching by the end of the day.

"Here." He stepped forward. "This lady is right. It is much harder to see the cookies on the bottom shelf." Without waiting for permission, he slid out the metal trays of cookies, setting them on the counter. Then he scooted the loaves of bread down in their place, where Rhoda had put them to start with.

"Caleb." Rhoda's glance strayed toward the office. Isaac was frowning from his desk chair.

"What are you doing?" he called in *Deutsch*.

"Moving things back where they belong," Caleb responded pleasantly. He smiled at the customer, who smiled back.

"That's much better," she said. "You know what? I forgot about those wonderful chocolate chip cookies with the pecans. Give me a dozen of those, too. My grandchildren are visiting, so I want plenty on hand."

While Rhoda added the cookies to the lady's box, Caleb inspected the window frame. It didn't need replacing, after all, but the bottom piece was badly scratched. Refinishing that would give him a good excuse to be in the front today.

"I need wood stain and sandpaper," he announced. "I'll be back in a minute."

"I would speak to you before you go." Isaac was standing at his office door.

Caleb barely glanced at him. "I'd really like to get this job started."

Isaac lowered his brows, and Rhoda made a soft, anxious noise. She shot Caleb a pleading look, then forced a smile as she handed the box of cookies to her customer.

"Have fun with your grandchildren," she said. "Next?"

"Caleb," Isaac insisted sternly.

Caleb recognized the tone in his father-in-law's voice. He'd heard it dozens of times over the years, and it always meant the same thing. He was in trouble.

He set his jaw. Fine. If Isaac wanted to talk, they'd talk. He walked into the office, and Isaac shut the door behind him.

"If this is about me moving those cookies, you should trust your daughter's instincts. She placed them on the top shelf for a reason. They've sold better ever since."

"It is not about the cookies. It is about you." Isaac sank into the chair behind the desk. "Why are you hanging around here?"

That, Caleb reflected, was a loaded question. He answered with one of his own. "Where else should I be?"

"Talking to your bishop. Or rather, listening to him. You should be preparing your heart to make your confession, not fiddling with odd jobs. That is," Isaac went on, "if you plan to stay in Johns Mill and do right by my daughter and my grandchildren. Do you?"

Caleb set his jaw. "When I've made my plans, I'll let you know. Is that all?"

Isaac's expression darkened. He opened his mouth, but before he could speak, there was a hurried knock on the door. Rhoda cracked it open.

"Caleb?" Her eyes were wide, and her voice sounded strained. "There is—someone here asking for you. *Daed,* I think you'd best come, too." It's—"

"Stephen Abbott," the voice boomed behind her. "Mr. Hochstedler, could you come out here, please? I'd appreciate a word with you."

For a second, Caleb froze. As he started for the door, Isaac grabbed his arm.

"No good will come from losing your temper with this man. Best you don't talk with him at all."

"Oh, I'll talk with him." Caleb was at the door in two strides.

"Please," Rhoda whispered as he passed. "Be careful. He's brought along a reporter and another man with a camera."

Sure enough, a reporter and a cameraman stood beside Trevor's father.

"Go in the office and shut the door," he murmured to Rhoda in *Deutsch*. "And don't come back out until I say."

"Please," she said again. "Don't."

Caleb nudged her toward the door. "Do as I ask," he said gently. "There's no reason for you to be in the middle of this."

He turned to face Stephen Abbott. The attorney was smirking, clearly pleased with himself.

"If you want to talk to me, turn off that camera," Caleb said.

"I understand." Abbott raised his hand in a conciliatory gesture. "You folks don't like cameras. I apologize. These gentlemen want to get some footage prior to the release of the movie. And I'm sure you'll understand why I'd want to make sure that our conversation isn't . . . misrepresented in any way."

"Lied about, you mean," Caleb answered bluntly. "Well,

I'm not the liar in this room, Mr. Abbott. You are. You've been lying for over two years."

The group of customers swiveled their heads back to Abbott, their faces rapt.

"Caleb." Rhoda's desperate murmur came from behind him. She hadn't done as he'd asked, he realized with some irritation.

The attorney's smirk stayed in place, but there was a dangerous flicker in his eyes. "Rein in that famous temper of yours, Mr. Hochstedler. Not only are you upsetting your wife, but as an attorney, I'd advise you not to make inflammatory accusations without solid proof to back them up. Besides"—he raised his voice—"I'm here as a gesture of goodwill. I've been offered an advance screening of the movie *Plain Desperation*, and I want to personally invite you and the rest of your family to see the film with me."

"That we cannot do." Isaac answered before Caleb could. "We thank you for the invitation, but our faith prohibits going to see films."

Caleb clenched his jaw. He wished Isaac would stay out of this.

"That's a shame." Abbott turned to the group of gaping observers. "This movie will reveal the truth about what really happened in Johns Mill that tragic December morning. I hope you'll all go see it when it releases."

"We know what happened," Caleb said. "We've always known, because my sister was standing right beside my parents when your son shot them."

Isaac made a warning noise behind him. *Be silent*, his father-in-law was telling him.

"Your sister Miriam. Yes." The lawyer pulled a long face. "Poor girl. I believe she's since suffered a nervous breakdown, isn't that so? Not a very reliable witness unfortunately."

As Caleb took a step forward, he felt Rhoda grab his

arm, clamping on tight. He stopped short, unwilling to shake off her hand.

Stephen Abbott lifted a brow. "Temper, temper, Mr. Hochstedler. I assure you, I only want to see our community healed and this tragedy put behind us. There's more than one side to this story. The rest of your family understands that. Your brother and your sisters have offered their forgiveness to my family and their support to this film."

"Another lie. They have offered forgiveness because the church gives them no choice. But they have never supported this movie."

Abbott clucked his tongue in mock sympathy. "You've only recently returned home. Maybe you haven't had the time to talk to them. Your twin sister, Emma, met with the screenwriter of the film herself. Your other sister, Miriam, has met more than once with the actress portraying her in the movie, and her husband, your brother-in-law, worked for the film company, caring for their horses. You yourself witnessed your father-in-law, the bishop, and your brother Joseph welcoming my wife and me to your home the day of your parents' funerals. It meant a great deal to us that they understood so well that we, too, were victims. You are a son who has lost his parents, and we are parents who have lost a son."

Caleb gently removed Rhoda's fingers from his arm. She pleaded with him in breathless *Deutsch*, but he ignored her. He walked around the counter and had the satisfaction of seeing Stephen Abbott take a couple of steps backward.

"You've lost nothing," Caleb stated flatly. "Your son is alive, and you know exactly where he is. You've known all along."

Satisfaction dawned in the older man's eyes, and Caleb knew—just a second too late—that he'd been duped.

"Sadly, that's not true. I haven't known where my son was. I do, however, know exactly where he will be." The lawyer turned toward the crowd. "This morning my son reached out to me for the first time since he disappeared over two years ago, afraid for his life."

A collective gasp went up from the group.

"He wanted me to contact our local sheriff because he plans to turn himself in to the authorities. Hopefully this entire situation will soon be resolved."

The crowd erupted into a cacophony of noise, and the reporter, who'd been standing by silently, stepped up, his face alight with amazement.

"Trevor's turning himself in?" The young man pulled out a phone and began pressing buttons. "We've got to get this on tonight's broadcast."

"Caleb," Rhoda's voice came from somewhere behind him. "Did you hear him? Trevor's giving up! It's over. It's finally over."

Caleb didn't look in her direction. He was watching Stephen Abbott the way he'd watch a rattlesnake.

"He's twisting the truth." Abbott wasn't the only one who could speak loudly enough to be heard. "He didn't hear from his son just this morning. Like I said, he's been in touch with him all along. A friend of mine, Milt Masterson, had already heard about this stunt they're planning and told me about it."

"What?" The new note in Rhoda's voice made him turn. Her face was drained of color, her brow crinkled. "Milt told you Trevor was turning himself in?"

"Yes. This is some kind of spectacle, Rhoda, timed to go along with the release of the movie."

"But you *knew*?" Rhoda seemed to have forgotten the people in the bakery. Her eyes were fixed on his, hurt and disbelief in her expression. "You knew about this, and you didn't tell me?"

Behind him, he heard Stephen Abbott tsk his tongue. "Seems pretty clear who's the one hiding things. So sorry, ma'am. I'll be happy to talk to you if you'd like. Fill you in on the details I know."

That did it.

"You'll not speak to my wife." Caleb rounded the corner of the counter. The people crowded around Abbott scattered like cockroaches. The lawyer backed up again, but he wasn't quick enough. In three seconds, Caleb had him by the collar and one arm, walking him forcefully out of the bakery.

He kicked the door open with one boot and propelled the lawyer through it. He didn't shove hard, but Abbott went down in a heap on the sidewalk.

Caleb was suddenly conscious of all the phones pointed in his direction.

"No, no," Trevor's father protested as people hurried to help him up. "I'm all right, just a little bruised. My own fault. My family knows all too well how some of these Hochstedlers react when you speak to one of their wives—or one of their daughters. Obviously this visit, well intentioned as it was, wasn't a good idea. I apologize."

His tone was rueful. Regretful. Almost humorous. But as he turned away from Caleb to face the camera, triumph shone in his eyes.

Chapter Twenty-Eight

THAT AFTERNOON ABRAM KING LISTENED TO ISAAC'S description of what had happened, a frown deepening on his face. He set his fork on the apartment's kitchen table next to his cinnamon roll. He'd taken only two bites, proof that he was deeply troubled.

"This," he said, "is not *gut*."

"Not *gut*? It is sin. It is violence." Isaac spoke firmly, without glancing at Caleb.

Caleb studied his father-in-law's disapproving face, then his gaze slid to Rhoda. She sat miserably beside her father, her hands folded in her lap. She wouldn't look at him, either.

His chest tightened. This felt familiar.

"What have you to say, Caleb?" Abram asked.

He cleared his throat. "I lost my temper. I shouldn't have. But I did, and I'm sorry."

Abram nodded, and Caleb saw something in the bishop's eyes—the last thing he'd expected to see.

Approval.

But before Abram could speak, Isaac made an impatient noise.

"You should certainly be sorry. The question is, are you sorry enough? To me, this behavior today is evidence that your heart has not changed. That should surprise no one since you've spent so much time out among the *Englisch*. Do you know what he has been doing?" The question was directed at Abram. "He has been working with a man who tracks down other men for money. My *dochder* has told me this."

"I know." Abram's voice was calm, but Caleb noticed the tiniest hint of irritation in the other man's plump face. Could be the bishop was getting a little tired of Isaac, too. "Caleb has told me this himself."

"Then you must surely see that this man's shunning was well justified."

Abram cleared his throat carefully. "What I see is that mistakes have been made."

"A mistake? He put hands on this *Englischer* and threw him down on the sidewalk. In front of cameras, no less." Abram shook his head emphatically. "He cannot be allowed to live among us like this when he shows no signs of repentance. Not in a home with young children. Think of the influence he will have upon them and the tragedy he might bring down on their souls. It cannot be allowed."

Abram let a few seconds of silence pass before he spoke. "I have heard you, Isaac. Perhaps now it would be better if Caleb and I talked privately."

Isaac didn't look happy about this suggestion, but he rose to his feet. "Come along, Rhoda," he said. "Work is the best answer to trouble. We will go downstairs and reopen the bakery."

"That's not a good idea," Caleb protested quickly. "After what's happened, there'll be likely more reporters coming by, asking questions."

"Thanks to you, *ja*. I'm sure there will be. But we will not be answering them. Some of us know how to behave." With that parting shot, Isaac shepherded Rhoda toward the steps.

"Rhoda," Caleb said desperately. She hesitated, looking over her shoulder at him, her face troubled. Abram cleared his throat.

"Let your *fraw* go downstairs and work with her father. There will be no more disturbances today, most likely, so long as you keep yourself out of sight. Stephen Abbott has done what he wished to do."

Surprised, Caleb shifted in his chair to face Abram. "You think so, too? That this was all some game he was playing?"

"I think it was planned, *ja*. But if it was a game, then you lost it, along with your temper. Surely, you see this."

Caleb blew out a breath. "I do see it. Now."

"So does everyone else. I have been told that a video of this has been played on the news and that many people are watching it on the internet. You do not come off so well, and there is growing sympathy for Trevor and his father."

"Which is exactly why Stephen Abbott came here to bait me in front of the cameras."

"He knew how you would respond, and you did not disappoint him." Abram studied him, his brow wrinkled. "I could talk, maybe, about the dangers of losing control of your temper. But I expect you have heard such things before, many times, so I think I will save my breath."

The bishop looked tired, and Caleb shifted uncomfortably in his chair. He hadn't disappointed Stephen Abbott, and that fact made him mad. But he *had* disappointed Abram, and that . . .

That bothered him a good deal more than he would have expected.

"Losing my temper was a *schtupid* thing to do, I admit

that. But it was all staged, him coming here, inviting us to that movie when he must have known Plain people don't go to movies. Although maybe one of us should go."

Abram considered him thoughtfully. "That is not allowed."

"How can we deal with the lies in that movie if we don't even know what they are?"

"We are not supposed to deal with them. We are not to take any notice of them at all."

"The rest of the world is certain sure going to take notice, and we'll have to deal with what happens when they do. We should be able to defend ourselves. That's more important than following a set of ridiculous rules."

"Those ridiculous rules are the best defense we have right now." Abram spoke with an unusual sharpness. "The guidelines in the *Ordnung* are like a fence surrounding us," the bishop went on more calmly. "You grew up on a farm, ain't so? You should see this easily enough. What is the purpose of a fence?"

"To keep animals penned in. But men are not animals."

"Are we not?" The bishop raised an eyebrow. "You have spent enough time in the world to know that men often behave like animals. Worse, even."

Caleb couldn't argue with that, so he kept silent. The bishop continued, "A fence is built to keep the animals safe, *ja?* To keep them where there is food, water, and shelter and the care of an overseer. But it also serves to keep danger out."

Caleb tamped down his impatience. Joseph had said something similar. That he saw the rules as a protection, keeping danger out and goodness in. "Maybe so. But fences are not enough by themselves. When there's danger, they must be guarded."

"This is so. And for now, for this time and in this place, *Gott* has seen fit to make that my job. To guard these fences." Abram rubbed his temples. "Why, I do not know.

I feel ill-suited to such a task, and many people share that opinion. Your father-in-law, for instance. He thinks I have failed to act wisely in dealing with you and his daughter, and I am not sure he is wrong. It is well known I have a soft heart when it comes to prodigals. Maybe too soft. I hoped that, given enough time and enough kindness, your heart would change. But hopes are like soap bubbles. They can only last so long. If they aren't replaced by something more solid, they burst into nothing."

Soap bubbles? Caleb shifted irritably in his seat. "You're not making much sense."

"Probably not." Abram smiled sadly. "I'm stepping around the truth as if it was a fresh cow pat, but you're the only man in the community who would tell me so. Well," he amended, "except for your father-in-law. You two have more in common than you think."

"Since we're being honest, I'll tell you I hope you're wrong about that."

"Isaac has drawn a hard line with you," Abram conceded. "Harder most likely than he normally would, because he's protecting his daughter and his grandchildren. We all have our blind spots, especially when it comes to those we love. Still, Isaac is a wise man, and I respect his opinion."

"You'd do better respecting your own opinion. You're a better bishop than he ever was."

Abram chuckled. "Taking your opinion about Isaac—or bishops in general—is like asking the cat's opinion of the dog. The truth is, while I trust the Lord's wisdom, I can't help but believe that other men would be far more effective in this job than I." He cocked his head and considered Caleb. "You, for instance, would make a remarkable bishop."

"Me?" Caleb sputtered a disbelieving laugh. "Are you trying to make a joke?"

One side of Abram's mouth crooked up in a smile. "*Nee*, I am not joking. You've been given a strength of will that is rarely seen, and you want to use that strength to fight for goodness and protect those you love. All this is *Gott*'s good purpose for you, and fine qualities for any church leader to have, if coupled with self-control."

Caleb lifted an eyebrow. "I don't think I would go around saying that if I were you. You're not likely to find many who agree with you."

"Time will tell," Abram answered. "Perhaps they—and you—will be surprised one day. *Gott* has great need of such men, given the world we live in. Men who stand up for what is right, no matter the personal cost. Men"—he winked—"who will guard the fence well. Of course, there is a cost. Such a man will have a hard time submitting his will, even to *Gott*. But . . ." The older man leaned forward and tapped his finger on the desk, punctuating each word as he spoke it. "Submission. Is. Necessary." He leaned back in his chair. "A man's greatest strength is always also his greatest weakness. What *Gott* wishes to use for His purposes, the enemy will always try to turn to his own. It is up to you to prevent that by following the Lord as faithfully as you can."

Caleb studied him silently, turning over the idea in his mind. Him as a bishop—or in any sort of church leadership—that was laughable. But his mind went back to what Milt had said about this place being special. Set apart. A haven, kept clean and good. Well worth sheltering and protecting.

Maybe there was something to what Abram was saying.

"Do you know what wonders me?" the bishop asked.

"What?"

"Not once have you spoken of Stephen Abbott's news—that his son is turning himself in." The bishop cocked his head sideways, studying Caleb thoughtfully. "It seems to me that not the movie nor the reporters would be first in your thoughts just now."

"I'm not sure it will actually happen."

Abram shrugged. "Who can be sure of anything? Still. You have paid a high price, it seems to me, trying to bring this to pass. Now it is possible the day has come. It wonders me that this is not giving you more satisfaction. If," he went on, "bringing this man to justice was as important to you as it seemed to be." He waited a second. "Does it trouble you that you had no hand in bringing this about? That you did not have a chance to deal with this young man yourself? Because if so, it was not justice you were seeking but vengeance. Or does it worry you what people will say—that your efforts and all the pain you have caused—have been wasted? Because that has more to do with pride than with justice for your parents."

Caleb didn't like these questions. He wasn't sure how to answer them, and he didn't want to think too closely about them, either.

"I don't trust Trevor or his father," he said.

"You don't trust. *Ja*." The bishop heaved a sigh. "What a man chooses to trust and not to trust can be a problem. You did not trust the church's judgment in this matter. They advised prayer and forgiveness and going on with your life. You leaned on your own understanding. Now—if Trevor does turn himself in as planned—it will seem that your way was no better than ours. And yet it cost you—and your wife—a very high price."

Caleb surveyed him with narrowed eyes. "Is this an 'I told you so' speech?"

"It is an observation. Sometimes *Gott* allows us to do what we want so that we learn a lesson. About Him. And also about ourselves and the costs of following our own will. It is a hard way to learn, but"—Abram shrugged—"it can be effective. If we allow it to be." He rose to his feet with a grunt of effort. "The Lord is a much better teacher than I, and He has given you plenty to think about. Once you've settled these questions in your own mind, come find me and we will talk again. In the meantime, I will be praying for you and for your family. And also," he added quietly, "for Trevor Abbott and his."

Silently Caleb followed Abram down the steps, letting the bishop out the back door. He glanced toward the store area. Rhoda and her father were both behind the counter, although there were only a couple of customers lined up.

Rhoda looked over her shoulder and caught his eye. She murmured something to her father, who frowned. For once she ignored his protests, walking quickly toward Caleb.

"We need to talk," she said.

He sighed. *Ja*, he supposed they did. "Upstairs?"

Rhoda cast an apprehensive look toward her father's back. "Maybe better someplace else where we won't be so likely to be interrupted. *Daed*," she called, "I'm taking a short break. I'll be back in a little while."

She took Caleb's arm and drew him out the back door before her father could argue. Once outside the building, she hesitated as if unsure where to go.

"Let's walk down and check on Maude," Caleb suggested. The road to Edna's farm was one they'd walked many times together.

Rhoda nodded. "All right."

Caleb took the spot on the inside of the quiet two-lane road so that she wouldn't be near the traffic. Not that there was likely to be much, and mostly buggies anyhow.

He glanced at her face. Something about her expression made him decide to bide his time and let her speak first. It took her longer than he thought it would. They were nearly to the farm before she spoke.

"Why didn't you tell me Trevor was planning to turn himself in?"

Caleb smothered a sigh. "Abram wanted to know the same thing. Neither of you have wanted to listen before when I talked about Trevor."

Rhoda had been watching her feet during the entire walk, but now she slanted a sideways glance at him.

"That's not the reason," she stated.

No, it wasn't. Caleb looked across the green fields, bright and cheerful in the midday sun.

"I wasn't sure what to tell you," he said. "I don't trust this. I think Trevor's up to something and so does Milt. I don't believe he'll go through with it."

She stopped in the road, gazing over the fields. An oak tree overhead dappled her with the shifting shadows of its leaves. Even in the shade, he could make out the fine lines around her eyes, lines that hadn't been there when they'd walked this road together in the old days.

She took a deep breath. "I will tell you what I think. I think maybe deep down you don't want Trevor to turn himself in because chasing him has distracted you from grieving for your parents. And because it's given you the chance to do what you truly wanted."

He started to argue but reined himself in. He needed to step very carefully. "What is it you think I truly wanted, Rhoda?"

"To leave." She seemed surprised by the question. "Not to be Plain anymore. I think you always wanted that, Caleb. Everybody expected you'd leave one day, even your own parents."

He supposed that was true. "But then I fell in love with you. If Trevor hadn't killed my parents, I'd have stayed, Rhoda."

"Maybe you would have stayed," Rhoda said. "But would you have been content?"

He'd wondered himself how happy he could have been living Plain for the rest of his life. He'd wondered it more than once.

"I don't know. I only know I was very happy with you," he said.

Rhoda was still gazing over the rolling pastures, but he didn't think she was seeing them. She was deep in her own thoughts.

"Happy comes and goes," she said after a minute. "It's contentment that lasts. I think if you'd truly been content, you wouldn't have left after your parents died. Sorrows come to everyone, Caleb. Look at my own parents, praying over and over again for more *kinder* but never having anyone but me."

"You were enough."

"For them maybe. But I was not enough for you. I always feared I wouldn't be. And in the end, I wasn't. Not enough to keep you anyhow."

"That's not true, Rhoda." He needed her to believe him. "This was never about how I felt about you. I struggled to square up my beliefs with the church, but I never struggled with loving you."

"It was the wrong kind of love, then. Love should be such a strong and happy thing. Marriage is supposed to be a blessing. I know it takes work and compromise and all that. But it's meant to be a comfort and a joy to both people. Ours . . ." She shook her head, and for the first time her face crumpled. "Didn't work out that way," she whispered.

"That was my fault, not yours."

"I believed that for a long time," she admitted. "That if you'd been honest about your doubts at the start, things would have been better for both of us. But this morning I've been thinking about that advice Milt gave you."

"What advice?"

"If you want to know the truth, don't listen to what people say. Watch what they do. You've been telling me the truth from the start, Caleb, without exactly meaning to. You told everybody the truth all along. We just didn't want to hear it." She finally looked up at him then. "I've blamed you for hurting me. For leaving. Everyone has. My parents, our friends, even your own family has felt you did wrong. But you were not the only one at fault."

"If you mean because you didn't tell me about the twins—"

"That was wrong, but I'm talking about before. You made a big mistake when you joined the church just so I could marry you. But"—she took a breath—"I made mistakes, too, because deep down in my heart I knew that's what you were doing. I was even proud, thinking I was bringing you into the church. That was wrong, but I told myself it would be all right because I loved you so much, and I believed you loved me."

"I did. I do."

"My father also made many mistakes, and it's true, I shouldn't have listened when he cautioned me not to tell you about our babies. I'm sorry about that."

"Rhoda—"

"But," she went on resolutely, "he was right about one thing. I thought that our love could fix everything, but *Daed* knew better. It can't, Caleb. I built my love for you on the way you made me feel when you looked at me, on how handsome you were, and how brave. Sweet things, but the wrong things to build a marriage on. Faith is what builds strong families, Caleb. A shared faith in *Gott* has to come first. Then the faith in each other. The church had it right all along. We're the ones who got it backwards."

The quiet sadness in her voice made him want to assure her that he could find some way to change that—to change himself. But that's what he'd done before, and it sure hadn't worked out so well. So instead, he asked a question.

"What do we do about it?"

Rhoda drew in a long, slow breath. "I think first we forgive each other. Then we find some way to live our lives so that our children don't suffer too much for our mistakes." She looked up at him. "That may be hard because you and I are very different people. But I know this. You are not an easy man, Caleb, but you are a fair one. You will not hurt us more than you can help. I will try not to hurt you, either, nor blame you for being the man that you are. If you can't live Plain, I'll accept it. We'll figure out some way that you can see the children and be a part of their lives."

"Your father won't like that idea."

"It will not be his decision to make." She spoke simply but firmly, and he found that he believed her.

Isaac, he realized, would likely not be getting his way half so often with his daughter in the future. He couldn't help feeling a little satisfied about that.

"But, Rhoda, you know, if I don't stay . . ." He left the sentence unfinished. They both knew what sort of a life that would leave for her.

She didn't flinch. "If you go, I will trust my community and my faith to meet my needs, and I'll learn to be content with the blessings *Gott* has given me. That will be good enough."

His heart was twisted up inside him, hurting so much that he couldn't think straight. It sounded like she was giving up on them, and he hadn't realized until this moment how much it had meant to him that she hadn't closed the door on their marriage. That her faith had kept her hoping for his return, no matter what he'd done or how much he'd hurt her.

"You deserve a lot better than just good enough," he managed.

She didn't smile, but there was a gentleness in her eyes. "You do, too. So when Trevor Abbott turns himself in a day after tomorrow, Caleb, go to the courthouse. See the end of this for yourself. Then you can start grieving for your parents maybe, instead of fighting for them. Afterwards, I'd like you to do something for me."

Anything. He'd do just about anything she asked him for right now. "What?"

"Ask yourself if you can live Plain with all your heart.

Not just the piece that belongs to me and the children. But all of it. When you know the answer to that question for certain sure, then we will talk again." She patted his arm. "Now you go check on Maude. I think I will walk back to the bakery. It's too busy to leave *Daed* working too long on his own. He's still not fully well. Besides," she added with a little laugh, "he doesn't do things the way I like them."

"I'll walk back with you."

"*Nee*, I will be all right." She reached out and squeezed his arm gently. She'd done the same thing the day of his parents' funerals, comforting him with a touch, reminding him that she was there. "I will be all right, Caleb," she repeated. "You don't have to worry."

She left him standing under the old tree and walked down the road toward the bakery. She didn't look back.

Chapter Twenty-Nine

ON FRIDAY MORNING, TREVOR WAS SUPPOSED TO ARrive at the courthouse around ten a.m., but a line formed on the sidewalk outside Lambright's Bakery well before they opened at seven. The waiting customers were all *Englischers,* and vans with brightly painted media logos lined the main street of Johns Mill.

It reminded Rhoda of those awful days after the shootings, only without the numbing bewilderment of grief and shock. At least they had plenty of experience with reporters now, so they weren't so *naerfich.*

They couldn't afford to be. There was too much to do.

Rhoda's mother was keeping an eye on the twins upstairs while Rhoda, her father, and their two helpers, Edna and her granddaughter, Cora, worked furiously in the kitchen, their gloved fingers sticky with dough and icing. As the sun rose behind a sullen mass of clouds, the crowd swelled outside, and the kitchen air grew overly warm, heavy with the scents of cinnamon, coffee, and baking bread.

Caleb was fixing the window frame in the front of the bakery, sanding it and painting on the stain. Rhoda's father cast irritated looks in his son-in-law's direction and made remarks about the smell of varnish bothering customers.

Caleb ignored him. Rhoda knew why he'd chosen to finish this job today. He wanted to keep a sharp eye on the crowds and all the activity outside.

They hadn't talked much since their walk. She'd sensed he'd have liked to speak with her alone, but her parents and the twins had made that impossible.

She was grateful. She'd said what she needed to say already. She didn't want to explain everything in her heart again. Once had been plenty hard enough.

"Near time to open," Isaac said, startling Rhoda out of her thoughts. He was filling a display tray with the apple turnovers she'd iced earlier, perfectly browned and with lovely thin drizzles of white icing.

She needed to be focusing on her work, not woolgathering. There was too much on hand. But fortunately, things seemed to be moving along well.

Edna was busy baking cookies in the smaller oven. Rhoda had mixed up three tubs of dough—snickerdoodle, cranberry walnut, and chocolate pecan—and refrigerated them last night. All Edna had to do was scoop it out and bake it. Edna appeared delighted with her simple task, and it was going well. She was working hard, switching out the cookie sheets with an important air. Her granddaughter, Cora, was handling more difficult tasks nearby, and more than once Rhoda had seen her step in to help when her grandmother began to get muddled.

She would see if Cora could come regularly and try to have the two working at the same time. That would be another problem solved—if she could stop her father from second-guessing her decision. It was convenient to have her parents' skilled help, but she had to admit, she missed the days when she'd been running the bakery on her own.

She squashed that disloyal thought as Caleb poked his head into the kitchen. His face was grim.

"The line outside's at least forty people long," he warned. "And it's mostly reporters."

"They'll be wanting coffee," Isaac said. "And plenty of it. Best pour what's made out there into a carafe and start another pot. You may as well not even bother with the decaffeinated. They never want that. I remember from back at the first, when—"

Her father fell silent, glancing at Caleb, who still stood in the doorway. Rhoda's fingers tightened on the icing bag she was holding, causing a big sugary plop to fall on the cherry turnover she'd been drizzling.

All these reporters crowding around again, the hubbub and the talk and the curiosity. It must rake up all sorts of painful feelings for Caleb. This would be a hard day for all the Hochstedlers.

But hopefully one of the last difficult days. Once Trevor was safely in custody and the excitement about the movie had faded, their world could start to heal again, this time for good.

For the rest of the family, at least.

For her and the twins, so much depended on Caleb's choice. She'd meant what she'd said, though. Whatever her future held, with *Gott*'s help, she would learn to be content with it.

"These are done." Her father straightened, winced, and rubbed his back. "Unlock the door," he instructed Caleb. "They'll be heading over to the courthouse in an hour or so, and we'll need to get them all served before that."

"It's a lot of people," Caleb warned. "I'm still not sure this is a *gut* idea. Sam and Emma have closed for the week."

Rhoda stayed silent. She wouldn't argue, although she didn't think it was the same thing. The store had been the site of the tragedy, and Emma was the girl Trevor had fixated on. Of course they would have to close. The bakery had nothing to do with it.

Besides, once Caleb left to go to the courthouse himself, she'd rather be busy working than sitting around fretting. She wasn't sure what he might do when he saw Trevor in person for the first time since his parents' murders. She'd lain awake half the night praying over it.

Still, she sensed that it was something Caleb needed to do, and she was glad he planned to go.

Isaac cleared his throat. "Caleb is right. We will stay open only long enough to serve the customers waiting. When it gets close to ten, they will go to the courthouse. Then we will close and stay so for the rest of the day."

The busy background noises went silent as everyone in the bakery froze. They exchanged quick, incredulous glances. Isaac was agreeing with his son-in-law?

"We could sell plenty today, *ja*," he admitted, misunderstanding their astonishment. "Usually crowds are *gut* news for business. But there is a great deal of excitement and high feelings just now. When you have those things and many people pushed together, there is often trouble. That we do not need, not for any amount of money. Besides, we are connected to the Hochstedlers by marriage, and today they are not thinking of profit, nor should they be. We will follow their example. We will drive over to Joseph's once we are finished here and spend time with them in prayer for this troubled young man and his family."

Rhoda didn't know what to think. Her father had never agreed with Caleb before. Caleb was looking at her father with the same disbelief she felt herself.

"*Denki*," he said after a moment. "That is kind of you."

"It is what is right to do," her father replied simply. "For the family. Family comes before everything else, except *Gott*."

"*Ja*," Caleb agreed. "That is so."

Isaac gave his son-in-law a short nod. Then he slid the tray of turnovers into the display cabinet.

On the wrong shelf, Rhoda noticed with a rueful smile. But she didn't mind. For once in their lives, her husband and her father had agreed about something.

The minute the door was unlocked, customers poured in. The next few hours were rushed as they served one impatient *Englischer* after another. Rhoda was too busy working to pay attention to much else, but she was aware of Caleb hanging around, out of sight but nearby, keeping an eye on her.

A few reporters tried asking Rhoda and Isaac how they felt about Trevor and the movie, some even offering to show parts of the film on their phones for a reaction. Thankfully, when their attempts were ignored, even the pushiest accepted their coffee and pastries and went on their way.

Fifteen minutes before ten o'clock, Caleb beckoned her father into the kitchen for a quiet conversation. A few seconds later, Caleb slipped through the crowd still waiting in line inside, turned the sign to **CLOSED**, and flipped the lock. His appearance caused a brief flurry among the reporters who recognized him, and several shouted questions.

Rhoda held her breath, but to her relief, Caleb paid them no attention. He elbowed his way back into the kitchen, and a moment later Cora appeared. She stationed herself at the door, unlocking it and letting the customers out after they'd collected their orders.

As she finished serving those remaining in line, Rhoda cast a few regretful glances out the window at the latecomers who walked up to check the sign and then wandered away. Missed business was never a happy thing. But her father was right, and she was ashamed she hadn't seen it for herself.

This was not a day to focus on profits. Today was a solemn day, a day when a man who'd caused a tremendous amount of hurt would finally step up to accept the consequences for his actions.

Cora let the last customer out of the door just as Caleb walked back into the kitchen. Rhoda caught her breath, her heart sinking. He was dressed *Englisch*, in the shirt and jeans he'd worn the first day back.

"I guess I'll be going," he said.

"You'd be better off staying here," Isaac muttered. "No good will come of you going to that courthouse. Your feelings are already stirred up. Likely someone will try to bait you into losing your temper again so that they can make a story out of it."

"I'm going." Caleb's tone was firm but polite. "I won't be talking to anybody, but I need to see this for myself. I changed clothes so I'm not so likely to be noticed." That part seemed more directed at Rhoda than at Isaac, but her father answered.

"You'll be less likely to be picked out of the crowd dressed so, for certain sure. No Plain folks will be there, not if they have the sense *Gott* gave a goose."

Caleb ignored him. "Lock the door after me," he told Rhoda. "And keep it locked. I'm still not sure how this is going to go."

"It will go the way the Lord intends," Isaac stated. "We must all trust in that."

Caleb kept his eyes on Rhoda. "I'll come back here, after," he told her. It sounded like a promise, and her heart lifted just a little.

"I will be here," she said, "waiting for you."

Their eyes connected. For a second she thought he was going to say something else. Then he glanced at Isaac and at Edna and Cora, who were pretending not to pay any attention but not doing such a good job of it. His eyes came back to hers briefly. Then, without another word, he slipped out the back door.

Rhoda's hands shook as she cleaned the kitchen. Edna and Cora left after finishing up a few tasks, leaving her alone with her father.

They worked together in silence as the clock ticked past the hour when Trevor was supposed to surrender. Rhoda felt jumpy and uneasy, and she wished it was all over.

"You have put the vanilla in the refrigerator instead of the cupboard." Isaac removed the brown bottle. "Mind yourself, *dochder*."

"I'm worried about Caleb," she admitted.

Isaac sighed. He looked tired, Rhoda thought. The morning's busy pace had been hard on him. "*Ja*, this I know. I am worried, too. But we cannot save him from his own foolishness."

"This is partly my foolishness, *Daed*. I told him yesterday that he should go see Trevor surrender for himself. I thought he needed to do that, that it might help him to be certain in his mind about what he wants to do next. Now I think maybe it wasn't so wise."

"He would have gone, I think, no matter what you said." Her father looked at her, his expression concerned. "What I said to him earlier is true for you as well. Whatever happens today will be what *Gott* intends. You must be prepared to accept it, just like him."

Rhoda knew that was true, and she'd spent a good part of her restless night praying for the strength to do that very thing. "You and *Mamm* can go ahead on to the Hochstedlers'," she suggested. "Caleb brought Maude over earlier, and she's hitched up outside. I can finish up here by myself, and you'll be better off to get on the road before the business at the courthouse is finished."

Isaac shook his head. "Best you come with us."

Rhoda finished drying a mixing bowl and set it on the worktable beside the sink. Then she turned to face her father.

"*Nee*," she said. "I have told Caleb I will be waiting here for him after this is over, and I will be."

Isaac dismissed this objection with a wave of his hand. "You can write him a note. He will understand, and Joseph, Emma, and Miriam will appreciate your company and your support today. That is where Caleb should be himself, and—"

"But that is not where he has chosen to be." Rhoda took a breath and stood up a little straighter. "Joseph, Emma, and Miriam have each other and their own families and you to help them through this day. Caleb has only me and the twins."

"That is his choice, to separate himself from his family." Her father was frowning at her.

"*Ja.*" Rhoda tilted up her chin. "And this is my choice." She hesitated, but she might as well say the rest of it. She'd been putting this off long enough. "Caleb has done many wrong things, *Daed.* I know this. He knows it, too. He struggles with his temper and his pride and his doubts. He's not a perfect man. But I am not perfect, either."

"Of course not. But, *dochder*—"

"Please." Rhoda's voice was shaking. She'd never interrupted her father before, but this had to be said before she lost her nerve. "Let me finish. I know I answer to *Gott* before I answer to Caleb. And I have tried to do this faithfully. But"—she swallowed—"whatever Caleb has done, whatever he will do, he is still my husband. And I must answer to him before I answer to you."

For a second her father stared at her, his brows drawn together in a worried line. "Rhoda," he began.

That was as far as he got.

"She is right, Isaac."

Ida stood at the bottom of the steps, holding Vonnie and Eli's hands. She looked at her husband, her expression both sad and firm. "It was right and good for us to step in when Caleb was gone. Rhoda needed us. And if he leaves again"—she turned to her daughter—"then we will be here to help you all we can. But he has not left yet. We must not interfere. We must give them space and see what *Gott* will do."

Both of them looked at Ida with surprise. She looked back steadily. "Think, Isaac," she added softly. "Think what you would tell another wife in Rhoda's place, if she was not your own daughter. What you *have* said, many times."

Isaac stared at his determined wife, who so rarely set herself against him. The confidence vanished from his face, and he looked suddenly so old and so uncertain that it tugged at Rhoda's heart.

But still, she was deeply thankful that her mother had spoken.

"All right," he said after a moment. "We will all stay here, then, until Caleb comes back."

"*Nee, Daed.* I don't know how Caleb will be feeling, and he and I will need to talk privately. The Hochstedlers are expecting you, and they will appreciate your company, yours and *Mamm*'s. The twins and I will stay here, and we will see you at suppertime."

For a second, she thought her father might argue, but her mother spoke softly. Just one word.

"Isaac."

He studied his wife for another long second. When he turned back to Rhoda, she held her breath.

"We will see you at supper." To her surprise, he gathered her up into a strong hug.

When he released her, she was blinking back tears, and she thought she saw a suspicious sparkle in his eyes as well.

"Come along," he said gruffly to his wife. "We will get going before all this nonsense is over with and the roads get busy again. That mare of Rhoda's is old and slow, and we'll need plenty of time. Best we start looking for another horse soon. I will talk to Reuben about that this afternoon."

"Whatever you think best, Isaac," her mother said quietly. She glanced at Rhoda, her gaze communicating what she wouldn't say aloud. *I have done what I can for you.* Then she leaned over and gave the twins a kiss each before following her husband out the door.

Rhoda stood in the kitchen for a minute, her heart pounding. Well, thanks to *Mamm*, that had gone better than she'd expected. She turned to the twins with a smile.

"Come on," she said brightly. "You may pick out a cookie each, and then we will go upstairs, and *Mamm* will read you a story while we wait for *Daed* to come back."

The twins were happy with that, and a few moments later they were upstairs in the apartment reading a storybook. They were halfway through when Rhoda heard the door downstairs.

Caleb was back.

She glanced up at the clock, surprised. It was only just past ten. Things at the courthouse must have gone real smoothly for him to be back already. That was a relief. As she heard him starting up the steps, she breathed a silent prayer of thanks—and a plea.

Because now, they would see what Caleb had decided.

She closed the book, her heart pounding. "*Daed* is here," she said. "We will finish the rest of this story later."

As the door opened, she smoothed her hair and tried her best to smile.

Chapter Thirty

LAW ENFORCEMENT OFFICERS MILLED AROUND THE crowded courthouse lawn, barking instructions and herding people away from a small platform that had been erected near the steps of the old brick building. Sweat stains darkened their khaki uniforms. The sky was overcast with threatening, bottom-heavy clouds, and the air was unpleasantly muggy.

Reporters jockeyed for the best positions, testing out their equipment. Men in suits congregated near the front, their faces self-consciously solemn. Caleb suspected they were local politicians, drawn by the cameras like flies to fresh manure.

Stephen Abbott was nowhere in sight, and Caleb wondered if maybe he and Trevor were already inside the courthouse. The doors to the building were blocked off, and people were being asked to show identification before they could enter.

Isaac had been right. There were no Plain people in the crowd at all. Mostly it seemed to be news crews, but there were a few people with posterboard signs leaning against their legs. The signs said things like **FREE TREVOR** and **ABUSE IS PLAIN WRONG**. One declared **TREVOR AND EMMA 4-EVER**. Several, he noticed, bore big photographs of Caleb, his eyes squinted with anger, his mouth open.

No doubt those photos had been taken during his argument with Stephen Abbott. He understood now why Trevor's father had been so delighted when Caleb had lost his temper. He'd given them exactly what they needed.

Disgusted, he looked up at the clock displayed on the small tower at the top of the courthouse roof. Ten minutes after ten o'clock, past time for this to start.

He wanted this to be done. Over. Afterward he planned to take a few minutes and get away by himself, someplace quiet so he could do some thinking, like Rhoda had asked.

He might do some praying, too.

His father-in-law's remark about all this working out as *Gott* intended had stuck with him. The truth was, he'd been thinking about God a lot lately. He'd even done some talking to Him, and while he couldn't say he'd heard any real answers yet, he had to admit, he'd felt . . . something.

What he'd felt, exactly, was hard to describe. The nearest he could come to it was how he'd felt as a *youngie*, when he'd complained to his father about something or someone that had him riled up. He'd pour out his anger and his grievances, and *Daed* would listen silently, often barely speaking at all, usually while he worked on some task in the barn.

Once, Caleb had impatiently asked *Daed* why he wasn't talking back, and his father had looked at him, a weary patience in his eyes.

You're not ready yet to listen to anybody but yourself. When you are, then I'll speak.

Ja, that was the closest he could come to how he was feeling now. As if God was there but silent, waiting for him to be ready to listen.

"Excuse me."

Caleb jumped and turned. A young *Englisch* man with shaggy hair took a quick step backward.

"Whoa. Sorry. Didn't mean to startle you." He stuck out his hand. "Eric Chandler. I'm a friend of Naomi and Joseph's. I have a message for you."

Caleb frowned. *Ja*, he remembered Rhoda telling him something about this fellow. About how an *Englischer* had helped Joseph and Naomi find a way to pay for Naomi's heart operation, the one that had finally given her back her health. She'd said the man was a reporter, but a kind person. When other reporters had made pests of themselves on Joseph's wedding day, this Eric had stood with the other Plain men, using his own body as a barrier to protect the boundaries of the property.

He accepted the offered hand. "Caleb—" he started, but Eric shook his head and leaned in close.

"I wouldn't go saying my name out loud if I were you. This place is crawling with reporters, and if somebody whispers a secret, we can hear it from four counties over." The other man's eyes skimmed his clothing. "Smart to dress like that, though I wouldn't count on it keeping you from being recognized. That video of you throwing Stephen Abbott out of that bakery's gone viral, and it's . . . uh . . . pretty controversial."

"*Ja,* I've seen the signs they're holding up. They seem to think I'm worse than Trevor."

"A lot of them do, yeah. I expect that was the reason Abbott went to the bakery in the first place. People nowadays think with their feelings, and even judges can be afraid to buck strong public opinion. He's stacking the deck in Trevor's favor, best he can."

"And I helped him do it by losing my temper," Caleb said grimly.

Eric didn't disagree. "Don't beat yourself up too much. Abbott's a slick guy, and as a lawyer, he's learned how to push people's buttons to his advantage. But I'd keep my head down around here and stay on the edge of the crowd so you can get away quick if you need to."

He was probably right about that. "You said you had a message? From Naomi and Joseph?"

"I have a message, but not from them. The bishop sent me. He's on the other side of the courthouse, and he wants a word with you."

Caleb sighed. He liked Abram surprisingly well, considering the man was a bishop, but he didn't have time for him today.

Eric must have picked up on his reluctance. "He said to tell you it wouldn't take long. He's on his way to Joseph and Naomi's house himself."

And being an Amish bishop, he assumed that Caleb would jump at his bidding. Which, if he planned to stay here with Rhoda, he'd have to do, for the rest of his life.

That was nonnegotiable—and a sobering thought.

He glanced toward the courthouse. Nothing had changed, except that the clock had ticked another five minutes forward.

"They're running late," Eric explained. "They gave my crew a heads-up just before ten o'clock that there'd be a delay. Said it'd be closer to ten thirty. I don't think you'll miss anything, not if you hurry."

"All right. Thanks."

"No problem. You have a phone?" Eric pulled his out of a pocket. "These delays always run longer than they tell you. If they say half an hour, you're usually looking at an hour at least. But I can text you if they surprise me and get started sooner."

Caleb reached for his jeans pocket. It was flat. Come to think of it, he couldn't remember the last time he'd carried his phone.

"I don't have one with me," he said. "I'll just have to be quick, I guess."

Eric nodded. "Okay. I need get back to my crew. And

listen." The other man seemed to have some trouble working out what he wanted to say. "I know it doesn't help much, but I'm really sorry about what happened to your family. I'm sorry how some of these media people have treated you, and I'm sorry about that stupid movie, too. I went to see it last night. Probably shouldn't have, but I was curious. Now I wish I hadn't gone. It was an embarrassment. Made me want to turn in my car keys, buy myself a buggy, and go Amish." He scanned the crowd. "Honestly, ever since I was here last time, I've kind of wished I could do that, and I'm not the only one. Some stuff would be really hard to give up, don't get me wrong. But what you folks have here . . ." He shook his head. "It's something special."

Caleb wasn't sure how to answer that. He cleared his throat. "I'd best go see the bishop."

"Sure." Eric offered an apologetic smile. "Sorry for rattling on. You probably hear a lot of that wannabe stuff from us *Englischers*. Good to meet you finally."

"You too."

As Caleb walked around the courthouse, he mulled over the conversation. This Eric seemed like a nice man. And like Milt, he was a *gut* friend.

Also like Milt, he seemed to have a sincere admiration for the Plain way of life.

A lot of *Englischers* did. Eric was right. Growing up, Caleb had wondered why. Plain life was hard work and full of rigid rules that made little sense. Who would choose such a thing over the freedom the *Englischers* reveled in?

Before Rhoda, when people made the mistake of commenting on such things to him, he'd set them straight quick. Would they want to muck stalls and sit through hours of church? Would they want to be told what colors they could wear or how much countertop they could install in their kitchens? Would they want to do without their televisions and their air-conditioning and their computers?

His father had overheard him once and later pulled

him aside and given him a talking-to. *Daed* had explained that some *Englischers* felt this way because there was something missing in the lives they had carved out for themselves.

Well, not something. One specific thing.

Daed had been very clear on that. *Unless Gott is at the center of a life, it means nothing. It produces nothing lasting. They sense this, so they think they want to be Plain. But they don't need to live like us. They only need to meet Gott for themselves and follow what He tells them, just as we do. That is job enough and purpose enough for anybody.*

Funny. He'd forgotten *Daed* saying that, although he'd heard variations on that sermon all during his growing-up years. Not that he'd paid much attention at the time.

Now he understood it better. Since he'd spent some time living outside the community, he could see why people like Milt and Eric were drawn to it. Why *Englischers* wanted to be a part of it.

There were a lot of troubles and oddities with Plain life. He'd be the last one to dispute that. But there was something else he couldn't dispute. Those rigid old rules, bulky and ill-fitting as they were, the ones he'd butted his head against for years . . . had done their job.

Not perfectly. And he still thought a few of them could be done away with. But they had held Plain communities together in a shifting sea of change and confusion and wickedness.

He rounded the corner of the courthouse. The back lawn was oddly deserted, only a few people milling about. He scanned the area looking for Abram's round figure, but there was only one Plain man there, standing with his back to Caleb, studying a war memorial, and this man was tall and thin. Definitely not Abram.

He turned, and Caleb blinked, confused.

Isaac.

The bishop, Eric had said. But, of course, when Eric had been here before, Isaac had been serving as bishop in Johns Mill.

A simple mistake but an uncomfortable one. Caleb had been preparing himself for a talk with Abram. A talk with Isaac was a very different thing.

"Caleb." Isaac's forehead was deeply creased, a sure sign that his father-in-law was troubled.

Caleb's heart skipped one painful beat. "Is everything all right with Rhoda and the children?"

Isaac waved away his concern. "*Ja,* they are fine. They are back at the bakery waiting for you. Ida and I wanted them to come with us to your brother's home, where the rest of your family is gathering." He paused, looking uncomfortable.

"She should have gone with you. I don't know how long this is going to take. It's already been pushed back a half hour."

"Rhoda wanted to wait for you. She felt you might want to speak to her privately once this is over with. I was tempted to argue with her, but Ida—" His father-in-law stopped short and sighed. "Marriage is a funny thing."

Caleb lifted his eyebrows, momentarily distracted from his impatience. "Is it?"

"*Ja*. A man must care and provide for his wife and children. We are the heads of our households, and that is a solemn responsibility before *Gott*. The women give us their trust, and we must do our best to lead them well." His gaze came back to settle on Caleb's face. "I have tried to do my part, and Ida has always done hers. Rhoda too. She has always been a *gut* and obedient daughter."

Rhoda had certainly been that, all right. Where exactly was Isaac heading with this? Caleb had no idea, and time was ticking by.

"But sometimes, in my zeal to lead my family well, I forget that *Gott* has given me this woman . . . this particular woman . . . for a reason. And that I should listen to her carefully when she has an opinion, especially when it differs from my own. We would have liked to have had more children, Ida and I. A son, perhaps. We love Rhoda very much, of course. But we had so much room in our hearts . . ." He shook his head. "Ida has always blamed herself for this because of what the doctors have said. But I have told her it was *Gott*'s will for us. Today, Ida helped me to see that maybe one reason *Gott* limited us in this way is because I am not such a wise father."

Caleb stared at his father-in-law, his mind stunned to blankness. He couldn't imagine Ida ever hinting such a thing to her husband. And he certainly couldn't see Isaac believing it.

"When you have only the one child," Isaac went on, "it is hard to let go. To accept that they have grown up and now must answer directly to *Gott*. And of course, in a woman's case, to her husband." He squared his thin shoulders. "Ida asked me to think what I would say to a father in my own position. I have spoken many times to families with strife, and always I said the same thing. Respect each other. Show love and kindness, and remember the guidelines *Gott* has set, the rules that He has put in place so that our families can prosper and be a blessing to each other. But when it came to my own family, I ignored those rules, particularly the one that states that when a couple is married, they must step away from their parents and live a new life together. I think maybe I was one of the reasons you were so willing to leave your church and your marriage. When I realized this, I had to come and speak to you, right away."

"I . . . appreciate that." Caleb wasn't sure what else he could say. He was ill-prepared for this conversation. He'd never expected to hear such things from Isaac.

"I was wrong, and I am sorry," his father-in-law said. "Although I do not think I was wrong about everything."

Ah. This sounded more familiar.

"I did not think you would make a good husband for my daughter. I believed you would hurt her, and so you have. But that choice was not mine to make. Something," Isaac added, sounding a little more like himself, "that you knew quite well. One would think that a man with your strength of will might have made some point of it. If you had done so, perhaps it would not have taken me quite so long to figure it out."

Caleb lifted an eyebrow. "You're saying I should have argued with you? Set my will against yours? The bishop of the community? I'd done that before, and it never got me anyplace but in bigger trouble."

"Maybe you have a point," Isaac considered. "But as I told . . . someone . . . recently, a man is only a man, and sometimes we make mistakes." He looked back up at Caleb. "Ida says I am not always so *gut* at listening, especially not when I have my mind made up. When it came to you, my mind was definitely made up. But," he continued, "now that you are married, your place comes before mine where Rhoda is concerned, and I had no right to step between you, nor to speak badly of you to her. But I did these things." The older man straightened his shoulders. "So I came here to ask for your forgiveness."

Caleb knew the answer to that—the only answer that could be given when someone confessed a wrong and asked for your forgiveness. And there was no doubt that Isaac was sincere. He wouldn't be looking half so uncomfortable right now if he weren't.

"You are forgiven," Caleb said.

"*Denki.*" Isaac looked relieved. "I want you to know that whatever happens between you and Rhoda in the future, I will not be speaking of you disrespectfully. Not to her, nor to the children. It has become a habit, so Ida is going to help me remember."

A habit. Caleb felt a completely inappropriate desire to laugh. He choked it down. "That's good of her," he said.

"She is a good woman," Isaac answered. "And," he added, "so is Rhoda."

"That's true."

"No man can be deserving of such a blessing as a wife like that," Isaac went on. "But that doesn't mean he should not try his best."

"You're right. And I will do that, Isaac." Caleb stuck out his hand. "I will try my best to be a man who deserves Rhoda, even though I know I never can be."

Isaac accepted the handshake. "*Gut.* We have this settled between us. Now I'd best get back to my *fraw.* I left her waiting in the buggy down by Mary Yoder's store. She is likely growing hot and impatient, and I am already in enough trouble for one day." To Caleb's astonishment, his father-in-law winked at him. "Besides, here comes that *Englisch* reporter, looking for you, no doubt. Things must be about to start."

Eric was headed in their direction, walking fast. "I'd better get back there," Caleb muttered.

"I cannot stay longer myself," Isaac said. "As I said, Ida is waiting, and we promised your family we would be there to pray with them, and we are already late. I do not think this is a very *schmaert* place for you or me to be today. Even so, since you are determined to be here, if I could, I would stand with you. I will be praying for you, my son, that this day may bring you some peace."

My son. Isaac had never called him that before. "Thank you, Isaac."

His father-in-law nodded and turned to go. He made only four steps before looking back over his shoulder.

"But for pity's sake, don't do anything *schtupid.*"

Then he strode off down the street, leaving Caleb fighting a smile.

"Hey!" Eric called.

Caleb started in the *Englischer*'s direction. "I'm coming!"

"No need," Eric said, jogging closer. "That's what I came

to tell you. They've canceled the whole thing until further notice."

"What? Why? Because rain's coming? He looked up at the sullen clouds. "It'll storm maybe, but it'll pass soon enough."

"No, it's nothing to do with the weather. I've made a couple of friends on the police force, so I asked around." Eric shot him a wary look. "I'm a reporter, remember. That's what we do. Anyway, turns out there was some sort of glitch. Trevor's dad was supposed to bring him in. That was the deal. No law enforcement until they were at the courthouse."

"In front of the cameras," Caleb said, disgusted.

"Right. But Trevor gave his dad the slip. Mr. Abbott showed up alone, and he's being grilled by the police now. They're about to send the deputies out to sweep the town looking for Trevor. They think he's somewhere close by. Abbott's been pleading with them, claiming his son's on the brink of some kind of psychotic break."

Caleb's heart went cold. That was what Milt had feared. What he said made bad things happen.

And Rhoda was alone at the bakery. And their children were with her.

Caleb took off across the courthouse lawn.

Chapter Thirty-One

"MAKE THAT KID SHUT UP!" TREVOR RUBBED HIS forehead with the butt of his gun as thunder rumbled in the distance. "I can't think with him crying like that."

"Shh." Rhoda drew Eli closer. She and the twins were huddled on the small couch while Trevor paced the apartment.

It had been such a shock when Trevor had walked into the apartment. Her parents must not have locked the back door when they left. Locking doors wasn't a habit they were accustomed to. She knew that. She should have checked the lock herself before bringing the children upstairs. Caleb had expressly told her to lock that door before he left. Lock it and keep it locked, he'd said.

She hadn't. She'd been horribly careless, and whatever happened now would be her fault.

Trevor had ordered them to sit down and had searched the apartment, looking for Caleb. Rhoda had been torn between wishing her husband were there and being thankful he wasn't. It was quickly clear that Trevor had lost his ability to reason, and she knew the gun he kept waving around was intended for Caleb.

Although she feared Trevor would use it on them if she couldn't keep the twins quiet. Vonnie was trembling like a leaf and whimpering. Eli was shaking, too—but with fury. Caleb's son was too much like his father to whimper.

"Go away!" the little boy shouted in *Deutsch*, and her heart jumped. Trevor scowled.

"What did he say?"

"Nothing. He's just upset," Rhoda soothed desperately.

Trevor's eyes narrowed. "Make him speak English."

"He doesn't know English. Our children don't learn that until they go to school."

"Then tell him to be quiet," Trevor muttered. He started pacing again.

"You must not shout at the man," she murmured in *Deutsch*. "We must sit here quietly."

Eli pushed his lips out stubbornly, but she sensed the fear behind his defiance. The whole room was thick with it.

"*Daed*," Vonnie whimpered into Rhoda's dress. "*Daed*."

Rhoda swallowed around the lump in her throat. "It will be all right," she whispered, tightening her arms around the twins. "*Gott* will take care of us."

Trevor slammed his fist against the wall, making them all jump. "Where is he?"

"I told you, he is gone for the day." She wasn't sure what to tell Trevor about Caleb's whereabouts, but she had to do what she could to keep their paths from crossing.

She'd heard the story of how Trevor had shown up in the barn at Sam's *aent*'s house the summer when Emma had lived there. Trevor had waved a gun around then, too, but Sam had calmed him down and convinced him to leave.

She was hoping she could do the same thing. Once she did, she'd bolt every door and window in the building, and she'd never ever scoff about Caleb's love of locks and alarms again. He could add as many as he liked. The more, the better.

"You are frightening the children," Rhoda said, trying to sound calm and reasonable. "They have done nothing wrong, and—"

"They're his," Trevor spat. "And all this is his fault. Whatever happens to them or to you, it's his fault, not mine. You understand?"

Whatever happens. A chill tickled down her back.

"*Nee*, I mean, no," she corrected hastily. "I don't understand. Why is this Caleb's fault?"

"He's been chasing me." Trevor dropped into a chair and stared at her, his face tight with anger. "Didn't you know that?"

Well, yes. "I know my husband has been away from home for some time," she admitted cautiously.

"Following me. Everywhere I went. I had to keep moving all the time."

"That must have been very hard."

"It was." For the first time, his expression softened—not much but a little. "It was really hard."

He sounded like a child whining. Rhoda took hold of her courage.

"I am sorry."

He looked surprised at the apology, but his eyes narrowed. "No, you're not. Nobody's sorry for me. The whole world hates me. Nobody understands. Dad said they would once the movie was out, but it's just as bad as ever. Now they all want me to go to a hospital."

"A hospital?"

"That's what they said. Better than jail. It's what my parents have been pushing all along. At first, they thought there wouldn't be much chance of it. No way to get a fair trial, my dad said, because everybody thinks Amish people are so sweet. Nobody would be willing to take my side. But

Dad's smart. He's been working all this time to swing things our way. This whole movie thing was his idea. He kept saying we needed to stay on top of the story, spin it the way it needed to go."

"He must love you very much."

Trevor scoffed. "He wants to be a state senator. That's why he's trying to fix this. He's mad at me because I messed up his chances of winning the election."

Mad. Rhoda tried to wrap her bewildered brain around this idea, that a father would be *mad* at his son for murdering two innocent people. Not devastated, not horrified.

Mad.

Because he wanted a certain job, and his son's sin had messed that up.

So many feelings were crowding into her heart right now. Fear, confusion, a desperation to protect her children. But mixed in was genuine sympathy for this boy.

He really did look like a boy, still with pimples on his cheeks. And although he hadn't shaved lately, the stubble was spotty. He was pale, too, as if he spent too much time indoors, and his shoulders were narrow, not wide and strong as a man's should be.

What she'd told Caleb was true. Trevor was only a boy who had done a terrible, horrible thing. But she'd also said she wasn't afraid of him. That part had turned out not to be true.

She feared this boy very much. The wildness and despair in his eyes terrified her.

An instinct told her to keep him talking.

"It is very hard to have your father mad at you," she said. "I know. And you are an only child, *ja?*"

He blinked, his brows drawing together. "Yeah."

"I am, too. That makes it harder, I think. All my friends came from big families, and their parents' attention was scattered between lots of children. My parents had only me.

It was lonesome. When my friends were angry with their parents, they could talk to their brothers and sisters. I didn't have anybody to talk to."

"Me neither. Except my friends online. And Emma. She understood everything." His face wrinkled, and Rhoda's heart dipped.

Talking about Emma wasn't a good idea. Rhoda fumbled desperately for something to say that would distract him.

"I upset my father, too," she blurted out. "I understand how that feels."

Trevor looked at her, a glimmer of interest in his eyes. "What'd you do?"

Rhoda decided to trust in the truth. "It was when I married Caleb. My father didn't like him."

Trevor's eyebrows went up, and he leaned back in the chair. Rhoda tried not to look at the gun resting on his knee. He was holding it loosely now, but his finger was still curled around the trigger.

She didn't know much about guns. She had no brothers, and her father had been too busy to hunt. But even she knew a finger on a trigger was a dangerous thing.

"He didn't like Caleb?"

"Caleb was always in trouble as a boy. My father was the bishop of our community, so he often had to deal with the problems Caleb caused. They didn't get along."

"I thought you people always stuck together. I didn't know you didn't like each other."

"People are people," Rhoda pointed out gently. "So sometimes, *ja,* there are problems between us, just like there are in your families."

Trevor appeared to think that over. "But you married him anyway, even though your father didn't want you to."

"I did."

"And your father let you."

"*Ja*, he did. He wasn't happy, but he did not stand in our way."

"I really liked Emma. I might've wanted to marry her one day. Probably." He leaned forward, his face more animated, and Rhoda noticed his hand tightening on the gun. "Well, I wanted to be her boyfriend first." He looked slightly embarrassed. "You know what that means? Like dating?"

"Yes," she said. "When young people spend time together to see if they would be a good fit for marriage. We also do this."

"But her father said no. He acted like there wasn't even a chance, that how I felt about her didn't matter. He laughed about it. He laughed about me. I wish she'd had a father like yours."

She certain sure wasn't going to tell him, but Isaac, Rhoda knew, would have taken a much sterner approach to an *Englisch* boy flirting with his daughter than Elijah Hochstedler had. Her father-in-law had been a kind and a gentle man, with a great deal of patience and a *gut* sense of humor. He could be firm when he needed to be, but Rhoda had never seen him lose his temper or be unkind to anyone.

"If she'd had a father like yours, none of this would have happened." Trevor jumped up out of the chair and started pacing again.

Rhoda's mouth had gone dry. This conversation wasn't heading in a good direction, but she wasn't sure what she could do or say to move things to safer ground.

"He was right, though," Trevor was saying. "Your father. You made a mistake marrying Caleb Hochstedler. He's nothing but trouble. I had a pretty good place for a while. Out on the beach. I like the ocean. And there was good Wi-Fi, so I was able to do some gaming. And then my father hears that Emma's brother is trying to find me. Our private investigator said somebody was asking a lot of questions, and I had to keep moving. They shut down all my accounts, too, and I lost all my progress."

Although Rhoda didn't understand half what he was talking about, she nodded as if she did.

"I was almost looking forward to going to the hospital, you know? Figured I could stay there awhile. My mom kept promising it was going to be a good place. My dad was pulling strings, talking to people he knew. He knows a lot of judges, and people owe him favors. It was going to be all right. But then I found out that they won't let me have a computer. Like at all."

"Oh." She tried to look sympathetic. "That's too bad."

"I'm not going there. Nobody can make me. If my dad tries, I'll start talking, and he can kiss the idea of being a senator goodbye. I'm done with doctors and pills. I'm going to get another place on the beach somewhere, with good Wi-Fi and a better computer. And this time I'll stay there. But I can't do that if Emma's brother keeps chasing me." His voice broke on the last sentence, and his pacing picked up a notch. "He's got to stop. I'm going to stop him."

Rhoda's heart pounded hard, and she sat up straight and stiff. She could feel the blood draining from her face.

Partly because of what Trevor had just said. It was clear what he was planning to do, and that he wasn't capable of thinking rationally. Anything—absolutely anything—could set him off. Having this man and his gun in the same room as her children made her blood run cold.

That was partly why. The other reason was because she had heard something. A quick, quiet noise that she recognized.

The sound of the back door opening.

"I will tell him what you've said." She raised her voice as much as she dared, praying Caleb would hear her—and that for once, he would listen. "You can put your gun away. There's no need to hurt anyone else. I will tell Caleb that he must stop looking for you. I will tell him that he must stay far away from you, that you are dangerous and will hurt him if he tries to find you again. Now," she said, pitching her voice more loudly, "you should go downstairs and out the back door where nobody will see you. Then you can get away."

"He won't listen to you." He paused, looking conflicted. "Will he?"

There was a sliver of hope in his voice, and Rhoda clung to that. "Things are different now," she assured him. "I need Caleb to stay here because of the children. If he's busy being a father, he won't have time to chase you anymore." Trevor looked unconvinced, so she added, "It is a good solution. And Emma was kind to you. She wouldn't want you to hurt her brother. Did you know he's her twin?"

"Of course I know that! I know everything about Emma. She's married now," he said sadly.

Rhoda nodded cautiously. "*Ja*, she is."

"I wanted them to send me pictures of her. But they wouldn't. She's off limits. But my father doesn't like your husband much. He says he likes to cause trouble. They were keeping an eye on you when you came back here, trying to figure out if you knew where he was and were telling him stuff. The private detective took a lot of pictures of you. I got my mother to send me some. She does whatever I ask her to do."

"I think you'd better go, Trevor." Rhoda was listening as hard as she could, but she hadn't heard another noise. *Please, Gott. Please, let this man leave. And let Caleb have the sense to hide so he won't be seen. Please keep us all safe.* "If you want to get away, you'll have to go quick."

Trevor crossed to look out the window, shoving the curtains aside with the barrel of the gun. "There's nobody out there."

"This is a bakery, and it's nearly lunchtime. People will wonder why we're not open." She was skirting around the truth a little, but surely *Gott* would understand.

She needed to get Trevor out of here. She was certain

Caleb was downstairs, and she knew her husband. He'd already have been in the apartment except for the gun. He didn't want to risk rushing in, no doubt fearing Trevor would hurt her or the children if he did.

But he wouldn't wait much longer. She felt sure of that.

Trevor frowned. "There's a sign in the window saying you'll be closed all day. Are you trying some kind of funny business? You'd better not." The expression on his face was petulant, not unlike Eli's when he was hungry and tired.

An idea occurred to her. It frightened her, but it was the only thing she could think of. "I'm not trying to be funny. I'm *naerfich*. Nervous," she explained. "And hungry. We're all hungry. We've not had lunch. The children will be quieter if they eat something. You're probably hungry, too. Why don't I fix you a sandwich?"

As she spoke, she held her breath and slowly rose to her feet, praying her plan would work.

Chapter Thirty-Two

CALEB WAS ALMOST AT THE TOP OF THE STAIRCASE. He took another step and winced at the soft creak. Moving so slowly was killing him. He wanted to be *in* the apartment and between Rhoda and Trevor, but if he messed up now, he didn't want to imagine what could happen. He tightened his fists and forced himself to wait—and listen.

He'd heard Rhoda lifting her voice when she'd talked about the gun. She knew he was here, and she was warning him to be careful and smart. Maybe she expected him to hide or to go get help, but he wasn't leaving her and the children alone with Trevor.

He'd seen how bad things could get when somebody was cornered. Simple situations could turn violent in seconds.

He leaned closer to the door. The storm had broken overhead, and it was hard to hear over the pelting rain. Rhoda was chattering about food, false cheerfulness in her voice. She was doing her best to calm Trevor down and distract him. It was a smart idea, but he couldn't tell if it was working. Trevor wasn't answering her, and the children were unnaturally quiet.

The children. Icy fear touched his heart, and he clenched his jaw. If Trevor hurt Rhoda or the twins . . .

Please, Gott. Help me to know what to do.

Oddly, the short, desperate prayer cleared the panic out of his mind. And suddenly, clearly, he knew exactly what he had to do.

He took a silent breath and pushed aside his fear and his fury.

And he listened.

He heard the scoot of a chair across the floor of the kitchen and the clink of a plate. Rhoda said something about a sandwich.

No answer from Trevor. Surely he wasn't sitting down at a table and eating. People didn't break into an apartment and hold folks at gunpoint and then eat a sandwich.

But then, Trevor was unpredictable. And if he was eating . . .

Maybe that would give Caleb an opening.

Think.

A memory stirred—Milt's first piece of advice about dealing with the bail jumpers they chased.

You got to take charge of the situation and calm 'em down. You know how the police officers call the folks they're arresting "ma'am" and "sir" and act professional? They're running the show, and they make sure you know it. But they ain't screaming or yelling or jumping out at you, neither. Guy you're after, he knows he's messed up. He knows this is bad. He's already on the edge, and these ain't folks known for good decisions on their best days. Situation like that, you got to have enough sense for the both of you.

If Trevor was in the kitchen, where were the twins? Where was Rhoda? Maybe if Caleb eased open the door just a crack, he could see. Then he could figure out the best thing to do. He could—

"Where is it?" Trevor shouted over the loud bang of a chair falling flat on the floor. "What'd you do with my gun?"

As Rhoda cried out and the twins began to wail, Caleb burst through the door.

He scanned the room in a split second. Trevor was standing by the kitchen table, his back to the living room. A sandwich with three bites missing was on a plate in front of him. The twins were behind him seated on the couch, screaming.

Rhoda stood across the table from him, holding two small plastic plates with sandwiches cut into four pieces. Her eyes were wide with fear, but she choked out, "Under the plate in the sink."

In *Deutsch*. She was speaking in *Deutsch*, telling him where the gun was so that Trevor wouldn't understand.

He moved fast, while Trevor was still trying to process what was happening.

"What are you saying?" he yelled at Rhoda as Caleb sprinted past him.

A dishtowel was draped over a plate sitting in the sink, propped up at an odd angle. He slid his hand underneath it and found a pistol. He pulled it out just as Trevor started toward him.

"*Nee*," Caleb said, surprised by how calm his voice sounded. "You'd best stay where you are."

Trevor stopped short. His eyes were wide and wild, flitting from one side of the room to the other. Caleb had seen looks like that before, mostly when they went after people who'd skipped bail over drug charges. Those were always dicey because even though the people weren't usually violent, they also weren't thinking straight when they were high.

Trevor turned toward Eli and Vonnie, who were both

wailing. "Shut up!" he screamed. "Everybody shut up!" He took a step toward the twins, and Rhoda made a terrified sound and moved toward the children. As she passed him, Trevor reached out and grabbed her arm.

Fury sparked in Caleb's heart. He lifted the pistol. "Let my wife go."

"No." Trevor's eyes were wide with fear. "If I do, you'll shoot me."

"Not if you let her go." When Trevor didn't move, Caleb added, "But if you don't, I make no promises."

Slowly Trevor released Rhoda's sleeve and she ran to gather the twins in her arms. She looked at Caleb, her face as white as skimmed milk.

"Go downstairs," he told her in *Deutsch*. "Take the children and get out of the building."

"Caleb—" She didn't want to leave him. The agony on her face made that clear.

"The children," he repeated. "Take the children away."

She looked down at the twins. They had their faces buried in her dress, sobbing. When she looked back up at him, the agony was still there, but her face was set.

She looked into his eyes for one long moment. Then she shepherded the twins toward the door.

"Where's she going? She can't leave!" Trevor's voice grew shriller. He turned in Rhoda's direction, and she gasped.

"Don't move again," Caleb commanded quietly. "She and the little ones are leaving. You and I are staying."

Trevor froze where he was, his thin chest heaving with frantic breaths. He looked, Caleb thought, like a cornered coyote, lean at the end of a long winter. Skinny and moth-eaten. A coward, but vicious and deadly to anything smaller than him.

Rhoda paused at the door. He felt her eyes on him, and he knew how they would look. Pleading. Frightened.

He didn't glance in her direction. He couldn't, not right now.

"Go on," he told her. "Don't stay in the bakery. Get far away."

"Caleb, please."

"Please do what I tell you."

She went. He waited, watching Trevor closely until he heard the door shut downstairs.

She was out. She and the children were safe. He drew a breath and sent a heartfelt prayer of thanks to God.

"Go on." Trevor's voice sounded as if he was about to cry. "Shoot me. That's what you want to do, isn't it? You want to kill me. Well, go ahead! Do it! I don't care anymore!"

Caleb stayed silent, studying the young man in front of him. He didn't think that was true. He didn't think this boy truly wanted to die.

But he wasn't far from it maybe.

He'd barely remembered Trevor before that awful day in December. He and Joseph had done some work at the Abbotts' home—kitchen cabinets. A big job, lots of money. Joseph had been pleased because he was working hard to build up his woodworking business back then.

It had been a couple weeks of steady work. They'd known Stephen Abbott had a son, but they'd barely seen him. When they did, he'd seemed bashful and pale. Lazy, too, they'd thought, hiding in his room most of the day. They'd not thought much of him.

But he'd looked a lot healthier and happier then than he did now.

"I found the pictures of my wife in your closet," Caleb said. "It wasn't so smart of you to leave those behind."

Trevor was breathing heavily, too much white showing in his eyes. "I wanted you to find them," he said. "I knew you would."

"How did you know that?"

"Because," Trevor went on bitterly, "you were always right behind me. You're why I had to leave. I was all set up there. It wasn't great, but it wasn't so bad. I could do my gaming there. I was rebuilding my life."

"Rebuilding your life. By playing games on your computer?"

"They're important to me!" Trevor screamed the words like an angry child. "Why can't anybody understand that? My parents don't, and neither do those stupid doctors at the hospital. I told my father I'd go. But it's no deal if I can't even have a computer!" His yells subsided into heavy breaths that sounded like half sobs.

"That's why you didn't turn yourself in?"

Trevor didn't answer, but Caleb took his silence as a yes. He shook his head slowly.

"You killed my parents. Do you know, they never met their grandchildren? They would have liked to have seen them." Caleb shifted the weight of the gun in his hand. "My son could have learned a lot from my father. He was a better *daed* than I will likely ever be."

"He wasn't! He wasn't a good father. He was stupid and narrow-minded, keeping me and Emma apart. I'm glad I shot him." Trevor stared at him defiantly. His whole body was shaking, but whether with fear or anger, Caleb couldn't tell.

And at the moment, he didn't much care. His finger curved gently around the trigger of the gun. "Are you glad you shot my mother, too?"

Now there was a spark of something different in Trevor's eyes. Regret maybe? Shame? Caleb wasn't sure.

"She was screaming at me. Yelling something I couldn't understand, talking like you people do. I . . . I didn't mean to shoot her. I just . . . did."

As Caleb listened, a wave of angry sorrow swamped him. *Ja*, that was what *Mamm* would have done. She would have yelled. *Mamm* had never taken trouble calmly. She went after it with a broom and a feisty attitude.

Daed used to needle her about that whenever Caleb got

into trouble, telling her what was in the cat was always in the kittens.

He swallowed a mouthful of sour bile before he could speak. "You have taken so much from us. And now you are upset because you can't play computer games in the hospital."

"You don't understand! It's a stupid rule!"

A stupid rule. How many times had those same words come out of his own mouth? In *Deutsch* maybe, but still.

It was the same. Both the words—and the defiance behind them.

"Some rules seem stupid," Caleb said slowly, "but that is sometimes because we do not understand them. We do not see what they are protecting us from."

"I don't need protecting from a computer. That's what—" Trevor ran a hand through his hair and wiped his running nose on the sleeve of his shirt. "That's what keeps me going. The gaming and the friends who don't . . . don't know what I did . . . They don't know who I am . . ."

"But you know. Maybe you need to face what you did. And stop running from it."

"I can't stop running if you won't stop chasing me!"

Trevor argued like a child because he thought like a child, Caleb realized. He wasn't capable of reasoning well. Something was terribly wrong with him. Likely always had been, leaving him dangerous but also miserable, angry, and confused.

Caleb suddenly remembered a milk cow they'd had, years back. Odd thing. She had been kicked in the head during a scuffle, and after that, she walked in circles in the pasture, over and over again, her head at an odd angle. He'd been about seven when that had happened, and he'd laughed at the funny cow.

Daed had brought him up sharp. *It isn't funny*, he'd said. *It is sad to see an animal hurt so. She can't help it any more than your kossin Henry can help not being able to walk or do for himself since his accident, any more than Amos Byer can help not recognizing his own children now that he has grown very old. They are not healthy in their heads, and they deserve both our pity and our help.*

Caleb looked at Trevor and wondered what *Daed* would be saying now. He didn't have to wonder long. He knew with a certainty that surprised and sobered him.

"I will not be chasing you anymore." Before he could think better of it, he walked to the window overlooking the alley and pushed it open. He flung the pistol out as far as he could and heard it rustle through the bushes.

When he turned around, Trevor was staring at him.

"What'd you do that for?"

"Amish people don't use such guns," he said simply. "Rifles, yes, for hunting food. But not pistols, because they are only meant to hurt people."

Trevor scanned his outfit. "But you're not Amish anymore."

"I'm not dressed Plain right now, but my clothes only tell others who I am. I have not been acting like it lately, but in my heart, I am Amish." He made a short, wry noise, almost a laugh. "More Amish than I thought I was, seems like."

Trevor seemed to be thinking this over. "Does that mean you're going to let me go?"

"To the hospital, *ja*," Caleb said quietly. "Soon people will come, and they will take you there. And you should listen to the doctors and take the medicines they give you. And pray for the strength to obey all the rules they set for you, even the stupid ones. That is the path forward for you, and it is the only one that will take you anyplace worth going."

Trevor seemed to be listening. "And you won't chase me anymore?"

"No. I will not." He took a breath. "I forgive you for what you did."

Trevor frowned. "I don't believe you."

"That's all right." This time Caleb did laugh, but there was no humor in it. "I don't believe myself. And I will have to keep on forgiving you. Every day. But I will do it."

"Why?"

Caleb looked at him. There were so many ways to answer that question. Because the bitterness he'd carried had done nothing but harm him and those he cared about. Because the bishop was going to make certain sure of that forgiveness before they offered Caleb any forgiveness of his own.

But mostly because *Gott*, the God who had just answered a desperate man's prayer, required it. And such a *Gott* came first. And after Him, Rhoda and the children.

Trevor couldn't understand that. Not yet. Maybe not ever, depending on how good those doctors and medicines turned out to be.

"Because that's the path forward for me," Caleb answered simply. "And it's the only one leading anyplace worth going."

Trevor stood looking at him uncertainly for a minute. He wiped at his nose and then nodded at the table.

"Can I finish my sandwich before they get here?"

"*Ja*, sure." Caleb leaned over and set the fallen chair right side up. "Sit down and eat."

"Can I have something to drink, too?"

Caleb moved toward the refrigerator. "*Ja*. I will pour you a glass of milk. It is fresh, but not so *gut* as the milk my *daed* sold from his dairy. There will never again be any milk so good as that. But the milk we have here today will do."

They were there still, sitting together at the table, when the police came up the stairs.

Chapter Thirty-Three

"MA'AM?"

A young man in a crisp uniform walked over to speak to her, and Rhoda rose from the chair she was sitting in, one she'd tucked into the bakery for elderly customers.

"May I see my husband now?"

"Not just yet. They want me to tell you that they're bringing the subject down. Once he's cleared out, they'll need to ask your husband a few questions, and then you can see him. Okay?"

Rhoda swallowed hard and nodded. "All right. Thank you."

"You're welcome." He offered her a polite smile before walking back to join the others.

Several policemen were in the bakery right now, milling around and talking on radios. So far they'd been very kind to her. When she'd returned alone after leaving the twins with Mary Yoder, they'd immediately allowed her to come inside, away from the reporters clustering outside the bakery. Then an older officer had taken her statement in the office, a plump female officer standing silently nearby.

At first she'd felt compassionate toward the man because he kept asking her the same questions in slightly different ways. She explained three times how she'd put the plate over the gun when she'd served Trevor his sandwich, picking it up and holding it against the dish as she walked to the sink. Maybe this poor fellow was like Edna, getting older and having some troubles with his memory.

Belatedly she'd realized he was doing it on purpose, trying to make certain sure she was telling the truth. She must have passed the test because finally he'd closed his notebook and nodded. "That's all for now. But if we have more questions later, you'll come in and answer them for us, won't you?"

He'd sounded a good deal friendlier than he had to start with. She'd nodded. "Of course."

He'd smiled hopefully. "I don't suppose you've got any cookies around that you'd be willing to sell to a hungry man. I missed my lunch."

She'd missed hers, too, but she couldn't have swallowed a bite. Not until she saw for herself that Caleb was all right. "I will give them to you," she said. "To all of you. With my thanks."

She'd been allowed to get down the containers of leftover cookies they'd put away that morning and start some coffee perking. Afterward they'd asked her to please have a seat again, so she had.

Someone knocked on the window behind her, and she jumped. She turned around and saw Abram peering in, his round face unusually solemn. He made gestures indicating that he wanted to come inside.

Rhoda bit her lip. She couldn't unlock the door. The policemen wouldn't like that, she was certain. But she couldn't ignore the bishop, either. She rose and walked to the older man, waiting respectfully until he'd finished speaking.

"Excuse me? That man there"—she pointed to the window—"is my bishop. Like our pastor. May he please come in and sit with me while I wait?"

The older man squinted at the window, then nodded to one of the younger officers. "Let him in."

Abram squeezed inside—no easy feat since the officer seemed determined to open the door only as much as absolutely necessary. He took the chair next to hers and listened intently as she explained in *Deutsch* everything that had happened.

"It is *Gott*'s providence," he said over and over. "*Gott*'s great mercy that you and the children are all right. And Caleb, too?"

She nodded. "They say so. I was not supposed to listen maybe, but I heard them say he threw the gun out the window. One of the men went and collected it from the shrubs behind the dumpster."

"He threw the gun away." Relief and joy warmed Abram's face. "That is very *gut*. Very, very *gut*. And the young man? Trevor? He, too, is all right?"

She remembered the wildness and despair in Trevor's face and shook her head. "He is alive. But no. I do not think he is all right. I don't believe he has been all right for a very long time."

"We must pray for him," Abram said, a fierceness in his eyes that didn't match the gentle roundness of his face. "There are many kinds of prodigals, many ways for a *youngie* to become lost to *Gott* and to himself. *Ja*, we will pray." He looked at her. "And for your *mann*, too. I know it seems as if this is over now, but in a way, for Caleb, it is only beginning. Now that this part of it is finished, he must face what he ran away from."

Rhoda's heart dipped. "Me, you mean?"

Abram blinked at her, surprised. Then he chuckled. "*Nee*, I did not mean you. I meant his doubts about the church and his sorrow over his parents' deaths. He never grieved them, I think. He moved straight into his anger and stayed there as long as he could. You must give him time to work through those things. And then . . ."

"And then what?"

"And then we will see," Abram answered gently.

They sat silently together watching as the officers brought Trevor down. He seemed subdued, his hands in handcuffs behind his back. He didn't struggle or cry out, but as he came out of the doorway, he glanced in Rhoda's direction.

Their eyes connected. He didn't speak, though, and within a few seconds, the officers had hustled him out of sight.

The reporters must have figured out that something was happening behind the bakery, because the people crowded around the front of the store took off at a run. They were too late. Police cars, lights blinking and sirens wailing, rolled away down the street, leaving them behind.

Rhoda and Abram watched as the disappointed reporters scrambled to get into vans and trucks. One by one, they drove away, following the police cars.

Rhoda blinked at the street, empty and silent. It was as if the whole day hadn't even happened.

The younger officer came over, looking embarrassed.

"Ma'am," he said uneasily. "Your husband—we . . . uh . . . we're done with him. But he . . . uh . . . he said to tell you he needed a minute to himself before he spoke with you. He just went out the back door there."

Rhoda stood, confused. Caleb didn't want to see her? That seemed . . . it seemed very wrong.

"I'm really sorry," the officer was saying, "but we couldn't detain him."

"That is not your fault," she answered absently. She thought she knew where Caleb was going. She wasn't certain . . . but she thought maybe she knew.

She was going there, too. Right now.

She turned to Abram. "I believe I know where he is, and I need to talk to him. Will you stay here until the officers get finished?"

"Of course I can do that. But, Rhoda, remember. You mustn't expect too much of Caleb right now, *ja?* Maybe it would be better even to let him have this time to himself. Let him come to you when he is ready."

Rhoda had never in her life argued with a bishop, but she braced herself and shook her head. "*Nee*, Abram. Caleb has had over two years to himself already. If he's grieving, he can do it with me beside him. And if he doesn't want me there, then I'd best know that sooner rather than later."

To her surprise and relief, Abram accepted her answer with a nod. "I will stay here, then," he said. "And if you need me, if either of you need me, I will help all I can."

The comfort of his simple, sincere promise steadied her. "You have helped us both very much already, and I am grateful."

He smiled, but as he sank back into his seat, she couldn't help noticing the troubled expression on his face. He was so worried about them. She would find some way to really thank him, to help this kind man understand that, whatever happened next, she would always be grateful because he'd tried so hard to help.

She was almost to the back door when the idea occurred to her. She turned.

"Abram?"

"Ja?"

"There are cookies in the kitchen. They'll go to waste if they aren't eaten soon. Help yourself to all you want."

The last thing she saw as she walked out of the bakery was Abram beaming as he made his way toward the cookie box.

She walked briskly down the now-empty road, her heart pattering even more quickly than her shoes on the hot pavement. The threatening clouds had blown away after only a brief burst of rain, and the early summer afternoon sparkled around her, beautiful and bright.

But inside she couldn't help worrying.

It wasn't a good sign for Caleb to run off like this. It couldn't be. Maybe Abram had been right to tell her to wait for him.

But she'd meant what she'd said. She'd waited long enough. And right now she needed to see Caleb with her own eyes, see that he was healthy and well and whole. Until she did, she wouldn't be able to take a deep breath, much less think sensible thoughts.

When she came to their old special spot in the bend of the road, she veered off into the woods, following the narrow path. Sure enough, Caleb was there in their old meadow sitting on the fallen log.

Relief washed through her so forcefully that her knees nearly buckled. He was all right. He was truly all right.

He got to his feet as she approached, his expression apprehensive.

"I'm sorry," he said when she was close enough to hear. "I know we need to talk, but there was something I had to do first."

"What?" She stopped a few feet away, folding her arms across her chest. As grateful as she was for his safety, she couldn't help feeling a little irritated. "What was so important that you had to see to it before you could talk to me after this terrible day we've had?"

"I had to pray."

"I was waiting and worrying—" She broke off to stare at him.

"I know." He walked toward her, pine needles crunching under his boots, and took her hands in his. "I know you were waiting for me and worried about me, and I wanted to talk to you. But I needed to do this first. I'm sorry."

She shook her head, struggling for words. "Don't be," she managed finally. "Don't be sorry."

"I had to thank *Gott*," Caleb said simply. "I could have lost you today. You and Eli and Vonnie. It was a very near thing, I think."

"I think so, too," she whispered, and his hands tightened over hers.

"I could have lost myself just as easily. If I had shot him . . . I wanted to, there for a minute, when he was talking about shooting *Daed*. About—" He had to stop for a second. "About *Mamm* yelling at him." Caleb's face went grim and hard. "I wanted to."

"But you didn't."

"*Nee*, I didn't." He went silent. The only sound was a bird trilling happily up in the treetops somewhere, as if there were nothing scary or harsh in the world at all. No guns, no death, no hard decisions to make. As if everything was just as it was supposed to be.

"I saw Trevor today," he said finally. "For what he was. I think I'd built him up in my mind . . . I hated him. And I feared what he might do. But when I saw him . . ." He shook his head roughly. "He wasn't what I expected."

"I understand what you mean, I think. He was like a raccoon that came in our yard one day when I was a girl. It was broad daylight, and it was acting so strangely that it scared me. *Daed* told me it was very dangerous because it had a sickness. That is the way Trevor is, I think."

Caleb was watching her closely. He nodded. "I think so, *ja*." He looked away, and she saw the muscles of his neck move as he swallowed. "I came here to ask for *Gott*'s forgiveness. That had to come first." He took a breath. "And, Rhoda, I will ask for the church's forgiveness, too. But before that, I want to ask for yours."

"There is no need, Caleb." She freed one hand from his and reached up to stroke his face, just above the beard he'd started growing the day of their marriage.

He reached up and caught her hand, pressing it against his cheek. "*Ja*, Rhoda, there is. I am sorry I hurt you. Sorry

I left you. Sorry for everything you went through without me. And if you can forgive me—"

"Caleb," she hurried to say, "you are already forgiven."

"I don't deserve it." His voice was ragged. "But I'll take it. And I'll spend the rest of my life trying to make these past two and a half years up to you. I'm going to give you and the children my best, Rhoda. With *Gott*'s help, I'm going to make you happy."

He sounded grimly determined, as if their happiness were something he would hunt down and drag back home. She laughed out loud and had the satisfaction of seeing his eyes lighten to a warmer shade of green.

"I'll do my best to make you happy, too, Caleb. I made my share of mistakes, and you weren't wrong that I put my father before you sometimes. But that won't happen anymore. *Daed* won't be coming between us again."

"*Nee*, I don't think he will," Caleb said slowly. "Do you know, he apologized to me today. He stopped special at the courthouse to do it. He asked my forgiveness." He shook his head. "That was a surprise."

Rhoda's eyes brimmed. "*Daed* is a *gut* man. He makes his mistakes, too. But when *Gott*—or my *mamm*—shows him his faults, he listens and he tries to make things right." She smiled up at him. "You're a lot like him, I think."

There'd been a time not too long ago when that would have made her husband's eyes shoot sparks. But now he only shook his head. "I'm not. I don't have his faith, nor Abram's kindness, nor my *bruder*'s steadiness. But I'm going to pray to *Gott* that He will make me more like them."

That grim determination was in his voice again, but this time Rhoda didn't laugh. "Not me. I will pray different. I have no wish to be married to a copy of my father, nor Abram. Nor," she added firmly, "your brother. I will pray that the Lord will shape my husband into the man He designed him to be. Such a man . . ." She trailed off and smiled. "Such a man will be a blessing and a strength to his family as no other could ever be."

His eyes traced her face like a touch. "I have a long way to go before I'm much of a blessing to you or anybody else. I need to get things straight with the church as soon as I can."

"That won't be easy," she reminded softly.

"I don't care. I'll do whatever I have to do. The first thing is to talk to Abram and get the process started."

"I left him at the bakery. If we hurry, we can catch him before he leaves, and you can set up a time to meet."

Caleb reached up and tucked a strand of hair under her *kapp.* For all his talk of hurry, he didn't seem to be in any particular rush to leave. "Do you think he'll still be there?"

Rhoda laughed. "I told him he could have all the cookies he wanted. So, *ja,* I think he will, if we start back now."

"Then we'd better go." He leaned close to her. "It doesn't matter how hard it is, Rhoda. Whatever he tells me to do, I'll do. I'm coming home with my whole heart. All of it. From this moment on."

She believed him. She smiled. Her father—and the rest of Johns Mill—were in for a big surprise.

"You," she said, "are going to be a force to be reckoned with, Caleb Hochstedler."

"I am not so sure about that," he whispered, leaning down. "But with *Gott*'s help and you by my side, I will be a happier man than I could ever deserve to be. That much I know."

He kissed her as the bird up in the treetops sang merrily, and the sunlit leaves flittered above them, as green as his eyes, washed clean by the storm.

Epilogue

WHERE HAD RHODA SLIPPED OFF TO?

On a late afternoon in early October, Caleb scanned his new home, searching for his wife. The house was crowded with family and friends chattering and bustling about getting ready for the celebratory potluck supper.

What they were celebrating, exactly, wasn't clear—but only because there were so many things to choose from. For one thing, Rhoda and Caleb had finally moved in to their new house, although they'd bought the small farm from Edna over a month ago.

There'd been a lot of minor repairs to make, things that had been left untended to since Edna's husband's death. Edna and her granddaughter, Cora, had happily moved into the apartment over Lambright's Bakery, and Rhoda, Caleb, and the twins had crowded in with Joseph and Naomi for the past four weeks.

He'd not been too excited about that, but in the end, it had worked out real well. Somehow, spending those weeks back in the house where he'd grown up had finished the healing process that had begun when he and Trevor had sat side by side at the kitchen table.

"Caleb?" Joseph stopped beside him for a moment. "Talk to Eben Zook when you get the chance. He needs more shelves put in the store, and I told him you'd be the one to handle that."

"I will, but I hope he's not in any hurry for them. I have so many orders already that I won't be able to fit him in for at least a month."

Joseph smiled. "That's a fine problem to have. Get to them when you can. He'll understand." Then he moved on to talk to old David Miller.

Caleb's new job was another reason for celebration. He'd been helping Joseph in the woodworking shop while he looked for permanent work. It had seemed the least he could do, considering all his brother had done for Rhoda and the twins.

His job search hadn't lasted long. Three weeks ago, his brother had suggested they partner together in the business, with Joseph making furniture and Caleb crafting and installing cabinets and doing house repairs.

The partnership was a generous offer and a *gut* fit. And there was something special about working alongside his brother in the old dairy barn where they'd spent so much of their boyhoods. Maybe they worked with oak and hickory now instead of with cows, but there was a comfortable familiarity about the arrangement, right down to their good-natured squabbling over Caleb's mess-making in Joseph's neat-as-a-pin shop.

He noticed Emma sitting near an open window fanning her face. The October air already had a fall crispness to it, but her pregnancy had made her very hot-natured. He walked over.

"Have you seen Rhoda anywhere?"

"In the kitchen," Emma said. "She's fixing up something to help me with the nausea."

Caleb frowned, concerned. “I thought you were feeling better. Is this normal, to be so sick?”

Emma chuckled weakly. “For me it is. For Rhoda, too, she says. And I am lots better; it’s just all these food smells mixed together are bothering me some.”

She did look a little green. “Maybe I’d better get Sam.”

“Oh, please don’t. He’s already fussing over me too much. I’ve got to get the house packed up for our move in two weeks, and he won’t let me lift so much as a frying pan. Anyhow, I’m fine, truly. Tell Rhoda I’m going to sit out on the porch for a bit. Once I’m outside in the air, I’ll be all right, I’m sure.”

She got up, waving away his offered arm, and went out the front door. He watched until he was sure she was safely seated in a rocking chair, and then he went in search of Rhoda.

Sure enough, he found her in the kitchen peering into the oven. Women were flitting in and out as they finished getting the tables ready, and she didn’t seem to notice him coming up behind her.

He leaned down beside her and murmured, “What are you cooking? There’s food enough here already to feed the whole town for a week.”

She jumped, startled, and then smiled, her brown eyes warm and sparkling. “I mixed up some special cookies for Emma. They’re near done.”

“*Ja,* she said to tell you she was on the porch. Something about the smell of the food making her feel sicker.”

Rhoda nodded sympathetically. “That always did me in, too. These cookies should help. They’re a special recipe I learned from my aunt, only I tweaked ’em a bit to make them taste better. They’re not so sweet, and they really help settle the stomach.”

She leaned over again, made a satisfied sound, and pulled the tray out of the oven. She used a spatula to move the hot cookies to a waiting plate. "Would you take these to her? I made extra so she can take some home, too. Tell her just to nibble them real slow at first. That's what I did when I was so sick with the twins."

He looked at his pretty wife, her cheeks rosy with the heat from the oven, happily taking time out of her own party to help her sister-in-law. "I wish I'd been there to fuss over you the way Sam fusses over Emma."

She gave him a sweet smile. "You'll be there the next time," she said. "If *Gott* answers my prayers, you'll have plenty of chances to make that up to me."

"And I'll take 'em. Every single one," he promised.

"At least we have plenty of room now," Rhoda said happily. "This is such a wonderful house! Close enough to the bakery and not a far drive for you out to Joseph's, either."

"Not far at all, and most of my work will be in town anyhow, working for different folks. And I promise, I'll get that *dawdi haus* built for Isaac and Ida as soon as I can." This particular house hadn't come with the separate living space for elderly relatives, but Caleb had sketched out the plans for it when he and Rhoda had discussed buying the place.

Since Rhoda was an only child, she'd be the one caring for her parents when they aged, and usually such arrangements worked better when the older folks had their own apartment connected to the main house. Even so, it would be close quarters, but thankfully he and Isaac had been getting along much better lately, especially since Caleb's confession and reinstatement in the church.

"About that. It seems you can take your time. *Mamm* just told me that, for now, she and *Daed* have decided to rent Sam and Emma's little house, now that they're moving."

He was surprised. "They're going to stay out at his *aent*'s old place?"

"To rent at first, and later maybe to buy, if it suits." Sam and Emma were moving to Sam's old family home, where there was more room for their growing family. "I think it'll suit real well," Rhoda said. "*Mamm* loves the house, and she says after living with relatives for years, she'll enjoy her peace and quiet for a time. They'll drive in so *Daed* can help at the bakery and so she can keep the twins for me some when I'm working."

"And you're happy with them living so far out of town?"

"For now. *Daed*'s health is improving, and the place is small and easy to keep up. Plus, there's Birdie just next door."

"Did I hear my name? I thought my ears were burning." Emma's *Englisch* neighbor, Birdie Marshall, swooped into the kitchen and picked up a tray of pickles. "Talking about my new neighbors, are you? I was just talking to Ida, and I think we'll get along great. Not that I won't miss Emma and Sam something fierce, but I knew they wouldn't be able to stay in that tiny house too long. It was never meant for a young family, but I think it'll be perfect for your parents. Don't you worry a bit. I'm just next door, and I'll be happy to drive them to doctor's appointments and such. And they're welcome to use my phone whenever they need to. Caleb?"

"Ja?"

"Who's that man there? The one with the long gray hair?" Birdie pointed out the kitchen window. "Reuben said he's a friend of yours?"

"That's Milt Masterson. I used to work for him. Why?"

"I was just curious because he was asking about a place in Johns Mill he could rent. Lydia Zook mentioned it to me, thinking I might know of something. I do, but I wasn't sure. He looks a little . . . eccentric," Birdie said. "I mean with that hair and those tattoos and scars and all." She studied Milt through the window. He was standing near Reuben, scratching at the stubble on his chin, looking over the fields.

His fields. Caleb smiled. "You need have no fear of Milt.

He's a real *gut* man, and honest. He'll make a fine addition to the town."

"Good to hear. As it happens, I do know of a place or two for rent. I suppose I could tell him about them." She tilted her head. "You know, he's really rather handsome in a dangerous sort of way, isn't he? Well"—she seemed suddenly flustered—"I suppose I'd better get these pickles out. Ann King sent me after them, and she'll be wondering what happened."

She hurried back out to the living room, pickle tray in hand.

"See?" Rhoda was saying. "I think my parents will be very happy living next door to Birdie. And honestly . . ." Her eyes twinkled up at him. "I'm hoping for a few years alone with my *mann* before they come to live with us."

He glanced around. Nobody seemed to be paying them too much attention, so he leaned in for a kiss.

"Caleb!" Sam's voice boomed behind him, and he reluctantly pulled back. His brother-in-law came through the door, already as confident finding his way around this house as he was at his own. "Eben Zook's looking for you. Something about cabinets. Are those fresh cookies I smell, Rhoda?"

"*Ja*, special ones for Emma to help her stomach."

"Is she feeling sick again?" Sam's face clouded.

"She'll be all right once she eats some of these," Rhoda assured him. "She's sitting on the porch." She offered the plate, and Sam accepted it and promptly disappeared.

Caleb grinned. Emma was going to have to put up with a bit more fussing. Rhoda quickly began dividing the remaining cookies between two small containers.

"What are you doing?"

"Getting these packaged up so they can be taken home."

Caleb looked at them and lifted an eyebrow. "Two containers?"

"One for Emma. One for—somebody else," Rhoda murmured, a smile playing around her lips. She nodded out the window, where Miriam was walking toward Reuben and Milt. "This family's growing by leaps and bounds."

Caleb watched his younger sister with a sense of awed disbelief. So, little Miriam was going to be a *mamm*, too. "It sure is. You and I are falling behind. We're going to have to do our best to keep up." Rhoda shot him a warning look, but that sweet smile was playing around her lips again.

He leaned closer.

"Here you two are!" Abram King called from the doorway.

"Don't mention the cookies," Rhoda whispered urgently, snapping tops on the containers quickly. "And if he sees them, please distract him. Otherwise there'll be none left for your sisters."

"The women have the tables all ready for the first seating." Abram walked into the kitchen, his round face beaming. "I was sent to collect you. Isn't this a wonderful day? Such a blessing to have the family all together. And so much *gut* food, too."

Caleb smiled, pushing away his impatience. "It is a blessing, for certain sure."

"A hard-earned one for you, I know." Abram shook his head. "And the answer to so many prayers. But we still have more to pray for. Did you hear? Stephen Abbott is under investigation. Trevor has admitted that his father was helping him hide all those many months." Abram tsked his tongue. "Such a shame. But at least Trevor seems to be getting the treatment he needs, and we will be praying for his parents. I will go and visit Stephen soon and see if I can offer any comfort. Perhaps," he added, "you might come with me on that visit, Caleb?"

Rhoda stiffened beside him. "Of course," he said calmly. "Just tell me when, and I will make the time. And I will be praying for the Abbotts, too."

"*Gut*," Abram said approvingly. "You will be a comfort to that family that I, perhaps, cannot be. *Gott* has taken all your hurts and grief and turned them to good, just as He promises to do. How happy your parents would be, Caleb, to see all their children and grandchildren now. It is just as they say. Every oak starts as an acorn, and every miracle starts as a problem. I would certain sure call your family's joy a miracle, wouldn't you?"

"*Ja*," Caleb said softly, looking into his wife's face. That little pucker was between her eyes again, and he grinned. She was worried about her cookies. "I would."

Naomi poked her head through the door. "It's time to eat," she said with a smile. She had Eli and Vonnie by the hands, and the twins beckoned to their parents.

"*Mamm! Daed!* Eat!"

Abram answered for them. "We are coming, little ones!" The bishop drew in a long, happy breath and went suddenly alert, like a dog on the trail of a rabbit. "I smell something." He sniffed. "What is it?"

Rhoda shifted quickly so that the cookies were behind her. "There's so much food in here," she hedged. "Who knows?"

"It smells like cookies, I think," Abram was saying. "Something sweet, for sure."

Rhoda sent Caleb a desperate look. *Help*, she mouthed as the older man peered around hopefully.

Caleb quirked an eyebrow. She wanted a bishop distracted? That he could do.

"Very sweet." He winked at his wife. "For sure." He bent closer.

She must have read his intention in his face because she scooted quickly out of kissing range. "Sweet things are for after supper," she said sternly. "You two go ahead and sit down now."

Abram gave one last hopeful sniff, then turned away. "Come, Caleb. We will sit together, *ja?*"

"Coming!" Caleb called behind him. But instead, as soon as the bishop was safely out of the kitchen, he turned back and swept Rhoda up into his arms.

"Caleb!" Her protest was softened by a laugh.

"I know. Sweet things are for after dinner, and kisses are for when bishops aren't sniffing around your kitchen." He leaned down until they were nose to nose. "But you know I've never been good at following rules."

He closed the last lingering space between them, and Rhoda's smile melted into the gentle warmth of his kiss.

ACKNOWLEDGMENTS

As always, I'm so grateful to Anna Mast, who has helped shape this series by providing personal insights into the Amish lifestyle and faith. Any errors in this area are entirely my own.

My heartfelt thanks to my fabulous critique partner, author Amy Grochowski, for working with me to polish this story and bring the Hochstedler series to its happy conclusion.

I'm blessed to work with an amazing agent, Jessica Alvarez of BookEnds Literary Agency, as well as an excellent editor, Anne Sowards of Berkley at Penguin Random House. Their incredible professional skills have been invaluable to this process, and I appreciate them both more than words can express.

I am deeply thankful for the love and support of my family and friends, who make my writing possible and my life an absolute joy.

Finally but most importantly, I offer this story back to the Author and Perfector of my faith, Jesus Christ, with my deepest gratitude.